PROMISED TO ANOTHER. CLAIMED BY HIM.

LET THEM *See*

"SHE'S MINE. AND NOBODY TOUCHES WHAT'S MINE."

Let Them See

Copyright © 2025 Bekki Vowles

Book Cover Design Bekki Vowles

First Edition 2025

Website: author.bekkivowles.co.uk

ISBN: 978-1-0686951-1-7

Editor: Sarah Baker @wordemporiumeditor

Alpha Reader: Nikki

For the women out there, who struggle to be themselves in a world full of judgment.

This is for you.

You can find your HEA. It doesn't matter what it looks like.

Content Warnings

Your well being and mental health mean a great deal to me; it's precious, and we need to look after it. I want nothing more than for you to enjoy this book with all the ups, downs, and shit that goes on in between these pages. So please take a look at the triggers and warning below:

Violence, Sexual/explicit content, Shaming, Trauma, Controlling Parents, Food Restriction, Controlled Life, Mild Abuse, Drugging, Choking.

If you are good with all of the above, read on and enjoy.

Acknowledgements

There are so many people I want to thank for being part of this journey. So many of you have been by my side, enjoying the ride of highs and lows with me.

Jenny, thanks for the strong coffees and reading aloud 'I Dreamt Of You' (the smutty bits) to whoever will listen, at the pub, cricket club, and James' workplace. I love you forever for this.

Anita, you are what you are, and I adore you for it. Your dirty mind is equal to mine. I could write a book just from our chats. (I won't, but I could). Thanks for everything.

Holly, you have been the best. You're the first person to read them. Thank you for all your advice, help and support. The side notes still make me laugh, if I can read them.

Aaron, my silent supporter, best friend, and husband, you are with me through it all, the late nights, the stress, the tears of sadness, and the tears of joy. The endless snacks you know make me happy. You are the one person I will always want by next to me, even if you are asleep.

Ruth, I'm so freaking glad I met you. My #bookwife, when I need advice you give it tome, honestly and thoughtfully. I just wish you lived closer. It's like I have known you a lifetime and it's been less than twelve months. Book talks with you are life. Thank you for everything.

Nikki, my awesome Alpha/Beta reader. I could not have asked for a better person to Beta read for me, you have helped me make this book what it is now, your advice was so valuable to me. You have all helped me to be a better writer. Thank you.

Sarah Baker, editor, and all-time spice queen. You have made this whole experience like a dream. Your words and notes on my manuscript encourage me to go further, be bolder, and just let rip on what the story needs. The little hearts you leave along the way make my day. There are not enough thank you's in the world to convey how I feel.

My boys, George and Harry, you are way too young to read my books. but I hope you will someday. I want you to know that you are both the best things in my life. You make me so happy, your smiles and cuddles melt me. Everything I do is for you.

Save the best till last. To my readers and supporters, and Street Team, what can I say. What I have would not be possible without you all. I can't thank you enough for everything you have done and keep doing for me. I write these for you.

Bekki xx

A little note from me...

When I became a mum, I had no idea just how much it would change my life. I struggled, I lost who I was and had no idea how to find it. It scared me.

But what I found in the chaos was friendships, other mums, and old friends who didn't hide how hard it was. People I could talk to, and in that I found clarity to be okay with the hard stuff, because it will pass. Our thoughts will become clearer, and we will find who we are in this moment. It'll change from time to time, but it's nothing to be scared of. If I hadn't become a mum, and struggled, I would never have found some of the best people I have in my life, trained as a life coach, and become an author.

Life sucks sometimes, but it makes you appreciate the good time so much more.

– Bekki Vowles x x

Be the change you want to see in the world.
~ Mahatma Gandhi

Contents

Chapter One

Ride

Cole

Fuck, that feels so good in between my legs; the steady purr, the vibration on my thighs, spurs me to move faster. Switching up a gear, my blood flows, calming the temper in my veins as I ride out on my motorbike. It's been far too long since I've been out. This poor girl's been sitting in the garage for over a month now with no one to ride her.

I don't have long until I'm back on duty. An hour to ride in the open air and feel the wind on my face. Driving out of town, I watch as the buildings get smaller, and the roads open up to lanes and countryside. The views grow more spectacular the further I go. Fields on one side, and on the other, the wide-open expanse of the sea.

This is what it's all about. I breathe in the air as it lashes against my face. The bike glides around corners, a little faster than it should, given the damp air from last night's fog. I need to make more time for this; another year or so and I'm off—getting out of the security business.

Seeing where the bike takes me.

Urging forward, I come full circle, winding back around to the small town that's been my home all my life, apart from my years spent away in the army. I pull over when I reach the hill that leads to the seafront and park outside Bruno's café. His bright orange scooter is parked out the front—his pride and joy. The bell dings when I walk inside, the door closing behind me. Busy already, the queue at least ten customers deep. "Buddy," Bruno greets me, with his wide smile and handlebar mustacho. I smile at the nickname he's given me, easing some of the constant tension I have from the woman I've been babysitting. "I saw you on the bike. It's been a while, huh?" he asks.

"Too long. What's got you getting the scooter out?" His smile widens as he glances out the front window towards his ride.

"I'm riding out with a few friends this afternoon. What can I get you?" His eyebrows lift in question.

"I'll take a dozen pastries for the guys. And a sweet Americano to go, please." Nodding, he gets to work, adding the pastries to bags so I can get them in my pack. It's only a short journey to the office so they should make it.

"Enjoy the ride out." Tapping my phone to the card reader to pay, I wait patiently for the coffee, then head out the front.

Leaning against my bike, my helmet propped on the seat, the black town car passes me, heading down the hill. It pulls up just in front of Magnolias—Charlie's shop. She also happens to be my friend Owen's wife. One of the other three guys I co-own Cerberus, our security company, with.

A familiar black Ford Raptor pulls up alongside it: Ethan's truck. He climbs out, checking out his surroundings, tipping his head in my direction, before he allows *Miss Byron* out of the car.

Catching a glimpse, as her long, bare, healed legs step from the car. Taking my last sip of coffee, I throw my cup in the bin beside me, climb on my bike, rev the ignition, and head to work.

Pulling into the secure underground car park, I take the lift up to the ground floor. Owen's been back a week since his wedding to Charlie. He's already on our asses about updates to the system that should have happened while he was away. He knows how busy we've been, even more so when we're a man down.

That's why I'm in this morning. I'll run what he needs, then start an update on the quiet list—old cases we keep an eye on. Reaching the reception desk, taking my bag from my back, I grab the pastries from my pack and place them in front of Jill, our receptionist. "These are for everyone, if I take them up," I say, pointing to the ceiling, where our offices are, "they'll tear them to shreds. If you do it, I know everyone will get one." She rolls her eyes.

"Well, good morning to you too, Cole. And yes, they're animals when it comes to Bruno's fine, sweet pastries." Jill hands me my post, and I make my way upstairs.

Swinging my bag on the couch in the corner of my office, I step into my ensuite. My suit already hanging up for me, ready to change into. Dropping my jeans to the floor, my white tee and leather jacket come off next, hanging them on the rail, I change into my steel-grey suit trousers and crisp, white shirt, which I keep open at the collar, not feeling a tie today. Buttoning up my matching waistcoat, I'm ready. The guy's rib me about the choice to wear a suit. I think I pull it off well. Maybe not as well as Ethan, but I think he may have been born in one.

Walking into the comms room, I find Owen already at the large desk we share. Sitting next to him, I log on using the retinal scanner I added a few weeks ago—an addition he loved—ensuring only the four of us can access the system. "Leon should be here soon," Owen says flatly. "I've got the schedules for the next few months ready to roll." His eyes stay fixed on the screen in front of him.

"Did Charlie kick you out this morning? You've not been in this early for a while," I tease, side eyeing him. It's nine am.

"Yeah." He sighs. "Said I need to learn to miss her. That some separation is good for us," he says, shaking his head in disbelief. He sounds miserable as fuck. You'd think the year they spent apart, while Owen recovered from his PTSD, would have been enough, but I guess not.

"Shit, man. It's killing me." Pausing what he's doing, he turns to me. "I've just spent the last week basking in the glory that she's my wife, fucking her whenever I wanted, however I wanted..." *Ew, that's too much for me to handle this time in the morning.*

"Stop the fuck right there. I do not want to know anymore. Wanker, she's like a fucking sister to me." I cringe, and Owen lets out a laugh. "I get you miss her already, but guess what? You get to go home to her every day," I add, knowing this will cheer him up.

"To fucking right, I do." He grins, then frowns. "Are you with anyone? You don't say much about your love life." He taps the touch screen to adjust a few settings on the facial recognition software.

"Not seeing anyone. I like the single life. It suits me and the job." I also remember it's been a long ass time since I've been with a woman. I have visions daily of one of the most beautiful women I have ever seen. The things I'd do to that body of hers. The way I'd put her venomous mouth to good use. That being said, I'd never touch a woman like *her.*

If it wasn't for everything she stood for, she'd be my perfect woman.

"Let me know if it changes," Owen says, looking at me like he knows better.

"If what changes?" Leon asks, strolling into the room.

"My love life," I tell him, glancing up at him when he sets his laptop down next to me.

"Yes, my friend." He slaps my shoulder, chuckling. "You've not been laid in six months." He states, casual as anything, my jaw drops, while my dick agrees solemnly.

"What the fuck, man? How would even know that?" I'm taken aback at just how much this man knows; it's freaky sometimes.

"The last one you slept with was that brunette from that clothes shop at the bottom of the street, next to the gallery. Before that there was that stripper who went a little stalker on you." Owen's laughing so hard now that tears run down his cheeks.

"How do you even?" He has superpowers, that has to be it. "No, don't answer that... schedules, Owen for the love of fucking"—poor choice of works for the current conversation—"talk about the schedules and not my shitting love life," I grunt.

"Lack of love life is a better description." Owen howls beside me, wiping the tears from his face.

"Tossers, both of you. Now schedules before I leave you both to it," I add, grumpily. I don't need any reminders that my dick's not had any action in a while. *I fucking know.*

Owen sends us the schedules that ping into my email.

Taking a moment to check where I'll be and who I'm covering, I can see we're still on a rotation for Miss Arianna Byron. My deceitful cock twitches as my skin itches just thinking about her. She's fire and ice rolled into one prissy princess. Still daddy's little girl at the age of twenty-five. Makes me sick.

"Same as ever with the Bryon cover," Owen informs us.

Looking over the schedule, to distract myself, I can already see the gaps I'll have to be able to take the bike out more.

"What has your face smiling so much?" Leon asks, I can't help it, my ride this morning was just what I needed.

"I took the bike out for a ride this morning, it's been a while since I've been out, it felt good." I answer, my bike to me is like Owen's carpentry to him. It soothes my mind.

"Do you need more free time?" Owen asks, his eyes questioning me.

"No, I'm good." That's why I'm still with these guys. These two may run most of the daily stuff, but we all have an equal share of this company, they give me the time and space I need. I'd never work anywhere else. They're my unit brothers. In it together.

Chapter Two

Glimpse

Arianna

My phone's been vibrating off the hook since my alarm went off this morning, at five-thirty. Always early. It's followed by my schedule notifications for what today will bring. No rest for the wicked. If only I was allowed to be wicked for just a little while. Like the women in my books: devilish, fun, outgoing, successful. Or even normal, whatever that looks like.

I get glimpses of life outside of mine. People watching is good for my soul. I can live through others until, *hmm... never mind*. I'm ignoring them all for at least a few more moments before I have to shut myself down for the day ahead. A few moments to think for myself. Heaven.

Moving my head to the side, I watch Gi, my father's housekeeper, enter my room, and start setting out my outfits for the day. First, my gym wear, then the outfit for the 'show my face in the community' photos I'm told my father wants. Then a conservative dress for the charity event I have later this evening. Nothing I would actually choose to wear.

"Thanks, Gi." There's a slight note of sarcasm in my voice.

Here we go. The moment I step out of bed, it all starts. My heart sinks like it does every morning I wake to the same routine.

"Is this it, this morning?" I hold up the bright green protein shake she brought in with her in front of me. My face mirrors my thoughts of how disgusting it's going to taste

"I'm just following orders. I'll pack you something better for the car journey. Sneak it to you somehow." Gianna's a deep-rooted Italian woman, with greying dark brown hair, and curves for miles. Giving me the food that's on my diet plan kills her. Still, she always finds a way to feed me, even if it's against the rules.

"I don't know what I'd do without you, Gi." I smile, taking the first sip, and wincing slightly. *Good grief, that's horrible.*

"You'd starve." Her hand flaps towards the shake. I drink it down in one, it's the only way to get it done without heaving. Swinging my legs out the side of the bed, I start towards the shower, giving her a quick kiss on the cheek before I close the door behind me.

"Your new personal trainer is already waiting for you in the gym. Don't make him wait," she shouts after me. My stomach twists when I open the door back up, sticking my head out a little, frowning. "What happened to Tom?" I ask sadly, covering my body with the door.

"He questioned your father about your diet. Told him it wasn't enough with the workout regime they have you on," she says, walking towards my bedroom door. "I should have warned him," she mutters to herself. My shoulders sag. I hate that this happens. Gi feels guilty for him being fired. I do too. Unfortunately, if you question my life, you don't get to stick around to see it.

"I'd better not get attached to this one," I say matter-of-factly. "Can you do me a favour and send him a message from me? Just say thank you, and I'm sorry." Nodding, she leaves the room.

Sitting back in the town car against the tan leather seats, on my way to the small town just outside where I live in the middle of nowhere, I'm exhausted after the workout the new guy put me through this morning.

Dec, my driver, slides down the divider that separates us and hands me a parcel wrapped in brown paper, I take it from his outstretched hands and open the most delicious-smelling chocolate pastries. Handing him the second piece of chocolate heaven, he thanks me, eating as we drive down the hill to my first location of the day.

Waiting until I have the go ahead from Dec, I ready myself to step out of the car, there's no play between us today. All business.

Ethan, my security guard for the last week, opens the door and greets me with a sort of extended blink. He doesn't smile, never does. Very rarely speaks, but he's a gentleman all the same. And that I appreciate. He's part of my external security. One of three I have on rotation as soon as I step out of the house grounds.

Press gather around the car, no doubt, having been notified of my trip. Flashes almost blind me. Raising my hand to cover my eyes, I don't answer the questions they shout, just smile politely, and move forward. They don't seem to have boundaries or respect mine. Anything to get a photo of me doing something I shouldn't. It doesn't happen often, or it's an exaggerated truth, spun to gain more views on my social media profile, which will inevitably create more sales from the brands I represent. You'd think I was an A-list celebrity the way they follow me, not just a social media influencer.

Yes, I have millions of followers, but it's my father's influence as a high-profile judge that keeps the public interested.

I've been in the public eye for as long as I can remember, creating an image of the perfect family life, while all the paid partnerships we have make the money my father loves.

The agenda for today is to be seen. *Stupid, I know.* I have a few shops in mind. I guess they were suggested too, by the PR firm that manage me, and I guess my father. I don't know the reasons why, I'm here. I just do as I'm told. But I'd like to visit them anyway. I did a little research last night and Magnolias, the flower shop I'm standing in front of, is holding walk in workshops today to make an autumn wreath. Then there's the bookstore I'm excited about. I'd love to add another classic edition to my collection. Then, I'm going to the café on the hill for coffee and cake.

You won't be able to eat in there.

Internally sighing at the truth, the smell of flowers hits me in a wave of earthy freshness when I step inside the shop. Taking a deep breath, I take in the vibrancy of the space.

"It smells amazing, doesn't it?" a woman with white-blonde hair says from behind the counter.

"It most certainly does," I agree with a genuine smile.

"Morning, Ethan," she says with a playful grin for him. They must know each other because he grunts at her in response. Weird, I'd never put them as friends.

"I thought it was just me he grunted at," I say, side eyeing him from where he stands by the door. He doesn't move a muscle.

"Oh no, that's Ethan's normal tone, but I think he's internally doing an eye roll." I chuckle. "What can I help you with today?" she asks kindly.

"I'd like some of the brightest flowers you have, please. Would you mind if I took some photos of the shop?" I say, pointing the photographer outside, then taking my phone from the small bag I have.

"Sure, I'll ask Layla to get the flowers for you. She'll have a preference for what's her favourite today. I've got a meeting just about to start, so you'll have to excuse me. I'll send her out. It was lovely to meet you." She waves.

"Thank you. You too." She walks away, and I take a few images on my phone of the shop for myself. A minute later, a young woman walks out; a messy bun on top of her head, beautiful caramel skin, and a voluptuous figure. My eyes scan her frame, comparing myself to her. I think I'm jealous. I may not be that way inclined, but it doesn't mean I can't appreciate an amazing figure when I see one.

It makes me wonder what my own figure would look like if I didn't have to workout so much or drink green protein shakes. *Would I have curves?*

"Hola, let's see," she says, with an accent. "My flowers of the day are these amazing Gerberas." She's not looked up yet. "Did you know each and every flower has its own meaning." She's not asking me a question. "It's more to do with the colours than the actual flowers. These have only really been around in this country since the nineteenth century." Her enthusiasm for what she does is inspiring. She keeps talking, focusing on the flowers. "They were discovered, in—"

"Layla," Ethan bellows, shutting her up. She looks up, a little shocked. *Layla.* The name suits her.

"Ethan?" Her eyes flit to him first, seemingly shocked by his outburst. His eyes glance at me and then lock with hers again, as if giving her a silent message. Her mouth pops open in a small O shape. "*Oh mi dias,* Arianna Byron."

"Please excuse Ethan," I reassure her. "He's rude, I was enjoying learning about the Gerbera." Layla flushes red.

"I'm so sorry," she says, looking down at her feet.

"There's no need to be sorry. Please carry on. I asked the other lady for some of your brightest flowers," I say encouragingly.

"Charlie?" She frowns slightly. "She didn't say who you were. Just said a customer. If she'd told me, I would have never—" I step forward, interrupting her.

"Please do not be anything other than who you are."

"Right," she says, looking at me like I've made her day. "Flowers... what would you like?" She waves over the full shelves beside her.

"I'm going to leave that up to you, but I would like them wrapped in yellow, if possible. It's her favourite colour."

"Are they for a special occasion?" Layla asks, her hand flying to her mouth as the words leave. "I'm sorry. You don't have to answer that," she rushes out as she starts picking up flowers from the vases around the shop.

"It's okay. There's no special occasion. They're just for someone special." After the chocolate heaven Gi made for me and Dec this morning, she deserves these.

"Your mum?" I'm taken aback for a moment. I don't want to lie, but some things are better kept close to my chest. So, I just nod my confirmation. I feel Ethan's eyes on me, but he doesn't say anything.

Once outside, ignoring the press who are still hanging around, I pass the flowers to Dec as he opens the car door. Pausing, I take a look out into the road, and shake my head a little. Placing my hand on top of the car, I close the door, stepping away.

"I think I can walk to the next location. I can see the bookshop from here." I tell him. His eyes shoot to Ethan, who's standing next to me. Before they can say anything, I step around them, heading to the crossing a few meters away, directly in front of the shop. My bodyguards flank my sides within seconds. The press run past me to get a shot of me heading into... I look up to see the name again, The Book Nook. *Cute.*

It's just as I imagined: shelves stuffed with new and second hand books, cosy corners with soft, sinkable chairs ready to relax and read, and a small coffee stand next to the counter, so you can help yourself. *I love it.* Breathing in the relaxed atmosphere and the wonderful dusky smell of books, I walk over to the counter, watching a member of staff busy wrapping some books.

"Hi, I wondered if you could help me. I'm looking for a special edition copy of Jane Eyre," I ask. Placing the half-wrapped book on the side, he looks at me. "It's the edition with the sprayed edges."

"I'm sorry, Miss Byron," I wince at his use of my name when he doesn't know me. "We don't stock anything like that in the store." He looks apologetic, at least.

"Oh, that's okay. I wanted to ask on the off chance." I start to walk away, but he catches my attention when he speaks again.

"What if I can find it on the database we have, then I may be able to get it on order for you to collect, or we can have it delivered for you?" His eyes sparkle when I grin back at him.

I'd love to be able to collect it, to come back to sit and enjoy the space they have so wonderfully created, but not with my schedule and the restrictions I have in place. I know it won't be possible. A little twinge of sadness grips me, that I won't be able to make it back, at least not for a while anyway.

"May I have it delivered?"

"Of course, if you want to take a look around, I'll check when we can get it for you, and then I'll need to take some details." Pressing the keys on his computer, he gets to work on finding my book.

Glancing at the shelves, I'd love to take my time browsing. As much as I love the classics, I also love a good kinky romance book. It's my guilty pleaser. But with the cameras from the press outside, watching my every move, I daren't risk it. Unfortunately, my kind of books I can only read on my Kindle. I can only imagine the fallout if I actually looked at one on the shelf, let alone bought one, and walked the street with it in my hand. My father would go ballistic.

Reputation and image are everything.

To my father, it would symbolise an act of defiance. My rebellion against him and everything he stands for.

For now, it's just my thing. I like it that way.

"I've found one, we can have it delivered to your address by this week." I look over to the man at the desk who looks pleased with himself.

"Wonderful, thank you. How much do I owe you?"

"Um…" He looks almost too nervous to tell me, chewing on his lip. "It's… um, two-hundred and eighty-four pounds, please."

I take my purse from my bag and hand him my card. When he's all done, I take the receipt and thank him for his time. Walking to the door, pleased with my purchase. I'm ready to seek out those amazing cakes and pastries the café has to offer, but Ethan presses his hand to the door, stopping me.

"Ethan?" I ask, my eyes drawn to his hard but handsome face.

"Change of plans, Ari, sorry." My shoulder slump. "Oh." I know my father had something to do with this.

Chapter Three
Fun Police

Arianna

"So, sweet-cheeks, what are our plans for tonight?" Chrisy, my best friend, chimes when she walks through the door of my room. "And before you say it, no, we are not heading to that lame ass 'get together' Ace invited us to." Like any other social event, Ace, an old friend of ours from school, holds or invites us to, it's all about making connections, which is not the type of freedom Chrisy is looking for.

I had no intention to go out tonight.

"I have other ideas for our sexy as fuck ass tonight." My cheeks heat when she pulls me into a hug and slaps my *sexy as fuck ass* as she lets me go. "Ace has provided our cover for the night; we're free to roam this town." Smirking while she wiggles her eyebrows at me and sits on my bed.

"Why the hell did you ask me what our plans were tonight if you already knew what we were doing?" Chrisy loves the thrill of sneaking around. The risk has little consequence for her. She does it just because she can.

She shrugs while she takes off her jeans and jumper, changing into the dress she brought with her—a dress her father would really not approve of. It's bright red, short, and hugs her luscious figure in the right places. It's the perfect colour against her dark skin.

Digging into the huge tote bag she came with, she hands me a perfectly wrapped gift. The logo on the tape is from one of my favourite shops—but it's not on the approved list.

"I guess this a something Daddy dearest won't approve of?" I say sarcastically, my heart in my throat. There's an evil glint in her eyes, which means we are in for a hell of a night, and my security team is going to have their work cut out for them. Again.

If it wasn't for Chrisy, and her love for life, I would have no life at all. My father only approves of our friendship because she refused to leave my side through school, and her dad rose through the ranks of business to become one of the top three Fortune Five-hundred companies. My father likes money and status. While he continues to never personally acknowledge my existence unless it's to show off, reprimand me, or teach me what he thinks is a valuable lesson. All of which leaves me a little more fractured each time.

She pulls out a bottle of fizz from her bag.

"You know I can't drink that Chrisy, not after last time," I tell her, biting the inside of my cheek, my heart pounds with fear as my insides churn from the memories of what my father did last time he found me drinking.

Rolling her eyes, she shows me the bottle: *zero per cent alcohol* I read. "I guess I can," I add, when she hands me the plastic flute to pour for myself.

"I think of everything, honey." She sure does. "I'd never put you in that situation again, not after what your dear father did to you." Lunging forwards, I tackle her to the bed, hugging the shit out her, because I know she will always have my back.

She huffs, shoving me off. "Will your hot security team be ready for us?" Lying on the bed next to her, I bite my lip, thinking of the team that watches out for me, well one in particular anyway. Hot as sin, and a complete brute.

"Only if I let them know where we'll be," I say, turning to face her, "I'll let Ed know we're off to Ace's it's on my schedule, so he should believe me." Ed's the head of my father's security.

"Fucking schedules," she groans, hating how my life has turned out just as much as I do.

"Do you remember when we planned our life out? The things we wanted to do?" I say, as she squints at me, not knowing where I'm going with this conversation.

"I remember it all." She sighs. "The poster we made. Do you remember?" She squeals, jolting to sit up. I stay lying down, staring at the high ceiling.

"I do. We cut out all those images from the travel brochures you got, and stuck them on a huge sheet of paper." I grin, holding out my arms to mimic its size.

"We put glitter all over it. I remember it well, why?" she asks, frowning slightly. Taking a breath, I decide to say what I've been thinking. This has been on my mind for a while.

"I want you to see it all," I admit, quietly. "I want you to visit everywhere we ever planned, and I want you to tell me all about it." Screwing my eyes shut, I wait.

"Fuck off."

I burst out a gruff laugh, at her response.

"No way am I doing any of that without you." She stands, walking across the room, her shoulders bunched in annoyance.

"I'm sorry. I want to see them all too, but if you wait for me, it's not going to happen," I admit. She opens her mouth to protest. "We both know it," I say before she can get a word out. "We made those plans… twenty years ago, Chrisy." Nothing in my life has changed.

"Shit." It's a whisper, but I hear it.

"You went to uni, you got your degree. They wouldn't let me go." 'They' being my parents.

"I know, but—"

"No buts. I need you to see these things for me. I'm going to have to live through you," I say. I can see the unshed tears in her eyes as I fight back my own.

"On one condition?" she says, pointing at me.

"Name it."

"We pick one place neither of us will ever go without the other." I can see how serious she is.

"Deal."

"Because one day you will get out of here, and see the world for yourself, Ari. And he won't be able to stop you." I nod, but deep down I know there's not a chance of me escaping this life. Not really.

"Right, we can decide on our travel destination another day," she says, clapping her hands together to change the beat of the conversation. "Who's on team fun police tonight?"

"I don't know." It's been a few days since I've been out, so I've not needed them. "I guess it's tall, blond, and angry, as tall, dark, and fucking scary did the last shift." I know their names, but I like my way of describing them better. What's better is Chrisy knows exactly which ones I'm talking about. She smirks.

"I like all of them. I don't care which one is it. They all make me want to do very bad things to them, *for* them. I like being a bit naughty when they're around." Laughing at her, I know just what she means. It's exciting to see how far we can push them. It just so happens that tall, blond, and angry gets the brunt of what we do. It helps he's sexy as hell.

"Take a look then," she says excitedly, handing me the dress she's taken from the bag which I hold against myself.

"You didn't?" It's the dress we've been looking at for weeks online. I'm shaking with excitement, unable to take my eyes off the dress.

"I sure fucking did, sweet-cheeks," she whispers shouts at me.

"Oh, if my father ever sees this." My voice wobbles as panic starts to rise, but I shove it down. "He'll send me off to the nunnery for sure." I'm only half joking.

"Just make sure he never finds it, and if he does, tell him it's mine. That will really blow his mind." There's a look of what appears to be concern that flashes over her face, but she masks it quickly. We both know what my father would really do if he found out about any of my unsanctioned outfits.

Chrisy walks into my walk-in closet and opens the drawer that's full of unapproved underwear, hidden under the uglier than *Bridget Jones'* big ass underwear that's bought for me. All of which has been vetted by my mother, to ensure I keep to the good girl family image, both my parents demand.

"No. I can't wear that. Look at it." I gasp as she holds up a black lace bodysuit. It's beautiful, dipping low at the front, the bottom rising high on the hips, at least it will cover my backside. Just.

"Oh yes you can. You'll feel amazing . It's sexy, classy, and beautiful just like you." And I'll be almost naked, but who can argue with those words?

Heading to the office where Ed monitors the cameras, pulling the belt of my trench coat a little tighter so he can't see what I'm wearing. I open the door and slip inside leaving Chrisy in the hall behind me.

"Ari," he says not taking his eyes off the screens that show grainy images of the house and land outside.

"Every time, Ed." It's been a thing since I was little. I'd try and sneak up on him, but each time he would know I was there. Ed has worked for my family since I was little. He and Gianna are happily married and sometimes feel more like parents than my own ever do.

"Are you and Chrisy off to Aces?" His tone is deep and serious. He doesn't like Ace. He'd prefer it if I didn't go.

"Yep," I lie, he'll find out soon where we are really headed, but for now, I let him think I'm doing as I'm told.

"Dec's already outside. I'll walk both of you out." He eyes Chrisy who's leaning against the door frame behind me.

"I don't need an escort through the house, Ed" I tease. Sighing, Ed stands. There's no point trying to get him to stay put, this is what he does. He opens the top filing cabinet drawer and takes out two cans of pepper spray, throwing one to Chrisy, who just manages to catch it before it hits the floor.

"I've got a few of these now, thanks, Ed. This should keep Ace and his wandering hands away for at least fifteen minutes," she says with a straight face, adding it to her bag as she walks away towards the front door, leaving us alone.

"She's trouble. I'm glad you have her, Ari. She's good for you." Slipping his hand into his pocket, he pulls out a small keyring and places it in my palm, closing my fingers around it.

"Panic alarm. Keep it close," he adds wrapping his arms around me in a warm hug. I want to roll my eyes at him, but the threats my father receives from the criminals he's put behind bars, to us as a family and myself in particular are terrifying. I love that Ed makes me carry this stuff. It means he cares, even if he is being paid to do a job. Smiling into his chest, I hug him back. It's rare that I feel cared for like this, so I hug him a little harder.

"Be safe Ari," he says, with a swift kiss to the top of my head. He releases me and I pull my belted coat a little tighter around me, making sure my dress is covered. He's only going to worry more, if he knew I was going out dressed like... well, like this.

Chapter Four

Flirt

Arianna

After giving Dec our new destination in the car, he grumbled something I wasn't able to hear and drove us here. I know he'll contact Cerberus as soon as we step out of the car and tell them where I am. I don't blame him. It just means I have about forty minutes before they arrive. Then my fun will either start or be over.

Leaving my coat in the car, we make it through the bright red doors of Club Adore just in time to see the dancers do their thing on stage. I've only been here once before. The whole theme of the place is to include you or a select few in the dances they perform each night. It's amazing, I only watched last time, but Chrisy got up and danced with them. I wasn't brave enough. I stood in awe at her zest for life.

But tonight, I want to. I want to feel life. I want to just *feel*.

Chrisy winks at the bouncers as we pass through the crowd of people near the stage already gathered hoping to be picked. Chrisy waves at one of the dancers to get his attention. "Ru saved us a spot." I'm guessing Ru is the male dancer who's making his way over to us.

He takes Chrisy's hand and leads her up the stairs while I stand watching them. Another dancer appears out of nowhere and offers me his hand. I take it, nerves bundling in my stomach.

Climbing the small set of stairs to the stage, we slip right in next to the other dancers already in full swing to a song I don't know. Pulling close, he bends down, discreetly asking if it's okay for him to dance with me like the others are. I nod, my voice stuck in my throat.

His hands are on my waist, guiding my hips as we move to the beat of the music, draping my arms around his neck; it's like that scene from Dirty Dancing. I feel sexy, something I've not felt before this moment.

This is what Chrisy meant by being naughty tonight. In this dress, I'm sure I'm giving the crowd an eyeful. Dancing like there is no one watching, I enjoy the feel of the professional dancer's hands on me as we move together. Swaying me, touching me, the thrill's addictive. Then I feel it. The shiver down my spine. I know he's here. I always know when tall, blond, and angry arrives. That he's watching me.

It's like a ripple across my skin as soon as he walks into the room. I know he won't be happy, but guess what? He's never fucking happy. I know he hates me, I know he hates what I am. Rich, unemployed, uneducated. A socialite who lives for the cameras. But do I care? Not in the slightest, because what he thinks makes no difference.

Catching Chrisy's attention, I grab her by the waist and pull her towards me. "He's here," I murmur into her ear. "Fancy a bit of fun?" I ask and her eyes light up. We position ourselves in front of our partners, our backs to their fronts. Moving closer together, our dance partners follow our lead. Hands trail our bodies as we dance. Christy's hands on my waist trail down, over my sides, skimming my dress, her hands are joined by Ru's, who's now behind me, skimming my thigh. I raise my hands in the air, swaying to the beat of "Dirty Thoughts", by Chloe Adam. Thoughts of whose hands I'd like on me race through my mind.

"You can come here again, Miss Byron," my dancer says, my heart sinking a little because, of course he knows who I am.

"Thank you." My eyes lock with Chrisy's as she plays with the hem of my dress, edging it a little higher. Only stopping when she reaches the hemline of my lace bodysuit. The guys step away as they move on to the next guest dancers. Spinning myself around, I kiss her cheek, mouthing a thank you before we move to the side of the stage. Stepping down from the stage, hands appear from a couple of guys who help us make a gracious exit.

Chrisy loves the attention, and this is where she shines; lapping it up when the guy who helped her down wraps a hand around her waist and goes in for a kiss. I revel in her freedom. The buzz of what we just did cursing through my skin. But now I know his eyes are on me, the tingle in my spine intensifies. I want to look, but won't. I won't give him the satisfaction. When the guy who helped me down leans in, expecting the same reaction as Chrisy gave his friend, I back away. There's only so much I'm willing to put at risk for one night.

As I head towards the bar, they follow. Chrisy and the new guy still all over each other, his friend looking a little miffed.

"You don't have to stick around," I whisper in his ear, his hand coming to the small of my back as we approach the bar.

"I know, but I have to stick with this one. He likes to get himself into trouble." Laughing with him, an intense shiver ripples up my spine, leaving me a little breathless. He's close, his gaze on my back right where my new friend's hand lays over my sheer dress. I ignore it and motion towards Chrisy. "Funny you should say that, I have friend just like that. I'm Ari," I offer.

"Alden," he replies with a smile. "That's my best friend, Avery."

"Chrisy," I say, pointing towards where she's perched on the bar stool, still kissing Alden's best friend.

After ordering a couple of waters, we make our way to the table in the VIP area Chrisy booked for us. Alden moves to sit down after Avery and Chrisy, leaving a space for me and I sit. I spot him; beautiful, angry, hazel eyes meet mine.

Cole, tall, blond, and angry as ever, stalking towards me, us. My stomach flips. I don't move, placing my hand on the new guy's arm. It's an innocent touch. My eyes flicker to the way Cole's fists clench at his sides, pushing past people to get to me.

"Oh shit," I hear Chrisy gasp, "Captain America's angry." I can't look at her. I know her smile will have faded a little. But I grin, knowing it'll annoy him further.

Reaching me, he doesn't even look me in the eye, instead, he curls his large hand around my wrist. His touch is soft, surprising me. My eyes lower to his fingers, unable to take my gaze away from where we're connected.

Cole pulls me to one side, away from the others, my feet following.

His jaw is hard, teeth clenched. As he stands over me, wearing an impeccable black suit, which stretches across his chest. It outlines *everything*.

"You need to be careful what you're doing *Miss Bryon*." Never Arianna, or Ari, just *Miss Bryon*. He spits it out like he hates the way it sounds on his lips, almost as if it leaves a bitter taste every time he says it.

Talk about a rollercoaster ride of highs and lows. Not even an hour into our night out and I've ridden my high, to hit my low. This is why any sort of relationship is out of the question.

There was one time, when I thought a relationship was real, but that... didn't work out. If that's what happens when I'm in a relationship, never again.

"Excuse me?" I seethe. He knows just how to ignite the fire in me, I see it in his smirk. It just goads me. I pull my wrist from his grasp and his hand falls to his side. His fingers shake away the feel of me like he can't stand to touch me.

"You know exactly what I mean, Miss Byron." He really has a way of getting under my skin. I like it more than I should.

"No, actually, I don't know what you mean." I huff, but his face is stone.

"There are cameras here tonight, this DJ is huge," he hisses, his mask slipping, showing the anger through his impressive façade. Leaning down, edging closer, he gets in my face. "You need to watch yourself." His tone is clipped and to the point. "And after that little stunt," he points to the stage, "wearing that," his eyes burn holes into my outfit, "have some self-respect."

I shrink back internally, swallowing a lump of sadness. His words hurt, tearing me apart. It's not like I haven't heard them before, but... from him. They cut a little deeper. *I don't know why.* Maybe his disdain for the life I have runs a little deeper than I thought. I can feel the fight leaving me.

"Right, I hear you loud and clear, Captain Furious." My chest squeezes a little, knowing that my night has come to an end sooner than I wanted it to.

"Ari, is everything okay?" Looking over my shoulder, Alden is watching with interest and concern. It's cute but unnecessary. Squaring my shoulders and standing a little taller, I turn to face him, placing *her* back into the room: the woman everyone sees instead of me.

"Thank you, Alden. I'm okay, meet Captain Furious, my security for the night." Alden steps closer, holding out his hand, but Cole makes no move to return the gesture. Alden drops his hand when Cole growls at him. Alden swallows, his nerves clear, but smiles at me anyway. Cute. But I don't feel anything for him.

"Captain Furious likes to suck the fun out of everything I do." The smile I give Alden is small and sad, polite even. I look at Chrisy, who has been watching intently.

"I'm heading home. You coming?" I know she won't.

"No, I'm staying with... what's your name?" She giggles, leaning onto her new friend.

"Avery." He smiles, kissing her cheek.

"I'm staying with Avery."

"Okay, text me when you're home." I walk toward the main doors, not looking back.

"Where's your coat?" Cole mumbles when we step outside. I don't answer.

I don't want him to see the sadness I have inside right now, so I switch on my sass. He's slipping off his jacket and I'm confused why. It's cold out here. "Hey,

Cap," I say walking backwards, "were you born with a stick up your backside, or is it something someone rammed up there for you?" He stops walking, swinging his jacket over his shoulder. As Dec pulls the car up beside me, he opens the car door for me when it pulls up alongside us. His dark, fiery, hazel eyes lower to mine, looking at me with something akin to dislike only stronger.

Whatever.

"Right, just as I thought. Go give yourself a few tugs of your tool, tonight cap, it may bring a smile to your face, using your right hand for something other than to ruin my night." I don't wait for a response; I know I won't get one. Climbing in the car, he closes it behind me. I leave him standing there.

Chapter Five

Sweat

Cole

I hit the punch bags as hard as I can as sweat drips down my bare back and chest. I don't know how long I've been at this; I just know I needed to let go of this frustration. An overwhelming irritation, infatuation, and hard on, I have for Miss *fucking* Byron.

Smack.

She had the audacity to tell me to go fuck myself.

Smack.

I don't remember the last time someone had the guts to tell me to do that.

Smack. The way she moved her body, fuck. The thought makes my breathing harder from more than just my workout.

Smack, punch, fucking *smack.* The way she swayed her hips, rocked them, showing her perfect ass. Beautiful. *Smack.*

If I wasn't so pissed that she put herself in another compromising position that could ruin her precious reputation, potentially ruining her, and everything she's built for herself as an influencer, I'd have laughed in her face. But she did. Again. That's why I keep hitting this bag. The entitled little... *smack.* I hit the bag again, erasing the names I want to call her, but can't.

There's something about her when she lets rip at me.

I fucking love it.

Getting under her skin, I mean, making her react, lose her shit. Fuck, it makes me want to piss her off just for the fun of it.

What the fuck is wrong with me?

She has everything handed to her, and she just wants to throw it all away on some night out. I was right, she has no self-respect. No respect for what she has. It makes me sick.

When I walked into the club last night after my call from Dec. I knew where she was instantly, I'm drawn to her in a way I don't understand, maybe it's her recklessness, her need to put herself in harm's way. Mixed with my need to do my job fucking well, protect and serve, that's what I was born to do.

It's in my blood.

She's infuriating to the point of obsession.

I can feel it now, the blood rushing through my system when I watched that little fucker with his hands all over her, grinding up against her. I saw red, but I had to fucking wait to get to her. Security wouldn't let me up there to grab her from the stage. Said it would be bad press for everyone involved. He was right, it would have been. So, I watched as she dry humped him in front of hundreds of people. I watched as her dress became almost god-damn-fucking see through when the light hit it and I almost dropped to the floor at the sight of her underwear.

My deceitful cock growing harder than steel at the sight of the lace covering her, my eyes drawn to her full tits.

She looked different. Freer almost. It's a look I've not seen before.

I watched her body move as she danced with this stranger, her head falling back onto his chest. I wanted to rip his fucking head off. Worst of all, I wanted it to be me... my hands on her body, feeling her breath quicken when I touched the hem of her dress, sliding it up... *Fuck.*

Smack. Why can't she see what she's doing is insanely dangerous for who she is? Drawing unwanted attention.

I had to step in. It's my job.

"What's the bag done to piss you off today?" Leon asks, coming into view as I roundhouse kick the leather.

"Nothing," I answer, kicking again, the bag groaning in protest.

"Yeah, sure. You always kick the shit out of the bag on Saturday morning before you run drills with fifteen teenage kids." He laughs that deep fucking annoying laugh he has. He's dressed ready for a training session with one of Xander's guys. Xander owns this place with Charlie's brothers, Christian and Corban. I stop my assault on the bag, my chest heaving. He's right, I don't do this.

She does this to me.

"Fine." Grunting as I lower my gloved hands, admitting defeat early. I know he won't give up until he gets it out of me. He's been relentless since Owen suffered through his PTSD and took off for a year. Leon's not forgiven himself for not trying harder with him. "The pampered princess got herself into a situation last night," I seethe. "Then had the guts to fucking tell me to go fuck myself, and it pissed me off."

"She cursed at you?" His frown deepens, looking confused. "You must have pissed her off. Ari never swears." *Ari? What the fuck?*

"You're on first name basis with her?" I ask, trying to keep my annoyance to myself. Leon nods at me like it's a stupid question.

"Of course I am. We all are."

Fuck, I knew she hated me just as much as I dislike her. This just proves she does most of this shit to wind me up. And I hate that it works.

Every. Fucking. Time.

"She rubs me the wrong way," I grit out, wanting to end this conversation. The more I think of her the more I... never mind.

"No shit, we never would have guessed; you've had it out for her the moment you laid eyes on her." Facing the bag again, I take another swing. Feeling the ripple of my muscles as I connect with the bag. Leon at my side, watching.

"She doesn't even call *me*, yesterday, Dec had to call me and tell me where she was, I was waiting at that dumb fuck Ace's place for her to turn up." The punch bags really getting it now. "That's where she was supposed to be last night, Leon, at a safe place." My chest aches. "It annoys the fuck out of me." My tone's harsh but he knows it's not aimed at him. "How am I meant to do my job when she keeps sneaking around? I was forty minutes behind her, Leon." *Smack.* Leon takes the handheld pads off the bench beside him, holding them up ready for me.

My body already feels exhausted, but I've got more to give. "She has no idea what could have happened. The danger she put herself in." Turning to face him, I hit the pad he holds out for me. *Smack.* "Fucking irresponsible." I grunt as I hit it again. Leon bracing with each hit I make. The fucking knob's smiling at me.

I followed her home, obviously not done with torturing myself. I watched her sneak into her own home last night. *She's twenty-five, for fuck's sake, why is she sneaking in?*

"Help me understand, my friend, I feel like I'm missing something." My right hand connects with his left, in a jab, we have sequenced in a well-rehearsed routine.

"I don't understand why she's the way she is. She has everything, the perfect life, it's all handed to her on a silver platter, or fucking spoon, whatever the saying is." Swiping the sweat from my forehead, I kick out this time, Leon blocks it.

"Do you need to understand?" He has a point. Why do I need to understand?

I punch the pad Leon's holding out harder, but he doesn't even flinch. "Fuck," I shout.

"She's just a job, Cole. Maybe you need to keep that in mind next time." He's right, for whatever reason, I'm in my head about it all. About her.

"Thanks, I needed that." I shrug away, grabbing my towel from the floor and wiping my face and chest down.

"You still on call?" he asks, but he knows I am.

"Yeah, for the next few weeks. At least." I groan, dropping my towel next to my bag on the floor.

"Looks like you're being summoned," Leon says, pointing to where my phone is lying on the top of my bag. *Shit.*

Pulling the gloves off, I reach for my phone. It's a text from Dec with details of where I need to rush to next—another unscheduled stop from Miss Byron.

After the quickest shower and throwing on my suit over my still damp body, I'm in my truck, speeding through the streets to see what the princess has in store for me today.

Chapter Six

Suck it Up

Arianna

"I'm so excited I have an interview today," Chrisy shouts down the phone when I answer. I'm lying on my bed recovering from today's extreme gym session. It's the same every morning. It always takes me a while to recover.

"Tell me all about it." I pause, then ask, "How long have you known about the interview?" She groans.

"A few weeks. I was so worried to tell you, it could mean some big changes for me."

"Big changes?" My heart's beating faster at what she could mean. "Tell me about it then," I tell her. If she's excited, I am too.

"It's for this new firm. I was head-hunted," she chimes proudly. "It's my dream job, Ari. They said it includes an apartment, car, and bonuses." Chrisy completed her master's degree in marketing a few years ago and has been working for a local firm ever since. "If I'm accepted, they even said they will cover all the moving costs."

"Moving costs?" My heart sinks a little. "Where is it?" I'd never stop her chasing her dreams, she knows that, but I'll be devastated she isn't near me.

"Liverpool."

Liverpool? My shoulders sag. That's like over four hours away—by car, and I can't drive. I'm glad she can't see me.

Suck it up, Ari, this is her dream job.

"At least you'll still be in the country. It sounds perfect. Just what you've always wanted." I'm keeping my tone as positive as I can.

"It is, Ari," she says, her voice a little sad. "I don't even have it yet. I may not even get it."

"Hey, that job's meant for you, right? Then go get it. I have every faith that by the end of the interview, you'll be packing your bags." My chest caves. It could really happen. "Plus, you said they head-hunted you. They must like what they see." I reassure her the best I can. I know what she'll do if I break down. I'm not holding her back.

"I *am* brilliant at what I do." I laugh at that. "I'm going to give it my all."

"Good, because if they don't hire you, then I may have to have a few words with them for being so utterly stupid." It's her turn to laugh now.

"I'll let them know I come highly recommended by my best friend. Anyway, I have to go and get ready. I told work I needed the time off to have this interview. I'm sure they didn't know what to do. They just wished me luck. Poor bastards may be a little lost without me."

"Let me know how it goes. I can't wait to hear all about it," I say, grinning while biting the inside of my cheek to keep it together.

"I'll call you later when I'm done."

Disconnecting my call with Chrisy, I stay on the bed for a while as the realisation sinks in that I may not have my best friend as close as I'm used to. Deciding I'll stay in and just chill. I need to check the social pages for any evidence of our night out, not that I can do anything about it, but I can at least brace myself for the fallout that will come with it.

After his cruel words yesterday, the hate he has for me seeps through every time I see him. I know what he thinks of me and my life style.

He has disapproval and disgust written all over his face with every encounter. I know I could show him the real me, but he's come to his own conclusions about who he thinks I am. I don't want him to see the real me anyway. According to him, the girl born with a silver spoon in her mouth. I'm a spoilt brat. The worst thing is, he's not wrong in his conclusions. I have been born into privilege. From the outside looking in, I could have or do anything I wanted.

I think the best solution would be to ask Ed if he will look at getting another firm to cover my security detail.

I'm on the way to the kitchen to get my fruit bowl for my movie, when the sound of the doorbell swings me in the opposite direction. I call out to Gianna that I'll get it. Everyone may think I'm a pampered princess, but I don't mind getting the door if I'm passing.

Looking on the video display, the face that greets me is terrifying. My father's business partner looks into the camera with a scowl on his ugly face. I take back everything I just said. This man can stay there. I'll take Captain Furious for the rest of my life before I speak to this man. My heart hammers in my chest and I have to shake my hands to get rid of the fear that's gripped me. This man scares the pants off me. For good reason. Pausing for a moment, I need to gather myself to face him.

I lean against the dark wall of the hall, internally groaning, chastising myself for telling Gi I would get the door. Stupid, stupid me. Next time I'll check before I tell her I'll do it. He can stand out there for a while and wait. It will aggravate him to no end, but that man seems to have a permanent sour expression, most likely from years of being the biggest dickhead known to mankind. And that's putting it kindly. Combined with a continuous black mood, his chauvinistic and misogynistic tendencies (his way of life) are the icing on his foul rotten, tobacco and whisky-smelling cake. My stomach rolls just thinking of the smell whenever he's too close.

I'm working up the courage to open it when Gianna walks around the corner, rushing a little, but still ever the professional. Most likely wondering why the door's not been opened yet. She rolls her eyes when she sees who's on the screen. We have a mutual hatred for this man, only Gianna can cover her contempt better than I can. Putting on my best princess fake smile, I take hold of the handle and open the door.

Not taking a breath.

He doesn't even wait for me to open the door fully, before shoving his way inside, barging into me in the process, and almost knocking me over. Steadying myself on the door, I bit my lip to hold in my reaction.

"Where's your father?" he scolds, like it's my fault he's not standing in front of him. "It's lovely to see you too Mr Carmichael," I murmur, the sound of his name making my skin crawl. I point in the direction of my father's office, assuming he's in.

Mr Carmichael strides forward, shoving me out of the way, my shoulder smashing against the wall as he passes, the gold edged mirror digging in just to hurt me further. Wincing, keeping my distance, I stay quiet.

Without any sort of acknowledgment, he walks towards the office. There's a saying about people like him and my parents, something about flies and shit, and being attracted to each other. I'm not sure who's the shit and who's the fly; I just know I hate being around any of them.

"Arsehole," I whisper under my breath, rubbing my now aching shoulder, before closing the door with force.

He spins back around and stares at me, his eyes pinning me in place. I freeze. He storms back towards where I still stand and takes my bicep in a grip that will probably bruise. I blink back the tears. I won't let him see me cry, even though it hurts like crazy.

"You have no idea how much of an arsehole I can be, *Miss* Byron." My skin prickles and I stumble backwards, trying to shake off his grip. Gi calls his name and he releases his hold on me as if he didn't realise she was witness to his actions.

Gianna guides him away, glancing over her shoulder, concern in her face. That woman has balls of steel. I don't think I would ever intervene when he was speaking. I'd be too afraid of what he might do.

I've heard the rumours about Mr Carmichael, and what he does to women in his life, he's brutal and unforgiving. Mr Robert Carmichael has no morals, none. Everyone is beneath him. He's willing to do anything to gain the power he craves to stay on top.

That, I think is one of the scariest things you can see in a person, everyone is disposable to him. Or at the very least has a value. Until you don't.

I look down at my arm, red marks dotting my skin, growing darker by the minute. I'll have to cover them up tomorrow. Changing my mind about staying in the house, I pick up my jacket and purse and make my way to find Ed. Popping my head into the security office, I find Gianna and Edward chatting.

"I'm heading out to the gallery," I tell them. Ed nods his agreement, while Gianna stands, coming towards me. There's nothing in my schedule today. Even if I'm expected to do as I'm told most of the time, I have been given the privilege of visiting the gallery when I'm on my time.

"It's a good idea with that man in the house." Her fingers grace my hand. "Did he hurt you?" she asks, looking at my arm, shaking my head in answer, I won't tell them he did. There's not a lot they could do about it anyway.

"Have you told the guys at Cerberus you're heading out? Will they meet you there?" Ed asks, ducking his head to look me in the eyes. I roll my eyes. I can't lie to this man, he's been too good to me.

"I will, I like to make things... hard for them." I laugh. Turning to walk away, he calls through the door, "I'll let the team know where you're headed." I understand why I have them, but it doesn't mean I want them to follow me everywhere I go. It's suffocating.

Chapter Seven

Freedom

Arianna

When Dec pulls the car into the drive a few minutes later, I step out the front door in my pale blue jeans, white *Blondie* tee, and bright pink blazer. I've left my dark brown hair loose; wavey from leaving it to dry on its own this morning. Chrisy hates I can do that with hair. Hers goes frizzy when she leaves it to dry.

Pulling open the handle to the car door, I get settled inside. Dec rolls his eyes at me in the rear-view mirror, something he does a lot when I get my own door. One good thing, I don't see Captain Furious anywhere. Good, maybe I'll be able to see this exhibit without his interference, and his gorgeous face darkening my mood further.

The gallery has good security. Ed knows them well, meaning I can go when I'm able to.

I rub my arm subconsciously, feeling the tender skin underneath. Opening the small fridge, I find a small bottle of sparkling white wine and a single glass waiting for me. It's alcohol-free, but it feels like a little luxury.

Taking the glass from its fixing on the built-in shelf, Declan waits for me to pour the golden liquid into the glass before he moves the car off the driveway. I see so many people drinking alcohol, enjoying just a glass or two; it seems like a normal thing to do, but in my father's eyes it's disgraceful for his daughter to

39

even take a sip, an act of defiance against him. My father drinks, I've seen his impressive collection of high priced, high end whisky. I'm allowed to pretend, to keep up appearances, but if I was ever found to have drunk any, he'd know about it, and unfortunately, so would I.

Dec knows me well. He's been driving me for years. I've always had Declan and Edward by my side until about a year ago, when it all changed.

I don't understand why things changed. Why my father stopped them, but he did, and overnight, I was left vulnerable. My own father stopped all my security and I was left reeling in what could happen to me with no security around.

My father has a lot of enemies being a judge. I've had a few verbally attack me while I've been out. It's sobering when someone blames you for something your father's done; targeting me to get to my father. When the guys from Cerberus were hired twelve months ago, it was agreed that they would have nothing to do with Ed's team, an outside team when I'm not in the house. I knew that it was Ed and Gi who arranged it; they went out of their way to help me. My chest tightens with guilt and gratitude for what they've done for me. They'd arranged for them to be by my side, protecting me. Worried for my safety when my own parents weren't. Even if I hate it, I know it makes Gi and Ed happy that I have someone looking out for me. But I do like to make them work for it.

I knew it was coming out of Gi and Ed's pay cheques. I decided there and then it wasn't good enough. How could I let them do that for me?

I couldn't.

Using the allowance, I started giving them money every month. Repaying the money they're spending to protect me. It takes a huge chunk—over two-thirds—I'm sure it's costing more than that, but I can't let my parents suspect I have no money, I still need the illusion in place. If I didn't, it would bring more unwanted questions my way.

I couldn't let them pay for it, even if I don't want the security, I'll keep it. I'll never admit it out loud, but having them around has been useful. If I'm really going for it, they make me feel safe. Who knows what could happen? I'll still have my fun though, however stupid it is.

My freedom has restrictions, iron bars almost. An illusion of freedom with none of the benefits. It's twisted. I can go out, like now, and see anyone on the recommended list—people with influence, social status, or money. I can go where I want, again on the recommended list. There's a list of respectable places I can go out at night, that I should be attending. A schedule. If I go anywhere else the repercussions are somewhat... barbaric or archaic? I found out the hard way just how barbaric they could be once.

I close my eyes at the awful memory as it tries to filter into the present.

I didn't see anyone for three months. Not a soul. Nothing but the same four walls. I was taken to a room and held there, locked away, until I agreed to be more agreeable. There's only one thing that came from those three months of pain and isolation, apart from my new fear of being locked in small spaces–my new-found determination to see life, in any way I can. Live through others if I need to. I'm not scared of going back there, I'm scared of not being able to live a life I know I should. Shutting that memory back into its box, I take my final sip of the fruity sparkling wine.

I feel more watched now than I ever have been. My parents' feigned interest in me is unwavering.

My every move recorded, monitored, and scrutinised.

Trapped in a gilded castle.

A perfectly fabricated life.

Declan pulls up to the front of the gallery, I hop out before he gets the chance to open my door for me.

"Ari, you do realise it's part of my job to open the door for you and assist you out." Dec groans, smirking at me. This is what we do. A little light banter between us. It's comforting to be playful with him.

"I'm not an old decrepit lady yet, Declan," I tease. "And as long as I can stand and use all of my limbs, I'll be opening my own doors, *and* getting out all by myself." He laughs, shutting the door behind me with a soft thud.

"I'll look forward to seeing you old and decrepit, Miss." I openly laugh at him.

"One to you, that was brilliant."

He discreetly fist pumps the air as I walk towards the entrance of the gallery. "Oh, Miss Byron, Mr Grant was informed of your impromptu trip. He's waiting for you inside, checking out the space. He'll be out in a few moments for you.

"Wonderful," I say sarcastically. Cole Grant is waiting inside for me. "Thank you, Dec," I add with a little more sincerity. It's anything but. I don't want them here.

Pausing before I push open the door, I consider turning around and getting back in the car, but decide against it. Instead, knowing the trouble I could get in, I head for the cocktail bar down the road I remember Chrisy telling me about. I'll grab a few drinks before I head back to the gallery. Make them sweat a bit. What's the point in living if you can't live, or take a risk every now and then?

Walking away from the gallery, my heart beating wildly. Dec knows better than to make a scene, leaning against his car, he shakes his head, while pulling out his phone. He won't call my name. I don't look back and I'm out of sight before anyone can see me, making a little detour, along the way to keep them on their toes when they attempt to find me.

I think I like making him chase me a little too much.

I've never been in this place before, but Chrisy's raved about how good it is for months, begging me to come. We've just not had the chance yet. We might not if she gets this job. Forcing myself to keep the smile on my face, I refuse to feel sorry for myself when my best friend has the world at her fingertips.

High tables and leather stools are scattered around the room, the bar rustic and industrial, with a hint of bling. It works. Understated opulence.

Perching myself onto a high stool, I look over the menu. The cocktails sound amazing, but I opt for the non-alcoholic one, placing my order with the girl behind the bar.

I watch as she pours, shakes, and adds various liquids in bright colours into a mixer, before eventually tipping it over dry ice into my lavish glass. As she adds the liquid, it plumes with icy smoke, spilling and flowing all over the counter. Sliding it towards me, she hands me the glass straw.

"Enjoy," she adds before she moves down the bar to serve someone else.

I've been here for fifteen minutes already. I'm sure I'll be greeted by an annoyed, grumpy bodyguard when either he finds me or I decide to go back to the gallery.

Smiling to myself, I'll enjoy this; not just the drink, but the little slice of freedom I've made. It's not often or ever really, that I get to sit by myself with no one around, watching me. It feels good. A little scary, if I'm honest. *I'm alone here.* I have all day with nothing to do and no-one to see. As long as I keep out of trouble, or of sight of the press, I'll be okay.

You hope.

Lifting my glass, I take a sip of my drink.

"A bit early to be hitting the hard stuff, isn't it? Especially when you're here alone." The question startles me. There's so much innuendo in both of his words. I'm not sure how to answer.

Shifting slightly in my seat, glancing around to see who and where the questions came from, I spot the guy. He's slightly older, sitting a few chairs down holding a tumbler of what looks like whiskey. I offer him the fake smile I'm well practiced in before turning my attention back to my drink, hopefully giving him the message that I'm not interested in having a conversation. I'm here to piss off my security team. Right on cue, my phone vibrates in my bag. Reaching for it, I read it without opening the app. I'll give it a few minutes before I answer.

Fun Police: Where the fuck are you?

God damn it. My stomach flips flops knowing he's looking for me. I knew he would look for me, but knowing he's actually doing it are very different feelings.

Me: Swearing's not very professional of you.

Fun Police: I will swear when you run off like that.

Makes me wonder what he really wants to say, but won't. When the dots appear and disappear like they are now I wonder if he's deleting and re-typing.

Me: I didn't run.

Fun Police: Not the point. Tell me where you are.

Me: I'm sure you can use your skills to find me.

Fun Police: Just tell me where you are.

Where would be the fun in that?

I'm not sure what happens when he's around me. I change, I get this attitude, I want to lash out, I want to say what's on my mind, I want to give him abuse. I'm only like this with him, and it scares me just how much I like it.

Me: Isn't that what you're supposed to be the best at, Cole? Isn't finding people your skill? Or have you lost it?

Dots appear and disappear on the screen again.

I don't get another message. I watch as the dots on the screen appear and disappear, and after a few seconds, they stop. An image of him standing in the street looking frustrated and angry in his dark, fine, fitted three-piece suit, with his phone crushed in his hand, crosses my mind. Chuckling to myself, I take another sip of my drink.

I can only imagine the look on his face right now. Hazel eyes furious, his lip curled in a sneer. The rumble of his throat as he growls and clenches his fists. His muscled arms tensing under his shirt, stretching the material. It sends a weird sensation to my lower stomach. *Butterflies?* He hates me, and doing this shit to him really winds him up. If he wasn't such an uptight stalker all the time, I'd take it easy on him, like I've started to do with the others. I actually enjoy their company.

Sighing, he can't even use my name in a message. It's still *Miss Bryon.*

Looking up, I catch the eyes of the guy sitting at the bar, "If I'm here in the day drinking by myself, what's your reason for being here?" I ask. This is so not me, but I want to really get under Cole's skin. He seems to hate it when I talk to anyone outside of my circle of... people. Being in any conversation with anyone seems to really send him over the edge.

"I wanted to drown my sorrows," he says, looking like his world has ended. His dark eyes look tired, and his pierced eyebrow is drawn down. "Thought a drink would help," he adds like he needs an excuse.

"Drinking never helps."

"If you're in a good mood, I'll leave you to it. I would hate to bring you down from your high." I take a second to think about it.

"I'm not on a high."

He drops his head, looking into his drink.

"I'm trying to really annoy someone, and this," I motion to the bar, "is the best way to do it before he finds me." Shrugging, I pick up my drink and take a sip.

"Wow, who's chasing you?" he asks, his pierced brow lifted in interest.

"You first. Why are you drowning your sorrows?"

"Can I?" He points to the empty seat next to me.

"Of course." He picks up his drink before standing and coming to sit next to me.

"I had a fight with my boyfriend, a serious one." I didn't expect that. That should teach me for being so judgmental. I thought I was being hit on. Laughable really. People have only ever wanted to date me for my name, my money and what it could do for them. Not that it's ever actually happened.

"I'm sorry, that's has to suck. What happened?" I ask, then realise that was way too personal. "You don't have to answer that, you don't know me." Embarrassed I take another sip of my drink.

"I know who you are, but that's okay."

I'll never get used to random strangers knowing who I am. I guess that's what you get when your father and mother live in the society pages, and headline news for the cases he covers.

"Now it's my turn to apologise. I've made you uncomfortable." Dropping his head into his hands, he ruffles his hair.

"It's okay, I just never get used to people knowing who I am, when I have no idea who they are. It's a little unsettling sometimes."

"Right, that makes sense, sorry." He winces.

"Carry on, I'd still like to hear about your boyfriend." Giving him an encouraging nod, we settle into easy conversation.

"He told me I love my work more than anything else in my life. That all he wants is to spend more time with me, and at every turn, I'll go to work instead of being with him." His eyes drop to his drink, you can tell he's reliving the moment.

"Okay, no judgments, but you thought coming to a bar by yourself was the answer? Is it true… what he said?" He signals to the girl behind the bar for another drink.

"Harsh, but yes, I really do love my job."

"More than you love him?" I ask.

"No way, I'm working hard for us, so we can have everything we have ever wanted." He's proud of that, the way he puffs up his chest. It's honourable. Makes me wonder if… I could ever feel that way?

"Did you tell him that? I'm sure if you did, he'd be able to see just how much you're doing it for you both." He looks confused for a moment before he rests his head on the bar.

"No, I basically threw a tantrum and walked out." Chuckling, he lifts his head again. I like him. In a different life, we could be friends.

That's the second time you've said that about someone recently. *Layla*. The girl at the flower shop. I really liked her.

"At least you're honest. What do you do?" I ask. I want to know more. This is the most real conversation I've had outside of Chrisy in forever.

"You're making me see the error of my ways. Thank you. I need to speak to him don't I?" I nod. "To answer your question, I run a building firm, built it from scratch. It's my life."

"That's amazing. Some people don't appreciate the work that needs to be put into it," I add. "Not that I would know anything about that." I sigh. "Not with my lifestyle." He laughs.

"At least you're honest about it. Others in your position like to live up to the princess hype. You seem different in person."

"Never believe what you read in the papers. They make me out to be some kind of spoilt princess" I have no idea why I'm speaking so freely to this guy. These are normally my inside thoughts. The smile and my mask of indifference are normally my front.

"It's a good job I like to get to know people before I make my opinions of them, and I think I'll wait a little longer to make my opinion of you, Arianna." I cringe.

"It still freaks me out when people I don't know use my name." He looks ready to apologise. "It's okay," I add.

"Let me introduce myself. I'm Kye West. It's nice to meet you in person." We shake hands then he tells me more about himself and how he's going to make it up to his boyfriend with a weekend away at one of his favourite spots.

The air shifts and I know Cole's found me. Controlling my breath, I carry on as if my insides aren't leaping for joy that he's here. All heads are turning towards the door at the main entrance, apart from mine.

"And if it doesn't work out, I'll start with whoever that is that's just walked through the door. He is a fine specimen of a man. I don't even think my boyfriend would mind."

"Let me guess, tall?" He nods while looking him up and down.

"Blond, the perfect combination of just got out of bed styled hair?" He nods again, side eyeing me with a grin while he faces my visitor's direction.

"Hmm... looks really annoyed?" I know angry looks good on him.

"Beautiful hazel eyes? Looks hot even when angry?" I add.

"Yes, I'd love to be on the other end of the scowl. Imagine what he would do to you?" I bite my lip, having imagined that very situation over and over again. Taking me over his knee, making me pay for my behaviour. Swallowing the need rising in me, I feel my cheeks flush from the vivid images in my mind. I cross my legs in an effort to fight off the tension that's throbbing there. *Oh, my god.* I drink a little more of my cocktail in an attempt to distract myself.

"Is he heading in our direction yet?" I ask quietly.

"Yep, I actually think he's trying to compose himself. Who is he?" he asks, looking between us.

"Oh, I have many names for him, not all of them nice. Captain Furious is, for lack of a better word, my bodyguard, personal security, however you want to say it." Knowing my time is almost over, I quickly ask the server for another drink. I know it annoys him when he assumes I'm drinking.

"Holy fuck."

"Yes, I was seeing how long it would take him to find me. I gave him the slip and came here." I shrug. Sounds stupid when I say it out loud.

"Why would you hide from him?" He looks confused.

"I like to keep them on their toes."

"But... why would you want to run from him? I'd let him pick me up and put me over his shoulder. He could spank my ass whenever he wanted," he says, with a wicked glint in his eyes. I almost spit out my drink. He's not holding back.

Lowering my voice, I whisper, "Kye, the man hates everything about me, and makes no qualms about hiding his dislike."

"That sucks, but at least he's good eye candy for the rest of us... oh shit, incoming."

Right on cue, Cole appears next to me, hand in his pockets, the vein in his neck throbbing. You can see he's trying to contain his hate towards me. He's failing miserably. I'm trying not to look too closely, but this man affects me. My knickers are already wet, and he's only walked into the bar.

"Cap, it's good to see you. Where have you been?" It's Kye's turn to hold his drink in while laughing at my obvious disdain towards Cole

"Where the fuck…" Cole takes a huge breath, his chest rising and giving everyone a show at just how toned his chest is through his shirt, the buttons visibly straining to be set free. "*Miss Byron*," he says through gritted teeth, not looking in my direction, but scowling at Kye, "I have spent the last twenty-eight minutes trying to find out where you decided to disappear off too." The tension radiating off of him is intense. You can almost feel the waves. "Are you planning on staying here all afternoon and *drinking* with your new friend?" *Judgmental arsehole*. Swallowing the tightness in my throat, I lift my chin.

There are no questions about what I'm drinking. He assumes it's alcohol, he assumes I'm here to get myself under a man. My stomach tightens at just how much he dislikes me. Without even trying to get to know me. It hurts, even though it shouldn't. I'm trying my best to not let his simple words affect me, but it's too late.

They hurt.

"I've not considered how long I'll stay, just that I was enjoying myself, until you arrived, yet again, to spoil my free time with your fun police drama." Wetting my top lip, I watch his eyes track the movement. I'm not the best at comebacks or thinking on the spot.

"Oh shit," Kye says through his stifled laughter, Cole darts his eyes towards Kye, glaring at him with such distaste, it silences him instantly.

"And who the fuck are you?" Cole hisses through his clenched jaw, positioning himself between me and Kye. And fuck me, Kye's eyes go a little wider, he actually smiles.

I have an awful feeling he's going to do something devious. Kye stands from his bar stool, coming round to me, his hand landing on my jean-covered knee. "I'm Ari's new *friend*." Oh, he's going there. "Didn't this little fox tell you about me? We've been having a wild time together this afternoon." I have to hold back my shock, keeping my face as straight as I can.. Kye's hand skims up my leg a little further. His face is so suggestive, it gives Cole the completely wrong impression of our time together. Actually, it's an impression he already has of what I'm doing here. What's the harm in playing into it?

Cole's fingers gently wrap around my arm, his eyes pleading with me to move. I slip off the stool, standing chest to chest with him—eyes to chest is more accurate. Wincing slightly from the bruises already forming on my arm from my run in with Mr Carmichael. His eyes catch mine and he drops my arm, obviously noticing my discomfort, and frowns slightly.

Walking us back, away from Kye. His big, strong hands come to my waist as he moves me behind him, placing himself firmly between myself and Kye this time. "What the hell," I protest, not disliking been manhandled by him as his fingers flex on my waist. I should hate him putting his hands on me. I mean, who does he think he is to walk in here and just move me around like that? And this butt-wipe is destined to be kneed in the nads if he carries on.

"Get your hands off me, and move away," I scold as his fingers glide down my hips. *Oh god,* that felt too good. Tingles rush my lower half. Cole's head whips around to stare me down, his eyes overflowing with contempt. "What is your problem?" I almost yell, but I don't want to draw any more attention than I already have.

"You," he grits out through clenched teeth. Internally flinching, I should be used to the venom he spews my way. I've had years of practice hiding my reactions from my parents, so hiding them from him is no different. "I'm here to watch you don't get yourself into any trouble." The angular curve of his jaw is set in a hard line, his eyes flick to Kye.

This whole moment makes my skin prickle with something akin to anger. Why does he have to be this way when things could be so different if he could just... I don't know, be able to like me?

I've had enough.

"No," I say calmly, meeting his beautifully hatful eyes. "Your job is to make sure I'm safe from others." I'm raising my voice. I can't help it; I'm starting to gain the looks of others drinking in this place. "Not to march over here and pull me away from having fun, having a *life*, and talking to guys." I hate how he smells so good. Like eucalyptus and leather with hints of something I can't make out; something that's *him*.

He places his mouth so close to my ear, his breath flutters across my skin. We're not touching, but I can feel him everywhere. I want to back away, but I can't.

"I will remove you from any situation I feel that is putting you in danger. That's my job, princess." I stiffen. The words from his lips guts me like a knife slicing me wide open. My skin prickles for all the wrong reasons. The last time a man used that word on me, it was to humiliate me. Crossing my arms protectively over my chest as some kind of defence against his words.

He thinks I'm entitled. I'll show him just how entitled I can be. My shoulders rise and fall, breathing in the rush of confidence that surges towards me. Turning my head, just as he did to me, my lips brush his ear, I swear he shivers when I let out a breath. Tutting at him. I quietly add, "Watch your mouth, Mr Grant. You want me to behave like everyone else I know, but I'll show you just how much trouble I can be." I don't know what's come over me. I didn't want to say these words, and I have no idea how to actually act like the entitled *princess* he thinks I am.

"Don't push me, princess." I bristle at that name again. Huffing a laugh at his words. I turn my head away. "You forget, I enjoy pushing your buttons, Cole." I step away, gathering myself for what I'm going to say next.

"Get your hands away from me, go back to your position by the door, and don't disturb me unless I actually need help." I hate everything I just said. I hate myself for even saying them. An image of my father pops into my head as these are words he has no issue throwing around. Turning around I leave him behind me, silent in my wake. I sit back down at the bar, right next to Kye, reaching for my glass, my hands shaking. Kye places his hand on mine, his caring eyes catch mine in unspoken support. Blowing out a shaky breath, I pick up my cherry-flavoured mocktail and drink it down in one.

Chapter Eight

Infuriating

Cole

I'm confused as fuck, frowning at the way she flinched when I pulled her away. It wasn't hard, but I instantly regretted the hold I had on her. All I wanted to do was get her to safety.

And away from him.

I'm dumbfounded. That's how I fucking feel right now. Her words. She put me in my place for the second time in as many days. She used them against me, but this time I just stood there and had to stop my fingers from gripping her waist again. But, *fuck*, she felt good when I pulled her off the chair. Her supple, tender flesh under my fingers. The heat she elicited through my body made my dick throb.

When her damp lips edged closer to my ear, her hot breath sent fucking waves through me, I shuddered in a way that made me swell in my boxers. I wanted to sink my fingers back into her, to pull her closer, to feel every inch of her. The way her lips felt when they brushed my ear, everything stopped.

It's infuriating. I want to drag her away, place her in my truck, and drive her back home, where I know she'll be away from him; safe. Until she decides to do another vanishing act, that is. I need to get a grip.

Pulling out my phone when it vibrates in my pocket, I'm still standing where Arianna told me to. Fucking told me to, and I went like a little puppy.

"Yeah," I answer, seeing Ethan's name flash on the screen.

"Just checking in. Leon said she called last minute again, but she was gone when you got there. Do you have eyes on Ari, Cole?" *What is it with this first name shit?*

"Yes, took me twenty-eight minutes, but I found her drinking in the cocktail bar down the road."

"Ari doesn't drink, Cole. Check your facts," he says with an edge in his voice.

"If she doesn't drink then why does she have a cocktail in her hand?"

"Mocktails," he states matter-of-factly. Now I feel like an even bigger dick than I did before. Why didn't I check before I assumed she was drinking?

"I need you to take my place this afternoon. I can't fucking stand to be around her." I'm saying the words, but I'm not sure I mean them. She's messing with my head.

"Strong words, Cole. What's she done now?"

"She's just been a princess. She's sat with some arsehole. If the press catches wind of this, it'll be all over the papers and websites. You know how they like to twist stories."

"That I do. Do you want me to check him out? I can pop into the office and do a full check on him?"

"Nah, I'll do it later."

"I need you to swap with me," I ask again. She's rattled me. I need some space.

"Sorry, no can do. Got to go home for a bit. Had a late one last night and I've only just signed off."

"Shit, sorry, I didn't realise. Everything okay?"

"All good, the event just went on for longer than we thought. The mayor decided he wanted to be the last to leave." I can tell by the slight inflection in his tone that he's annoyed.

"Is anyone else free?" I question.

"No, Leon and Owen are out. We don't have anyone free. Busy is good," he deadpans.

"Okay, thanks anyway." My chest tightens.

"Also, Leon said your dad called."

"Fuck." Dread fills my stomach.

"If you need anything, call me." His voice a slither softer. They all know the trouble I have with my parents, They're divorced, but my dad will forever look after my mom; even after what she did to him. I can only guess what's happened if he's calling the office, looking for me. "I'll head round when I'm done here," I tell him.

Hanging up the phone, she's still with that dickhead. He put his hands on her in public. She'll regret anything she does with him tomorrow. *If I let it go that far.* My eyes never left her.

She has every right to her opinion, but she's wrong. I'll do everything in my power to keep her out of trouble, like it or not, I'll be there for her when she needs me.

Reaching for my phone again, I send a quick message to Leon, about the next few months' schedule for Miss Bryon. I'll need a detailed list, of her comings and goings if I'm going to be on full time duty.

I have to admit I like seeing her get angry.

I knew what these types of men want from someone like her. They are all about the take, they want to use her to get a foot on the social ladder, they'll take until she's nothing left to give.

This one also wants in her fucking knickers, and she going to let him. I fucking hate it. I hate that she letting him use her. *Why the fuck do I care?* Balling my fist at my side, I try to focus on anything else. But then I hear it; she's laughing. I've never heard her laugh before. I'm stunned for a moment just listening, to the sound. It's *nice.* Taking a step forward when the guy moves closer to her, standing he brushes a piece of hair from her face, the smile she gives him is encouraging, he leans in further, bringing his face so close to hers, I want to pull her away. I can't make out what he's saying, instinctively I take another step closer to them, I'll be there in a second if he tries to do anything to her. Her eyes flick to mine for the briefest of moments, a smile tugging on her lips for a split second before it's gone, replaced with the look I know so well, defiance, trouble.

This guy slowly moves around to stand at the back of her stool. She turns to face him over her shoulder and kisses him on the cheek. Leaving her bright pink lipstick mark on his cheek.

Fuck, that does something to me, her hot pink lips, they'd look stunning wrapped around my cock. Clearing my throat and the image of my cock stained with the colour of her lips.

What in the hell was that? I almost stop walking, that thought. Fuck.

He's gone before I get to them, "Loverboy didn't even buy you a drink?" Tapping the card on the machine, she turns towards me.

"Despite what you think, I'm more than happy to pay my way in all areas of my life."

"Yeah, I'll believe it when I see it, maybe if you had any sort of self-worth, you'd get a job or at least an education." She flinches, I know I shouldn't have said it. Even I know that was harsh. Her head snaps towards mine. Shit that was out of line even for me, there's no way I'm taking them back though. Nothing I have just said isn't true.

"I'm done." she says simply, no anger in her voice, no venom in her words. "You can consider yourself and your team fired." Easing herself from the stool she's been perched on, she calmly walks out the front door, the press shouting her name, demanding a quick photo.

I step to her side, she may have just fired me, but there's no way I'll let that happen. We walk in silence, her in front and me tagging behind, scanning the area. My eyes drift to her every few seconds, over her body, and the way she walks in those high heels, the way her arse moves with each step.

Walking up to the entrance of the gallery, the doorman opens up for her, and she steps in, saying something to him as she passes.

"I'm sorry, sir, Miss Byron has told us you are to be stopped from entering the building." I freeze, watching her walk further inside, out of view.

The look I give him makes him call for back up as he probably thinks I'm going to be trouble.

"What? I'm Miss Byron's security. You know I am?" Shit, that's the second time she's left me feeling like this today: dumbfounded.

"Sir, if you could please step back outside, you can wait for her there."

And I do.

Chapter Nine

Fire Me

Cole

"Dad," I shout through the living room when I walk into the house I grew up in, the doors never locked. No matter how many times I tell him it's not safe, he still leaves it unsecured. It's reassuring and reckless, but he just wants me to know I always have a home here. After I came back from the army, I had nothing until the business started paying out. Being here helped me heal from the trauma me, Ethan, Owen, and Leon, all suffered through when we lost six members of our unit on our last tour.

We were betrayed by one of our own—Mendez. He was responsible for the loss of our friends' lives that day. He knew it too; the last words he whispered were, 'Tell her I'm sorry,' before he passed away. He had no family that we knew of, so we assumed he meant someone in the unit, but it was too late to find out. Coming back here, being with my dad, my friends close by, was all I needed to ease me back into civilian life. Owen, Leon, and Ethan created a business and brought me into the fold.

"Where you at?" I ask a little louder. I can hear Dad's muffled voice coming from the back garden. Walking through the hall, my childhood pictures line the wall as I make my way out back through the kitchen.

Opening the patio door, I step out, leaning against the frame, watching him on the phone, talking animatedly to whoever is on the other end. His free hand slides through his greying hair, tugging at it slightly when he gets to the top. He's trying to keep calm, puffing his cheeks out to steady his breath. I've seen this look a thousand times, usually aimed at me for some of the shit I used to get into.

Before it all went to hell, then his focus changed. All of that frustration aimed at someone else. Someone I should have been close to, but never was.

I have a feeling I know who's on the other end of the phone. My guard instantly goes up. I'm here for Dad, no one else. I won't bow down to her, she won't get any pity from me. She chose that life.

Dad turns and his shoulders drop when he sees me standing there. He half smiles, but it doesn't reach his eyes. I'd give anything to see a genuine smile on his face. Since she left us, he's not been the same. I think he lost a little bit of himself when my mother decided to trade my dad in for a different model. Not younger, not older, just one with more money, a lot more money.

It almost killed him watching her leave us.

Yep, that's definitely my mom on the other end of the phone. I'm not sure I want to know what she's done this time. Even after everything she put us through, she still calls my dad and he answers every goddamn-fucking-time. She got over my dad pretty damn fast, moving on to the next guy. Since then she's always been the same. She's on her third husband, fourth, if you include my dad. Each and every time she divorces one of them, it's because what they had was not enough. She'll rattle off why this husband is getting boring, bitch about them, then move on to the next. With absolutely no concern over how it makes my dad feel, how she's ripping out his fucking heart just to chase the money or the right social circles.

Fucking bitch.

She may be my mom, but only in blood. I don't have to love her, or even like her.

She gave up her right to be a parent when she left us when I was fifteen. My dad side eyes me, shaking his head at something she just said. "I'll ask, but you know what the answer will be, Tan. I don't like you putting me in the middle." He sighs, giving in to whatever demand she just made of him.

It's a running joke between my dad and me, that he should start a support group for the survivors of Tanya Grant, or would it be Tanya Stevens now? Dad hangs up the phone and then sits on the chair on the small patio, rubbing his face with his hands.

"What's the issue this time, Dad? Something new and shiny caught her eye?" I add sarcastically, squeezing my palms together.

"She seeing someone else or wants to be. The current husband has no idea yet. Says he's so rich he has his own boat and helicopter. He's everything she's been looking for. Her words, not mine." He huffs a disbelieving breath.

"How many times has she called you in the last twenty-four hours?" Dad squints at me then rests his head back on the chair like he's giving in.

"Enough that I've had very little sleep because of the constant stream of texts with links showing me just how much this man has. She has absolutely no self-respect."

"I don't know why you even answer, Dad," I say honestly. I take my seat, mimicking his pose.

"I have my reasons, son." I have a good idea what they are, not that he would ever tell me. We are all the family she has. "Is that why you called the office? To tell me Tanya getting another divorce." He gave up a long time ago trying to get me to call her mom.

"That, and she's asked to see you." I tilt my head back, turning my gaze to the sky.

I've not seen or spoken to her in years. I stopped when I left to join the army. It was best for everyone involved.

"Why?"

"She didn't say, just that it was important, and you should go and see her next week. I think she said Tuesday."

"You can relay the very solid no, not a chance in hell, back to her." My tone is flat as I close my eyes.

"Son, please, it's been years. Maybe she just wants to see you?" I'd call him delusional, but he still holds hope for us when I know there's none.

"I'm not seeing her, Dad. You know how I feel about her, after she left us high and dry, we..." I have to take a deep breath to get my thoughts straight, "we hit rock bottom, Dad. We almost lost the house, and she didn't give a fuck about either of us." He shifts next to me and his hand grabs my arm, squeezing in support.

"I know, son, and if it wasn't for you working part-time while going to school, then going into the army, we would have lost it all." I've never told him that's when I learnt to do all the tech stuff, my part time job at a local shop, didn't earn much. What I earned on the side, digging into company files and outing people for what they were doing earnt me good money. It kept us in this house. When the army offered me a position, I jumped at the chance. Offering me the chance to do what I was doing for my country, and make more than what I was earning, with travel thrown in. I never looked back.

"Sorry, Dad, it just pisses me off. I'm not seeing her. I won't," I say, clenching my jaw tightly.

"I know. I told her as much. I'll tell her you said no." This is dragging him down. I can see the bags under his eyes.

"Fucking hell." The tension rises in my muscles, guilt plaguing my chest, as I think of how I can make it better for him, but I haven't. Now I'm annoyed for another reason. She'll take it upon herself to pester him until I say yes. He's hardly sleeping as it is, she'll get worse until she gets her way. Rolling my eyes at myself, I can't stand it. Fisting my hands together, I do what has to be the right thing, I've left him to deal with her for long enough, on his own. "Fine, I'll do it." I'm up and out of the chair before the last words leave my mouth.

"What? But you just said..."

"I'm doing it for you, Dad, not for *her*. She'll make your life hell if I say no." He drops his head.

"She will, but I hate that you're doing this."

"It's about time we teamed up to deal with her." My dad just nods. "It's okay."

"I appreciate it, Cole. She can be hell when she gets an idea in her head." He's not wrong.

He stands from his chair and walks into the house, leaving me to my own thoughts. He hates this as much as I do, but we both know she's relentless when she wants something. This is the best solution, but it will be on my terms. When I hear the door open again, he hands me a bottle of beer. "One before you head off, son."

"Thanks, Dad." Taking the bottle from his hand, I twist off the cap.

"If I'm going to see her for the first time in almost thirteen years, I'll pick the date, time, and location," I say, grinding my teeth at the thought.

"Do you want her number? To sort it out?" Raising my eyebrows at him, he immediately holds his hands up in defeat.

"Don't push it, Dad," I joke, taking a sip of my beer.

Frustrating women seem to be part and parcel of my life. At least I'm getting paid to handle one of them. The other? Well, I guess we'll have to see how that goes.

Chapter Ten
Change

Arianna

"I'm so sorry, Ari." Chrisy's sobbing at me. My chest's tight. We've been on the phone for the last thirty minutes. I'm just about holding it together. I feel sick.

"I—" She tries to talk, but I cut her off.

"It's okay." I'm doing my best to sound normal when I'm anything but. "I knew you would get this job. It was made for you." My tone is hopeful when I'm not. "We both knew when you did, you'd be moving away." My heart hurts. I don't know how I'll do this without her. "You should be happy about this, not crying down the phone to me." God, I want to be happy for her. I am. Truly. Chrisy deserves this.

"But..." I feel it deep in my stomach; if I even cave a little she'll stay. I won't let that happen. I don't care how much my life will suck not having her here to get me out of this hellhole, I'm not holding her back.

Forcing myself to get through this, grateful it's not a video call, I sit a little straighter. If the life I lead has taught me anything, it's that I can put on a believable act.

"So, what, you won't be here for my birthday, I'll still speak to you. We can video call." My only friend is moving away.

Leaving me behind.

On my own.

"Don't give me that shit, Ari. I know this is breaking you just as much as it is me. I know you remember. I know the real you." She sobs again, and I have to bite my lip so I don't do the same. "Speaking about it all and it actually happening are two very different things, Ari. I'm going to miss the fuck out of you."

"I'm..." Do I tell her the truth? I may as well I'm already losing her. "I'm going to be a little lost without you, Chrisy, but I want this for you so much. I want you to go for all the right reasons." My voice wobbles.

"Fuck, sweet-cheeks. I didn't think it would be this soon. I thought we would have time, at least to see each other again before I left. Will you be okay?" I know what she is asking, and if I'm honest, I don't know the answer. She's always been the light at the end of my day, seeing her face appear at my door or on the odd occasion, through my window when she's climbed the tree in front of the balcony just to check on me.

"Honestly..." I can't imagine not really seeing her. The loneliness I already feel is overwhelming. When you remove Chrisy from my life, I don't know what I have left. "It will be different. I'll be okay," I force out.

"Shit, I know what you're really thinking. I hate that you have the life you do. Our dreams, Ari," she cries. "Fucking wankers." I feel lifeless, heavy with what's going to come.

"Chrisy, I still have you, just not in my face every day." This entices a low chuckle from her. "I'm not going to deny that it's going to be really hard without you, but that said... the quicker you move, the faster you can live the life you have always wanted. I'll still be here. That's something you can always count on." Pausing for a moment, to gather my thoughts. "And you have all that travelling to get started on. I want so many postcards and video calls, you'll be sick of me."

"If I'm not sick of you now, I never will be, Ari."

"Aww, I love you like the sister I never had and always wanted."

"I love you too, Ari. A sister in every way." I smile at this.

"I'm sorry, I know I should be happy, but I'm a little gutted you're not crying with me." My little chuckle turns into a cry.

"That's better," she says, cry-laughing with me.

"One day we'll meet in paradise: the Italian coast?"

"Deal, sweet-cheeks," she adds. My smile is genuine, thinking of discovering a new place with her by my side.

"I'm going to miss you so much, Chrisy," I say eventually. "Will you call me before you leave? And when you get there. Even if I can't answer, I want to know everything."

"Done. Look after yourself, Ari, please."

"I will. I promise." *Or I'll try.*

As soon as she hangs up, I break down.

"Ten more minutes on the treadmill, that'll be ten miles, then we're onto strength," this new guy, Adam, says over the music in our home gym. I don't have the energy today. I feel drained after last night's crying session. I knew there was no choice but to turn up. I'm not performing as well as I normally would. My speed has dipped and there won't be a PB today. "Did you eat before you came here?" Oh no, he asking questions, my heart skips a beat, as worry starts to set in.

"Yes, a shake from the plan," I say, trying to catch my breath, for a second, before I clear my throat, forcing a smile.

"What plan?" He looks confused.

"What do you mean? You should have been given my diet plan when you started?" His face scrunches.

"No," he says, obviously confused at my statement. "Diet plan?" he adds. "Like to lose weight?" His eyes drift over my already small frame.

"I'm on a strict plan. It's all approved by my dietitian." I say, I think it is anyway, although I can't be sure. Slowing my pace on the running machine, he hits the red button, bringing the track to a stop.

"The fact that I've not seen it, and your workout plan is physically demanding, doesn't fill me with confidence that this is right for you." He grumbles as I step off the machine. I sigh, as I grab my towel from the bench and wipe myself down.

"I'm healthy. I just had a bit of a rough night last night. I'll be back on form tomorrow." I move to the next section as he removes the weights from the rack on the wall ready for me.

"I'll have to get a copy of the diet plan." he adds, making a note on his phone. Reaching out, I place my hand on his arm. He looks at me, seemingly surprised by the contact.

"Look," I say, being as quiet as I can, "the last guy, Tom," he nods in recognition, "he asked questions, and they fired him. I don't want that to happen again. Okay." Dropping my hand, I pick up one of the weights and sit on the bench. "I'm fine. I'm healthy, I promise." He doesn't look like he believes me. Lying back on the bench, I get ready for the first round of reps. He kneels next to me, leaning in close.

"There's more to this, isn't there?" he whispers in between counts.

"Yes," I whisper back, "but it's not your concern. Please just forget about it," I beg, repeating the sit-ups with the weight against my chest.

"I can't, but I won't say anything."

I can only hope he keeps his word.

With my freshly made shake in hand, I head to Ed's office on tired, shaky legs, sipping it as I go. Once I've asked him about hiring another firm, I'll head back to my room for a while. I have a get together this afternoon. I don't want to go. It will be just like any other outing: fake friends, fake smiles. *Fake, fake, fake.*

I catch Ed in the hall, slipping on his jacket. "Are you heading out? I was hoping to ask you a favour," I ask.

"Ask away, we leave in fifteen minutes," he says, buttoning it up, he looks like a MIB agent. Only he's not fighting aliens.

"We?" I question. "Me and your parents, plus the full team." Right, the idea of being all alone causes a conflict. I'll feel relaxed that my parents aren't here, but also so alone. I hate it. "I've asked Dec to come by." So, still alone, Dec's not allowed in the house, as he's not security anymore. He was fired when my dad changed things. Now he's my driver. He'll sit outside.

"Right."

"What's this favour you need?" he asks, holding my arm, waiting for me to speak.

"I fired Cole yesterday, so we need to hire another company to do the security for me."

"Ari, you can't just…" There is a menacing laugh behind me. A tone I know well, that can only belong to one person. Ed looks up over my head but doesn't say anything, his expression sombre, before it turns to steel. Panicking, I have to gulp down my fear.

My mother.

I freeze. I don't remember the last time I actually saw her. A month? Maybe more. Turning, I catch my first look. She's poised on the stairs, looking down on us like a viper ready to pounce. Dressed in red, her bottle blonde hair groomed and curled to overdone perfection. If she fills her lips anymore, she looks like a trout I think she aiming for. I have to take a guess that she's frowning at me, but she's had so much Botox you can't tell. But her eyes say what her face can't, raking over me, her matching red pout lifts a fraction in a sneer.

"What's this about?" Her question is aimed at Ed. Opening his mouth to speak, she gets in first, her eyes narrowing in my direction. "You don't need security. You don't matter," she snarls.

My mask slides into place, a cold sweat covering my body as humiliation sets in. I hold my expression as she descends the stairs. I don't say anything; it's not worth it.

"I don't know where your sense of self-importance comes from," she continues, "but you need to rain it in. You're not worth the money we spend on you. I can't wait till you leave."

What? I flinch back instinctively. *Leave?* My chest tightens. *Leave to go where?*

Dread washes over me. I have to remind myself to breathe. Are they sending me away again? With shaky hands, I move them to cover my stomach, holding the knot of fear she's just struck me with. I don't move. I shouldn't rise to her cruel words, but I need to know. I can't go through that again: Months of being alone, tormented for not living up to their standards.

What's the other option? Letting Gi and Ed suffer because of me? No. I'd do it for them.

I wish I stayed in bed. It's not even 11 am, and my heart and head want to burst.

"What do you mean, leave?" I ask trying to hide the fear from my voice. Ignoring me, she walks towards my father's office. I face the only man I look up to. "What's she talking about, Ed?"

"I don't know what she's talking about. If I did, I'd tell you. You know I would," he reassures me. She could just be messing with my head. I wouldn't put it past her.

"Back to your question." Taking my elbow in his hand, he guides me into the dining room, closing the door behind us. "You can't fire Cerberus. They're the best." My face falls.

"I already did, Ed. I want a new team." I need this small win today.

"Sorry, Ari. I had a call from Owen this morning. Whatever you said to Cole yesterday, he didn't take seriously." Closing my eyes, my stomach sinks. "There's been a change in the rotation." I shake my head, willing him not to say what I think he's going to, trepidation prickling my skin.

"What are you talking about?" Gulping, I watch the words spill from his mouth.

"Cole will be taking over your security. There won't be a rotation anymore. Just Cole." I feel my body cave, despair rising within me. I fired him, and he just... took control. Took it out of my control.

"You have to be kidding me," I hiss. I can't take this.

"Ari? They are the best. Something is going on here, and I want you safe. Please."

"Chrisy's moving away." I blurt out, sitting down in the window seat across from him.

"Fuck, Ari, I'm sorry."

"It's okay, just one more thing today wants to throw at me." Tucking my knees into my chest, I don't say another word. I should have known I have no control over anything. Maybe it's time I resigned myself to that fact.

Let myself be who they think I am.

I've got no fight left.

Chapter Eleven

Hard

Cole

"Cole, there's a difference between disliking her in here," Owen taps his temple, indicating inside thoughts, "and voicing it. Which is why I don't understand why you requested to be her full-time guard." He's looking at me from across the desk in my office.

"I was letting you all deal with my issues with her." It took me a while to think up a believable answer to why I wanted this. I didn't think he would accept getting under her skin, to justify my need to piss her off. "Avoiding her is not the answer. I want to spend more time with her." It freaks me out a little just how true that statement is. Pushing it to the side, I won't be dealing with that right now. "Sort out our differences, and all that." Owen is looking at me like I've grown two heads. I've done nothing but bitch about her since we started our security detail.

"Still don't really understand, but if that's your reasoning, then carry on. But, if this comes back on us in any way, shape or form, you're in for it," he threatens, only half joking.

"Serious words for a man who took off for a year without a word."

Owen storms forwards, planting his hands on my desk, leaning in my face. "I've already told you all how sorry I am. How I went about things, leaving like that was wrong, but I did it for all the right reasons." Clasping my hands together in my lap, I stare down at the floor as I look up at him. I'm a dick.

"Shit, I know. Sorry, that was uncalled for."

"No, I want to know how you feel about it all, Cole. I'll never disappear again. You, Leon, and Ethan are my family," he adds seriously.

"Don't forget Charlie on that list of yours, otherwise she'll kick your ass if she finds out you left her out," I joke. He rolls his eyes and takes a step back, sitting on the chair opposite the desk.

"What exactly is your issue with her anyway?"

"Miss Bryon... shit," how do I say this? "She has the same values as my... Tanya."

"Shit, that's fucking harsh, mate." He shakes his head, like he knows it's not true. "She's nothing like Tanya."

"Look at what she does. *Nothing*. Posts on her social media, gets paid to do it. She wants the money to live an easy life. She didn't even go to university, she's had every opportunity handed to her on a fucking silver platter, and all she does is dress up to go to lunch, visit places just to get in the papers. It's pathetic." Letting out a frustrated breath, I sit back.

"I think your wrong." He says. "But I'll give you a month to work it out, if not, I'm pulling you off. It's not healthy for either of you."

Shit, I only wanted to be nearer to her to piss her off. Now I have to make an effort. I'm not sure why, but I don't want to be booted off being her bodyguard. I like that she challenges me.

I really don't.

> **Me:** I'll meet Tanya this Saturday, 8pm, at The Brasserie.

Frowning at the open gate, I pull into the drive ahead of Miss Byron's house, I make my way up to the front steps and see Dec standing at the door. Parking behind the town car he drives for her, I get out, before I make it a step closer, he's already walking towards me.

"Dec," I say extending my hand to him.

"Cole," he says, taking my hand in a firm handshake. His eyes flick to the gate he must have forgotten to close.

"What are you doing out here? Won't she let you in?" I mock, tipping my head towards the huge dark front doors.

"I'm not allowed in. Not since they fired me as security, anyway. Ed asked me to watch the house while they're all out."

What? Frowning at him in confusion, I take a step back to survey the house. *Why would he need to watch the house? Where are they?*

"I'm sure you're not needed out here. Ed's team will watch out for her while she's in there." He follows my gaze and then grimaces, shaking his head.

"Cole, there's no team in there," he says a little too flippantly and my heart does this small leap. "It's just Ari."

"She has no security? She's here alone?" What the actual fuck? That makes no sense. Her father's team is top notch. Not as good as us, but close.

"Explain it to me, Dec, because right now, I don't get it," I rush out. They are paying us to protect her. Why not have us cover the house when they leave?

"I don't know the details," he sighs. "But just under twelve months ago, I was fired as her personal security. Ed didn't say much, he never does when it comes to her parents. I was told I would be her driver. Rules were put in place about where I was and wasn't allowed. I was never to accompany her outside of driving her to where they told her to be. All I know is that when her parents leave, she's left by herself. No security, no protection." You can see he's angry, his pale skin has turned red under his collar, his fists thrust into his trouser pockets.

Her parents removed her security. Why?

What does he mean, where they tell her to be?

And she's left by herself.

"What the fuck?" I'm so confused. Everything in me is screaming to call the guys and sort this situation out. It doesn't make sense. What she's shown me of her life, the money, the stuff, a man like her father has to get threats to him and his family. How can her parents abandon her like that? Her father's values on family, honesty, and pride make the news. He's always on about how important they are to him and his wife. There must be some valid reason for him to leave his daughter alone. I just can't think of why he would. There has to be one and I'll look for it.

"I shouldn't be telling you this, but they have a seriously fucked-up relationship. They…" Before he can explain, the front door opens and Arianna steps out. My hackles go up, but this time for very different reason. It pisses me off that she's just fucking steps out. Anything could happen to her. She's in the public eye for fuck's sake.

Scanning the grounds, I feel a little out of control, adrenaline shooting through my body. I had no idea I needed to protect her coming out of her own home. I thought she was already safe. Moving quickly, I jog up the steps to meet her half way, keeping an eye on my surroundings in my peripheral, but my gaze falls on her. I watch her tanned legs walk down each step to meet me. I can't draw my eyes away from her. Fuck, she looks good.

I don't know if it's a thing, but she looks too perfect. Her outfit makes me what to fist her hair in my hands until it's untamed. I want her to look at me from where I've placed her on her knees, her skin flushed with arousal… fuck, my cock's wide awake now, begging me to get her in the back of the car and see how far she's willing go.

Stop.

Shaking my head, trying to rid my mind of the images she conjures so easily, Dec frowns at me as we all move towards the car.

"Afternoon, gentleman," she says. She stands by the door of the car and smooths her hands down her black silk skirt, looking everywhere but at us. Dec moves around her, opening the door with a sad smile. I've watched them long enough to know this is out of character for her, they always have a little joke.

What's changed?

We take separate cars. I step out of mine after we arrive on the busy street and head inside the overpriced tearoom to ensure it's safe. I head back out just in time to find him opening the door for her. He looks sombre, deflated almost. I'll have to have a chat with him later. Get some details on what is going on.

Turning on the fake as fuck charm, she thanks Declan, then turns to me. I expect her to hurl some abuse at me for ignoring her firing me, and putting myself on full detail. But she stands a little taller and says, "When you're ready, Mr Grant, I'll take your lead." It surprises the shit out me so much, I don't say a word back, just nod like a dickhead.

All I can do is watch her every move, and everything around her. It all feels wrong.

I don't know what's going on, but I will find out.

Chapter Twelve

Fake

Arianna

Oh my god, I want to tear my eyes out. I don't feel anything. I hate this. Sitting here listening to them—Chastity, April, and Cathy, my so-called *friends*; people my parents want me to be associated with because they want me to be like them.

All I can hear is...

"Look what daddy bought me."

"It's so expensive, I made him buy me one in every colour."

"I told them I had to have it, and the next day it arrived. All I had to was pout my lips."

Fake smiles, fake lips, fake boobs, fake nails, Cathy even has fake cheeks, something she is proud to tell anyone about. I feel she may get a free treatment from her surgeon if she recommends enough people.

This is the life I've resigned myself to. So, I sit through it.

I don't hate them, they're just the product of parents and husbands who have too much money and too little time to spend with each other. Things, stuff, becomes a way to gain the attention they crave. This is how they think life should be.

And I can't stand it.

Am I a hypocrite? Most likely. I've been raised in the same environment. Only I don't ask for anything. Everything I have is so my parents can show the world that they care about me. That I have everything I could ever want.

When all I want is my freedom. I suppose it's a dream when I'm living in a nightmare.

The waitress comes over and places our tower of forbidden food on the table. We each take a small cake and place it on our delicate plates. At this point, the three of them have already drank a bottle and a half of champagne and we've only been here twenty-five minutes. I'm calculating how long I have to stay. I want to go, stick on my fluffy pyjamas, and climb into bed. And I have every intention of doing so soon.

Can I last another hour? Can I make an excuse to leave without it getting back to my father that I left early? I'd be forced to do something else, just as equally boring or pretentious. I'd receive the sharp end of his tongue or the back of his hand for disrespecting him. I'll sit for as long as I can.

No. That's the sad truth of my life. If I want to live like really live, I need to do something.

Cole

God these people are everything I hate about having money; they scream wealth and privilege. After what Dec said at the house, I've started to question everything I know about her and everything I have seen her do. Like right now.

She's sitting at the round table with her friends, drink in hand but not actually drinking. She'll lift the glass to her plump, pink lips, and take a sip, yet the level stays the same and she never tops it up like the others have. *Why isn't she drinking?*

Why not order water or a soft drink? Why pretend?

No one at the table has paid any attention to her, they are too busy talking to themselves to realise she's only spoken a few non-committal words the entire time.

Watching the waitress place a tower of tiny cupcakes on the table, they all hesitantly reach for one. Each watching to see who will take a bite first.

Miss Bryon's movements are fluid and well-practiced. She may be sitting in the pink and white chair, but she's not here; her mind's checked out. *Why have I never seen it before?*

Too wrapped up in my own shit.

To wrapped up in judging her, you're an arsehole.

Taking her phone from her purse, I watch her fingers fly across the screen. Then place it face down on the table. Who's she messaging?

And why the fuck do I care?

Not even a second later I get my answer, as my phone pings in my hand.

> **Miss Byron:** I want to leave, please call Dec to pull the car around.

> **Me:** As you wish, Cupcake.

She flips the phone over and I see the smallest tip of her lips as she glances my way. Fuck, it floors me. I made Arianna Byron almost smile.

Chapter Thirteen

Damage

Cole

"Get in the damn car, guys." I sigh at Owen and Jack, one of our best friends and best customers, he owns The Manor Hotel, where we're headed tonight, and quite a few other businesses around the world. I've managed to get them to come out tonight with me for a meal. It's been a few weeks since we had the same night off, and I want to make the most of it with some fine food and good company. I've been sitting in the truck for almost ten minutes waiting for them. I wanted to drive just in case Miss Byron decides to break free. Her schedule says she has nothing on tonight, but that's never stopped her before. I'll be able to jump in the truck and track her down if she decides to change her mind.

Tipping my head back against the head rest, I stare at the roof of my truck, my patience wearing thin. I know if I have to go inside, we won't make our reservations. In hindsight, I don't suppose it matters when I'm having dinner with the owner.

"If I have to get out of the car and drag the two of you away, I will send your wives *those* photos of your stag dos."

"Fuck off," Owen hollers over his shoulder as he kisses Charlie. Again. "There is nothing my wife hasn't seen from that day." He sounds so secure in that knowledge, but it gets his ass moving quicker than I expected, with Jack trailing behind him. The girls chuckle, closing the cottage door behind them.

Owen climbs in the front next to me, strapping himself in. Jack hops in the back.

"If you ever show anyone *those* images," Owen mimics my tone, "I'll hunt you down and kill you myself."

"What he said," Jack adds, sitting back ready to get going.

"You're both soft for your women, you know that?" I mutter. It's a new side of them that I'm getting used to.

"Yeah, I don't care, mate. I'm all for it. You'll be next," Owen says with a wink.

"Oh yeah, who's the lady?" Jack asks with excitement in his tone.

"There is no lady," I fire back, trying to shut this conversation down. "I like things the way they are, free and single." I smile, but something feels off when I say it.

"Umm, you sure do. What did Leon say about your last hook-up? How long has it been?" Owen remarks from next to me.

"Just because I'm going through a little dry spell, doesn't mean it's not what I want." Six months is long ass time not to have slept with a woman.

"So, who is it then?" Jack asks, eyes wide staring at me in the mirror as I look into it. I love these guys, they are my brothers, but sometimes I want to shoot them myself. It would be much quieter, but I'd miss them after a while. Not that I would ever tell them that.

"I'll tell you later. You'll be as shocked as I was when Leon told me," Owen says.

"Leon can't have told you about anyone, because there is *no one*." I huff at my own frustration.

Jack orders us a round of drinks, and we sit just off the reception in the lounge area, waiting to be seated. I like this spot; you can see everything that's going on.

"I have something serious I need to ask," I dive in. Jack and Owen exchange a look.

"What do you know about Judge Byron?" Jack scrunches his brow and sighs before getting comfortable in the chair.

"Why, what did you want to know?" Jack asks.

"I have my reasons," I reply, wanting to keep it close to my chest for now. "Anything you can give me would help," I say. I don't know what I'm looking for yet, but I think I'll know when I find it.

"Okay, we run in the same financial circles. He loves money, I mean really loves money, and I think he'll do anything to get it. There was a rumour going around he had some sort of connection with club Praise, but it's just a rumour." He tilts his head, frowning. "When it comes down to it, I wouldn't trust him. Not that he's ever given me any reason not to. Why?" he asks again. Owen's silent, taking it all in as the waitress places our drinks on the small table in front of us.

"I came across some information yesterday that just doesn't make sense to me," I answer honestly.

Owen sets his drink down. "Why didn't you ask me this yesterday?"

"I only got off duty this afternoon. I had a long night."

"What, did she sneak off again? What did she do this time?" he groans, shaking his head at me, a smile creeping onto his face.

"She didn't do anything," I say a bit too harshly, "but I had to watch her house last night. I only left when Ed's team and her parents got back to the property."

"What do you mean? Where was Ed's team?" Owen asks sounding tense. The house is all on Ed's team, or so we thought. He never told us any different. We assumed this was taken care of.

"That's the thing, Miss Byron, has zero security when her parents leave. She's left alone with nothing and no one to protect her." It makes me so fucking angry she's left vulnerable like that.

"Was it just last night?"

"I don't think so. I think it's been like that since we were hired. Maybe before then."

"Fuck, we've been watching her for what? Eleven months? Shit." Pulling out his phone from his jean pocket, he types out a message then puts it on the table.

"What else? You wouldn't be asking if that was the only thing. You looked into a few things, didn't you?" I did. I can't help myself.

"I need to dig a little more. What I found out about her dad is nothing we don't already know. But Miss Byron. Her whole life doesn't make sense..." Sucking in a breath, I fill my chest, letting it go with the next words. "A fake life. She's their daughter, the paper trails and digital signatures don't add up to what we see."

"What do you mean?" Jack asks, edging forward in his seat as if he's making sure no one can overhear us.

"Remind me what his slogan is, when he's in court," I ask them both.

"Um... something about family values, putting them first?" Jack answers.

"Yeah, family, honesty, and pride. The only family he put's first is his wife. Every holiday they have ever taken has just been the two of them, every Christmas they fly out to some island somewhere, and leave Miss Byron behind."

"That's fucked up," Jack offers.

"It gets worse. She has nothing in her name. Not her phone, no credit cards, even her bank account is shared with her father. Her social accounts are managed, she doesn't even have access to them..."

"Not one?" Owen asks.

"No, nothing, worst still... and this is where it gets fucked up," I say, lowering my tone. "Her parents don't seem to have any communications with her, they are only seen with her, when it's seems to be important to him. I checked the call records, not one call from either her mom or dad. Not even on Christmas."

"Shit, man. It's all fake?" Owen asks, puffing out his cheeks, obviously trying to digest everything I just said.

"Add that he's left his own daughter vulnerable, and it's Ed who's paying for her security from us. That's twisted," Owen says, shoving a hand through his hair.

"I agree, it's messed up," I confirm.

"I've messaged Ed for a meeting tomorrow. I'll let you know what time. We'll get to the bottom of this. We can always arrange cover where there are gaps," Owen says.

"Already done… I'm concerned, O, what are they really hiding? Every family has its issues, but why paint a picture of her having this big fancy open life, a great family when there's no calls between them, no holidays together." That's putting it lightly. "Jack, can you keep your ear to the ground about him or any of his associates."

"Sure, I'll ask around."

The guys slip back into their normal banter after that, but I can't forget what I've learnt this afternoon. It's playing on my mind, is everything I know about her life, a lie? I'm not really listening to their conversation when Jack blurts out.

"Oh my god, it's her, isn't it? Arianna Byron is your lady?" Jack announces, and I don't know what to say.

"Fuck, no… she's fucking beautiful, and intriguing… not the point."

Owen smirks, quietly laughing at my reaction, while Jack looks at me like I've given him the best secret in the world. "Whatever. Think what you like." I huff, annoyed at them for a reason I don't understand.

"Oh, yes," Jack whisper shouts like a kid at Christmas. "She's here. Did you know she was coming here tonight? Is that why you asked us out this morning?" What?

"This wasn't on her schedule." My heart rate picks up, as I watch her father and mother walk in and talk to Mary, the manager of The Manor, behind the front desk. "She should be home," I say to myself, as Arianna, slowly walks in, keeping a few paces behind them. Gripping the arms of the chair, I just stare at her as she gets closer, her eyes wandering over the interior of the building. What's she doing here? Looking around, I don't see any of Ed's team. Where are they? They should be here too if we weren't notified.

She comes to a stop when she reaches us, watching us all, the beautiful smile she was wearing as she looked around, now gone. Replaced with a look I can only describe as blank. I can't take my eyes off her, exploring her fine figure in her stunning blue dress. My grip on the chair tightens. I want to reach out and touch the slight curve of her waist, feel her warm skin beneath my fingers. But she still looks off. Not the Ari I've seen when she's out with Chrisy and she has no idea I'm watching. Too put together, this is a whole different person. This is Arianna showing us who she wants us to see. Or who her parents want her to be. Her only giveaway that she's not comfortable is that she's picking the skin on her fingers, and I don't think she realises she's doing it. She looks exactly like she did yesterday: a face full of fake smiles. Only there's an edge of worry to her veil of indifference.

Chapter Fourteen

Birthday

Arianna

It's my birthday today, and I feel like shit. Instead of celebrating like a normal twenty-six-year-old, I'm here with my parents. An email arrived in my inbox late this afternoon, informing me we'd be going out to dinner at a local restaurant, so my father could be seen supporting local businesses.

Not a word about it being my birthday.

Attached as always was a list of requirements: what to wear, how to behave, what to talk about, or not speak at all unless spoken to. It soured my already fragile mood. Basically, act like I'm not there, but be seen with them so they can act like I'm important to them. *Do they remember it's my birthday?*

Holding in a sigh, I listen to my father tell us how important this 'meeting' is. *Meeting.* I'm surprised I'm even in the same car as them. I was shoved into the corner of the town car, while my parents spread out, enjoying a glass of fizz. One I wasn't offered to join in with. Fidgeting with the hem of my dress, I do my best to blend into the background. Silently.

I imagine how other people celebrate their birthdays: friends, family food, cards from loved ones, with a handwritten note inside. I would imagine they'd have genuine smiles lighting up their faces.

I can only imagine.

I received a small cake from Gi and Ed this morning. She'd put it in a box, ready for when I came back to my room from the gym. *Pathetic, isn't it?*

I didn't eat it. Couldn't stomach it.

"Is *that* what you chose to wear this evening?" My mother's snide comment shocks me out of my daydream. And so, it begins. I remain still, looking down.

"Yes, mother. It's what..." I'm cut off reminding her it's what she told me to wear when she tutus.

"Well, you don't look like any daughter of ours in *that awful* blue dress." I actually like what I have on tonight. Maybe that's the problem.

"You must have put on weight. It doesn't even fit you. Look darling," she says to my father, who's busy looking at his phone. He takes a moment to look up.

"I can see," he agrees. She scans my body, shaking her head in disgust. Actually, I've lost weight over the last few days, but I don't bother answering her back. They can have their opinions of me, even if it does feel like another deep dent in my already damaged amour.

I cried today. Sobbed actually, for many reasons, but mainly for the life I wish I was able to have.

Even Cole was different with me yesterday too, I think he likes this version of me more. Easier to handle. Easier to control. Is this the self-respect he was looking for when he made that comment at the club? He was definitely much calmer around me. I feel numb. This is what everyone seems to want, but me.

I remember the way his hands flexed like he couldn't wait to tame me. Too late Cap, I'm already there, they beat you to it.

Chrisy once asked me why I couldn't leave. It was an argument actually, all out of how much she cares for me. She said she'd help me escape my confines, but I told her I had already tried to leave, to run. It was the night they locked me away; the night they told me I wouldn't be leaving until I was more agreeable. It's not something I'll be trying again, not for the long term anyway.

The car makes its way down the country roads. Our house is on the outskirts of a small seaside town. It's beautiful, I just don't get to see it much.

I researched where we're going tonight. I've heard so many good things about The Manor Hotels' restaurant, and its head chef Marco. Apparently, his desserts are to die for. Sadly, I won't be able to eat any if I'm dining with my parents, especially after my mother's last comment. But I can look.

As much as I hate spending time with my parents, I am pleased I get to see somewhere new, with great architecture; restored to perfection.

My parents don't speak to me again. A small perk. They exit the car first, with a groan of disapproval aimed my way, and head for the entrance. They don't even glance to see if I'm with them.

Taking a step to exit the car, Dec offers me his hand as I climb out. Winking at me, he whispers 'happy birthday' just for me to hear. I offer him a small smile in return. I still feel guilty for not talking to him yesterday, I just don't have the enthusiasm to joke around.

Taking each step as slowly as I can, I follow my parents into The Manors' entrance, and my father asks the lady at the front desk if his guest has arrived yet.

Dread fills me as we wait to be seated, listening to my father's demands for drinks, while my mother complains about how old this place is.

I think it's beautiful.

"Will they even have The Macallan you like darling?" she drones, acting like this place isn't good enough for them.

I'm actually ashamed to be with them, so I stay back a little further.

"We have an excellent range of Macallan's behind the bar Mrs Byron." Biting my lip to hold back the smile, as one of The Manor managers, 'Mary' as her name badge says, moves around the counter to take us to our table.

My skin prickles deliciously, like it knows I'm being watched. Sending a warm rush over my skin. A weirdly comforting feeling that only one person can bring. *Cole*. But why would he be here? For a fleeting moment, a smile pulls on my lips, I'm almost so excited to see him that I daren't look around. I need to be perfect tonight. Knowing he could be here makes me feel safer. *Huh.* My heart skitters with anticipation.

Tonight's just going to get worse now she's been caught out making a snide comment about their range of drinks. She'll make it her mission to find fault with everything. Guilt plagues me. I feel sorry for the staff already.

Walking past reception, the sound of laughter catches my attention. Turning my head, my eyes immediately search for where the noise is coming from, wanting to see someone enjoying my day. The moment I see the small group of men smiling and joking in the lounge area my steps slow, the slight dread I felt a moment ago seizing my limbs.

Just seeing Cole, relaxed and enjoying himself, smiling like that, big, and free, the laugh he lets out as I stand here, is deep and beautiful, making me smile for the first time today.

I like what I see.

My heart aches for what they have.

I'm still staring when the laughter stops, and all eyes land on me. My smile drops, jolting me back to reality. They all look so... mad. Can they dislike me that much? My mask falls back into place.

"Good evening, gentleman. Mr Lucas, this place is beautiful," I say to the owner of the restaurant as my eyes sweep the grace of the lounge area.

"Thank you, Miss Bryon. I hope you enjoy your evening." I'm very sure I won't enjoy the company, but I have every faith I will enjoy the food and the view.

I don't realise I've completely stopped, until my mother, grips my arm. "Arianna, get a hold of yourself. And don't embarrass your father," she chastises, pulling me to move.

There are so many things I want to say, like, get your hand off me, let me speak, let me enjoy something. Have you even remembered it's my birthday? But I don't. I do what I'm told.

I feel my father's eyes on me before I look over to him, his nostrils flaring at me. Lowering my head, I move one foot in front of the other and walk towards our table without another word or look in Cole's direction.

"Robert," my mother coos and my attention snaps from the beautiful view of the green manicured lawn slopping down towards the ocean as I hear the name of the man I hate. The man who left bruises on my arm I had to cover with makeup tonight. My father stands to shake his hand, gesturing for him to take a seat next to me. He pulls it closer to mine with his tobacco-stained fingers and I have to force myself not to lean away.

His leg brushes mine as he sits down, it takes everything I have to not visibly heave.

Robert Carmichael is the only reason this evening could have got worse. And here he is, joining us for dinner. No one talks to me, as they talk over why they're here. I'm ignored for the most part, and I'm okay with that. I'd rather be ignored than have to speak with him or have their attention on me.

Our waiter arrives and asks if we are ready to order.

After my parents decide what they want to eat, Robert orders the steak I've been eyeing with all the trimming and a bottle of the Château Hosanna Pomerol 2008 to accompany the meal. I'm just about the say I'll have the same, when he cuts me off, placing his hand over mine, forcing it to the table. Holding back a gasp, as pain shoots through my hand. My chest heaves as try to stay calm, I daren't move or say anything. *What's happening?*

"She'll have the side salad, no dressing, with grilled chicken, and tap water." Sucking in a breath, my eyes lower to where he's got my hand in his sweaty grip. My disappointment must show, because he squeezes my hand hard, putting me back in my place. I don't even flinch. I won't let him know he's scaring me.

Unfortunately, having food ordered for me is normal, but I'm shocked that it's my father's business partner ordering for me, and putting his hands on me in public. "She needs to lose a little weight. She's let herself go," he hisses, chastising me while running his eyes over my chest and stomach. My breath gets caught in my throat, unable to process what he's just said.

My parents actually laugh and I have to bite my tongue at the retort edging to slip out. It's not just an, oh, he's made a *joke*, let's cover it up with laughter. No, they actually laugh out loud. Tears form in my eyes. It amuses them that he's humiliated me.

These people are my parents.

Swallowing it down, I rise in my seat like nothing can affect me, while another piece of me dies inside.

My façade is breaking.

My father decides then to start talking about work, and Robert finally lets go of my hand. Relief washes over me and a shaky breath leaves my lips as I flex my fingers before wiping them on the napkin. I'd do anything to rid myself of the feel of him.

The table across from ours gets cleared, just as our drinks are served, ready for the next party to enjoy their food. I watch in fascination as they set the table with ease, making it look as elegant as the dining area itself. My fascination turns to horror as one by one, the three men who glared at me earlier sit at the newly laid table. If I was with anyone else, I'd take my time appreciating the view of each man, but Cole steals my attention, seating himself directly in my line of sight. I watch as he grips the table, showing the flex of his forearms under his rolled up shirt sleeves. Oh-my-god. This is not the time or place to be turned by a man's arms. Crossing my legs under the table, I squeeze my thighs together. In my peripheral, I see Owen sit to his left, and Mr Lucas to his right. I don't want to tear my eyes away, but I have to.

Dropping my gaze to the napkin I'm placing on my lap, I try and focus on just how I can make this evening not get any worse. I bite the inside of my lip so hard I taste the bitter copper tang of blood as it coats my tongue.

Closing my eyes for a split second, I try to smile, I don't want them anywhere near me, or this table. To them, I'm nothing but a drama queen, a spoilt daddy's girl, and I don't want them to think anything else.

My father knows of the men across the table from us but considers them of little importance. If he realised how well respected they are in the community, maybe he'd think twice about how he'll represent himself tonight. The small-minded man who thinks he's better than anyone else in this small town. Unfortunately, the jealousy my father holds for those with more money than him outweighs any respect he'll hold for them and what they've achieved. Only making him more bitter, and disrespectful towards them.

Internally panicking, I know what these dinners are like, no one hears what goes on, what happens when I don't behave, in a way that's perfect for them, the way they speak to me, and treat me, it's for my ears and eyes only. I want to keep it that way.

On the rare occasions we're seen together, we're surrounded by like minded people, people my father chooses for company, who don't see his behaviour as anything but normal. I'll always stay quiet, and do as I'm told. The trouble is, I never get it right, I try, I really do, but they find new things to pick at. New things to find displeasing, new ways to cut me down, to make me feel small.

They're going to see it all.

I don't want their pity. I want them to see who I want them to see this version of me. No-one gets to see this. Not even Chrisy. I can already feel Cole's eyes on me, yet they don't say a word. They sit at their table in silence, looking at the menu, frowning.

I sit silent, messing with the skin on my fingers, only speaking when spoken to, until our starters arrive. While everyone at my table eats, but me, I sneak a look at the table across from us and I'm met with piercing hazel eyes focused on me. Cole's jaw is clenched so hard I can see the muscle straining in his cheek. Even sitting at a separate table, I can feel the ripple of anger aimed my way.

I swallow my unease.

A cold hand grips my arm, as Robert's fingers dig into my flesh. *Shit, he caught me looking at Cole.* I try to pull my arm free, but he holds tighter.

"You need to learn your place." Robert's cold tone slicks my ear as he continues to reprimand me. "Remember what happened last time you stepped out of line?" I take in a calming breath. *How does he know about that?* Biting the inside of my cheek, I remember vividly, shuddering at the thoughts that try to crash my reality. If I let them win, I'll fall. Managing to push them down, I take another breath.

"Tell me more about our birthday girl, Thomas. I can't wait to get to know her." Robert says arrogantly from beside me. *What? Why does he want to get to know me?* My heart races, but I can't question anything, and I have a million of them. My mind flicks back to the off hand comment my mother made, that I'll be leaving soon.

I don't want to put the pieces together, *leaving, he wants to get to know me? No.* I can't and won't let myself think it.

I know Cole's eyes are focused on me, but I can't look. I'm too scared.

Scared for what his eyes have seen and will judge me for, scared for why Robert Carmichael wants to get to know me. Scared they'll see through it all.

"This one." My father says with such ridicule, I can already sense the humiliation coming, swallowing down the emotion that wants to overpower me.

He's about to crush me. It's his favourite thing to do. He'll make me say what happened.

"Why don't you tell Robert, Arianna, tell him all about *it*," he says, pointing at me with his knife in hand.

"I had what you'd say was an..." It physically pains me to say this but if I say this how I want, then I'll be punished later for it. "Unrealistic image of what I could have for myself," I say, lowering my head as he takes my mother's hand. At least this way my parents wont have to voice what they did.

"Go on, tell Robert what happened." My mother hangs on his every word. "She came to me when she was..."

"I was fourteen, Father," I answer for him. Why would I need an education when I'm a woman with money? A man will rule my life, that's his point. I don't and never will have power. It's a simple fact to him. "I came to you with a folder filled with all this information." My mother laughs with my father, and my eyes dart up, hoping the men on the other table have forgotten my existence.

Nope, still there.

My heart's racing. I don't want them listening. My father's loud. It's just his natural volume. Cole's eyes flick to my empty place setting, His hand grips his drink, lifting it up, taking a sip. He's listening.

I continue with my own self torture, "It was a waste time, useless, all of it," I say, hating myself a little more. "It was information about a university I wanted to attend when I left school." Boom there it is. My stomach rolls. My father laughs harder, my mother and Robert joining in on my humiliation.

I don't move, internally shrinking in my seat, wishing a hole to open up underneath me. He'll make me tell this story over and over again, he loves the humiliation it brings me. I'm just some stupid girl who happens to be his daughter, and no daughter of his will ever aspire to be anything but a good doting daughter. And if I'm lucky one day, 'someone will have me against their better judgment' (his words) as a wife. My only use is to look good, be good, and, if I'm lucky I'll bear children. My nausea rises the more I listen.

My father glares at me. "Tell Robert, Arianna. Don't stop there. We were just getting to the good part," he says, when what he wants to say is, 'tell him what you stupidly thought you could be'.

I wish he would speak just a little quieter, or not speak at all would be perfect. Looking away from Cole, I can't watch. I won't meet his gaze.

"Such a *stupid* girl, whatever was she thinking," my mother adds, quietly chuckling along with my father as he waits for me to say it.

"Let me guess. A fucking beautician?" Robert's tone is so condescending that my teeth sink into my bottom lip to keep myself from crying in front of them.

I had aspirations, dreams, but they would be shot down, chipped away, until I gave up.

"No," he says, lowering his tone, "even worse. I don't know where she even got the useless idea, ridiculous." My father's amused.

My breathing is unsteady, shaky almost. Closing my eyes, I listen.

Shame coats my skin, sinking deeper, with every passing second.

I'm ashamed of my life. Of all the false assumptions I've let the world believe.

I open my eyes. My life is what it is. I can't get away from it. But I can at least have some respect for myself. I may regret my next words, but I want to voice them. I'm not sure why, but I want Cole to know I planned my life to be very different from what it is now. This life was not my choice, but it's what I have, and what I have to live with. Looking up, Cole's hazel eyes seek mine, his brow furrowed in question. I want him to hear it from my lips.

"I wanted to be an architect," I tell him with pride, a smile gracing my lips, watching for any signs of amusement, but he grins. I'm lost in him, his face softening, and the world slips away. Just us. He sees me. My whole body lights up with the warmth of his gaze. I'm taken aback by how good it feels, my pulse quickens for an entirely different reason.

I hear a scoff beside me, taking my focus from Cole. I turn to see Robert's angry eyes laser-focused on me. He smirks in my face, my so-called family joining in with them. My smile falls, just like my heart.

"Did you not teach her what her role is in this life, Thomas?" Robert asks, his tone serious.

"She'll find out soon enough." My father grins, his humourless words fill the space as he wipes his mouth, leaving me with more questions I'm unable to answer.

Robert's aged face gets so close I can smell the tobacco on his breath, tinged with something bitter. I try my best to keep my face as neutral as I can. "I'll have to teach you to remember your place in my world."

His world? My parents ignore us or don't care that he's talking to me like this. His cold, callused hand slips onto my thigh.

I stop breathing.

He glides it up to the thicker part of my thigh. Forcing my legs together, I try to stop him without making a scene. My hands grab his arm, hoping he'll release me, but he continues to feel his way up my leg. A whimper escapes my lips as he reaches higher. I'm not strong enough to push his hand away. My eyes dart down as a sharp pain radiates through my skin. He's really doing this right here, right now, in the middle of the restaurant.

I want to look at Cole for help, plead with my eyes for him to help me, *I want to... I just can't. I can't move, I can't force the words out.* No matter how much I want to.

I want to leave. It will be hell for me at the house. My father will blame me for making a scene. He'll blame me for not accepting Robert's actions. *I'll be the one he blames whatever happens.*

So why take it? If they're going to punish me anyway, the least I can do is stand up for myself. Isn't it?

I don't have to take this.

Sucking in a breath, I lean closer to him, a small bit of fight kicking in.

"Remove your hand or I'll make a scene." My voice is shaky and low but I doubt he wants a scene. Feeling a little braver, I move my chair back and his hand lifts to his wine glass like nothing happened.

Pushing my chair further back, I slip my bag from the back and head for the restroom, my leg stinging as my dress brushes the tender skin beneath it.

I don't make it to the restrooms. Instead, I lean against the wall in the hall, out of view from everyone. I need a moment. To breathe, to think, to scream silently in my own despair. Leaning over, my hands on my knees letting out a shaky, breathy cry.

Happy birthday to me.

Taking my phone from my bag, I shoot Declan a message to pick me up and head outside. I need to hear a friendly voice. Chrisy should be in her new place now. I just hope she picks up.

"Birthday Girl," she practically yells down the phone. "Why are you calling? I thought you were out for a meal with the hated parents tonight?"

"They added a guest to the list, and let's just say, my evening has not gone well, and I don't see that changing anytime soon."

"Oh shit." Her voice has gone serious. "Who did they invite to dinner, Ari?" she asks, anger tangling with her words.

"The epitome of evil, smelling of tobacco and whisky." She knows who I'm talking about.

"Fuck." She knows it's bad. I don't have to say anything else. "What's he done? Are you okay?"

"I'm fine. I just needed a breather. I have Dec picking me up at nine-thirty."

"That's over an hour away, Ari. Can't you get away sooner?"

"No, I have to go back in there. We both know that." She sighs. Hearing her on the other end of the phone helps settle my nerves.

"Shit, I hate this for you. I should have stayed with you, Ari. I'm so sorry."

"Don't you dare apologise, Chrisy." I force the words out. "I would have had to come here anyway it wouldn't have made any difference." Hanging my head, I let out a shaky sigh.

"I know, but I could have been there to hug you."

"You're still here for me."

"It's not the same, though, is it?" It's definitely not the same.

"No, but I wouldn't change that you left."

"Don't spend too long with him. Just his name gives me the creeps, I can't imagine what having to sit with him at the table feels like."

"Not with him, next to him." I run my hand over my leg and wince at the sting.

"Has he hurt you? You sound... I don't know, upset. Worse than upset." No one can hear, so I'm honest.

"Yes."

"Fuck, Ari, what are you going to do? You can't go back in there. What if he hurts you again? What did he do?" She's angry. It sounds like she's forcing the words out between her teeth.

"I'll be okay," I say, unconvinced by my words.

"Okay, sweet-cheeks. Call me as soon as Dec picks you up. I want to know you're safe. Please?" she pleads.

"Of course, I will. Love you, Chrisy." Hanging up I stay there for a moment, really thinking about escaping, walking out, and never coming back. I know what will happen if I do that.

Chapter Fifteen

Celebrations

Cole

We watched Arianna walk into the restaurant. For the first time tonight, I saw a genuine smile on her lips as she walked in, I can only assume, it had nothing to with the people she was with, and everything to do with this place and then us. The way she looked at us, me and the guys sitting here laughing. Her plump pink lips quirking upwards. Stunning that's what I'd call the smile she gave me... us. It stumped me for a moment.

I watched the smile slip away, only to be replaced with indifference; her cool façade coming back into place, and then her mother scolding her, after she spoke a few words to us, before she bent her head and followed.

To say I'm seeing things a little clearer is an understatement.

Everything I knew about her before yesterday, I found out from websites, social media accounts, news sites, and gossip.

I realise now I don't know her at all.

"It's plain as day, isn't it?" Owen says, shaking his head.

"What?" I ask, Jack and Owen's attention on Arianna's retreating form.

"That her life is controlled." He sounds aggravated.

"Yeah. How did we miss it?" I'm not really asking. We already know. She's good at letting us see what she wants us to see.

"What are you going to do about it, Cole?" Jack asks, picking up his drink and leaning back in his chair.

"Something. I don't know what, but I'll do something." My muscles tense, quickly nodding in his direction.

"Good. If I can help let me know."

"O, I want to join you in that meeting with Ed," I state.

He smiles in reply. "I already included you on the email." They each give me a look I can't decipher.

I want to follow her, make sure she's okay. I'll find everything I need to know. I'll find the truth if it kills me.

When we took our seats at the table opposite Arianna and her parents, I knew we'd get a show—the flashy side of her life, the expensive drinks, fine food, talk of business, and what they have that others don't.

Everything I hate. Everything my mother left us for. What I don't expect is Robert Carmichael to be sat right next to her. Like really *fucking* close to her. Something curls around my insides, hardening my features in the process.

We didn't see him arrive. *How long has he been here?*

Taking the menu from Mary, Jack discreetly asks her to keep him updated on Arianna's table. She nods, towards his phone. "Keep it close, and I already have something," she whispers.

"Okay, I will." He looks at her, and she gives him a sad smile as she leaves.

A few minutes later, Mary sends a voice message through, Jack places an ear pod in his ear, listening while he pretends to read the menu.

My eyes catch Arianna's for the first time. She's hiding something, her eyes and body language send completely different signals. Jack huffs out a frustrated breath but doesn't say anything.

Owen listens to the message next, his face hardening. "Who told Mary this?" Owen asks. Jack looks at his phone. "Aiden, their waiter," he adds quietly, not that they'll hear us over how loud her father is. I'm desperate to hear what Mary knows. Owen and Jack's reaction wasn't bad, but I can tell that it made them uncomfortable.

"Let me listen?" I say, reaching for the ear pod.

"Just remember where we are, okay?" Owen, quietly lectures.

"How bad it is?" I ask as I place the pod in my ear.

"Mr Carmichael grabbed her hand hard when she went to order, interrupting her before she got a chance to speak. He told us she would have a salad, grilled chicken, and a water as she's let herself go." My whole body tenses. I'm scowling in their direction, my fist gripping the menu.

No one has the right to order for her, she can eat what the fuck she wants to, but to tell her *that...* fuck no. Not just to say it to her face, but in front of a stranger, that's fucking sick.

"She just sat there and took it, like this was normal." The message ends but all I see is red clouding my vision.

Handing the ear pod back to Jack, we're all watching their table now.

"Jack, give me your phone," I say, holding my hand out ready. He unlocks it and hands it over without question. I type out a message to Mary before I hand it back. He reads the message, showing it to Owen as he smirks, adding, "I'd do the same." Owen agrees with him.

Arianna looks up, her eyes catching mine, only to be pulled away when Robert grabs her arm.

"Don't," Owen mutters from my side. My hands grip the seat of the chair, I can't take my eyes off her. I need him to take his fucking hands off her. He leans in closer, saying something I can't hear. Arianna flinches as his hand tightens around her arm.

"Cole," Owen warns me. She says nothing. Is this normal for her? *People treating her like this?* "If we intervein, we don't know if we'll make it worse."

Jack dips his head, agreeing with Owen.

I catch Robert asking about the birthday girl. Her father laughs.

Fuck me, it's her fucking birthday.

Disbelief rages through me, a knot forming in my stomach. The next few minutes are all a blur, I catch the snippets of words from her father as they pass demeaning words around: delusional, useless, and stupid.

My eyes never leave her as my anger levels reach fever pitch at the way they're speaking, making her do this to herself. It's cruel. She sits a little straighter, determination overriding the sadness etched into her face, ebbing its way to the surface.

"I wanted to be an architect." There is so much pride in those few words. She smiles, it's small, but I take it. It's mine. A moment between the two of us. I smile back, the rooms ours.

It's all over in flash. The words 'her role in life' and 'she'll find out soon enough' creep into our bubble. Her father laughs, and she breaks eye contact. Carmichael leans into her space, closer this time. I have to watch as her face pales, gulping down a cry, she tries to hide the shock covering her features. Her eyes dart down, lips parting. I can't see what he's doing, but I know he's doing something to her. Under that fucking table.

Slamming my hands on the table, I brace my legs ready to move, to get her away from Carmichael, but Owen stops me. There's fucking tears in her eyes. Arianna whispers something to Carmichael before she gets up, walking away like nothing's happened.

"Give it a second, then head out the other door," Jack whispers, tilting his head to the side doors.

I can barely contain myself as I wait, letting out a breath when I can finally take off after Arianna.

Chapter Sixteen

It Changes Eveything

Cole

I feel like a fucking stalker. I watched her in the hallway, after I left the table, knowing she needed to be alone. Following her outside, standing in the shadows, I keep watching.

She lets her mask slip, tears falling as she speaks to someone on the phone. I have an uncontrollable urge to take her into my arms and make everything okay. I want to hold her tight and make sure she's safe.

I don't know what to do with that.

Forcing myself to stay routed to the spot, as she wipes her tears away with trembling fingers.

Finishing the call, she sighs heavily and I need to check she's alright.

Moving from the shadows I step in front of her.

"Ar… Miss Byron," I murmur, not wanting to startle her. She stills, looking up at me. We're bathed in semi-darkness, only the faint glow of light from The Manor highlighting her features.

"Mr Grant, what can I do for you?" Her voice is small like she's lost her energy to argue with me today. Anger sparks in my chest, I like the fight she has in her, and it tears at me now, that I can't see it.

"What happened in there?" I demand, regretting my tone instantly.

"What do you mean?" she states, her hand covering the arm that prick grabbed like she's trying to cover it up.

I want her to tell me everything, I want her to tell me the truth, after what I just saw and heard in there, I want it all.

"Tell me," I ask, in the calmest voice I can muster. I feel anything but calm right now. I can see it in the way she squares her shoulders that she's building up her defences as we speak; she won't tell me anything.

Moving closer, I crouch down in front of her, the smell of her perfume permeating my senses. I hold back a groan, she smells good enough to eat. Like strawberries and cream, with a hint of vanilla. Resting my hand on either side of her legs, caging her in, she lets out a faint gasp from her parted lips. I have to force myself not to lean in further as she flicks her tongue over her bottom lip. I want to taste them, suck them between my own, feel her tongue on mine. Fuck, she's sexy as hell.

"I'm having a blast celebrating, can't you see?" Fuck there she goes—the princess coming out to play. I peel her fingers from her arm, inspecting the marks there, following the outline of what looks like finger-sized bruises with a gentle touch. "Cole." My name on her lips sounds like a promise or maybe a cry for help.

"Who did this to you?" I'm trying my best to restrain myself. "I want to know who left these marks on your perfect skin." Inspecting them even in this dim light, I can tell they are a day or so old.

She shrinks into herself. The last few times we've been together, she's stood up to me, got in my face and put me in my place. I want *that* Arianna.

"Don't," I scold when she tries to push my fingers away. "I watched him hurt you." Grinding my teeth, my muscles ripple with anger. "What's going on?" I ask again, almost begging this time. She stays quiet as she fidgets with her nails.

"You want to know what's going on?" she whispers. I stay quiet but hold her eyes with mine, my hands wrapped softly around her slender wrists. Her pulse hammers under my fingers as sparks fly over my skin, almost taking my breath away. "I'm here celebrating my birthday with my... family, and an extra guest I don't really care for."

"I gathered that much. Follow me," I order as I stand. I'm expecting a fight, or for her sexy ass to walk in the opposite direction, but she follows me, actually fucking follows me. I don't touch her, just in case we're seen. Walking towards the seafront on the back lawns of The Manor, away from the restaurant windows, I check over my shoulder to make sure no one is around but us.

Taking her cold hand in mine, our fingers interlace. Breathing easier with the trust she putting in me, I hold tight as I lead her towards the covered hedge archway, blocking us from the view of anyone walking past.

"What are you doing?" she questions her eyes darting around when we come to a standstill.

"We're safe here, I promise." I clutch her hand a little firmer to reassure her, my thumb grazing her knuckles. She scoffs, clearly not believing me, but keeps her hand in mine. "That's the thing, Mr Grant, I'm not safe anywhere..." It feels like the first honest answer she's ever given. My chest caves. Fuck, have I not made her feel safe?

"You're safe with me. Always." Ari's eyes hold my gaze like she's trying to figure out if I'm telling the truth. "I'd never let anything happen to you." I mean every single one of those words, their truth searing a path in my chest, unlocking feelings I've kept hidden, and unable to admit to even myself. Now they are staring back at me with such force, I have to simmer them down before they boil over.

"Okay." Her shoulders slump, not really relaxing, but more like she's giving in.

"I heard what your father said..."

She blanches back slightly but I hold her firm, I won't let her waver. It changes nothing in how I've promised to keep her safe, and everything in how I feel towards her.

"No," her voice wobbles, "Oh, my god... you must think I'm..." She lets out a pained sigh.

"I don't think any less of you, Ari, if that's what you're thinking." I'm proud of her. "You spoke up and that took so much determination." Her eyes shine in the dim light as I hold her closer.

"I hoped you didn't hear anything. I'm sorry about that." She drops her eyes a fraction in a look of defeat.

"Don't fucking apologise for him," I warn and I get a small smile in return.

"Then I guess you know, or have guessed that my privileged life has some... restrictions." she says quietly, lowering her gaze further, letting out the tension in her shoulders as she speaks.

"What I just heard was nothing like a restriction. I don't know what it was. Explain it to me." I tilt her chin up with my finger, her dark emotion-filled eyes meeting mine.

"I can't. If they find out... I can't," she whispers.

"You can, please. I need to understand," I plead, cupping her cheek with my hand. Her eyes flick to mine, pausing before she leans into my touch. Fuck, the warmth of her skin on mine sends a shudder down my spine. She fits perfectly against my palm. I'd tear the world apart to keep her safe. Grazing her cheek with my thumb, I close my eyes, relishing at our closeness.

Her hand rises to my chest, her fingers brushing against my shirt. My body comes alive.

"In there, before you got up, when you smiled that beautiful fucking smile at me, what happened? You froze." She lets out a deep breath, it rushes against my cheek, making my skin tingle. "Arianna." My heart triples its beat.

I can't think past her lips and how they'd feel against mine. Soft, warm. I lick my own in response, gulping down a breath. Our chemistry colliding.

"Cole." It short circuits everything inside me. I can't stop myself leaning in, her sweet scent surrounding me.

I shouldn't, but I can't stop.

"Fuck it," I mouth against her lips. I wait for her to move away or tell me to back off, but she doesn't so I do the only thing I can think about, pressing my mouth to hers in a tentative kiss. A small breathless moan escapes her, sending my senses into overdrive.

I need more. My lips fall to hers again, my tongue edging over the seam, seeking entry. Wanting, no needing, her so badly I can hardly breathe.

Her lips part and I take that as my sign that she wants this as much as me.

Sinking my hand into her thick waves, at the back of her neck, holding her in place, I devour her. Her breasts press against my chest and I feel her nipples harden. Groaning my satisfaction at the feel of her, as she moans hers. Her movement's match my own as our tongues dance slowly searching for more. I'm harder than I've ever been, pressing myself into her stomach. I capture her whimper, as I pull her closer. Ari relaxes into me, making my need for her greater. I want to take more, but I'll let her lead. I'll take anything I can get. It's slow, sensual and I'm so fucking hard it's painful. Arianna deepens our kiss, and I can't hold back anymore. My arm sweeps around her, erasing any space between us. Her hands franticly pull at my shirt as she arches into me. I let myself take what I need, devouring her mouth with my own. Sweeping my tongue with hers, our lips crushed together, barely breathing. I'm not religious, but dear fucking god, she is the sweetest thing I have ever tasted.

Applying the slightest pressure to the nap of her neck with my hand, I caress her skin beneath the mass of dark hair, tilting her head up just a fraction, consuming every inch of her mouth. Groaning when she matches me move for move. It's frantic and messy, but so fucking right, I never want to let her go. I take her lips between my teeth and nip. I take every swipe of her tongue, every whimper like it's my last.

It's Arianna who eventually breaks our kiss. My forehead rests on hers, needing to keep her close while our breathing evens out.

"You said my full name," she whispers with a half smile.

"What?" I've said her name a thousand times.

"Whenever you're with me it's always Miss Byron." She steps back.

"Honestly. I wanted to hear how it sounded." I catch her before she can step further away from me.

"And how did it sound, Cole?" Her finger traces her lips which are swollen from our kiss.

"Fuck, like god-damn heaven baby. It's nothing compared to hearing my name fall from on your lips." Even in the dark, I can see the flush creep up her neck.

"I need to get back." She sounds worried.

"Arianna?" She still hasn't answered my question about what happened tonight.

"I have to, Cole. I'm sorry." Shaking her head, she moves away.

"Please, help me understand. Please." I'm begging.

"I can't help you understand when I don't fully get it myself, Cole."

"We need to talk about this, Arianna."

She hums, closing her eyes as if she likes the sound of her name coming from my mouth. She begins to walk away, but I snake my arm around her waist, pulling her back. She stumbles and lands her palms flat on my chest.

"I won't leave you alone, Ari," I say, trying to reassure her as firmly as I can.

"Well tonight, Mr Grant, you're not on duty, so enjoy your night. Please, leave me to the rest of my evening," she says calmly, slipping back into the Ari who hides her true self away. Her walls firmly back in place as she steps back.

I let her go, but everything has changed.

I want more of her lips on mine, to feel her hands on my bare skin, but most of all, I want the truth.

And I intend to get all of it.

Chapter Seventeen

Gesture

Arianna

I can't even begin to process what just happened. He kissed me.

I touch my lips again, where he's left a permanent tingle.

But now I'm back to reality. Robert is at my side, glaring at me, but I just don't care. The sting of Robert's touch has faded to nothing. Replaced with the feel of Cole.

I'm lost in my own world. And how he made me come alive.

When our food arrives, I'm taken aback when a mouth-watering steak is placed in front of me. "I'm sorry, this is not what I was ordered," I say confused as I move it to my right, thinking it must be Robert's. He makes that noise again, scoffing like I'd be so lucky to have a meal like his, but the waiter moves it back in front of me before he places an identical meal in front of Robert.

I look up and catch Cole's wink while he mouths 'Happy Birthday'.

The beautiful bastard bought me a steak.

Chapter Eighteen

Reality Check

Cole

> **Me:** Morning, Cupcake.

I want Arianna to know I'm here. I need her to talk to me. I'm desperate for it. I need to know how bad things are before I overstep. My head has been pounding with tension from the moment I saw her yesterday. Angry at myself for missing all the signs. I need to ride, clear my head, so I can think straight, but I can't. Not yet. There's no time.

My phone buzzes on the desk and I'm instantly annoyed it's not Arianna.

> **Dad:** Come when you're done later. I want to know everything.

I let out a sigh. I'd forgotten about meeting Tanya, tonight. Just another thing to increase my tension.

> **Me:** I'll see how I feel when I finish up.

> **Dad:** Okay, when you're ready.

Putting my phone back down, I push the thoughts of Tanya and my dad to one side. I need to focus and get to the bottom of what's going on with Arianna's dad, and her safety. Edward, will be here soon. I've also asked Dec to come in separately. I want Ethan with me on this, his presence alone will cause them both to shit themselves. As much as I like both Ed and Dec, I need answers and I'm willing to get them any way I can.

"What time's he due to arrive?" Ethan asks, striding into my office, coffee in hand, placing another on my desk, and sliding it over to me.

"Half an hour or so, I think? Ed was a bit vague on time," I reply.

"Do you trust him?" Ethan's always serious, but his undertone right now is curious.

"He's never given me a reason not to until Dec told me about her lack of security."

"And Declan?" He's also a man of few words.

"I trust him. He seems to care for her. I caught him driving past the house a few times the other night when she was home alone. I think he worries."

"I think Arianna trusts him, and Ed," he says sitting down.

Yawning, I reach for the coffee, the bitter liquid hot against my tongue when I take a sip. It's the shot I need after another long night. Ethan looks at me, obviously surveying my creased clothes.

After I dropped the guys back home last night, I went back to my place and took a long ass cold shower, trying to ease the raging hard on I seem to permanently have whenever I'm around Ari.

I had to fuck my right hand when the cold shower didn't work. Just at the thought of her lips on mine. The soft moans she made when my tongue swept her mouth. I'll admit the images spiralled into wanting to see that pink lipstick spread over my dick while I fucked her mouth. I'm getting a semi just thinking about her lips wrapped around my cock. After that, I drove past her house and checked in with the team I've put on twenty-four-hour duty. I'm not leaving anything to chance.

"I still can't get my head round that her own father left her so fucking vulnerable," I tell him.

"Did you sleep?" he asks.

"I caught an hour on there," I say, tilting my head towards the sofa in the corner of my office. "I jumped back onto the system after that."

"She'll hate that you're looking into her life without her knowing."

"What makes you say that?"

"She has her pride, Cole." I have no choice; she won't talk, not yet anyway.

"When you spoke to her last night, what did she tell you?" he asks.

"Nothing, I didn't get that far." *I kissed her instead.*

"How far did you get Cole?" He leans forward, a knowing look coming across his face. I don't regret a thing.

"No idea what you're talking about." He just smirks, raising his dark brows at me. "Fine, I kissed her."

"Knew it." He slaps his hand on his thigh excitedly. "Owen owes me fifty quid."

"What?"

"Grab a shower and change. He's on his way. We'll meet you at the centre table in ten."

Ed walks in twenty minutes later. We didn't brief him on why we needed the meeting, just that we needed to update a few things.

"What's this about?" Ed asks, eyeing myself, Owen and Ethan seated around the table covered in information I've been able to dig up over the last couple of nights.

"We have some questions. Ed. Take a seat." I say.

"Cole found out about Miss Byron's lack of security the other day, and we have some concerns." Owen takes control, ever the professional. Ed's shoulders rise a little as he sits.

"Don't bullshit us, Ed, we've known you too long for that." I glance at Ethan, who shifts just a fraction in his seat. He'll step in if we need him to, but I'm a great hacker, one of the best actually. So that's how I'll find what I need. Not that he needs to know that.

"There's no need for that—" Ed says, his eyes firmly on Ethan. He'll be disappointed he doesn't get to play today, but I'm sure he'll find someone to interrogate later. "—I'll tell you anything I can."

"Start with why the fuck Arianna is left alone when you and your team leave? And why we were never informed for twelve *fucking* months." Anger laces every word as I say them.

"It's Miss Byron to you, Mr Grant." Ethan's shifts forwards at his tone, letting Ed know that this is not the time or the place for petty shit.

"I'll call her anything I goddamn want to." I smirk at him. "Now answer my fucking questions." You can see the moment he realises he has no choice but to tell us the truth.

"What you need to understand is that her relationship with her parents is... *shit*. None existent. But she is like a daughter to me and Gi. From the moment they brought her home, I knew I could never leave her." He pauses, glancing up to the ceiling. "They left her in the fucking car and just walked into the house." His jaw tenses at the memory. "I was twenty-seven. They didn't give a shit."

We all consider that for moment, the reality of the situation that her parents left her in the car as a baby.

"After that, I was told to hire a nanny for her, but when he saw the cost, he said she wasn't worth the money. She was raised by staff coming in and out of her life for years. Only one stayed. Gianna. When she started working for the family, we dated. After we were married, we decided Arianna would be our unofficial kid." He's tense in his seat, eyes sad for the little girl he had to bring up.

"If she means that much to you, then why the hell has she been left alone?" Ed sits there, dragging his hands down his face and jaw.

"Because her fucking father values money more than anything else in this life. I'm stuck because if I say anything, I'm out and then who will she have?" he yells, his fists banging on the table in frustration.

"Okay, let's calm down. We can sort this out," Owen adds, trying to defuse the tension in the room.

"Right," Ed says, clamping his hands together as he sucks in a deep breath like he's calming his anger at the situation. "He won't let anyone but my team on their property unless they are picking her up. No one is allowed to step foot in the house. Not even Dec."

"How have you been watching out for her?" Ethan questions.

"I've been able to monitor the cameras. Inside and out. She knows to call Dec if anything happens. He'll be there within a minute." He gives us a look because he knows it's not enough.

"Why is Declan doing this?" It's puzzled me since I saw him drive by the other night.

"Dec cares, sees her as friend, a sister almost." That's fair I think, but something is still not sitting right about it.

"What about her parents? Why do they do this?" Owen adds.

"I don't know, they've never cared. Saw her as an opportunity... to make money, clean up his reputation. Since he partnered up with Carmichael, he's been doing some weird shit when it comes to Ari." Dropping his head, he runs his hand over his greying hair. "He took away all of her security, no explanation. I tried to tell him it was a bad idea. With the number of threats she gets because of him, she's a target. He didn't give a shit. Never has. Threatened to fire me and Gi if I said anything about it again." He sighs. "That's why I came to you. You have no idea what her life is like. It's fucked up."

"You have no option but to leave her, without security. If you don't, she'll be worse off. Is that what you're saying?" Owen confirms.

"Exactly that," he says gravely.

"From now on, you need to keep me... us updated with her parents coming and goings. We'll help fill in the blanks when you can't be there." I won't tell him that I've got her permanent cover.

"I appreciate it, but if you step foot onto his property while she's there, it won't be you who deals with the consequences." A clear warning for us to stay out; something I have no intention of doing.

"I don't give a shit what happens to you as long as she's safe," I say, my voice raising slightly the more he pisses me off.

"You're naïve as fuck sometimes." Balking at the comment, he can't mean us? Can he? "I'm not talking about me, arsehole. I'm talking about Ari. Everything that happens, good or bad, her father finds a way to make her pay. *She'll* suffer. Why do you think she acts the way she does." It's not a question, a sudden feeling of cold covers my skin, I get it. I wish like fuck I didn't, squeezing my eyes shut, I don't want to believe it, I don't understand it. Silence encompasses the table.

"Why do you think he's like this with her?" Ethan asks.

"Fuck, I can only guess. She's been through so much all at the hands of her so-called parents. But she makes him money has done for a long time. Before she arrived at the house, his reputation was going downhill. He got involved with some shady shit. Owed a lot of people money. Once the press found out he had a kid, he played it to his advantage. Started making money from photos, brand ops. Nothing much at first but then it grew. The public loved her, and she been his easy money ever since. Whatever he did worked, because by the time she turned sixteen, he didn't owe a penny. He was able to recover his reputation with the family image without being a family. Image and money are *everything* to him."

"He controls her?" Ethan asks.

"Everything she does is all controlled by him. From the moment she wakes, it's all about him: what she wears, what she eats, drinks. He makes millions every year from what Ari brings in," he admits, clenching his hands together, over his head.

"You mean she makes millions?" I frown.

"No, she doesn't see a penny." Jesus. My heart's in my stomach.

"You have to be kidding me?" Owens says through gritted teeth.

"Then how does she buy the things she does?" Ethan asks.

"She has an allowance; an amount she has to spend to keep up appearances. That's the only part of her life that's not monitored."

"Not monitored?" My chest rises and falls, trying to keep my anger in check.

"A PR team manage her," Ed explains.

"Manage her?" I know I'm just repeating him, but *fuck*.

Standing, I walk back into my office, needing a minute to myself. I can't hear any more of this shit. Did my actions last night cause her problems today? She's not texted me back. Fuck! Instantly grabbing my phone from my pocket, I text her.

> **Me:** Cupcake? I need to know you're ok.

I wait.

Nothing.

"Did you see her this morning?" I say, storming back into the room, tugging on my collar.

"No, but Gi may have done. Why?" Ed replies. A small amount of relief courses through me, but I can't tell him why.

"Oh, fuck," Owen mouths. I don't think anyone saw our kiss, but they saw the steak arrive and the way she looked at me when it did.

"Was she okay?" Stuffing my hands into my pockets. I pace round the table.

"I've not seen Gi to ask her, she's been busy, I assume Ari's staying in her room today. That's not unusual." Rolling my shoulders, I breathe a little easier, knowing someone may have seen her.

"Even after a meal out with her parents and Mr Carmichael?" I say, looking over to him for confirmation.

"What meal out?" Ed's eyes go wide.

"We had the pleasure of watching them at The Manor." His face turns white as a sheet.

Ed stands abruptly. "I knew her father was up to something he told me and Gianna to go home."

"Why would he hide the meal from you?" I ask. Ed swallows loudly as he takes out his phone, leaving my question unanswered as he makes a call.

"Check on her," he demands down the phone. "He was there last night, with them. Make sure she's okay." Having no idea who's on the other end of the call, we can only guess it's his wife, Gi.

"Okay, not since this morning—" More silence. "—fucking bastards." His jaw clenched, he mutters, "I'm on my way."

Shoving his phone in his pocket, he moves towards the door. "I have to go, I need to be there."

"What happened?" I ask, but Ed ignores me. Ethan stands, rounding the table quickly, coming to stand right behind him. His hands come to Ed's shoulders, gripping them firmly until Ed winces from the pressure. Ed's a big man, but Ethan looms over him, tilting his head to the side. Whatever he's whispering to him, Ed shakes his head, and steps back away from Ethan.

"Okay, okay, I don't know yet, but she's refusing to leave her room. It's what she does when she wants to hide something from us." He looks around at us, breathing out before he speaks again, "In the past, he's... Carmichael, he's hurt her." I stand, fisting my hands, I shove them in my pockets before I lash out.

My pulse races, making me feverish. *Carmichael's hurt my girl.* I'll fucking end him before he can lay a finger on her again. Feeling the thrum of blood, rushing though me, I can't focus, I'm seeing red, who the fuck does he think he is. She's *mine*. No one touches what's mine. He's just found himself at the top of my shit list. Pacing the room, I'll take everything he has, and make him watch while he loses it all. He'll beg for forgiveness by the time I'm through with him.

Every eye falls to me when I grab a cup from the table and smash it to the floor. My chest rising and falling, I hold my hands up, showing my team I'm sorry. Ethan stands next to me, but I move away before he can touch me. I can't relax, no matter how hard I try. I need to get her out of there and safe. Only after I've put them behind bars, will I relax.

He knows he's fucking up, but is helpless to do anything about it. Caught between a rock and a hard place.

"Get her the fuck out of that goddamn house," I demand, yelling in his face. My pulse spikes as I fist his shirt.

"I can't, and she won't go." He groans, sounding defeated. I let go when Ethan's hand lands on my shoulder. Shaking it off, I move back.

"What the fuck do you mean?" I'm shaking with anger. "What the hell would she want to stay for?"

"I need to go." Ed all but runs out the door, leaving us all in a weird space, filled with tension, anger, and uncertainty. But most of all needing a lot more answers. I feel like the walls are closing in.

Is she too scared to leave? Before I can continue with that tormenting spiral of thoughts, Jill walks in.

"Guys, your next meeting is here." popping her head around the door from the stairs, taking in the scene, "Do you need me to ask him to wait?"

"No, send him in. He's part of this shit show," I snap, giving her an apologetic look as soon as the words leave my mouth.

She leaves, and seconds later Dec walks in.

"What's wrong with Ed? He looked like he was going to be sick," he asks, taking in the room.

"Carmichael," I say, offering him a seat. "Dec, man, why didn't you tell me how bad it was?" Looking at me, he sweeps his hand down his jumper.

"I really don't know the details. All I know is what her dad asks me to do." Gripping the wallet in my pocket, I squeeze that rather than his neck.

"So, fill me in, Dec. What do you do for Judge Byron?" My tone is bitter. I already want to floor him before he's told us anything else.

"Primarily, I'm her driver. About six months ago, I had a bonus come through with a message attached from some PR firm saying I need to watch Ari without being seen. Take her to where she needs to be, then watch what she does." Taking out his phone, he flicks through it, and when he finds what he's after he hands it to me. On the screen is an email from a firm called Hex PR with a list of stipulations explaining what they meant by 'watch her'. Reading through them I almost choke at the shit they want him to keep an eye out for.

"You can't be serious? This is fucking crazy." Handing the phone to Ethan, his reaction is the same as he scrolls through the list.

"A list of things I was to catch her out on."

"That's not just 'catching her', that's details they want of her *every* movement."

"The bookshop?" Ethan checks. I don't know what he's on about, but I think I'm about to find out.

"Yeah, that was me. I had to tell him she walked to the shop rather than let me drive her. If I hadn't, the journalist her father tipped off would have told him anyway. It was better it came from me than some stranger who's being paid to get the scoop on her.

"You're being paid to get a scoop on her." My voice raises with anger as I speak. *Fuck, why can't I keep my head straight?*

"He would have fired me," he retaliates, "and I'm the only one that can look out for her while she's home. I've spent weeks watching the house at night while no one else could."

"You're the reason her visit was cut short. Why she was told to leave?" Ethan asks. Dec slides his hands through his hair, quietly whispering a "yes" to the floor.

"It's okay," I can tell he feels shitty for it. "You're not the only one anymore," I console him because he's visibly upset.

"She doesn't know what *he* asked me to do Cole. I feel like I've betrayed her. She's like a little sister to me."

"Have you told him anything that would lead her to be hurt?" I'll fucking kill him if he has.

"Nah, man, I couldn't. I'd give him little bits, like the bookstore, or her buying something that's not approved." Dec shakes his head at the thought.

"Approved?" my heart sinks, when he confirms.

"She has pre-approved places she can visit in her own time." I can't listen anymore. I need to get out, but I can't.

"We need to get her out," I announce. I'll get on my bike now and get her.

"She won't leave." *This again.*

"Why? Ed said the same thing. Why won't she leave?" I demand.

"I don't know. Something happened when she was about eighteen. It was before my time, but from what I can gather, it was horrific."

"If she won't leave then what can we do?" I state. Ethan stands to come by my side.

"Nothing, we can't make her do something that she doesn't want to do." That's my worst fear. If she's too scared to leave, but also scared to stay, where does that leave her?

"I never said she didn't want to leave, she does. She just knows she can't. There a difference," Dec says, his head in his hands.

"Fuck."

Chapter Nineteen

In Person

Cole

Dad: She's there already. Can I at least give her your number? You're a big boy now. I know you can handle it.

Me: Don't you dare. I'm two minutes away.

Dad: I'm joking. Good luck. Call me after.

Dad: Better still come round, we'll have a drink. You may need it.

I don't message back.

The fact is, I've been sitting on my bike in the car park at the back of The Brasseries for the last twenty minutes. Today's been hell. I don't want to see Tanya, my mom, after all these years. I know she wants something from me. She only ever wants me when she needs something. Normally a request for me to find something out about one of her potential husbands. Always asks through Dad though, never in person. I never do it. Not once have I given her what she wants.

Maybe she thinks a change in tactics will get her what she wants. I'll give her fifteen minutes before she cracks and asks me. I'll have great satisfaction in telling her to get fucked again. Only this time to her face.

Resting my head on my arms over the handles of my bike, I'm not normally this angry, and frustrated, but it's all my fault. I judged. I didn't look into a client like I normally would.

I fucked up.

Apparently, I really fucking like her. I can't help but think of the one-eighty the past few days have been. *Arianna.* Fuck, she's always been sexy. Hands down the finest woman I've ever seen. Those lips, god-damn, those lips: plump, kissable and fuckable. My dick twitches at the thought. I hated everything else about her. Her wealth, her lack of self-respect, and self-preservation. Living for social events, being part of high society. Never wanting to better herself, with all the advantages she has. The arsehole men she'd hang around with, pawing her because of her name. But most of all, the way she put herself in danger just to get a quick high.

All those things, everything single one of them a fucking lie. A fucking lie to cover up what she's been going through. One she's trying to stick to.

Why?

I've been so fucking absorbed in my hate for her, and everything she stands for, that I didn't see the truth. I didn't see what was right in front of me. A woman struggling to be herself in a world that was controlled for her.

When I think back, I've seen glimpses of who she really is.

Strong minded. Tempting. Clever. Sexy as fuck.

I smirk at the thought of getting to know her, inside and out.

After Dec left the office this morning, Leon suggested I went for a ride to clear my head, while they looked into Hex PR. They were right, it helped... for about two minutes, before I had visions of riding over to her house and making her leave on the back of my bike. Legs spread around me, the heat of her core nestled into my back and ass, gripping my chest tightly as we rode away.

Groaning out loud, I shake my head in an attempt to shake Ari from my thoughts. Trouble is, I don't want to stop thinking about her, not until she's in my arms.

After our kiss, my imagination has been running wild with the possibilities, of what we would be like together. I mean together? It sounds ridiculous.

Doesn't it?

What the hell did that kiss do to me?

A thought pops into my head. Sitting upright, I pull my phone from my jacket.

> **Me:** Is her phone monitored?

> **O:** Hello to you too, and I'll check it out now.

> **Me:** Load a new one up anyway. She needs to be able to get in touch with us if anything happens. Having a backup will be perfect.

> **O:** Done. I'll make sure it can't be traced.

> **O:** Leon said your meeting Tanya.

> **Me:** How the fuck? I didn't tell him shit!

> **O:** Not my issue. Are you meeting her?

> **Me:** Yes.

I don't tell him I'm sitting in the car park willing myself to go in.

> **O:** What does she want this time?

> **Me:** I have no idea, but wanting to meet me is new.

Time to face the woman who gave birth to me.

I've not seen this woman in almost twelve years, but I spot her instantly, sitting at a table in the middle of the room. Instead of going to her, I head to the bar to get a drink.

"Mike," I say, greeting the manager and long time friend.

"Beer?" he asks, pulling a glass from the shelf ready to pour my usual.

"Not tonight, I'm meeting Tanya. Just a water, please," I tell him, looking over my shoulder at her.

"I wondered why she's here. I don't remember the last time she stepped foot in this place." Scrunching his face at me, he leans forward resting his elbows on the bar, "She didn't even say hi," he jokes. It's no secret what she did to my dad; him and Mike have been friends for years. I think Mike's held more of a grudge than my dad.

"Are you surprised?" I mock.

"No, a little offended maybe, but not surprised." He laughs. Before I can laugh along with him, he turns serious. "I'm here if you need me, Cole. Say the word, and I'll chuck her out on her arse."

"I don't think I'll be long, but I appreciate the offer." Mike hands me my glass of water. Turning, I watch Tanya, as I walk over. She looks uncomfortable. *Good.* Dressed like she's ready to head off to a fancy restaurant, rather than sitting in a family-style pub. More than likely in a dress that's worth more money than my bike.

Draped in jewellery from her ears to her fingers it's screaming 'I have more money than you' for anyone who wants to look. She doesn't have that sort of money; her husband does. I've checked. I'll never tell her just how well her son has done for himself. She'll just see me as something else to flaunt, to take advantage of, and buy her the things she wants.

"Tanya," I deadpan as I step by her side.

"Cole, *darling*." I cringe as she stands, wrapping her arms around my neck and kissing my cheek like we see each other every day. Standing stiff, I don't repay the false gesture. Peeling her arms from around me, I pull a chair from beneath the table and take a seat opposite her. Placing my drink in front of me. I wait for whatever she wants to say.

She just starts talking like we've never been apart; like she never abandoned me and Dad to chase money. My whole body tenses with every word. Sipping on my water, I think about Arianna and how I've never seen her wear any jewellery. Not even a bracelet. "... It's so good to see you, *darling*," she preens. "You must tell me about your job." I block her out, waiting for her to get to the point of why I'm here. Then decide otherwise.

"I'm good, thanks," I say sarcastically as she never asked. "So is my job." The very fact she asked *that* sets the tone of what she wants from me. What can she want from my work? Has she finally found out what I'm worth? Does she need me to look into someone? Holding my smile to myself, if she knew I paid off Dad's mortgage after years of struggling by himself because of her, She'll think I owed her the privilege.

"... I've been so busy with.... the ladies at the club... so expensive, I love it."

"Oh." I have no other words.

"... Working away so much... endless shopping... my new... this ring... my... my... my." It's all I hear. The way she speaks is irritating me to the point of pain. If I have to sit here and listen to this any longer, I'll lose my shit. I don't have to listen to this drivel. I place my hands on the table, making her jolt slightly at my sudden movement.

"Why am I here?" I ask, aggravated I'm even sitting here. She falters for a moment.

"I know your dad keeps you updated on my life, but I knew you would want to hear this from me." She sighs, feigning a look of care for me. There is nothing I want to hear from her that Dad can't relay.

"I doubt that," I state, picking up my drink, taking a sip of the cool water, ready to refuse anything she wants to ask.

"Don't be so silly. I'm your mother."

I scoff, almost choking on my drink.

"I know you want me to do well for myself. Of course you want to know about what's happening in my life," she says with a flip of her hand.

"Right." I let out an exasperated breath. "Spit it out then. I have things I need to do?" I may sound crass, but I don't give a shit. "Clive and I are getting a divorce." I know this, but I bet Clive has no idea.

"Does he know he's about to be dumped, and for a man with more money, I can only guess?" I ask as casually as I can.

"That's not fair, Cole," she says quietly, with an edge that tells me I've hit a nerve.

"Answer me. Does Clive know?" I ask again, my voice low.

"No, and that's not the point," she says gritting her teeth together.

"That's exactly the point, *Tanya*. What, does Clive not have enough money for you? Or has he told you no to buying something ridiculous?" She doesn't even flinch. The façade she's been putting on falls, letting me see the real woman behind the makeup and money.

"Before you get on your high horse," she sneers, pointing her finger at my chest, "and give me a lecture just like your *father* does." Fuck, I hate her even more for the way she says *father*. "I need something from you." *Here we go...* "But before I contact my lawyer, and start ball rolling in divorcing Clive's cheap ass." I shouldn't be shocked. I just can't get over that this is my *mum*.

"Nice, showing your true colours now, I see." She ignores me, moving on.

"I wanted a small favour from you." She pauses, looking around, like this is going to be the biggest secret, and she's letting me in on it. "I heard a rumour that you've been working for the Byron family. Is that right?"

"Oh-my-fucking-god." I move my seat back to leave, but she grabs my arm before I can get up.

"I want to meet her... Arianna." Absolutely not. She's never setting foot in the same room as Ari. "I need her to introduce me to..." I don't say anything, if I do, I'll confirm who I'm working for. I don't want to compromise anything. "Her father and then, Robert Carmichael." She literally swoons when she says his name.

Cringing, I sit back in the chair. She has to be kidding. I fucking knew it. She wants to use me. Curling my upper lip, I snarl. She doesn't notice, she's too busy vomiting everything she knows about him at me.

"I've tried to meet with him, but I'm not in the same circles as they are. It's near impossible to get Robert alone. And *she* was pictured with him the other night at dinner. He was all over her." Her lip raises with disgust; like it should have been her, not my beautiful Ari. "She doesn't deserve him." Huffing out my disbelief, I think 'try the other way around', he doesn't deserve her or anyone for that matter. "Robert deserves a real woman." My stomach churns, then clenches at what she's insinuating. She thinks she's more deserving; that Ari's so far beneath her, she doesn't deserve a man like Carmichael. "I need to get in there before..." she stops midsentence.

"Before what, Tanya?"

She cackles in my face like I'm missing something. It only winds me up further. Flexing my fingers in irritation, I wrap my hand around my glass, and tap my foot on the floor, doing my best to let the tension out any way I can.

"Before she can get her perfect nails into him."

What I want to do right now is give her a fucking truth bomb and let her know just what I think of *Robert fucking Carmichael*. But I won't.

"I'm done." I don't say anymore, she's not worth it. Standing, I wave bye to Mike and leave my mother speechless and probably seething that I wouldn't help.

I check my phone before I climb back on my bike, finding the message I've been desperate for.

Cupcake: I'll be fine.

Relief floods me, but only for a second. We all know when a woman says fine she means anything but.

Unfortunately, it only causes the unease in my stomach to twist further. I'm heading over to check in with the team around her house.

Me: I'm going to need you to be more than fine, Cupcake.

Me: You can sleep well. I'm watching over you.

I don't expect a reply, and I don't get one.

Chapter Twenty

A Life

Arianna

Hot, rough hands cover the length of my stomach, trailing their way deliciously down to the apex of my thighs. My breath catches. He's teasing the edge of my knickers as I lie on my side, in a bed covered in the softest sheets I've ever felt. I'm held tight against him. My back pressed to his hard front. Feeling his growing arousal pressing into my backside. He feels big; getting bigger by the second.

His hand grips the inside of my thigh, my breathing quickening when he parts my legs, lifting my leg over his strong toned thigh, exposing me. Teasing me with deft fingers. My heart flutters, *actually* flutters, from his touch.

Arching my back, I want more. My hands fall behind me, grabbing his firm ass, pressing him into me. He groans, kissing my neck. Warm lips meet my ear, his breath grazing my skin, sending a wave of ecstasy over my tired body, causing my nipples to tighten into hard peaks.

"Arianna," he whispers, his large hand reaching my core, possessively cupping me, holding onto my heat. His finger grazes lazily through my soaked slit as he parts me. "Is this for me Arianna?" He groans as he gathers my wetness, teasing my entrance before he circles my clit. Gasping at the sensations he's causing.

"I've only seen you like this in my mind, Arianna." His words are sweet and welcoming. My hips start to rock. I need him, I need the friction.

"Cupcake, I want to give you the life you deserve." *What?* My mind is hazy with sleep. I can't speak. I try but words fail me. I can only think of how much I want this. Of how much I want to tell him I want that to.

He slips two fingers deep inside me. *Oh, god.* My walls tighten around him and he groans in my ear. My entire body shivers with need as I arch into him, feeling his hard length pressed against my ass as he pumps his fingers in and out, tormenting me with their slow teasing. It makes my toes curl and I press myself back, needing more. His lips disappear from my neck, and I miss them already. Desperation takes over as I search for him.

Nothing.

"Ari…" I hear it. It's not the same voice, it's not his. Cole's. I want him to call me Cupcake, even though it's the worst nickname on the planet.

"Arianna." The feminine voice is a little more aggressive this time. Peeling my eyes open, I realise it's all a dream. My hands search the bed for him, finding it cold.

I'm alone. My heart plummets, realising nothing's changed. I have to gulp down the sadness that weighs heavy in my throat.

How can I miss him when he's never been here?

"You're late, you slept in," Gianna says from the other end of my room. Rushing around, she looks concerned as I never sleep in.

"Shit," I groan, shifting, my book falling to the side as I do. I fell asleep reading my smutty book. Quickly, I slide it under the covers before Gi sees it. No wonder I had such a wonderful dream. I can feel the slickness between my legs when I move. My neck flushes, hoping to god that I didn't say anything out loud while I was asleep.

"Ari," Gi warns, "keep that language to yourself." Taking in a sharp breath, as my bruised thigh connects with the mattress, I wince as I move to sit up.

"Are you okay?" A frown worries her face but I don't want to tell her what happened last night. She'll only worry more than she already does.

"I'm okay, I just caught my leg on the table yesterday when we went to dinner. It may have left a bruise."

"Let me see," she says, coming over the side of my bed.

"No, no, no." I panic, shuffling backwards. "It's okay. I promise, I just forgot I did it that's all," I say shooing her away as quickly as I can.

Gi's eyes sweep over me. "What dinner?"

"Oh, um." *Crap.* "I was summoned to have a meal with the parents last night." Her eyes soften as she lets out a sigh, my leg forgotten.

"I don't understand. Eddy was given time off?" The softness in her eyes turns to sadness, and then anger as her nostrils flare. "Who joined you Ari?" she asks, before sitting at the edge of my bed, gently taking my hand in hers.

"Gi, it was okay. I'm okay I promise," I try to reassure her.

"*He* was there, wasn't he? Mr Carmichael." Her accent gets thicker when she's angry.

"Yes. It was okay. It just so happened that Cole and Owen from Cerberus were there too." I smile.

"They were?" I nod and my smile genuine. It's the only thing that saved my night from being derailed when sat back at that table. Seeing him sit down a few minutes later, watching me as I ate the best fillet steak I have ever eaten. I didn't even care that Robert was complaining to the staff, trying to get my meal removed. Or that it was taken away from me before I finished. Or that he accused me of changing my own order when I removed myself from the table. I've never had anyone do something so nice for me before.

I don't see Gi after that, I stay in my room after my extra-long gym session, Punishment for the food i ate last night. I think i got off easy.

Waking up to the thought of Cole's hands on my body was hot. I have so many questions: Why did he kiss me? Why cross the line? Did he like it? It felt like he liked it.

My fire got doused quickly... the pain in my thigh, my talk with Gi. I'm an unstable roller-coaster waiting to be closed. I have a lot to think about today, while I hide the emotional mess that I am.

As much as Cole made me smile last night, what Robert Carmichael did, the pain he's willing to submit me to, at home and in public. It's terrifying. My parents watched while he hurt me. There's no way they didn't know. But Cole showed me a different side to himself yesterday. A caring side. There was nothing fake about any of it—the kiss, his words. He was worried about me. He even messaged me this morning like he wanted me to know he's thinking about me.

I haven't replied to him. Not because I don't want to, but because I have no idea where to go from here.

Last night changed a lot of things for me.

I need to think about how I want my life to be moving forward. I can't trust my parents to keep me safe, that's for sure. Them having control over me is one thing, but putting me in harm's way so publicly is another. I know I can't leave, but maybe I can stand up for myself in some way.

Even if it ends up as another story for my father to joke about, I have to try. I don't want to give up.

I want so much more than this pitiful existence.

Things need to change.

I need to talk to Gi today. I want to run a few things by her.

Chapter Twenty-One

A Wish

Arianna

"Popcorn with melted chocolate and crushed chocolate chip cookies, for you, miss," Gi says, holding out the huge bowl for me with a spoon, taking it from her outstretched hands, I wiggle a little to get my spot just right on the small two-seater sofa in my room.

Gianna and Ed, brought up the food, all hidden in boxes labelled with brands I need to unpack and try on. She's devious, having already brought up the new things with my washing earlier today. I laughed at the lengths she goes to get me actual food, rather than the smoothies and shakes my diet plan suggests I have.

I sit back, ready to watch The Holiday, with Ed one side of me and Gi the other. It's a tight fit, but I wouldn't have it any other way. I love that they are celebrating my birthday with me; even if it is a little belated.

I feel comfortable for the first time in days. "Thank you," I say quietly. I want them to know how much this means to me. "And for you, my love," Gi says to Ed, "some roasted peanuts and a bar of chocolate."

"What do you have?" I ask. Eyeing me, she pulls the bowl out of my reach, so I can't get a look at what she has. I know she's hiding something good. She always tops what I have.

"What is it? Show me," I tease. I can't move as my bowl will topple, and there is no way I'm letting this baby fall to the floor.

"I can tell you without looking, Ari." Ed tips his head up to the ceiling, closing his eyes. "Nachos, with half a tonne of cheddar cheese, spicy salsa, and guacamole. With some crème fresh to finish. All heated up in the oven, so she can get the cheese crispy and stringy."

"Wow, that's detailed," I say a little surprised, smiling at the same time.

"He's right. It's also one of his favourites because I know he'll only eat a few bits of what he has before he descends on mine." She scowls, but from the size of the bowl she's made, she has enough for the three of us and then some.

"Absolutely, my dear. You make the best nachos I've ever tasted. You may be Italian, but you love your Mexican food." His arm reaches around the back of the sofa to Gi, brushing her hair from her face. A pang of jealousy strikes my chest, looking at the two of them together. The connection feels so foreign to me. I'm envious that it's something I may never have.

"Wow," I say again, "maybe I should sit on the bed, while you two have a moment." Edging my way to move off, two hands land on me at the same time, keeping me in place.

"Not a chance, honey," Gi says, while Ed just smiles his big goofy grin at me.

"This night is for you, and after our movie, we have lots to plan and discuss if you really want to do this thing with your parents." After speaking with Gi earlier today about my plans for attending uni, she wasn't happy. I could see the sadness in her eyes. She knows I could be hurt in the process of asking; that I could be locked away again. But even while she hates it, she said she'd support me, which is all I want.

Almost two hours later, we're watching the closing credits of the film, when I have to swallow back the lump in my throat. A thought hitting me like a brick. "If he says no," I blurt, "where do I go after that?"

"You try again. Never give up. If it's a life you really want, you need to fight for it," Ed says. He's right, I do need to fight for it, and I will.

Squeezing myself off the sofa, I make myself comfy on the floor next to my bed and open up my laptop.

"Ready to get to work?" Ed offers, sitting on the edge of the sofa, hands clenched.

"I'm ready."

"Good, your dad is meticulous in everything he does. He'll find flaws and loopholes that you never will." *Oh shit. He's going straight for the jugular.* "You'll need an argument for each and every one of them." My hands start to shake as I type.

"Fuck," I say out loud, earning a playful eyebrow lift from Gi. My language has been getting a little more colourful lately. Only in private.

"You need to treat this like a business plan, and show him the benefits, costs advantages, and disadvantages of you doing it compared to not doing it. I'm going to put it bluntly, I hate using these words with you, but..." Taking a deep breath, he adds, "Even though you bring him in an obscene amount of money, some of that money has to go back on you and he hates it. Sees it as a waste." That is harsh, but true. He only tolerates it because I bring him in so much more. "That's all he cares about. The less you cost him, the less it will affect his bottom line. That will work in your favour." *We hope.*

"Edward." Gi scolds him, before giving me a side hug. "That was..."

"Needed, baby," he says, squeezing her knee. "You know what he's like. We all do. Money is his everything, along with status." He's not wrong. I'd hate to think how my life would be if I didn't earn him money. My body visibly shudders, and I hug myself a little for comfort.

"It's not like I didn't know this already. Ed's just helping me face a few facts." Not being wanted by my own family, that's definitely a fact of my life.

"So, what are you planning to start with?" Gi asks after a few moments, rubbing my arm as she sits down beside me.

"It needs to be something small, that will cost him nothing, but will also save him money in the long run." Damn it, I deflate slightly, knowing uni will be expensive, I need to think of something else.

"I can't ask him about going to university. That will cost him thousands. What about driving?" I say cautiously. "Ed, don't look at me like that." His eyes have gone wide.

"It's not that I think you couldn't, I know you are more than capable, I just…"

"He likes that you're safe being driven by someone else," Gi finishes for him.

"That, and it's someone *I* have picked, and put through extensive training to cover any sort of situation that could arise." He's so serious it's cute.

"You're not making this easy. Now I feel guilty for suggesting it."

"Let's look into the details, the costs, the benefits, lay it all out, I'm not saying no."

I literally squeal at him, diving to give him a hug. We'd topple over, but he holds me steady, hugging me back, Gi laughing in the background.

Standing up after I let him go, Ed walks towards the door of my room. "I'm off to watch the security feeds. I left Dec in charge while we did this. The kid needs to head home at some point." It's getting more frequent that he leaves Ed behind when he meets Mr Carmichael.

"Maybe I can ask Dec to give me a few lessons?"

The look I get from Ed when he spins around pins me in place.

"Abso-fucking-lutly not. If it goes well with your father, I'll be teaching you to drive," he declares before he storms out of the room.

"Well… um," I utter, a little lost for words.

"Um, indeed, sweetie. I guess you found some free lessons. You may need to word it right in your plan, so that you don't mention who will be teaching you, just that you have secured some free lessons with a professional."

Gi leaves me and I sit back on my bed, remembering I've still not replied to Cole.

Typing out my reply I hit send.

Me: I'll be fine.

And I really mean it. Whatever happens next, I'll still be here.

Cap: I'm going to need you to be more than fine, Cupcake.

My stomach does this weird little flutter, I'm reading it again when his second message comes through.

Cap: You can sleep well. I'm watching over you.

My whole body relaxes at the thought of Cole watching over me, looking out for me when others won't. I actually feel safe.

Chapter Twenty-Two

Ruse

Cole

Myself and Leon come up with a plan to get Arianna on her own without anyone finding out. We've faked a photoshoot at the house next to mine. It's an Airbnb and was available for the day, backing onto the beach. I arrived hours ago, checking the place out after an early briefing at the office.

It's only going to be the four of us. It's as safe as my own place and it's not overlooked, even in the garden. I've made sure Arianna can be herself here.

We're using Millie, Jack's wife's new range of eco-friendly clothing as a ruse. We'll take some photos, and get what they need. It's allowed us to get a private space, and a block of time for us to be alone *to talk*. While everyone thinks she's in the private garden or the house next door, I'll sneak her into mine, where we can talk more openly. *Hopefully,* she won't freak out that we made this happen.

For the first time in my life, I'm nervous about what might happen. I can't stay still, moving from room to room, checking, double checking, and triple checking how safe the location is.

I'm not expecting Arianna to open up about it all. I hope she does. *I need her to trust me.* I need a few answers. Namely, why she thinks she can't leave. It's been bugging the shit out of me since Ed and Dec said it the other day. And what I... *we* can do to help her out of this nightmare she seems to have been born into.

The way I'm feeling right now, I'm willing to risk anything to help her. I'll use all the resources we have to get her out. I have to get Arianna to agree. She's stubborn and I know she wants to do things her way. She needs to know I'm here to help anytime she wants or needs it.

Millie's been here for about an hour with Leon, she's currently laying out the blankets, and props in the garden, while Leon moves some loungers to set up what we hope to look like a photoshoot.

Her ETA is only a minute away and I'm eager to get her in here where I can see her. *Touch her.* I've hacked her phone so I can track her movements since the night at the restaurant. Something I should have done sooner. I need to know where she is at all times. It fucked with my head yesterday not seeing her, and not knowing she was okay.

I've spent so much time trying to get away from Arianna in the past, even I'm finding it hard to believe how I'm reacting right now.

She's mine.

Shit.

Ari has no idea it's us behind the photoshoot. Leon came up with the idea after we got a copy of her schedule, realising we would never be able to get her alone long enough for her to talk. We got Millie to offer the PR firm a hefty sum of money in return for our urgency. That was only yesterday. We've been added to her list of duties for today as a last-minute job. Not even Dec and Ed know it's us. The fewer people that know the truth, the better.

If she's being monitored, we have no idea if that includes messages and phone calls. I've added a signal jammer to both my house and this one just as a backup. You can be sure as shit guarantee that once she has her new phone in her hand today, I'll be expecting an answer every time I call or message.

Peering out the front door's spy hole, I catch sight of the black town car. Opening the door, I step out, making my way onto the driveway.

When Dec jumps out of the driver's seat, I wave him off, aiming to open Ari's door for her, but she beats me to it. She steps out in a pair of tight black jeans and an oversized blue hoodie. I almost stagger back, my pulse racing.

"Wow," I say, offering her my hand. I don't mean to say it out loud, but in all the time I've been watching her, I've never seen her dressed so casually. Even down to the high-top Nike trainers she's wearing. She's even more fucking stunning like this than she is dressed up. Arianna places her soft hand in mine as I help her out.

"What's wrong?" she asks as she takes her hand away.

"Nothing. I've just never seen you dressed like this."

Lowing her head, she frowns, taking a step to the side away from me, where I'm crowding her.

"Well, if I'm going to change outfits, there's not much point wearing what I'm... normally asked to wear." The way she says it has my anger flaring.

"I like this look on you," I hum into her ear as I press my hand to her back and lead her towards the house. "You have an effect on me, I've not felt for any other woman in a long time." Her hair grazes my cheek, as I speak. God, she smells good. Taking a long dark strand into my hand, I tug it lightly. And fuck she makes the quietest little gasp. Visions of her making that delicate noise as I bend her over my bike, wrapping the hair around my fist, pulling it as I fuck into her surge through my mind.

My dick has stood to attention the moment she got out of the car, straining against my suit trousers. It's hard as steel, urging me to unbutton her jeans, slide the zipper down, and slide my hand inside, just to feel her. Brush my fingers over her mound... Groaning loudly in her ear, I move to open the front door just to her side, I watch the way she reacts. Her eyes flicker closed for a second, then she glances down. Fuck, she just looked at my dick. "Visible for those who dare to look, Arianna," I say teasingly. Her cheeks redden with embarrassment at being caught.

Opening the front door, we walk through my hand still on her back. She turns to me, flashing me a smile that makes me weak at the knees. It's playful, and fuck, I want to see it all the time. When her eyes sweep over me as she bites her lip, she steps back, this time doing a full-on review of me, I let her look. Loving that she seems to be feeling confident today.

"I dare," she says and her sultry tone makes me want to bite that pretty mouth of hers. She peers around us, biting her lip, relaxing and seeming to be comfortable that were alone, she trails her finger down my chest, coming to a stop at belt buckle on my trousers. My whole body shudders at her touch, even through my shirt and jacket. My eyes on hers daring her to go further. I'm willing if she is.

Before I can react, she's turning away. Letting out a choked breath, my entire body on fire, I have to adjust my dick as I try to focus my vision because I've just almost shot my load in my boxers.

Who is this woman? This was not the woman I was expecting today. If this is the *real* Arianna, I'll make it my life's mission to see this side of her every day.

Quickening my pace, I catch up to her as she walks through the house and into the garden, via the bifold door. "What's changed?" I ask in confusion.

"Nothing's changed, Cole," she states, "You just don't know the real me, yet."

Yet.

"Show me who you really are, Cupcake," I reply.

"I will." I haven't even realised we're standing next to Leon and Millie until Ari reaches out and takes Millie's hand in a handshake. Leon tries to hide his laugh, coughing into his hand. He pulls out his phone, making a quick work of the message he types out. The low buzz in my pocket indicated he messaged me.

Bear: Whipped.

Me: You're a child.

"You must be Millie? From Millican?" Arianna offers. I see it, the moment she changes who she is in front of others. Oh right, I was supposed to tell her before we come out, about why she's really here.

"Yes, that's me," Millie says, and Leon laughs openly, moving towards Arianna, his big frame overshadowing us.

"My friend here has fucked up the plan already. He was supposed to tell you a few things before you came out." Arianna's looking between us, confused.

"You distracted me," I offer in a way as a resolve. She blushes, and it's so fucking cute.

"What's happening? Leon why are you here?" she asks, Millie steps away, giving us some peace, pulling Leon with her. "I need you to help with this," she says. "Jack says I'm not allowed to lift anything, now I'm pregnant," Millie says, rubbing her small bump tenderly. Leon moves quicky, keeping up with her as they walk away.

"Cole?" Ari asks worriedly.

"Arianna?" I joke. "This is all for you," I admit seriously.

"I know, it's work. I've been paid to be here."

"Not work," I say. "This is to give you some space." She looks around, her shoulders rise of full two inches as my words sink in.

"Why... I don't understand." She's pinching her fingers together anxiously. I take her hand in mine as her eyes dart around us, scouring the garden to see if anyone is watching. But her hand remains in mine, gripping my fingers with hers.

"You're safe, Cupcake." I know this isn't what she expected. I can only reassure her as best I can. "This," I say tilting my hand to the side to indicate the loungers and tables, "is not a real shoot."

"Cole, if it's not real, they'll find out, and I'll be..." Ari, says gulping down a breath. I hold her hand a little firmer in an attempt to bring her back to me.

"Finish that sentence, Cupcake. Tell me what will happen to you."

"What, no, nothing," she stammers. Her eyes fall to the floor and I know she's lying, but I'll get to the bottom of it all later.

"As fake as this is, you'll still have your photos taken. You will have proof that you were working. Millie will use them on her site and social media. And you have already been paid."

"Oh shit," she says quietly, and I can't help chuckling at her response.

"Arianna Byron, did you just swear at me?" Her hand flies to her mouth like she trying to take it back because she never swears. "I like it," I add. Lifting my hand, I tilt her head to the side so she can see I'm serious. "I'd like to see what other dirty things you can do with that mouth," I add. I don't have a chance in hell of my dick going down today. What I don't say out loud is that I can't wait to do all of the depraved things my overactive imagination has conjured up in the past... *year,* if I'm being honest. She doesn't say anything. She trying to hide her smile as her tongue flicks out to lick her bottom lip. I know she likes it.

Putting the dirty thoughts back into the box, I need to remember why we're here today. "Let's get this done, then we can talk, okay?" I say.

"Okay." I can tell she's still nervous about all of this. She's fidgeting with her hands again. But she'll see. After I call Millie back over, they head into the house, leaving me with Leon.

"I knew she was your lady." He smirks as he gets the camera ready.

"She's not my..." I try to deny what he's saying, but I can't.

"You can't deny it," he laughs. "You did all this for her, you've taken up twenty-four-hour watch in spite of having a team on her now. You spend any free time looking into what's really happening with her. The more you find out, the angrier you get. Plus, the fact you followed her out here like a god-damn dog on a lead, forgetting to tell her the real reason why she was here. Whipped, just like I said." god-damn-it... he's going to be like this all day.

"I don't even know how it happened," I admit, more to myself than him.

"Did you even do a sweep when she walked in?" Fuck. I hang my head briefly. I know she's safe, but I still have a job to do. I just can't take my mind off her.

"No, no, I didn't. Like I said, she distracted me." Crossing his arms over his chest, a smug smile settles on his face. "I don't know what's happening, Leon."

"I'm sure you'll figure it out eventually," he adds, slapping my back, jolting me forwards with the force.

"What I want to know is how she distracted you, is it anything I can replicate? I'd love to have a go on that bike of yours." I know he's fucking with me.

"Not telling you, no, and keep your hands off my fucking bike," I bite back.

Chapter Twenty-Three

For Me

Arianna

"Thanks, Leon," Millie chimes sweetly as Leon heads back down the stairs. Walking back through the door of the bedroom we're in, a moment later closing the door behind her. I still can't get my head around what's happening today. This is *for* me. Not for me to earn someone else money, or for me to be treated like a rag doll, passed around, dressed in clothes I don't like, and made up to look like someone I'm not.

This is *for me* to talk freely.

Other than when I'm with Chrisy, I don't remember a time I was ever able to do that. It's boggling my mind. It must be showing on my face because Millie sits next to me on the bed. Her kind face searching mine. "How are you doing?" she asks tentatively, taking a dress from the pile beside her, and fiddling with the fabric.

"Honestly, I don't know," I admit. "I have no idea what's happening," I add, blowing out a breath. I don't know this woman, but I get the feeling she cares. I feel comfortable just sitting next to her.

"Well, all I know is that Cole wanted to talk to you, but he knew he couldn't get you alone. Something about your schedule being a little too tightly packed. I'm paraphrasing," she says gently. "His words were a little more direct. I don't know all the details, and I don't need to know. *Unless* you want to tell me." I shake my head in response. My heart races a little faster. I think she suspects something, but I have no idea who she is really. "That's okay," she adds, settling the chaos that was starting to rise in my head.

"So, you don't really want me to wear your stuff, you're just doing it as a favour to Cole?" I ask, not knowing what to think.

"Oh, I want you to wear my stuff," she says seriously. "I've followed your accounts for a while. Business wise, you're an amazing investment. I just want you to *want* to wear it," she adds. I don't say anything for a moment, stunned by her admission.

It's a really simple question. One not many people would even think twice about, but it has me stumped. And I'm at a loss for words.

Do I want to wear them?

"No one has ever asked me that," I admit sadly. "Thinking back to all the photo shoots, galas, and events I've been dressed for, not a single person asked if *I* liked what I was wearing. Or if I *wanted* to wear it."

"That must suck, and did you? Like any of them, I mean?" she asks, curiously.

"Some of the dresses I liked, but some were more of..." I don't know how to put it without sounding ungrateful.

"More like you were being dressed to make someone else happy, rather than yourself?" A huff escapes me. Shit, that's exactly it.

"Yes, how did you guess?"

"I've had my fair share of shit over the years," she says, rubbing her hand over her baby bump.

"I'm sorry," I say, feeling like I've hit a sore point.

"There's no need for you to be sorry. Everything I went through led me right here. Right to a life I love. I wouldn't be able to do what I do now if it wasn't for what happened." Maybe that's a good way to look at things.

Everything happens for a reason. Right now, though, I'm not so sure.

"May I take a look at what you have? And can you tell me all about what you do? This was so short notice I didn't get a chance to look into your work." I say, in a hope of changing the direction that our conversation was going.

Millie explains how she went from an abusive relationship with her ex, who's now behind bars, to being with Jack and how her company 'Millican' is now a living, breathing positivity brand. Where forty per cent of each product sold goes to help support victims of abuse. The pure devotion she has for her work is beautiful. I really admire her.

I wish I had access to my money. I'd send every penny she paid for my time back to her, putting it to better use than lining my father's pockets. Maybe I can figure out a way to do it. Or make an anonymous donation. I'm sure I can if I keep back from spending what remains of my allowance.

"How much do you spend on things like this?" I ask trying to get a figure so I can pay her back.

"Oh," she looks confused for a moment, "anywhere between thirty and a hundred grand. It depends on what we know we can get out of it. Like, yours was the higher end because of your reach and following you have on social media. I know we can make that back just of the images you post when they're done." I inwardly groan. It's going to take me a little longer to give Millie the money back.

"Can you send me some of your other products, I'll happily promote anything you have. I'll pay for them. I don't want any freebies."

Her eyes sparkle, and I relax a little more, I think I've made a good impression, and for the right reasons. "Can we try this one first, while the sun's shining?" I ask, holding up a dress that actually makes me smile. It reminds me of the one Chrisy bought me last.

"Do you like it?" she asks, her face scrunched as she waits for me to reply.

"I love it, the colour's beautiful." It's a figure hugging pink bodycon dress with a sheer overlay and long sleeves. "It's so soft," I say holding it to my face.

"It is. All made from recycled and eco-friendly materials. Let's get you dressed, so we don't keep them waiting." I agree, standing from the bed ready to change.

"Do you want me to leave while you get dressed?" Millie asks, moving towards the door.

"No, you're okay. I've done these enough times to not be bothered when there's someone else in the room." Millie moves back and sits on the bed, pulling a few other outfits and showing them to me, as I agree to wear them next. All dresses, all beautiful, and all approved by me. I feel giddy just at the thought.

Taking my hoodie off, I place it on the bed and remove my trainers, socks, and then jeans. I catch Millie looking. There's nothing wrong with it, but she frowns, and I don't understand why until I realise what she's seen.

How could I have forgotten? My stomach twists painfully. I should have done something to hide them. Turning away to try and hide what's so very obviously five distinct purple bruises at the top of my thigh, lined with healing cuts on the tip of each one. Coupled with matching ones on my arm. My cheeks burn as shame washes over me, and I'm regretting my decision to have her stay in the room.

"What are these marks, Arianna?" Millie's voice is quiet but calm.

"Nothing, just a silly..."

She shakes her head and I stop talking.

"You're talking to the queen of just a *silly*, and *accidents* that were all *my* fault. Show me." I don't want to admit anything, but I know I can't hide what she's already seen. Walking over in just my underwear. I hold my arm out to her first. My insides churn at what she could possibly think of me when she's just told me about all the work she does to help women and men who suffer abuse. This is nothing like that though. I'm not being abused.

"These look recent." I nod, as she brushes her fingers over the bruising on my arm. "Are they sore?" Shaking my head in reply, I stay quiet, until she reaches for the ones on my leg.

"Those are…" I barely whisper.

"Have you cleaned them? I can see the nail marks." My head drops, embarrassment washing over me that I let this happen.

"Yes."

"Good. Does Cole know about these?" She's not judging me, just asking simple questions.

If I speak up now, what will happen?

"I think he might, but I'm not sure," I answer nervously, thinking back to the way he reacted at the restaurant when I went outside.

"Okay, here what's going to happen." Her voice is even softer than before. "I'm not going to ask you anything more. The dress you've chosen will cover them up. When we're done, Cole's going to take you next door. Something about his place being safer than this." Her eye's roll, easing the tension that built so quickly. "And you're going to tell him all about this. It has to come from you, Arianna."

My heart rate picks up, and my hands go a little clammy at the thought of freeing the words that have been trapped and I've been too ashamed to let out.

Like she can hear my thoughts, Millie continues, "I understand how you feel. Saying it out loud is scary, but once you do it, it'll be like a weight off your shoulders." I want to tell her and Cole everything, I really do, but there's still something stopping me.

"I don't know if he cares enough," I admit.

"Who Cole?"

'Yeah', I mouth.

"Oh, he cares, and I believe he has for a while." She beams like she knows something I don't. "He's just starting to see it for himself." Millie's smile is reassuring, giving me a little courage to do what needs to be done: To get this photoshoot done to the best of my ability and then tell him my truth.

Chapter Twenty-Four
My Truth

Arianna

An hour and a half later, after taking as many photos, in as many different settings as we can, they're shutting down the set. The images Leon and Millie took are a lot more natural than I'm used to, but the whole experience made me feel like I was actually part of something. It sparks the buzz for the way I want my future.

Cole only left my side about twenty minutes ago, when he walked back into the house, saying he had something he needed to do. I didn't take much notice, but as he reappears, I'm taken aback at how agitated he is. His shoulders are tense, fists clenched. I can see the vein in his neck throbbing from here. As he speaks to Leon, he looks angrier than I've ever seen him before.

I've made him angry.

I can't look away. My vision blurs for a second, but I force myself to focus on what's happening. I rub my chest, trying to calm my unease as Cole heads towards me, and I take a step back instinctively, gulping down my anxiety.

Leon stops him with a firm hand on his shoulder before he can go any further.

Millie starts talking to me, but I don't hear I word she says. Cole's glaring at me. My heart sinks. *What did I do?* His voice is raised, pointing in my direction. Cursing my father for something I don't quite catch, then Leon tells him to keep it down. I can't look away as they argue about something. My vision blurs again and I have to blink back the tears that threaten to spill. My father, he's done something.

Then it hits me. The anger, the looks, the glares.

They found out.

My father found out I'm here and it's not real. It takes everything I have not to double over when the weight of anxiety threatens to pull me down. I can't catch my breath.

I have to go.

It'll make everything worse if I stay. The consequences are too high, I have to take the fall. I won't let anything happen to them. My father will blame me, but I can't take the chance he won't lash out at them. They've been too kind. I'll tell my father it was all me.

"I'll be back in a second, I'll see what's going on," Millie says, before she walks over to where Leon and Cole are all talking about me.

Has my father done something already? Oh god, what if he's...

Shutting the thought down immediately, I go into automatic pilot. They all look at me briefly, quietening their voice when I pass by, making my way inside. Taking the stairs two at a time, in a rush to get my things and leave. I realise with a sob that I need to change and get back into my hoodie and jeans. I need to be quick about it. Walking into the bedroom I grab my clothes ready to change, when I hear a voice. My hands shake as I grab my things, before racing back towards the stairs, trying to be quiet. I can change in the car. The sooner I'm out of here the better things will be for them.

I hear the door slam at the front of the house. *Who left?* Making it to the bottom of the huge staircase, my feet bare, I'm stunned when Cole storms back through. his panicked eyes landing on me.

"Ari, thank fuck. I thought you left, without anyone to... never mind," he rushes out as he places a hand on the wall beside himself. He looks... *worried?* "You scared me," he says. I shake my head in confusion, *I scared him?*

"No, but I'm going now. Don't worry, I'll make it all okay. I'll make whatever he's done right. I'll direct it my way." His eyes flare with a new type of anger. "I won't let them..." *Hurt you*. I can't say the words out loud. "I promise."

"Ari, wait..." I try to push past him but he grabs my waist, his warm hands protectively stopping me from behind, stalling my escape. "Where are you going? Why are you running?" he says, spinning me around to face him.

"I need to stop them, Cole. Whatever they did to make you *that* angry, I'll sort it out. I'm so sorry." My speech is hurried. I take my phone out of the pile of clothes I have in my arm and open the screen ready to message Dec to pick me up. "I'll wait outside for Dec. I'm so sorry, I'll make it right." Pulling me closer, he invades my space, plucking my phone out of my hand before I have a chance to do anything.

"What will you make right Ari?" he asks calmly, as he slides it into his pocket.

"Whatever they've done to make you react that way. You were so angry. I won't let them take it out on you." I know I'm repeating myself, but I can't think of anything else to say.

He doesn't let me go.

"What are doing? I need to leave," I say. "Please let me go."

"No." His voice is strained, desperate almost, as he tries to get the words out through his clenched jaw. "Ari, you're not going anywhere."

"Okay," I agree, not knowing why.

He visibly relaxes, the tension easing off his shoulders. Is it because I'm in his arms and he knows I'm safe? Or is it that he caught me just in time before I could put myself into a reckless situation? I don't know what the answer is.

"I am angry," he says honestly, "and yes, they, your parents have made me so fucking angry I want to rip them to shreds for how they're treating you." He's angry on my behalf? "Cupcake, you're not leaving until I know what caused this. What made you want to run, beautiful?" Cole pulls me to him and my things fall to the floor as I crash into his chest. He doesn't give me time to answer.

"And I will *not,* now or ever, fucking let you put yourself in that situation for me."

"I don't understand, I thought..." I say as I melt further into his chest, my head resting over his heart. *He feels good.* His chin comes to rest on my head and he lets out a breath, that I feel skate across my scalp, sending a hot shiver down my spine.

"The way you reacted out there, I thought my father had found out about all of this. I thought he had done something to you or one of the guys." It comes out in a rush.

I could get used to this. Being honest while feeling so safe. Not that I could ever be with someone as kind and protective as Cole. My father wouldn't allow it. I'll take it for now though. I'll take as much as I can get.

"Ari, I'll explain. Let's go to my place, next door. I know you'll be safe there," he whispers as he places a soft kiss to my head. "Bring your clothes you can change there."

"They don't know?" I ask, looking up, needing some sort of answer, reassurance even. "Who?" he says.

"My parents. They don't know what's really happening here?"

"They don't know, I promise you." I feel it, relief saddled with the buzz of adrenaline. I don't say anything, I just let out a breath releasing all the tension from the last few minutes.

"Ari, they can't get to you while you're with me." Softening some more, I wrap my arms around his waist, seeking more of the comfort and safety he's offering. "Come on," he says, stepping back. I instantly feel the loss of his warmth but his hand slowly glides down my arm, entwining his fingers with mine, the trail leaving a path of electricity in its wake.

"Why are we going to another house? We could have stayed there," I ask as we walk between the properties. I'm a little confused, but I'm not complaining. Most of my fear has subsided, replaced with a slither of excitement at going somewhere with Cole, my dream coming back to me in a flash.

"No, I need you alone for this." I giggle, and he looks at me, a smile replacing the frown that was on his face a few moments ago. "Not like that, well... no. We need to clear a few things up before we do any of that."

"Any of what?" I ask shyly. Even when my mind screams *yes, give it to me.*

"After that kiss the other day, and the way you feel in my arms, there is no way we are not doing that again." And just like that, I can already feel the ghost of his lips on mine. A memory that will never leave me. The way he kissed me was divine.

A cold suppression starts creeping in, taking over, jolting me back to reality, with the icy memory of the last guy I kissed and had sex with. I could have never have guessed how that would have ended. I'm under no illusion they'd do it again if they found out about what Cole's doing for me today.

I can't do it again. Not for my sake, but for Gi and Ed, I can't risk them or their happiness. Trying to pull my hand away from his, I stop mid-step. "Ari?" His eyes questioning as his hands come up to my face, cupping each side gently.

"I can't, Cole," I choke out, his thumb traces my lower lip.

"Yes, you can." He's so matter-of-fact that I want to laugh at how simple he makes everything. I want to believe him.

"No, I can't it's too risky." Shaking my head, I disagree with him.

"You're capable of anything." I'm taken aback by the firmness in his voice. It's encouraging and I want to believe it. "I'll never make you do anything you don't want to, Ari." Taking his hand in mine, I kiss his palm, unable to stop myself.

"I like that." I smirk.

"You are..."

"No, I mean the way you call me Ari. I like it." Looking down at me, he sweeps his thumb over the pad of my bottom lip, parting them briefly as he pulls away.

"Get used to it. I'll never call you Miss Bryon again." I don't want him to. I feel a little more secure and confident in Cole and myself, just like I did this morning when I walked through the door and looked at his crotch.

Can I take this for myself today? If I'm safe like he says, there's no way anything can get back to them. A small spark lights in my chest.

"You have an effect on me too, Cole. Things I have never felt for another man." I repeat his earlier words back to him. Watching as his eyes hood, and his breathing deepens.

"Fuck, Cupcake, let's get you inside." Smirking at me, as he pulls me along the small winding path of the back garden, stamping down my own fear, refusing to let it spoil my fun.

Guiding me through the back door, I'm greeted by the warmest feeling. This kitchen is cosy; big but relaxing. "Sit," he demands, almost placing me on the chair at the rectangular table on the other side of the room.

"Tell me why you and me are risky?" He's jumping right in as he puts the kettle on. *Him and me,* it's an impossible thing. The rumbling of the water as it boils fills the room, allowing me a moment to think. I can't tell him why it's risky, can I? Biting the inside of my cheek hard, I consider what he's asking of me. The kettle clicks, and he pours a herbal tea. Camomile and honey, I think. Sweet and settling.

My favourite.

My heart flips, knowing he's trying to make me feel comfortable.

"So, tell me," he tells me again as he sets down the steaming cup.

"Cole," I warn, not sure if I can sit here under his intense, and worried gaze.

"The only risk is you not telling me what's happening behind that door when Dec drops you home." There's that word again: *home.* Pulling the chair out, he sits beside me, before dragging my chair so we're facing each other. Crossing my legs, I shift, placing my clutched hands on my knees. "Nothing happens when I get to the house." It's the truth; nothing happens. "I walk in, shower, go to my room." Cole just shakes his head like he knows better.

Because while nothing really happens at the house, other than the occasional run in with Robert Carmichael, it all happens when I leave.

His feet hook around the edge of the chair legs, trapping me, while he lifts my hands, inspecting where I'm pulling at the skin slightly. Distracting myself. A second later they spread over mine. Gentle and comforting. How did we get to this point in our relationship? Four days ago I disliked him, and him me.

"Answer me, honestly, Ari. Do you feel safe at home?" I can't look at him, my eyes dart down to our now entwined fingers. "Ari."

If I tell him the truth, will he help me? If I tell him my plan to ask my father for some independence, a small slice of something that's mine, will he help me pick up the pieces when he says no, and tries to ruin my life?

I doubt it. Cole may be my bodyguard, but even I know that's asking too much of him. If my father found out, he'd ruin him. When I look up, his hazel eyes bore into mine, begging me to tell him the truth, so I give it to him. I can't deny him my truth.

"No, I don't. I don't feel safe anywhere," I say on a shaky exhale. Looking him directly in the eyes, I steel myself a little.

"I'll keep you safe." He leans forward and there's a deep, unmistakable shake in my chest as my body gives in to him. Like a balm to my broken soul. There's no doubt in my mind he means what he says. "You really mean that don't you?" I whisper.

"Yes," he swallows, like he's nervous to admit it.

"Why?" I ask tentatively, licking my bottom lip. His eyes track the movement. I can see the streaks of colours in his eyes, greens and browns intertwined to create a galaxy of colour so unique to Cole, they could be an illusion.

"I've always wanted you to be safe, baby. It's seared into my blood to protect you. Every time you leave your house, I *need* to know where you are. I'm only satisfied when it's my eyes on you. I want you to know I'm watching, I always will be." Oh, how did this turn so quickly? I mean that's a lot to digest from one sentence. I may need a minute. He's smirking at me again like he can read my thoughts.

"Because it's your job?"

"No," he says a little sternly, the vein in his neck coming to life telling me that the fact I even asked the question annoys him. "It may have started like that, baby, but right now, it so much more. I want to protect you. And not just as your bodyguard." He just called me baby. *Baby. Twice.*

"Oh." I feel like I'm in a wind tunnel, everything is happening so fast, and I'm getting swept away in the best possible way.

"Yeah, it's a shock to me too."

I giggle, and he smiles.

"I need to hear more of that, Cupcake. You don't laugh enough." My cheeks instantly flame. This whole conversation is so intimate. I like it.

He leans in to kiss me. As soon as his lips touch mine, my stomach clenches with an intense need. Closing my eyes, my mind relaxes as my world descends into a safe place. A safe place where Cole sees me, feels me, and lets me be me. His soft lips are barely a kiss, a fleeting touch. It's over before it really begins, leaving me wanting more.

"You have been, every time, Cole," I whisper as he pulls away. "When I wanted to lose myself and forget my life you brought me back to reality. Before anyone found out and could punish me for what I'd done." He sucks in a breath, and I realise what I've said. Only I can't take it back. *And I don't want to.*

"What did you want to forget, Ari." I close my eyes for a brief second and his warm hand rests on my thigh, his thumb gently grazing the bruises he doesn't know are there. Millie told me to tell him, maybe this is the best way, to show him. Looking down where his hand lies on the truth I've been hiding.

I brush the back of his hand lightly with the tips of my fingers. My heart beating wildly in my chest at what I'm about to admit to a man I've kind of loved to hate since the first time we met.

I move his hand and my dress slowly up my thigh, spreading my legs a fraction, so he's able see the full extent of what Robert Carmichael did to me at the table in the restaurant. In front of my parents and a room full of people. Where I fled the table, only for the man right in front of me to catch me, ground me, and kiss me.

Unspoken words pass between us. There's nothing sexual about what happening and we both know it. Offering him a sad smile, I plead with my eyes for him to look down, where I know the bruising is now exposed.

His gaze slowly lowers And I know the moment he sees it. His sharp intake of air feels suffocating. His fingertips dust over the marks, causing me to flinch despite the softness of his touch. So many emotions swirl over his features, competing for attention, I just watch as the hate, sadness and anger play out.

"I was right there when he did this, wasn't I? Sitting right across from you?" A pained expression crosses his face, his lips turning down in regret as he lets go of a heavy sigh. I don't need to answer. "I should have known. I'm so sorry, Ari."

"There's nothing you could have done, Cole," I say, lightly touching his cheek, his stubble grazing the pads of my fingers as he leans into my touch.

"I sat and watched as they all laid into you, and did nothing to stop it. What sort of person does that make me?" He's upset. Tears well in my eyes. I can't hide them. He feels this for me.

"No, no... please don't do this, that night may have been one of the worst but you turned it into something I'll never forget." I don't want him feeling like this. "I ate chips," I quip. Only he grimaces like I've just made it worse.

"I could have got you out of there. The moment you walked in, the way they spoke to you, I hated it. I wanted to drag you away then. I could have stopped this from happening." He's trying to take the blame.

"No, you couldn't," I admit, licking a tear that's fallen over my lips.

"Don't give me that shit, Ari..." he starts, but I won't have it.

"No." I stand, and he stands with me, grasping my shoulders softly, holding me in place. "What you don't understand, is that if you had done that, it would have been so much worse."

"How can it be worse than this, look at your fucking leg... he literally put his filthy hands on you. Bruised and cut your beautiful skin." His voice breaks. I raise my voice to match his. I won't let him blame himself for this. It's mine to own.

"I know what they'll do if I don't behave in a way that's acceptable to them, they'd try to break me again." My anger is rising, my arms gesturing outwards with the need to release the frustration that's building inside. Forcing him to let go of my shoulders. "Cole." A small whimper escapes my lips. "They would have taken me away again," I shout, the pressure in my chest almost suffocating me. "They would have locked me away... brutal, so fucking brutal, the pain." Gasping at the memory, I try to continue, "What he did is nothing compared to that." All my fight deflates as I watch for Cole's reaction. I stumble back, the chair clashing with my legs.

"What the hell are you talking about?" he says, shaking his head in a slow back and forth motion like he can't believe what I said. My hands come to my mouth, covering a cry. Oh God, I've never told a soul about any of this. Ed, Gi, and Chrisy know I was sent away, but they don't know the extent of what happened to me.

The torture they inflicted on me to just to get me to comply.

How do I even start? Maybe just the basics? I don't waste any time. If I don't do it now I never will.

"It was my twentieth birthday. I'd been seeing this guy, secretly of course. We wanted to move to the next step, so I asked Chrisy to help me sort it so we could be alone at a function we were invited to." He grunts, not moving from where he's stood.

"I hate the prick already," he says shoving one hand in his pocket, while the other reaches for mine. "It was all going fine. We were in the middle of... you know." I'm not shy about using the word *sex* or *fuck*, but they're not part of my daily vocab, so saying them out loud doesn't come easy to me.

"No, Ari, I don't know," he says clenching his jaw. "Tell me what you and *this* guy were in the middle of doing?" His nostrils flare as a storm I don't fully understand brews behind his eyes.

"I, we were in the middle of having sex."

"Fuck." I wonder how he would react if I told him it was my first time and only time.

"Anyway," I say with a little caution, "we were interrupted. I won't get into the details"

"No, please *do* tell me how this guy fucked you, and how *you* were exposed to other people, I'm going to take a wild guess, you had nothing on?" I'm a little stumped. I'm trying to tell him what he wanted to hear, and now this.

"Wow, not the point, Cole," I exclaim. I didn't expect him to behave like this, he's so hot and cold. Caring one moment, then whatever this is, the next.

"No, you're right. Not the point," he says, recovering a little. Dropping his hand, I reach down to take off the gold sandals that match the dress I'm wearing. Leaving them on the floor next to me. I take another step away I'm not ready to tell him anything, not while he's like this. My own anger rising, I won't be spoken to like this. I've let people walk all over me for too long. I don't have to listen to this.

"You don't have any right to judge me, Cole. You wanted to know what happened, well, fuck you, you've blown it."

"Cupcake." The corner of his mouth lifts, as if I've I said something that amuses him. My temper rises.

"You're confusing the fuck out of me. Don't you dare damn smile at me. Mr Grant." His name is emphasised to make my point.

"Don't fucking Mr Grant, me. I can't help it, I really like it when you lose your shit enough to swear at me. Keep it coming." *What? He wants me to lose my shit? Why would he want to see that?*

"No." I've had enough. Snatching my hoodie and jeans from the table, I move down the hall, my temper flowing into every step. I don't even know if he follows. The temper raging in my mind cutting off any noise around me.

Standing in the middle of the living room, I grab the soft hem of the dress, and pull it up and over my head, ready to change, and leave.

Chapter Twenty-Five

Shame

Cole

I'm fucking it all up without even trying, watching her walk away. I mean it's a great fucking view, epic actually, especially in that gold dress. How it hugs her ass, I want to sink my teeth in it so badly, run my tongue over the marks I create. *Sweet fucking Jesus*. I have issues. Really fucked up issues. I can't stop where my head goes when I see her like that. She just laid out what she been through: the pain, torture, hurt. I then get jealous, angry, and my fucked-up mind goes *there*, to how she sparks a flame in me when she can't hold in her temper. I'd have walked away too.

I would have knocked me out.

A three-way tug of war, lust, anger, and pride, fight it out in my body. Shoving my fisted hands into the pockets of my suit trousers, I have no idea how to handle any of this. My mouth seems to fucking run away with itself without checking in with my brain first. In the last few minutes, I have gone from having her lips on mine, to blazing fury, all doused with pride when she lets rip and swore at me.

She's showing me and only me who she really is, instead of the queen of masks she has been hiding behind all her life.

I'm an idiot, shit. Running my hand over my hair, I stride quietly through the hall looking for Ari, only to freeze when I get to the doorway of the living room.

She's taking off her dress. Her arms high, pulling the gold fabric over her head.

Fuck me.

I've imagined her like this more than I care to admit. She's been off limits, from my own doing for a long time. But seeing her now, my mind hasn't done her justice. I have to palm my dick, squeezing it a little to try and stop it from bursting through my trousers, because the sight of Ari right now, *my Ari,* is flooring me. The vision of her perfect tits in that almost see-through bra and matching knickers is leaving me lost for words.

I could look at her like this for hours, but she deserves to be admired for all the right reasons, with someone who appreciates her for who and what she is rather than how much money they can make off her.

I need to apologise. Beg for forgiveness. It came out wrong, and I need her to understand that. Especially now. When I want more than just a professional relationship.

"I'm sorry, I'd never judge you, Cupcake," I say, gripping the doorframe. Her eyes widen when she realises what I've just seen and I watch as the blush actually creeps over every fibre of her body.

"I'm sorry," I admit again. Arching an eyebrow in her direction, it strikes me she's not covering herself up. She's more confident than I expected, my soul lights up, and I love it. We're on equal ground; I'm not naked, but if she looked closely, she'll see just how I'm reacting to her, the outline of my cock prominent in my trousers. Groaning, I step forward.

"I heard you the first time," she adds, looking back at me with an angry glare.

"I don't know what came over me," I admit. It's a lie. Fuck, it's a huge lie. Breaking eye contact with her beautiful chocolate eyes, I hang my head, "Shit, yes, I do," I mumble. "I fucking hate the thought of another guy's hands on you.

Then, fuck, even now. When I've not even had the chance." I search her face for some sort of reaction. I'm unwavering in my plea. I want to look, I want to take her in.

When she doesn't move, or say a word, I relent.

"Could you please put some clothes on before I... just put some clothes on. Please, Ari." It comes out through gritted teeth.

"Sure," she says, still saying nothing about my outburst. Taking her jeans, Ari turns around and I glimpse the delicate curve of her arse in a fucking thong. *This is torture.* I want to touch her so badly. But I'll remain the gentleman, *for now.*

"You did that on purpose," I say when she bends to put her jeans on. "You're wearing a goddamn thong, Cupcake." She chuckles, grabbing her hoodie. "Devil." The tension that was there is replaced with something else, something easier... than whatever that was.

"I want to know everything." I'm getting as close as I can without touching her. "I'll keep my opinions to myself until you're finished." Meeting her toe to toe, I take the hoodie from her hand, and slip it over her head, my fingers grazing her breasts and stomach as I pull down to cover her. The hitch in her breath makes me smile—she's just as affected as I am by our proximity.

I kiss her. It's a hot, yet chaste kiss on her delicate lips. "I'll never hurt you, Ari," I say as my mouth leaves hers.

"I know." Her eyes flicker to mine, letting me know it's the truth, and fuck does that settle my soul, knowing she trusts me to keep her safe.

"Tell me, everything?" I ask, stepping away to lead her to the huge deep green sofa. We sit facing each other. Crossing her legs underneath her, she places her hands on her knees, worrying her fingers together. I cover them with mine, holding them there.

"Not a word until I'm finished, okay?"

"Where was I?" I ask nervously, still afraid to let him see the truth. I know I want things to change, and this has to be part of the process. I need to be able to come to terms with what happened. When I tell Cole, my heart knows that he won't let it happen again. He'll look for me if I disappear. He's already searched me out whenever I'm out of his sight. Closing my eyes I take an unsteady breath, letting the memory of that awful night come back to me.

Like the flick of a switch, every sensation, every emotion, the shame, the horror I felt, like a veil falling over me, all the vivid details like it was only yesterday my world shattered overnight.

"We were interrupted, not by one person, but by almost everyone at the party." My stomach churns at the memory. "They burst in." Sucking in a breath, I force the words out; words I've kept hidden. "Laughed, took photos, of me and him..."

"Fuck." It's faint but I can hear the hate as he says it, his body vibrating with tension as I continue.

"He set me up—the long game he called it—a practical joke, to touch the untouchable." Dropping my hands, Cole stands and starts pacing the room, but keeps his mouth firmly closed, respecting my wishes. Remembering as I lay there, my so called boyfriend at the time, on top of me still inside me, laughing. "I froze. I had no idea what to do. He was laughing along with them all. He left me on the bed, did up his trousers, walked over to his friends, and hooked his arm around another girl."

"I'd grabbed the blanket to cover myself up, but it was too late, they had what they needed." I remember what happened next. Cole looks confused for a moment and stops pacing, staring at me with such concern in his eyes that I want to kiss him for it.

"It was Chrisy who came to my rescue. I've never seen her look so fierce. She cupped my face, wiped away the tears, and told me she'd deal with it all."

I chuckle, remembering how she flew across the room. "She punched him in the face, broke his nose, and kicked him in the dick as he went down." I watch the smirk rise on Cole's handsome face. "Long story short, it got back to my parents. Only *they* believed I had orchestrated the whole thing. That it was me who seduced, humiliated, and assaulted him."

"Shit, Ari." He comes back over to me, taking me in his arms, and holding me tight to his chest. My arms wrap around him, this feels right. Natural. Only I have to force him away to finish the story.

"When I got back to the house... there was a group of men waiting outside the door that I'd never seen before. They followed me inside. Cole, I was so scared. My father appeared and hit me so hard, I fell to the floor. The men then dragged me away, kicking and screaming, to a place I never want to go back to." I don't tell him I would if it meant helping the people I care for. "I was taken away from everything I knew, no-one even tried to help me," I say, vividly remembering screaming for it until my throat and lungs burned. "My parents just stood by and watched, while I was repeatedly hit by the ones who held me down. They then laughed at me, my own parents." My chest shudders in a soundless cry.

"After they locked me away, I was subjected to things..." I close my eyes, remembering the way I was made to submit to the pain, "almost every day. The more I cried or screamed for them to stop, the more the men would hurt me. I soon learned to stay quiet. Every blow, every cruel word, every threat made me believe that there will never be another option for me. That this is my life and there is no getting away from it."

"I want to say so many things, baby, I just don't know where to start." He moves my hands to his heaving chest, I relish the warmth.

"The trouble is, I tried to be me. I wanted my parents to realise that I could still give them what they wanted, and have a little slice of life for myself. I wanted them to see that I was just your average woman, that there's nothing special about me."

"There's nothing average about you, Cupcake. You're far from that, so far from that. I'd say you're spectacular, and I'm only just beginning to get to know the real you." I press a gentle kiss to his lips. His soft exhale flutters across my skin, like its own caress.

"I wanted them to see that I could still make them all the money they wanted, I just wanted to be me while I did it. Only they locked me away for it. That was my mistake." I won't tell him that I'm going to start again. I'm going to try and be me, just on a smaller scale. I don't think I even realise that I've already started by being with Cole.

"What do you mean, they locked you away?"

"They were so disgusted that their daughter would offer herself up so willingly as a whore to be used, that they locked me away." His grip tightens on me, holding me while I relive one of the worst moments of my life. "I wasn't far away from them, in fact, I was so close. They had people hold me down and carry me away, to... a room, with nothing in it apart from a screen. A cell inside the walls of my father's estate, I had no idea even existed until that moment. They threw me in like I was nothing." These are the words I've never told a living soul before now. "They made me watch, on a small tv screen, when they told Gi and Ed that I'd been sent away to be punished for my actions. Told me their pain was my fault. I was made to listen and watch when my parents laughed at how I was tainted, and they'd have to think of another use for me now. That I'd disgraced myself and the family name." Cole's speechless, like he can't comprehend what they did. "I watched as Gianna's heart broke for me. I watched as Chrisy searched the house for me, while Gi broke down in despair at not knowing where I was, as Ed held it together by a thread, unable to help me." Closing my eyes, I see it for what it is. I'm not there now, I'm safe.

"In the end, I had no idea how long I was there. Each day would bring a new painful way to make me weak. Kicked, punched by people I didn't know, or just left in the endless darkness."

"Fuck, the sick bastards," he almost cries as he lunges towards me, sweeping me into his arms, holding me so tight I can hardly breathe. "Never again, Cupcake. I'll make sure of it," he promises, like a lifeline I never knew I needed.

"The thing is, Cole, I have no option. They threatened everyone I hold close, told me Gi would be sent back to Italy with nothing, and never allowed back in the country, and Ed—my father told me they could hold him here; ruin his happiness. My father even threatened Chrisy—people around me get fired on a regular basis when they start to care too much, that's why…"

"Don't you fucking dare say it. You can't deny this, us," he warns, as I swallow down his words. They warm me after the cold story of my past.

"I'm not denying anything, Cole. I know I like you, more than like you, but if they find out about you, *us,*" I say testing out how it feels on my lips. I like it. "They will ruin you and everything you hold close. Your business, family, friends. I'd never see you again. I don't think I could handle that." Pulling me closer, his hands wrapping around my waist. He lifts me onto his lap so I'm straddling his strong thighs, his forehead touches mine. "That's never going to happen. I'm not letting you go." he murmurs. I think it's more to himself than to me, but they ignite a pain in my chest. One I've felt before, having to witness the people around me break.

"Cole, please, I couldn't live with myself if…" The words won't come out. His eyes lift to mine, his knuckles brushing down my cheek, causing me to whimper at how caring this big man is towards me. I see it written in his eyes: the determination to set me free from this world my parents have created. To care for me.

"Let them see," he says. My breath catches in my throat, his words echoing the ones my mind has been searching for. "Let them see just how beautiful you are, inside and out." His voice is fierce, as he kisses the tip of my nose, then the top of my lip so gently, nipping at my lips. My lips meet his and he devours me. Fireworks light up my body like it's New Year's Eve. Moaning into his mouth, barely able to breathe with its intensity.

"Please," he says taking his lips from mine, "let them see you. I'll be with you every step of the way, baby." I wonder how I ever saw Cole differently. How I mistook this kind and considerate man, who only wants to protect me, for a gruff, angry man, ruining my life and fun. How could I have ever hated him? *I never hated him. He just had everything I ever wanted. And pissed me off in the process.* And right there and then I decide that I want more with this man. So, I kiss him back, pressing my lips to his, giving him everything I can without words.

Cole's strong, wide hands move up my back, sending tingles over my skin, his thumb grazing the side of my breast. My nipples harden at the slightest touch, and I moan into his mouth when his hands reach my waist. His fingers dig in beautifully, holding me, as Cole grinds his hardening length against my core. My eyes flutter closed at the delicious friction he's causing, feeling him beneath me, growing harder.

"Ari, do you want this?" he asks, breaking our kiss, but only for a second.

"Yes," I admit, I do, I really do, but I need to tell him first, "It's been a while since I was with someone."

"How long is a while, baby?"

"Oh, um, a few... years," I say sheepishly.

"What? How? Look at you, how is that possible..." His words fall away as he sits up a little straighter.

"*That*," I say, giving him a knowing look, "was the last time I had sex." Mortification runs through my veins, but I don't look away.

"Well shit, Ari?" Cole murmurs. The look on his face doesn't change, like I thought it would.

"It was also my first time," I admit sheepishly, unable to look him in the eyes this time, only sneaking a peak when he doesn't say anything.

"Fuck." he curses eventually, after what feels like the longest few seconds of my life. "If we do this, I don't want to hurt you. We'll take it slow, okay?" I chuckle a little. I may have only slept with one guy, but he assumes I'm innocent when I'm anything but.

"There's really no need. I had this very conversation with Chrisy after everything happened. She got this wicked grin, and a few days later, she proceeded to sneak in a huge variety of toys, to help with my situation." She'd hidden them all in various ways to conceal them from anyone willing to look too closely. She then went and made a false bottom in my underwear drawer to hide them.

"Toys?" his eyebrows raise, and the heat in his eyes intensifies. I feel like I'm on fire.

"Yep, toys, I have four in my little collection." I don't tell him that some of them aren't that little. "Also with the type of books I read, they've been put to good use."

"Holy shit," he says, looking uncomfortable as he reaches down between us and adjusts himself, making me smile.

"Are you okay?" I ask, looking him over. His body is tense, his grip tightening around my arse and hips as he palms them, causing my core to tighten.

"Cupcake, I've just listened to you tell me you have only ever slept with one man one time. Then you tell me you use toys to make yourself come." He lifts his hips, pressing himself into me. My chest heaves as I meet his hips, panting out a breath, as he leaves me lightheaded. I want him. Hard, thick, and hot. I tilt my head back, sucking in his air. "All of which I'm going to need to see and use on you." He thrusts upwards again. *Oh my god, yes.* My stomach tightens at the thought. "Then you tell me you read smutty books." I nod to confirm my choice in literature. "My dick was hard the moment your sexy arse straddled my lap. Feel it now baby." He grinds into me again, and this time I moan. "Like a fucking iron bar. It's all for you and your pleasure." His firm hands press my hips down, forcing my core to his length, creating the most delicious pressure I have ever felt. My hips jolt for more. I'm breathless.

"Do you trust me?" he asks, as my hips grind over his length. Trying to catch my breath, I don't even have to think of the answer: I do trust him. I think I always have. I knew he would always find me, no matter how reckless my actions were. I knew he would always come looking for me. Even if it pissed me off in the process, he was there. I knew I could fall and he would catch me.

I suck in a breath as Cole lifts me to my feet and waits for my answer.

"Yes," I say simply. He stands and the smile on his face intensifies. Taking my hand in his, he leads me towards the staircase. I don't feel scared, a little nervous, but this feels right. I feel settled with his hand holding mine. Like this, we, were inevitable somehow.

We're not slow in our steps and every few seconds he looks back as if he's checking I'm still there. We end up in a bedroom I assume is his.

Cole closes the door behind me with a soft thud, and his lips crash to mine in a possessive, passionate kiss I never want to end. Clasping his hands on the sensitive skin just above my jeans, my body liquid in his grip, as our lips become frenzied, my whole body giving into this man. His warmth penetrates my skin even through my hoodie.

"You're safe here with me, baby," he murmurs, breaking the intensity of our kiss as he moves us towards the bed.

"Cole..." I don't know what to say, but the need I feel is so good, so intense, it was never like this before. Knowing I can do this, kiss a man, feel a man I truly want to be with, all while being safe is something I have never been able to experience before.

It's heady, almost unbelievable. Maybe I am dreaming. If I am, I don't care. I'll wake up with the memory of this, and I'll treasure it just as much as I would if it were real life.

This is real Ari, take it, enjoy it, and never forget this moment.

"We're doing this the way it should have been done all those years ago, Ari." It's like he knows what I want without asking.

Laying me on the bed he hovers over me, kissing me deeper, our tongues fighting for everything we want to say.

"Okay" I breathe out, relaxing into the soft white covers.

"Are you sure?" he asks again.

"Yes, Cole, please." His mouth lands on mine as the last word leaves my lips as his hands work to undo my jeans. Impatient, I sit up and peel off my hoodie. He lets out a hungry growl of approval. Standing on the bed, with Cole at my feet. I remove my jeans and throw them on the floor.

My gaze wonders, over his still dressed frame, stood on the floor in front of me. Watching him unbutton his shirt is pure torture. My thighs and core clench at the sight of his bare, toned chest as it rises and falls with each breath he takes. My gaze drops when his hand comes to his belt and he flicks open buckle, removing it from the loops.

Why is that so hot?

My breathing stops, when he drops it to the floor with his shirt.

"Tease," I say licking my lips. He smirks, knowing full well the reaction my body is having at the sight of him. Unbuttoning his trousers, the zipper comes down next, and I'm ready to burst. Stifling a moan, my body shudders with so much need, wetness pools at my centre. I could have a full-blown orgasm just watching him.

I can't tear my eyes away when his trousers and boxers drop to the floor, watching his impressive cock stand to attention.

He's beautiful. Sculpted like a Greek god, and just as divine.

"Take them off, Cupcake. Show me just how beautiful you are. Just for me" I move to step down next to him, but he stops me. "No, stay there. I want to see you." I unclip my bra and let it fall.

"Holy shit, Ari." He gulps, taking his thick, heavy dick in his hand, stroking it firmly from root to tip. I feel his eyes everywhere, drinking me in. I slowly remove my thong. He climbs back onto the bed, lowering me back, down on the bed.

"You, okay?" he asks, and I love that he's checking, but there's no need. I want this just as much as he does.

"I'm good," I smile, as his body covers mine and his lips trace down my neck before latching on to my hardened nipple. Gasping, my back arches into him. "Cole, yes." His hand skims my side, igniting a trail of sparks as it moves. I open my legs a little wider for his huge frame and his fingers brush over my core, making me gasp.

"You like that, baby?" he asks, groaning, looking at me through hooded eyes.

"Yes." I don't sound like me. I'm breathy and needy. He's hardly touching me and I want to scream his name already. He does it again, this time grazing my clit, and I whimper.

"Fuck, baby, your so wet." He's looking down between my legs where his fingers play with my core. I all but keel over at his words. "Is this just for me?" he says. He takes a slow circle of my clit, and *good god,* I want him to push those fingers inside me. I want them so deep, I can feel him there for days after we're done here. This admittedly, would be a first for me. I've had my own fingers but never anyone else's. "Oh, god," I shout.

Adding a little pressure to my sensitive clit, Cole drags his thick finger down to my entrance—*please, please, please*—rimming and teasing where I desperately need him. "Has anyone else ever touched you here with their fingers, baby?" he asks, as the tip of his finger nudges my entrance, and my walls flutter in response.

"No." I gasp. Feeling hot in every cell of my body, as blood rushes to cover my skin in fine, pink hue.

"Fuck," he moans, his fingers adding a little more pressure, but not pushing inside. "Do you have any idea how fucking good it feels to be the first to fuck you with my fingers?" His words will be my undoing. "Cupcake, I'm going to make you come just like this."

"Please." Pushing two fingers inside me, my hips jolt, as I moan, but removes his fingers only seconds later, watching him, as he slides them back through my pussy, and up to his mouth.

"Watch me lick them clean, Ari." Wrapping his tongue around his two fingers he sucks them. His vibrant eyes, now dark with desire hold mine. Working his hand between us, my clit throbs as he presses firmly. Wet heat spreads over my thighs as his tongue dances over the seal of my lips. "Open," he demands. And I do as I'm told. Opening my mouth, his hot tongue slips in tasting myself on his tongue, it's dirty, and fuck if I don't want to taste more. His fingers trail their way down, pushing inside me.

"Oh, dear god," I murmur. I can't form any more words, I don't think they exist right now.

His fingers move slowly in and out of me, stretching me wide. It's never felt so good. I'm a writhing mess, sure I'm about to explode any second now. His body pins me in place as he extracts pure, unadulterated pleasure from every cell in my body. And when he curls his fingers to stroke my walls, Jesus-fucking-christ. He catches all my moans, with his greedy kisses.

"Are you going to come, baby?" he says as his mouth leaves mine, trailing soft kisses down my neck to the sensitive spot on my clavicle. My breath hitches, noticing my reaction, he does it again. I'm on the edge, he knows it.

"Yes." I moan, unable to contain myself.

"Then come for me, Ari," he says just as he adds another finger, forcing them so deep, the line between pleasure and pain blur, I tuck my head into the crook of his neck, it's to much and everything all at the same time. And I shatter like a glass vase hitting the floor.

"Fucking, fuck." My hands fist the sheets and my body bows as I chase the pleasure pulsing through me. "Cole." He brings me to the peak of the quickest and best high I have ever felt. His lips seal over my nipple and as he bites down, my orgasm rises again and I fall from the highest peak into a Cole-induced oblivion. Panting, unable to think of anything but us. *This.*

"Baby, I need to be inside you." he groans into my ear.

"Yes." I feel his thick, hot cock notch against my entrance.

"I'll go slow, baby, I'll make it so fucking good," he promises.

His forehead touches mine and he pushes inside me slowly. I tense at the intrusion as his girthy shaft stretches me, and he pauses.

"Relax, I promise, you're safe." I take in a breath and he pushes in further. The sting only lasts a moment, before it morphs into pleasure. "Almost there, Ari. Look at me." I don't remember closing my eyes, but when I open them, I see a world of hope in front of me.

"That's it, baby, just like that. Take me, take all of me." My walls clamp down around him as he bottoms out.

"Breathe, baby, please," he forces out, groaning. A light sheen of sweat coats his skin, just like mine.

"You feel so good," I tell him, and I do as he asked, relaxing into him.

"I think you were made for me," he utters, his hand moving to my hair.

"I think I was," I admit. Even with my limited experience, I know it doesn't always feel like this. "I need you to move."

Nodding at me, his lips graze mine and he pulls out, almost all the way, and slowly pushes back in. "Fuck, Ari, I'm not going to last. You feel fucking incredible," he says through a strained grunt, his eyes screwed tight shut like he's forcing himself not to come.

He plunges back into me, causing me to arch and whimper at the intensity of this whole situation. Sparks fly across my skin with each thrust, matching my pace with his. I need to feel him. I want him, all of him. Gripping the back of my neck he holds me in place, taking me higher, his heat inside of me so intense I can't take any more.

My walls begin to flutter I grab his ass, to keep him right where I need him. He doesn't disappoint, rubbing his cock, against my G-spot. My body lights up, warmth spreading through me. I start to tense, my legs shaking uncontrollably as my own pleasure builds with the rising high of my orgasm.

"Fuck, Ari, you're strangling my dick. It feels too good."

"I want to come inside you, say I can." My mind explodes with the possibilities.

"Yes, fuck yes, I want to feel your come, paint my walls." Shocking myself, my walls flutter as I take him deeper.

"Oh, my fucking god," he grunts, "you have a dirty mouth. Perfect, so fucking perfect."

"Shit," I scream as my walls take one final hit and clamp around him so hard he releases in me; his hot seed coating me, making me come harder.

Moans and gasps fill the room as we fall together. Resting his weight heavily on me, he goes to move, but I stop him.

There's a look of bewilderment on his face that I think matches my own. Pushing my hair from my face, Cole cups my cheek and places a tender kiss on my lips. Still wrapped around him, my hands leave his ass to stroke through his hair, watching his vibrant eyes soften. He shifts us so we lay facing each other, pulling out of me, working his fingers between my thighs, trailing them where our combined pleasure mixes.

"What are you doing?" Feeling sensitive, I moan at his touch.

"Feeling us." His finger plays at my entrance, pushing our release back inside me. I cry out, liking how it feels. "You like it?" he asks, his brows rising in question.

"Seems like I do." I laugh. "Um, I'm on the pill. It helps with my periods, so we're safe." It's a conversation we should have had first, but that moment has well and truly passed.

"Good," he offers. "I've never gone bare with anyone before, but the thought of not being able to feel you around my dick killed me." His fingers push inside me one last time.

"Good," I mimic. "I want to feel you come inside me every time." His smile brightens as he looks at my flushed face.

"So, you agree there's an *us*?" Kissing my lips, he rolls from the bed and stands, disappearing through a door to the left.

"I never denied there was an us." I say, stretching out on the bed, my muscles already feeling sore. Cole comes back with a washcloth, kneels between my legs and starts cleaning me.

"The sound of us sounds fucking amazing, doesn't it?" Dropping the wash-cloth on the floor, Cole, hovers over me again, kissing me like it's his last moment on Earth. When we part, we're both panting.

"We need to get back." I can hear this disappointment in his words. "We don't have long before Dec picks you up." Placing a kiss on my forehead, he reaches for his discarded clothes.

"I don't want to," I say, sadness creeping in.

"I hate this just as much as you." Walking back towards me, he lifts my chin. "I want to keep you in my bed, but we have a few things to deal with first." Cole hands me my things, and we get ready in silence.

"This is for you," he says handing me a phone when we get downstairs.

"Why? I have one." My brows pinch together in confusion.

"That one you have is being monitored. That's why I was so angry earlier." Just another thing to add to the long list of crappy things my parents do.

"Oh, I'm not surprised," I say, kissing him tenderly, to say thank you.

"We need to talk more Ari, this…" he points to the phone, "has my number in, as well as Ethan's, Owen's, and Leon's. If you want anything use this one, not yours."

"Okay. I will," I say, feeling the best I have in a long time.

"Cupcake, this was everything," he says before opening the backdoor and leading us back through the garden.

"Does this mean I can sext you later?"

"That was not my intention, but fuck, yes." We walk under the arch, smiling like dizzy kids.

God, does it feel good.

Chapter Twenty-Six

Two Forks

Arianna

Yesterday was wild. It's the only way I can describe this feeling of being alive. I can honestly say that I always felt the fear of being caught. I was always on edge, looking over my shoulder, withdrawn even. Knowing somehow my father could find out what I was up to. Now when I look over my shoulder, I know who I'll see.

Cole. Always watching.

Nothing could have burst my blissful bubble yesterday. I've never felt so free, so liberated. Sighing a little, I do feel a little guilty about Dec being kept out of all this. He's been there for me for a long time. But like Cole said, the fewer people that know the better. I'll be safer that way. When I got back, I spent the night going over my plans for my meeting with my father. It's frustrating how much I want to move on with my life. It won't even be moving on, more like starting a life. It's small steps and like Ed said, I still need to tread carefully.

But this is the beginning.

Only I can't get past my father's bitch of a secretary. Every time I call she lists the multiple reasons I'd be wasting his time. She then places me on hold, and like the stubborn, good girl I am, I wait, and wait and wait, then the line goes dead, and I have to start again. I won't be defeated, even if I do scream into my pillow every time.

I've emailed and called constantly today to get the meeting. But it's not happening. Maybe I need to be someone else for this. Make a meeting in someone else's name just to get in the door. Leaning back on my bed, I realise just how stupid that idea is. If I book it under someone else, I won't get in the courthouse, plus I want to be myself. That's the whole point after all. I'll keep trying. She'll get annoyed, and have to give up eventually. I just don't know when that will be.

Frustrating.

I've been texting and talking to Cole, on and off all day too. There's so much I need to know about that man. I didn't know he was in the army, although I should have guessed from the way he is. That's how he met Owen, Ethan, and Leon. He didn't give me any more details than that, but I get a feeling there's more to the story.

After doing a little research for myself, I can see they've made an impressive name for themselves in the security business. He even part owns a custom motorbike shop.

Putting my bookmark in my book, a gift from Chrisy before she left, I grin, imagining Cole as one of the MC bikers in the story. His bike between his legs. I've caught glimpses of his bike and I can only imagine what he would look like riding it. A small shiver runs up my spine thinking of the rumble of the engine between my thighs if we rode together.

Chuckling to myself, I reach for my drink on the bedside table, I'm ready for bed, in just knickers and a shirt, when my phone—my other one—buzzes with a message from under my pillow.

Cole: What you reading, Cupcake?

The nickname does things to me I can't describe, smiling, I read it again. *Wait, what?*

> **Ari:** How do you know I'm reading?

> **Cole:** It's your favourite thing to do, other than me. (*winky face emoji*) I'm taking a wild guess that you're reading, given you haven't moved from your room in over two hours.

What-the-ever-loving-hell? How the hell does he know I haven't moved in that long. Has it been that long? Glancing at the clock, I realise he's right. How the heck does he know? Sitting up straighter, I place my glass back down with a clunk, almost spilling it.

> **Me:** You're freaking me out. How do you know this?

> **Cole:** I'm watching you.

A thrill runs through me, bolting off the bed I look around, scanning my room for anything that could be a camera.

> **Cole:** Joking. I made you move that sexy ass though, didn't I?

Laughing, I hit video to call him, not wanting to spend any more time texting when we don't need to. My parents are out, there's no need to hide anything. Before he even gets a word out, I stick my tongue out at him, then flash him a cheeky grin.

"You really freaked me out. I thought you'd put a camera in my room somehow," I say giving him my best mock evil eyes.

"Well, I don't have a camera in your room," he admits, eyeing me through the screen, "but I have hacked into your father's security system, and I've been watching you move around the house. The only time I don't see you is when you're in your bedroom." My jaw drops, my mouth hanging open.

"Please, tell me you're not serious."

"I'm serious. You said you didn't feel safe at home." My heart softens just that little bit more towards this beautiful man.

"I said I didn't feel safe anywhere, there a difference," I state, sighing like it makes a difference.

"Still, this way I can make sure you're safe when you're home, *and* when you're not, I'll be there if you need me." His deep tone rumbles with each word.

"I'm not sure I believe you. My father's system is one of the best," I tease.

"It is one of the best because Cerberus installed it."

"Really?" I ask. "Isn't that some sort of violation, hacking into a private system?"

He laughs. "No," he says simply, "not when they are putting people, you, at risk." The smile's wiped from his face. "Your father should have read the terms a little more closely if he didn't want anyone hacking his system, it clearly says—*sort of*—that we can access the system when deemed fit. And we deemed it fit."

A nervous laugh escapes my lips. "Prove it," I ask, still not sure it's the truth. "What time did I have lunch today?" If he gets this right, I'll know for sure.

"Trick question, you didn't have any sort of food that I would deem acceptable for lunch, but you drank a very strange looking green drink at twelve-thirty-four, followed by some fruit. You also had one before your workout, which was impressive by the way."

"Okay, I believe you," I add, rolling my eyes at him. "That *was* my lunch," I whisper, reeling at how he's been watching my movements all day. "Won't you get in trouble for that?" I question, looking at his sculpted features, illuminated in the dark.

"I can assure you I won't get into trouble," he snickers. "Hacking is why I was recruited by the army. It's my specialty. Now I use it for other purposes." He looks amused, the spark in his eyes has come back after the annoyance of my lunch.

"Other purposes?" I mimic him, "What else have you hacked into?"

"I can't answer that."

"Just a hint of something. Come on, *please.*"

His eyes darken as I lick my lips, teasing them with my tongue. He lets out a deep breath, a sly grin creeping over his full mouth. Edging a little closer to the camera, he looks like he going to let me into a secret.

"I hacked into the camera footage of The Manor Hotel." My mouth hangs open as I gasp.

"Why would you do that? Aren't you friends with Mr Lucas?"

"I like to do things my way. It was also quicker." Nodding into the camera, I can see his point.

"Why The Manor? There can't be anything there of much interest."

"You hold my interest, Ari, and you were at The Manor." I'm blushing.

"I don't understand. Why?" I say, confused, as I chew my lip.

"I've been fascinated with you since the day I took the job. You've had a hold over me, Ari. I just didn't realise what it was until I saw you at that meal, saw the real you fighting to get out from beneath that veil you hide under." He pauses, letting out a low growl. "Then I kissed you." His eyes focus on my lips. "And when your sweet as fuck mouth kissed me back. I knew."

"What did you know, Cole?" I'm scared to listen, to see the truth in his expressions as he tells me.

"I knew I wanted to see the real you. God, Ari I'm desperate to get to know you. I see you, Ari. And I want the rest of the world to see the real you too."

"Cole." My words are a whisper but I can tell he hears me loud and clear. "No-one ever—"

"I know. There's just one thing I'm asking for, Ari." Dread fills me, everyone always wants something. Holding my breath I wait for the blow. "Show me first." Relief floods me. *He's not asking for anything from me.* He wants to see me, *the real me,* and wants to be the first one to see it. I can't focus, my eyes brimming with tears. I can't even express what those words do to me. I just stare at him, unable to voice just how much I needed to hear them. We're silent for a few moments before I can gather myself, my erratic heart beating widely.

"I'll show you," I promise, breaking the silence. The warmth in his eyes, spreads to the tilt of his lips.

"I got the video of our first kiss," he admits, my eyes shooting up the screen, at his change in tone. "That's why I hacked the footage at The Manor."

"How? I thought we were hidden?" I ask, thinking back to that moment. "You really, have it?"

"Yeah." He smirks. "I liked seeing the way you reacted to my touch, Ari. The way we came together." His tone is sultry and low.

"You've watched it?" I gasp. Stupid question, of course he has.

"More than once. I even fucked my hand over it, last night." The noise that leaves my mouth is a combination of shock and lust, like a gasped whimper. I love that he says these things out loud. There's no shame in his voice... pride maybe. His confidence inspires me. I want to be a bit more like that. And I will be.

"Oh-my-god, Cole." Maybe. "Can I see it?"

"Sure." He looks away for a moment before my phone dings with another message. "Save it for later," he adds.

"I will, did you really... touch yourself to it?" The thought turns me on so much, I have to squeeze my thighs tightly together in an attempt to ease the throb.

"Wait until you see us together, baby, you'll need to touch yourself too. Maybe we should watch it together. I'd like to see you touch yourself." My eyes go wide at just how serious he sounds about doing that.

"Don't be shy, baby. You can't tell me you haven't thought about what we did yesterday, because I have. It's been on constant replay in my head. And fuck, I want more of you." I can see him grinning in the dark, his wicked gaze drinking me in. I want more of him too.

"Tell me, Ari." His voice deepens making me shiver with need. "Where did that dirty mouth of yours come from when I fucked you yesterday?" My breath catches as my core lights up and my hips shift slightly on the bed, needing the friction.

Lying back on the bed, I hold the phone up high so he can still see me, my other hand toying with the edge of my knickers.

"I've been saving them for you, Cole." Pinning my lip between my teeth, my eyes roam over his face, waiting for his reaction, as my fingers tease the skin beneath the soft fabric of my underwear.

"I want them all, Ari. Are you a naughty girl?" he asks. My breath stutters, taking in his intense gaze as it trails over my face and the small peek of my breasts he can see.

"No, but I want to be," I admit. The more I speak with him, the more I feel like I'm becoming me. My fingers trail lower, skimming my clit, knowing he has no idea I'm touching myself.

"Fuck," he groans, "will you be my good girl?" His tone is full of tension and anticipation. "Are you touching yourself?" I can hear him moving, like he's jogging.

"Maybe." I tease, my eyes flutter closed, as my finger circles my tight bud, sending waves of pleasure over my skin. "Where are you?" I ask, on a whisper. My eyes focus back to the screen above my head.

"Outside," he says, his wicked smirk stretching wider.

"Outside?" Squinting to try and see where he is, I remove my hand from my knickers. "Why?" I ask, my cheeks reddening at what I was about to do over the phone.

"I wanted to check in on you."

"I feel better knowing you're out there." There is a glint in his eyes I don't quite understand. Shifting on the bed a little as I get comfortable, I look at him in the dark, waiting for him to say something. The tension in me building, I slide my fingers back to my knickers, continuing to play with my clit. A soft moan escapes my lips.

"Would you feel better if it was my fingers inside you?"

I get a feeling in my stomach that he's up to something. I still can't see where he is, he's standing in the shadows. I don't want to state the obvious, that yes, of course I would. His breathing's as laboured as mine.

"Yes, fuck, Cole. Yes," I pant.

"Tilt your head to the side and look out your window." My breath leaves me. I turn my head, only to see him sat on my balcony ledge.

I rush to the window and slide the balcony door open. He strides to meet me brimming with confidence, crushing his lips to mine like he can't get close enough.

"Now that's a greeting I could get used to." His rough hands kneed my ass, as they slide under the sheer fabric of my knickers.

"How did you do this? There are so many cameras here," I pant, pulling away even when I don't want to. Panic rises in my chest, like a bubble that needs to burst but won't. "What if someone saw you or catches us? Oh, my god, I just flung myself at you." The bubble in my chest expands, as my panic grows. I attempt to pull away and get some distance between us. Although, if someone from my father's team is watching the surveillance, it'll be too late.

Shit.

Cole cups my face, soothing the panic he can see rising.

"I'd never put you at risk," he says, placing a soft kiss on my lips. "Your father's security team left you alone. They may check the footage, but they won't see shit, Ari. I have many, many talents," he says, wiggling his eyebrows at me, settling the rising unease of potentially being caught. "You already know two of them," he says, "maybe three if you include the hacking thing," he admits while kissing the corner of my mouth and I grin.

"What are the other two?" I ask, teasing him. He has the decency to look wounded, faking a gasp. "Cupcake," he says firmly, "if you don't remember what I did to you yesterday in my house, in my bed, then maybe I need to remind you just what I can do to you with my special set of abilities." Lowing his voice to a seductive whisper he adds, "And how I can make you scream my name." Scooping me up in his arms, he marches us back through the sliding doors, closing them behind him.

This feels wrong, but only in the sense that we're in my room, in my parents' house, where they control everything I do. I know Gi's downstairs, although she should be leaving soon, so it will just be us. Striding into my room, Cole lowers my legs, placing me on the edge of my bed. The sheets are still a mess from my lazy two hours of reading.

Lowering himself to his knees in front of me, his trousers stretch over his thick thighs. He looks divine like this. *This huge powerful man, on his knees in front of me.* My skin tingles in response to the way he's looking at me right now; like he could eat me alive. A surge of unfamiliar power circles my chest, making my nipples instantly harden through my flimsy shirt, as I part my legs for him.

"Yesterday," he says, skimming his finger over my calf, "you admitted you'd only had sex once, and he was shit." His finger inches higher, causing the sensitive skin on my legs to prickle as the current of electricity surges right to my centre.

Holding back a moan, my lips part, as a shiver runs over my skin. "I never said he was shit, Cole, that was all you." I groan, knowing full well the man in question was shit in bed. I only have Cole to compare him too and there is no comparison. Cole wins hands down. His eyes flick to mine, both of us knowing the truth.

"Fine, he was shit, but I only have you to compare him to, so…" I squeak when his grip tightens around my thighs.

"What are you saying?" he grits out like his words are painful to say.

I shouldn't, but I can't resist. "Maybe I need to get some more experience under my belt. You know, a few more notches on my bed post so to speak." My hand traces where he grips my thigh. His head snaps up to meet mine, my pulse racing at the fierce look in his eyes.

"Ari, let me tell you something. If you thought having me remove every man in your orbit was bad before, just wait and see how bad I can get when I know what it feels like to have your tight, wet pussy, wrapped around my cock." *Holy hell, this man and his hot words.* Heat flashes over me, through me, and deep inside me. "I was joking, Cole," I breathe out.

"Cupcake. This right here," he says spreading my legs apart, and moving between them, cupping my core with his warm hand, "is mine. And no one gets to play with what's mine, Ari." His gaze is like steel, I have no intention of ever sleeping with anyone else. *Ever?* I'll deal with that thought later.

"Okay." I know it's not the right words, but what else can you say to that? I mean that got serious quick. Like really quick. "I don't want anyone else near me." Apparently, I *can* say something more appropriate, from the deep growl his throat makes a second later he approves. He bends down, kissing the inside of my thigh—*oh,* that feels so good—my brain fizzes out. Having his lips so close to my core, his hot breath is wreaking havoc on me.

"That's a given, Cupcake," he murmurs against my skin. His hand leaves my core, along with his lips, leaving an empty, unwanted sensation behind. I want to put my fingers through his hair and hold him to me. *Who am I?* Whoever this woman is coming to the surface, I like her. "Cole." Doing exactly what I want, my fingers spread through his soft blond hair, gripping, ready to pull him closer. He pulls away, causing my hands to fall to his shoulder.

"I want to be selfish," his lips quirk to the side, "and have one of your firsts." His head tilts like he's just reached a conclusion. "Fuck that," he moans, his unyielding eyes on me, "I want the rest of your firsts." With his words and his hands hot on my skin, I feel I may combust. It's like I'm starving and Cole is the only person able to feed me.

"You can have them," I stutter, closing my eyes, not giving a crap that it comes out a little needy. Because I am. I'm needy for him. My mind and body want everything he is handing to me. Even here in my room.

"What else didn't that bastard do to make you come?"

"He did nothing to make me come, Cole..." Pausing for a second, it would be a far shorter list to say what he did in fact do: no foreplay, just a few kisses, then wham-bam, put it in. Opening my eyes I stare down at him.

I actually think Cole would hunt him down and tear him a new one if I let that bit of information slip. "He didn't use his mouth on me, he didn't use his fingers... he didn't fuck me like you did. He didn't talk dirty to me, he didn't tease me. Oh, my god, Cole, there is so much he didn't do." Licking my lips, I catch my breath. Cole's fingers now dancing over my damp knickers. "It's all yours. Touch me," I hiss. His eyes snap to mine. Taking off his jacket, he rolls up his sleeves. Leaning forward, he places soft kisses on the inside of my thighs, driving me insane with need. Leaning back on my elbows, I'm unable to take the heat of his stare.

"Fuck, Ari, you're beautiful." Every breath is a tease on my clit as he slides my knickers to the side, exposing me as he strokes his finger through my soaking wet folds.

"Cole," I almost scream.

"Ari," he counters as his lips latch onto my clit at the same time he pushes two fingers inside me; sucking me so hard, I swear I see stars. *I hope Gi's gone home.* I don't want her to hear this. My stomach tenses as his fingers slowly move inside me, stroking that precious spot that makes me spiral. He works me like the devil needs to torment and tease the good from every living soul. My body is moving of its own accord. I can't stop, tethering on the edge of oblivion, ready to dive in to the pits of hell, just see what's on the other side and burst into flames.

"Fuck, Ari." I hear him undoing his belt. "I'm so fucking hard for you right now." Lifting my heavy head, my eyes unfocused I watch as he takes his cock in hand, fisting himself so hard he groans. The vibrations are enough to end me. I fall, my body convulsing as he licks and sucks, taking my clit between his lips and nipping at my sensitive bud, my orgasm hitting me with so much force I can't breathe.

"That's it, baby, come all over my face." Lapping up every drop, he drags out my orgasm further. Cole lifts me from the edge of my bed, placing me against the pillows. He lays down beside me, his shirt and trousers gone.

"Sleep, Ari. I'm here," he whispers, stroking my hair from my face.

Turning to face him, my hand strokes his chest. "I can't sleep, I have questions." He chuckles, kissing my heated cheeks.

"Like what?" he says dropping his lips to the tip of my nose.

"When did you get naked? Are you staying? I want you to stay. Why were you outside?" There are so many more, but I'll hold off for now. Settling in, I tuck my head into his shoulder, as he softly strokes my hair, so at odds with the man I thought he was.

"I'm staying, until I have to leave. But I'll be watching. I wanted to feel you next to me, I got undressed, after I made you came so hard you almost passed out. I wanted to give you something, that's why I was outside."

"You definitely gave it to me," I tease, snuggling into him while I can.

"That was an unexpected gift you gave me, not the other way around." He chides, stroking the skin along my waist.

"Oh, well, what do you want to give me," I trail my fingers down his bare chest.

"It's still outside." He gets up, walks to my balcony door as naked as the day he was born. I'll never get bored of that sight of his tight ass flexing with each step. Opening the door, he darts out into the cold night air, grabbing a small black box from the ledge, and brings it back inside.

"What is it?" I ask, sitting up on the bed.

"Hold out your hands." I do, loving the anticipation coursing through me. The box feels heavy as he drops it into my waiting hands.

"Open it, but you have to share it." He nods towards the box.

I notice The Manors Hotel logo stamped on the side. Frowning I open the box, just as he places two forks in from of me.

"Happy belated birthday, beautiful." he grins, as I peer inside, finding the most extravagant red velvet cake I have ever seen. Red layered with silky, butter cream icing.

Holy shit.

He bought me a birthday cake.

Chapter Twenty-Seven

Complicated

Cole

Waking up with Ari's ass snuggled against my crotch, my arms holding her against me, was the best way to start to any morning. I had no intention of falling asleep last night, but I did. After we ate the cake, she rode me like the queen I know she is, and we passed out in her huge bed, tangled together. It was fucking bliss.

When she shifted her ass against me in her sleep, I had no choice but to spread her legs and play with her pussy, until she woke up panting my name. Sliding my cock deep inside her was just the buttery icing on the cake.

I'm obsessed.

The way she feels wrapped around my cock memorizes me and the fact that she's gradually letting me see who she really is staggers me. She's woven herself into the fabric of my soul already. It made leaving her bed so much harder, she wrapped the sheets around herself and followed me to the balcony, kissing the shit out of me before I descended the tree and took off. Not before I took a backwards glance to see her watching me with a smile on her face.

Clearing the wall on the far side of the estate, I run the quarter of a mile down the road where I left my bike in the bushes. Taking off her cover, I swing my leg over, firing her up, she purrs like a dream. Making my way through the quiet roads, I head to the office, winding around the back roads, enjoying the ride.

It all feels better today.

Passing her father's town car as I drive away, looking back as it passes. I immediately want to turn around as I drive away. The rising need swirling through me to be with her every second of the day becoming far too real to what I'm able to do. I know I can't. I'll steal any moment I can. Their oblivious to who I am, and where I spent the night with his beautiful daughter in my arms.

A devilish smile crosses my face, thinking about how I'm going to fuck-up her parents' lives. I'll take pleasure in that too.

"What are you looking into?" Ethan asks from behind me, spinning around as he takes his place next to me. "I think I can guess, but I want to hear it from you."

"I'm going to get her out, Ethan," I say.

"Does she want that?"

"What the fuck? Of course she does." My voice rising.

"All I'm saying is, that she stayed for a reason. If you fuck with that, what will happen? What are the reasons she's stayed?" He's making me see what I need to do. It's so obvious.

"They threatened everyone she loves."

"What with? We need to know what we're up against if we're going to do this. We need to be prepared." Filling him in on the threats made towards Gianna, Ed and Dec. I keep looking for anything I can use against Byron and Carmichael. Knowing Ethan and I can make sure Gi, Ed and Dec safe if anything happens is the best next step.

I've spent the last few hours looking over Ari's schedules, tense as fuck, finding this shit worse the more I dig. The last ten years, it's been horrific. I've seen her university applications, she filed that were pulled by her father. Driving licence applications never processed. Every time she's made to do something for herself, it's been taken away. From the moment she wakes to the moment she goes to sleep, she's watched, controlled, and all while having any sense of self torn away.

My shoulders are so tense, I feel like I could snap. But Ethan in all his gruff glory, just made me smile for the first time since leaving Ari this morning.

"She told me she was taken away. I assumed it was a few days, maybe a week, but the only gap I've found in her schedule over the last ten years is three months, there's nothing. No meetings, no bank or card transactions, no original social media posts, they were all reused, from past jobs. It's like she fell off the face of the earth. No electronic trail, no paper one either." It's killing me that I know what happened during those months. I'd do anything to take away the pain of her past, and I'll do anything to ensure she never has to endure anything like that again.

Ethan's hands grip the arms of the chair, listening to me explain what I found. "Where did they take her?" There's a slight twitch in his eyes. He's angry just like me. I'm not sure how much longer I can watch without doing something about it.

"They locked her away, in a room somewhere on the estate, and made her watch the people she cared for fall apart. They hurt her, Ethan, really fucking hurt her."

"We need something on her parents? Is it just money, or does it go deeper than that?"

"Good fucking question. That's what I need to find out. I don't just want info on her parents. I want Robert Carmichael to go down too."

"We'll get her out," he states.

My phone digs with a notification telling me Ari's left her room. I hate watching her like this, but I have no other choice. I can be there if anything happens. And I'll have the evidence to prove it. Opening up the app, I see her walk the hallway, heading to the gym. She's already been today, why is she going again?

I pull up the feed to the big screen and open up her schedule, seeing they've added another workout for her. The ones she did yesterday, and this morning, were brutal. You'd think she was training for battle the things she's put through.

"What going on?" Ethan asks, looking from his laptop to me, with his eyebrow pinched together.

"I'm not sure, I'll message her." I know she connected the burner phone to her smartwatch, so she'll get the message.

Me: What going on?

Cupcake: You stalking me again Cole?

Me: Yes.

Her gaze flicks to the cameras where she gives me a faint smile.

Me: What's wrong?

Cupcake: The cleaning staff found the cake box this morning while I was at the gym. I'm off to be punished for indulging in gluttonous behaviour.

Cupcake: That's what my father said anyway *eyeroll emoji face*.

Picking up the closest thing to me, I throw it across the room. The pen holder smashes against the wall, sending its contents scattering to the floor. Ethan grabs me before I do any more damage.

"Show me." Handing him my phone, he reads the messages, cursing under his breath, while I slump back in my chair, rubbing my hands over my face, my stomach knotting with regret at being so careless.

"It's my fault," I admit. "I should have been more careful."

"Help me understand, Cole. Don't leave me out," he pleads.

"Last night, I took her a cake to celebrate her birthday. I didn't think about it, I just wanted to do something nice for her."

"Why is that such a big deal?" He looks confused as fuck, like I'm overreacting.

"It's not, she fucking loved it. We sat and ate it together. The issue is, I forgot just how much she's watched within her own home. Like you just read in those messages. It's what happens when she's found out that fucking kills me."

"Are there consequences to everything she does, that they don't approve of?"

"Yep, Ari's already worked out today, in fact, she works out for two hours every-fucking-morning. No rest days. It's torture what they make her do. And they're making her do it again."

"If anything, she needs to add a little weight, not lose it," he says. I know he means well, but I don't fucking care about his opinion. I'd have her, whatever she looked like. I type out a message.

> **Me:** I'm so sorry. It's all my fault.

> **Cupcake:** Don't you dare apologise, I would take every gym session they throw at me just to sit and eat cake with you again. It will be worth the exhaustion I'll feel later.

We both sit in silence and watch as her PT puts her through the passes, buy the time she done, she can hardly walk. The PT goes to help her up, but she shakes her head. Staying on the floor. He leaves, after punching the shit out of the bag.

It's not until an older woman comes in and hands her a protein shake that she moves slowly to a sitting position, leaning heavily against the wall for support. My blood boiling with anger. This has to stop.

Ethan's been pouring over every document we have, and finding articles on Carmichael and Thomas Bryon, ready to make a case to get the others on board for what we're planning.

In a few weeks, she'll be out living a life she wants. And I'll be right there next to her.

Chapter Twenty-Eight

Disgrace

Cole

"You," I shout from across the room. I fucking knew I recognised the bastard. I only came in here to work out, but now I'm itching for a fight. I thought after having to sit and watch Ari be put through the paces in the gym until she could barely stand, was enough to get me riled up. But seeing *this* guy, her fucking PT in my motherfucking gym, when I walk through the doors, has me ready to throw punches.

"Me?" the snivelling little prick says, stepping back from the guy he was talking to.

"Yes, you," I almost run over to him, my fists clenched. I get right in his face. He tries to back away, but I pin him to the wall, my arm coming to his throat. "You're a fucking disgrace," I shout, "How can you live with yourself." I hear people behind me talking and someone rushes to my side, but I'm too angry to notice who.

"What the hell?" The PT yells, his hands gripping my arm tightly.

"Don't give me that shit, you're her fucking PT. How could you?" I roar, my other hand gripping his shirt in my fist, so tightly my skin could spilt.

"Shit, who are you on about." His voice strains through the force of my arm on his neck, but I'm not fucking letting go, he needs to pay for this.

"Miss Byron," I say through clenched teeth. His eyes widen, understanding flowing over his face. Then I see it: remorse in his eyes. "You know what you've done, you arsehole," I seethe.

"I know. Fuck, I know." His whole body surrenders to the force I'm putting on him, sagging against the wall.

"I know you fucking know, dumb-ass. Tell me why you feel the need to put her through that every fucking day?"

"Cole, *step* away." I hear Charlie's voice but I just can't move. Not until I get answers.

"Cole, please?" Her hands come to my back and I feel myself relax a fraction.

"Fine," shoving the guy into the wall, I step away, as Charlie steps into my line of sight. "Take him to the office, I need to have a serious word with him," I grunt at her.

"It's not your gym, or mine, but sure I'll ask Shelly, see if we can use one of them." she walks away, with Ari's PT following behind, his head hung low, as he rubs his neck.

"Don't let him out of your sight," I shout after her. She turns, flipping me off as she pulls her phone out, more than likely telling Owen to get his arse down here.

Spinning around, I walk over to the punch bag and let rip my anger, laying my fists into the soft leather, ready to destroy anyone or anything that gets in my way.

I only stop when I hear my name being called, I was right she called Owen. He's stood right next to me waiting for me to finish kicking and punching the shit out of the bag.

He should be pleased it's not the person sat in that office.

"You'll ruin your suit man. That's at least a few grand down the drain." He's right, I took my jacket off in the car, but I'm still in my shirt, tie, and waistcoat.

"Fine." The temper I felt before seems to have faded.

"So, what did he do?" I tell him exactly what I told Ethan. The cake, the diet plan, the gruelling workouts until she can't move.

"Shit, we're working on a plan, right?" he asks.

"Yeah, we are, Ethan's on it, I need to let off some steam before I see her later. She's got to show her face at Bruno's."

"Okay, what time? Do you want me to handle this? You're going to need to hold on to that anger, it's not how we do things."

"I know, I just lost it for a moment, I'll be good." Slapping me on the back, I move away.

Fifteen minutes later were both sat opposite Theo, Ari's personal trainer, in one of the small offices Shelly the manager has let us use.

"I'm sorry, I knew who you were talking about, I just... panicked." he says before we even open our mouths to speak. "I don't know how much you know, but the whole situation is messed up."

"How?" I don't want him to know, I already know how messed up everything is. I need anything he can give me.

"I'll show you, look." He pulls out his phone, opening up an email. Handing it over I read through it all. Another set of instructions for them to follow. "I was pissed off the day I go there, I thought she'd fired her last PT, Tom, and I had no idea why, I thought she was just being a prissy little princess." Moving forward on my chair, I grip the edge of the table between us.

"Watch your fucking mouth." He told his hands up in defence.

"Sorry, I'm just... anyway. Turns out, it wasn't her. I think he started to care too much."

"What?" My mind goes to the worst-case scenario: did he hit on her, did he touch her? Owen's arm flies out in front of me, stopping me from leaping over the table.

"Calm the fuck down, Cole," he demands. Shooting him a look, I settle back in my chair, rage and anger curdling in my stomach.

"It's not like that, I promise. He saw what they were putting her through, turns out Tom started asking questions, he'd been with her a while, started to see what was happening, he knew she was struggling. Questioned her meals, told them she couldn't live like that, told them he was going to adjust her workouts to suit the meals, or the other way around. And they fired him for it." he all but vomits the words out. His hands shaking.

"That's doesn't make what you did any better."

"I know, I hate every second of it." lowering his head into his hands, his shoulders slump.

"Then explain why you still do it?" I'm seething inside, if it wasn't for Owen sitting next to me, I would have knocked him out by now.

"There's an understanding, Miss Byron knows what's expected, I've tried on so many occasions to change things but she won't have it. Gianna, the woman who runs the house, she warned me what would happen. She told me, she sneaks her food to compensate for anything she's missing." He looks almost relieved.

"Are you sure?" I ask.

"Yes, Tom even told me that Miss Byron has sent him money as a way of compensation for losing his contract." She's taking care of them. All of them. Sticking with a gruelling routine and lack of food, so they don't get fired, and when they do. She still makes sure they don't miss out.

"She did?" he nods, like he can't believe it himself.

"Yeah, through another account. I think it was hers. I drop everything to get there when they tell me to. Like earlier, I had to get a friend to cover my sessions. I can't risk getting fired. The next one they hire might not be as accommodating. It almost killed me earlier, she could hardly move, but I had to leave, At least this way, I can warn Gianna that Miss Bryon needs more."

"Fucking hell," Owen chimes in from my side, leaning forwards his elbows resting on the table.

"Who else has worked for them? And who are *them*?"

"There are at least three others that I know of, but there could be more I'll give you their names. As for who they are, I don't exactly know. It's not her parents, well not that I can see from the email address anyway, a PR firm." He scrolls through his phone again. "There are no calls, no people, just emails. It's not one we can reply to either. See." His lips twist, showing me the email address.

Hex PR. I'll find out who they are today.

"Thanks, I'm going to need to do something to your phone so I get the emails and trace them, is that okay?"

"Will it affect anything else?" he asks me cautiously.

"No, just your inbox, I'll remove it once I have what I need." I say calmly. I wouldn't blame him if he said no, not after the way I treated him.

"Okay sure, have-at-it." handing me his phone again, I do what I need to do, it'll copy all the emails on to my system. I should be able to track it from there see who's behind this. "Anything to help." He nods.

"For what it's worth, I'm sorry." He grimpses.

"Yeah, me too." With that we let him out and Charlie slips in, sitting on the table in front of Owen.

"Just how bad is it, Cole?"

"Bad, she protecting everyone she knows that cares about her. She'll never leave if she knows they're at risk of being hurt in anyway."

Chapter Twenty-Nine

Pit Stop

Arianna

I step out of the car, after accepting Dec's outstretched hand and Cole by my side immediately. His eyes only meet mine for second, but that's all I need. Calm washes over me. My mind's been playing tricks on me today, waiting for my parents or Gi, to ask how the cake box got into my room. But they seem more intent on doling out the punishment, than finding the cause, thank goodness.

My whole body's sore. I feel it with every step.

I've missed Cole today, stupid I know, but I have. When he woke me up this morning, all I wanted to do was stay in bed and enjoy being in his warmth. Today's flaunting is just that, me having some pictures taken at the cute sixties throwback café, called Bruno's. The one I missed out on when my trip got cut short. Stepping through the door, I'm taken aback, the vibe is out of this world. It's five in the afternoon, but it's busy. People queuing, chatting and eating. It's so *normal*, I love it. It's been so long since I've been around others just doing their daily things. I stop just inside the doorway, soaking it all in. I feel a hand at my back, and when I look over my shoulder, Cole urging me forward, so I walk into the café.

"Everything okay?" he whispers.

"Yes, just enjoying it while it lasts." I'm shoved to the side as someone barges through the door. Cole catches my arm to steady me, literally growling in the direction of the man spoiling my moment. Unfortunately, I recognise him and my smile changes. My photographer has arrived in all his rude and obnoxious glory. Cole frowns at me.

The photographer turns and looks through me like every time before.

"I have a list of shots we need," he grumbles, not even saying hello, "we need to be quick. I have better things to be doing." Keeping my mask firmly in place, I smile, while I hear Cole mumble under his breath. His hand slips to my side, it's intimate, his fingers gripping, letting me know he's here. I like it when he does that. Like he sees me, even when others don't.

When his hand leaves my side, he steps in front of me, his arm now like a barrier, protecting me from the photographer.

"Hey, buddy, how about you speak to Miss Byron with a bit of respect, then maybe we'll do the list you want. She *is* paying *you* right?" I have to bite my tongue to hide my grin.

"Mr?" I offer, waiting for the photographer to tell me his name, I remember it, but I want him to know I'm in charge not him.

"Smith," he offers, unpacking his camera and phone, placing them on an open table.

"Mr Smith, thank you for taking the time to come and do this today. I assume it was at my father's request?" He's been building up material for something, I've had to do one of these for almost every business on the high street here. Maybe he's going to run for mayor?

"No idea, I just had an email telling me where I needed to be." He looks annoyed. Watching Cole as his eyes flick to the table, assessing the equipment with a frown, like it's going to hurt me, and he needs to get rid of it.

"Did you have somewhere else you needed to be?" I'm being polite, finding out just how much time I have to be here. My calendar was blacked out a ninety-minute window. If I can get this done sooner than normal, maybe I can enjoy being here.

"Yes, it's my wedding anniversary and I was planning to—" I cut him off, I don't need him to continue.

"Let's get it over with, then, shall we. What's first on the list?" I ask.

"Just go about what you would normally do in a coffee shop, and I'll tick them off as we go," he grumbles, picking up the camera.

"Okay, I'll order the coffee then." Walking over the counter I wait in line and order four coffees and three cakes.

"Why so many cakes? You hungry?" Cole asks seriously as I take my seat at the wooden-topped table.

"Yes, but no. One for Mr Smith, one for Dec when we leave, and one for you."

"Where's yours?" he questions.

"I have no desire to undergo another gym session today," I tell him with a small smile.

"I'm on duty, baby." My eyes go wide at his slip of the tongue. "I don't need anything."

"I know you don't, cuddle muffin," I whisper back, knowing the photographer is out of earshot.

"Cuddle muffin?"

"Don't you like it? I thought it was sweet," I say, licking my bottom lip.

"I'm not sweet, Ari," he grumbles.

"Pumpkin?" He shakes his head.

"What about *sir*?" I rub my foot up his calf suggestively, making him shut his eyes just for split second, inhaling a shuddering breath.

"Ari," he warns, but I know for sure he likes it when his eyes open and the depth of colours highlights his desire. "Only in the bedroom. Now be a good girl and behave," he growls. My cheeks flush red, my mind imagining just how that will play out. Do I want to be a good girl, or do I want to see what he'll do if I'm a little naughty?

"Miss Byron, if you could just stand by the counter, that will be the last shot." Picking up my coffee, I move to the counter, sipping it as I stand, watching Cole the entire time.

"Arianna?"

Turning to see who calling my name, I catch Cole stiffen and start moving towards me.

"Kye?" I say, seeing the man I met in the cocktail bar, "Oh my gosh." He smiles brightly as he takes his takeaway drink from the guy behind the counter. "What are you doing here." Cole steps beside me, his glare firmly latched onto Kye.

"I see you still have your guard dog?" he whispers. Cole's hand moves like he's ready to pull me into him, claiming me somehow. But he stops, obviously remembering were in public. Disappointment simmers under my skin for a flicker of a second.

I remember that he has no idea that Kye's gay. Reaching out I touch Kye's arm. He leans in to kiss my cheek. You can practically feel the rage coming off Cole, his body vibrating.

"Are you just passing?" I ask, eyeing his cup.

"Yes, I'm off to finalise the menu for the charity concert I'm hosting this year."

"What are you raising money for? Can I help?" His eyes almost pop out of his head with excitement. "That would be amazing. It's the abuse awareness foundation. Some of the local businesses around here take it in turns every other year to set it up."

"That's amazing. I've just done a photoshoot with Millie from Milliecan for a similar cause," I add.

"I've heard so many nice things about her and the work she does."

"She's a wonderful person. I'm hoping to be an ambassador for her." I don't know where that came from, but just imagine if I could—using what I have to help and support others.

"Ari. Can I call you, please?" Kye asks.

"Yes." Taking a napkin, I write my number on it and hand it over, Cole glaring the entire time. Kye leans in, kissing me on the cheek again, laughing as he watches Cole. He leaves with a promise to call me. I swear Cole looks ready to kill him. A few seconds later, Mr Smith steps in telling me he's also finished. The café is almost empty as grabs his things and heads to the door.

Leaving me and Cole alone, sort of.

"What's wrong?" I ask, knowing full well that he's annoyed at my actions, but if he took the time to talk more and scowl less, he'd know about Kye. And maybe even enjoy his company as much as I do.

"I don't know what to make of him?" he admits.

"I like him, he's easy to talk to and friendly enough."

"He's handsy." I laugh at this, and in a moment of forgetfulness, I place my hand over his where it rests on the counter.

"He means nothing by it, Cole." I run my thumb over the veins on the back of his hand. His gaze lingers on my touch, his eyes softening just a little. He slips his hand from under mine, and I remember where we are. It was stupid of me to forget myself.

Clearing his throat, he takes my elbow, the flare of his touch making my skin tingle. "You have forty minutes before Dec comes back to pick you up. What would you like to do?"

"What would I like to do?" I'm confused by the question. Why is he asking me what I want to do?

"Yes, Ari, what would you, Arianna Bryon, like to do for the next forty minutes?" I really have to think about it.

"What would I like to do?" I repeat.

"That's what I asked, Ari, It's an easy question."

"Not as easy as you might think, Cole." A look of understanding crosses his face. "I want to stay."

"Okay."

"I'd like to get another drink," I tell him. "I'd like to sit at this table and just enjoy being here with you." His eyes darken as he steps closer.

"As you wish." He smirks, his voice so low it's almost like a vibration across my skin. Then he steps away, leaving me to watch his fine ass in perfectly fitted suit trousers walk back to the counter. I sit down on the leather seats while he orders me a caramel latte and a protein bar. My heart squeezes at his thoughtfulness. He knows I need the extra calories today.

"Your drink, miss," Cole says as he places my drink and bar on the table, but he doesn't sit down. It's only us and the man behind the counter now. It must be close to closing.

"Why are you still stood up? I want you to sit down with me," I tell him, looking up from my position, he towers above me. God, he looks good. Every woman in this place eyes him at some point since we walked in. He didn't look in their direction. His gaze constantly sweeping over the room, but always coming back to me.

Placing his hand on the table he leans into me, "If I sit down with you, Cupcake. I'll want to touch you. No. I would touch you, and I wouldn't be able to stop at the feel of you beneath my fingers." I can't breathe, my lungs seize, his intense eyes hold mine. "I'd spread your legs under this table, and fuck you with my fingers, just how I know you like it. Deep and slow." My core tightens, desire instantly heating between my legs. Cole lowers his tone further, barely audible to anyone else but me. "The way I'm feeling right now, I want to spank your ass for that little show you put on with Kye." I gasp. "Looking at your flushed cheeks, I think not touching you is torture enough for now." My heart's skittering, unable to keep a normal rhythm. "Are you wet for me, Ari?"

"Cole." I can only look at him.

"There it is. Let's see how long you can last before you beg me to touch you."

"Oh hell, Cole." He stands taking his place beside me again, scanning the room, looking like nothing has phased him. While I sit, dazed, turned on and so wet between my thighs, all I can think of is his hands, sliding through my folds.

I need him so badly, I could explode. My nipples feel like bullets, grazing my bra as I breathe. I'm sure you can see them through my shirt. Smiling like I've won the lottery, I giggle, actually giggle at the absurdity of all this. I want him to do it, I want him to make me come in this café.

Who am I?

When I stop myself laughing, his eyes are on me, shining with delight. I want to be brave, and daring and be everything I always held back on. When he scans the room slowly again, I shift in my seat, hitching my skirt high on my thighs, making sure no one can see, I quickly hook my fingers into the elastic of my thong. Sliding them down my legs, bending to retrieve them from around my ankles, I pull them free. Straightening my skirt. Before scrunching them in my hand to hide them.

Standing from my chair, he steps back to allow me room. Offering me his hand in the process.

"Bathroom?" I smile, putting my hand with my bunched-up thong into his.

"What's this?" he asks when I walk past him, my cheeks flush deeply, as realisation hits him, he moans deep in his chest. Peaking at them, before he pockets them. "Let me show you the way." Eyes dark, he strides behind me. When we get to the bathroom door, he pulls me into a different room. It's dark, with just the light from above the window lighting the room.

I don't get a chance to say anything, Cole hands grip my waist, as he pushes me to the wall. My back flat against the cold surface, he presses into me, his length, digging into my stomach.

"You're a naughty girl, Ari."

"Am I?" I breathe out.

"You know you are, Cupcake." Hot hands glid up my side cupping my breasts, I'm aching to have him touch me more. His thumbs flicking over my hard nipples. Moaning at the bolt of lightning that shoots from my nipples to my core, it lights me up.

"I need you, Cole." My hands tugging at the nape of his neck. Pulling his mouth to mine.

"This will be hard and quick Ari." *Oh my god.* I can't breathe. In a good, yes, fuck me now way.

"Yes, I need to feel you, Sir." Lifting my skirt, as his hand slips between my legs.

"Your so wet baby, do you like the thought of being spanked?" his rough fingers circle my clit and I almost lose it. Reaching down between us, I undo his belt, and untuck his black as night shirt. Flipping his button undone on his trousers, as he pushes two fingers deep inside me, my head falls back to the wall. He captures my moan, with his mouth, it's sloppy, frantic, and fuck I need it like I need to breath. Pumping his fingers in and out of me, my body aching with the need to come undone. Lowering his zipper, I push his trousers down, just enough to feel his beautiful cock, hot and heavy in my hand.

Taking a second, to feel the thrill running through my system, not just for what I'm doing right now with Cole, but for everything I want my life to be. Grasping him a little harder, brushing my thumb over his sensitive tip, he thrusts into my hand. Groaning as I fist him harder, stroking the palm of my hand up and down the glorious length of him.

"Turn around, now." He demands, his hand at my core moves to my waist turning me, before I get a chance to move. My hands sting as they hit the wall.

I'm flat up against it, my shoulders against my hands, as his hands stroke down my back, over my shirt. His touch searing, driving me crazy as he grips my hips just a little harder.

"Fuck, Ari," he breathes deeps, "I can't control myself around you." Pulling my hips back, he runs the tip of cock over my slit, jolting me to groan, when his cock notches at my entrance. Closing my eyes, my head rest on the wall, relishing every sensation, swiping through my body.

How have I gone so long without this? Would it be the same with someone else? Or is this just an us thing? The thought of being with someone turns my stomach, but the thought of Cole with someone else makes me feel a little crazy.

This is not the time for this.

"I don't want your control, Cole. I want you to fuck me, quick." I say, putting all of the thoughts to the back of my mind, because right now all I need is Cole inside me.

"Fucking hell." his tip still braced at my entrance; I don't want to wait. Pushing back, every pore in my body, craving what he's about to give me. He rests his head on my shoulder, each breath creates goosebumps over my flesh, his lips peppering my skin with kisses, when he surges forwards filling me so deep so quickly. I yelp at the delicious burn, my fingers try to grip the wall, but come up with nothing as he stretches me wide, still I'm pulsing around him. My desire for him as evident as ever, with how wet I'm becoming.

"Ari." he's asking if I'm good, he's tense and needs to know if he can move.

"I'm fine, fuck... you feel so good," grasping for air as I speak. Pressing my hands in to the wall in front of me.

"Quiet, Cupcake, I can't have anyone finding us here, I've already had to cover for you more than once." what does that mean? Before I can ask, his strong hand covers my mouth as he sets a punishing pace, slamming into me from behind. I'm already peaking, my eyes roll back, as my lids shut tight. Climbing and chasing my high, as he drives harder and harder into me. I love every second of it, my hands on the wall, my head resting on them. My whole body shifting with the ferocity of his movements. The way my body moves with his. He's so powerful, his steel thighs bracing against my own. I want to fall at his feet, and surrender everything I am to him.

"You..." I don't know what I'm trying to say, I can't focus on the words. My mind drawing a blank, with each formidable drive of his hips.

Cole's hand rubs over the soft cheek of my arse, still pounding into me, I'm lost in the most exquisite feeling, when I feel it a sharp sting as his hand connects to the soft flesh of my ass. My scream's muffled, as he does it again. I feel, oh god, I feel dirty and exposed and *good god,* I love it, my screams turn to moans when he does it again, each time soothing the tingling, sensitive skin, with his hand.

"Punishment, baby." I'm a whimpering mess, getting wetter by the second, "I knew you'd love it," he groans, into my neck as he cranes back over me, "feel how wet you are for me." removing one of my hands, from under my head, I reach between my legs to feel myself, he's right I'm drenched. He makes me feel this way. Only him. Taking my hand away, he grabs my wrist, bringing my fingers to his mouth, and sucks. Moaning when I feel him thicken inside me, as he wraps his tongue around them sucking them. Letting my hand go back its original place, to hold on to anything I can.

Cole reaches for my clit, pinching it between his fingers, my body skyrockets, the pleasure pain line blurred as fuck; I crave it.

"That's it, baby come all over my cock like the good girl you are." I want to scream, but I know I can't. There's a veil of sweat over my skin, glistening in the dark.

"Yes, Sir." I whimper, through his hand still covering my mouth.

"Jesus, fuck baby, say it again." he growls, slowing his pace for just a second.

"Sir, make me come." He presses into me so deep; I see stars. His fingers dig into my skin at my hips. I hope they leave bruises; I want to know that this was real tomorrow when I wake up. With one more push of his hips, his cock hit my G spot. I fall into a freefall I never want to see the end of. Fireworks, spread over me, and throughout my body, my wall clamp down on his cock, as he comes with me. Roaring into my ear, as he holds himself deep inside, covering my insides with his come. I feel it all, every drop as he fills me. His hands move from my hip, to circle my clit, easing me through my high, until I land. Only he cups me, holding us where we're joined together.

"This is mine, no one else's, mine Ari." its possessive and intense, and damn I like it.

"Yours." I murmur back, as he kisses down my spine.

It feels like forever before we pull apart. And I hate the empty feeling he leaves behind every time we do this. It's not even the fact that he's not inside me, it's that don't know when we be like this together again. Alone, no one but us.

"I need more of this Ari, I need more of you." He whispers holding me to him. "You need to be free, Ari" he pants, against my back, bringing me up right. Skating his hands over my shirt, smoothing it back into place, he adjusts my skirt, turning me around, before he tucks himself away, and buckles himself up. Taking me in his arms, he takes a tissue from somewhere and cleans in between my legs. Gasping at how sensitive I am.

"I want it, I want it so badly." My breath catches on the lump in my throat.

Snaking his arms around my waist, he pulls me closer. Resting his chin on my shoulder, I tilt my head to peer at him in the darkened room. A store cupboard, I can see the outlines of the shelving and boxes now. My high setting to a welcome buzz of emotions.

"We're working on a plan Ari, me and the guys." fear ricochets through me, like a ping pong ball at full speed. Stepping away.

"No, Cole, please, this is my life, it's fucked up I know it is, but I will never let them get to you, and if you help me in any way, and they find out…" I can't breathe, No. I can't let them do whatever it is they think they can. "They'll hurt you, they'll ruin everything you ever worked for Cole."

"They can't touch me, Ari. We want to do this, the more I look the more I find, and hate this life you have." His voice is thick and pleading. Reaching for me, his fingers interlace with mine.

"It's my life Cole, please don't ruin what this is, what this is becoming. I can't stand by and let them make good on their promises; to hurt the few people I have in my life."

Opening the door, with my free hand, I step back out into the small hallway of the café. It's still empty apart from a guy behind the counter. Cole drops my hand, and my heart drops with it. I hate this. Turning to him, I have to stop myself from grabbing his shirt and kissing him.

"I will get free. I don't know how long it will take, but it will happen."

"Then let us help," he pleads. What do I have to lose? *Everything.*

But what if it works?

"Okay," I say tentatively, looking at my hands, "but I want to know everything you're planning. I mean it, Cole. I'll tell you everything I know," I say, stepping into his space, he smells like sex and coffee. My chest's ready to burst with what this man is willing to put at risk. With our hand hidden from view, I place my finger in the palm of his hand, and he takes it, enveloping my finger with his hand. His eyes sparkle. A dimple on his cheek I've never seen before, as his smile deepens, into something I know is just for me.

"Done, the sooner the better, Cupcake, I want to take you on a real date." The smile on his face set off my own.

"To the escape plan."

"The escape plan." he mimics, shaking his head.

Chapter Thirty

Asking

Arianna

I've had an email confirmation for a meeting with my father.

I'm not ready for this.

I have to be ready for this. I've hounded her to get this. Now I have it, I can't think of one reason why I still want to go ahead with it.

You need this, Ari.

Even if Cole works out a plan, you need to do this for yourself.

A backup plan.

Reading the email, it's not even addressed to me by name, it's all to whom it may concern. *Bitch.* She really doesn't want me to see him. What difference does it make to her if I do or not? Oh-my-god, it's today. Glancing at my watch, my chest heaves as I realise it's in an hour. She's setting me up to fail. It'll take me at least thirty minutes to get there, and Dec's not even here. On top of that, I'm not dressed. I've only just come back from the gym. I look a mess. I'll be cutting it fine, that's for sure. Why does she hate me so much?

Firing off a message to Chrisy, I need some moral support while in a rush to get ready.

Me: Can you call me? I'm freaking TF out.

Chrisy: Yep. Give me a few. I'm just leaving a meeting. What's up?

Me: Just call me when you're free and I'll fill you in.

Chrisy: Alright, keep your knickers on, sweet cheeks.

I can't keep still. I'm sick to my stomach with nerves. I want this so badly, but all I keep doing is remembering what happened last time I asked my father for something important to me. I know Cole's working on a plan, not that he's told me anything about it yet. *Okay,* it's been like a day, but I already feel a little left out. Stripping as quickly as I can, I shoot a text to Dec to pick me up in fifteen minutes, then jump in the shower, leaving my hair unwashed. It will have to do.

Stepping out of the shower, I answer the phone after it's first ring. I don't even give Chrisy a chance to speak before I dive right in and spill my guts.

"I'm asking my father for driving lessons today. I feel sick. What if I vomit all over him before I get a chance to ask him and make my presentation. What happens if he laughs in my face like last time. Worse, what happens if he actually does what he did last time?" I pause, sucking a lung full of air in. I step into my closet, picking out the pre-prepared outfit. A deep pink trouser suit, with a black Cami top. Stylish, sexy but sophisticated. Perfect. *Oh my god,* my father will hate it. It's too late to change it now.

"Fucking hell, that's a shit-ton to unload on girl before she's had her fourth coffee of the day." Slipping on my knickers, I put her on speaker so I can get ready.

"I know. I just really needed to talk to you. Tell me why I'm doing this. I can't do it, Chris." I grab my bra and put that on next, hopping around like an idiot.

"Okay, okay, you're really doing this?"

"Yes," I squeak, pulling on my trousers.

"Right, what's changed?" She needs context I don't have time to go into.

"No time for that."

"Okay, fine, you want a life, right?"

"Yes, so badly." Slipping my cami over my head.

"You want to travel, see the world, on your own schedule?" That's it.

"Yes," I manage, as slide my jacket on, grabbing my shoes at the same time I almost fall over. I can't breathe, I think I'm hyperventilating; it's never happened before but I think this is it. I can't get air in. My face feels like it's going to explode along with my chest and stomach contents.

"Hold on, suck in some air, sweetness. Stick your head between your knees, and breathe deep." I do as I'm told, perching on the stool in my closet and tucking my head low. I breathe through my nose and mouth, feeling the effects after only a few seconds.

"Is that any better?" she asks.

"Yep, sort of," I say, my voice muffled still, because my heads still between my knees.

"I can't hear you, lie back on your bed and talk to me." I can hear her voice getting higher the more I panic.

"I need to move. I need to go," I rush out.

"Ari, you're scaring me. I need more from you." Sucking in another breath I stand, feeling a little light headed. Picking up my phone, I take Chrisy off speaker, striding towards my door, pulling my black patent heels on as I go, and grabbing my black trench coat from its hanger.

"I'm asking my dad for driving lessons today." she takes a deep breath. She knows what he said and did last time.

"Why driving lessons?" I can only imagine the frown on her face.

"It's all part of the greater plan," I whisper as I step out from my room, sliding my arms into my coat as I hold the phone under my chin. "To get me into university, start small, work my way up." I'm panting, goddamn, you'd think with all the extra workouts I've been put through, I'd at least be able to walk without getting out of breath.

"Solid plan. How are you approaching it?" I love this side of her, no judgment. She accepted my decision, no questions.

"God, I miss you," I say between breaths. "A business plan. I've even booked in a meeting with him at his office." Reaching the top of the stairs, I pause, taking a second to get my breath. Dec should be here in a minute, if he's not already.

"Really they let you…"

"No, I had to go through his secretary. It took a lot of stalking and persuasion to even get in his diary." Taking the first step down, I add, "They've only just let me know I have a slot, and it's in," pulling up my sleeve a fraction, I check the watch on my wrist, "forty-three minutes." My heart's pounding in my chest as I take a few steps.

"Fucking hell, that's… shameful, on their side, not yours. You're their daughter, for fuck's sake." She raises her voice, no doubt scaring anyone in her immediate vicinity.

"I know, but I wanted to do this right. If I had walked up to his office on any given day, he would have said no he didn't have time. Shooed me away, made excuses and laughed me off before I got a word out. At least now, in forty-two minutes, I have an allotted time to be in and out."

"Jesus Christ, how long did they give you?" She hates him just as much as I do.

"Fifteen minutes," I deadpan.

"Sounds like you've really thought about this. What's brought all this on?"

"You," I say shyly. My birthday meal, not admitting Cole played his huge part too. I don't want her to feel bad, or responsible, but I've always told her the truth.

"What do you mean? I don't get it." My heart squeezes.

"I mean, you've inspired me. I've watched you ask for what you want, do the things you love with the support you need. I've backed you all the way. I've watched you grow and become this fucking amazing businesswoman. Leave home, start a career, and be yourself." Now I'm on the verge of crying. Taking a breath, I attempt to settle my nerves.

"You're making me cry, for fuck's sake. I've got to go back into my meeting after this call," she says, sniffling down the phone.

"I'm sorry," I half chuckle, half cry with her. "I just want a tiny fraction of what you have. Even if it takes me years to get it, I want some of it."

"You, my fucking beautiful friend, are worth more than just a fraction of what you want. You deserve it all. Every single thing you want you should go and get," she almost yells.

"Stop, I can't cry. He'll see it and think I'm weak."

"Okay, time to put your big girl pants on, pull them up to your tits, and go ask your dad if you can learn to drive." It's about as positive as I'm going to get.

"I will…" I realise I've left the presentation upstairs. Jogging back to get it, I grab my laptop bag with the presentation tucked safely inside. "I've got to go down to his office in town, to see him, I'll need to leave in a few minutes," I huff, making my way back down again.

"Sweet-cheeks, do you remember the plan we put into place after you got the bad news last time?" Chrisy asks. I remember chuckling at the ridiculous plan we made.

"Yeah, I do. Why?"

"We still have that option," she says, teasing, but not.

"What? To hitch a ride to Rio, and live out our lives as boat tour guides?" The plan lives in my brain rent-free. Always makes me smile.

"Yeah, I mean why not?" Chrisy questions.

"Don't you remember what happened last time you went on a boat?"

"Yes, but I'd do it all again for you, plus there are pills for that now. I'm sure it would reduce the amount of sick that comes up, if not stop it." Bursting out laughing, I place the phone between my shoulder and ear smoothing my outfit in the mirror by the door.

"I never want to live through that again. We can make a new plan. What about Greece? I hear it's amazing over there."

"No boats, maybe we can become dancers, show off a little." I actually relax a little.

"Sounds good to me" Turning slightly, I catch Gi's reflection in the mirror. She's waiting for me. Dec's pulling up and I have every faith that Cole has been notified of my movements. If not, he'll have seen me leave my room. He'll be annoyed I didn't tell him, but he'll understand when I explain. Hopefully.

"I've got to go," Chrisy says "but be brave, ask. Don't back down. I know you can do this."

"Thanks, I really needed to hear that." We end our call, and I move towards Gi.

"Was that Chrisy?" she asks before handing me a travel mug. I think this woman is a mind reader.

"Yes, I needed to hear her voice; it worked. I'm smiling after almost having a full-blown panic attack." Gi looks so concerned, I know it's been playing on her mind what my father will say. She was with me after he gave his orders last time.

"I saw the notification," she says. I guess everyone got the email.

"I'll be fine, Gi, I promise. He can only say no." We both know he can do more than that. I'm just not going to think about what that could be if this goes wrong.

"Good, I've made you a camomile tea for your journey, I also want you to call me as soon as you're done." Hugging me one last time, she practically shoves me through the door while holding my hand. God, I wish she was my mom.

Pulling up to the courthouse, through the back entrance, Dec rolls to a stop, he moves like lightning to get to the door before me, bowing his head slightly when I take his out-stretched hand to exit to the car. "Thank you," I say on a laugh.

"I'll be here waiting for you. Cole is already here, just to your left." Looking over my shoulder I see him walking toward me. I'm not shocked to see him, I knew Dec would let him know I was here, just like he always has done. Why does he have to look like sin, wrapped up in a flipping suit? It makes me want to do things, very naughty things I know we'll both love.

Maybe I should have asked for Ethan to come with me; less of a distraction. Maybe I need the distraction?

"Great," I say with an eye roll. Dec chuckles, closing the car door behind me. Glancing at my watch, Dec must have broken a record getting here. He's given me an extra five minutes. I'll need to find my father's office and check myself in. Lost in thought for a moment, I feel him at my side, that ever-present tingle I get when he's around flares to life in my chest. I don't need to look. I feel a little calmer, knowing he's here, even if he has no idea why.

"Miss Byron?" He nods, his shadow casting over me.

I hear the question in his voice. I don't know if I can handle him right now. I need to keep focused or I'll lose my nerve and never ask. Turning to face him, I can't meet his eyes.

"Look, you don't have to come in with me. It's probably best you don't. This is the courthouse. There's plenty of security around, so I'll be fine. Wait with Dec outside." I don't want to be rude; I just need space from him.

"No can do, a courthouse is just as dangerous as anywhere else, even more so with all the criminals walking around," he adds, keeping pace with me. His hand coming the small of my back when we come through the door. "Besides, I want to know what you're up to."

I stop walking a few paces in, he immediately stays by my side, never missing a beat. "Please." He looks shocked at the word. "I can't handle you right now. I need to be able to breathe and I can't be around you." He stands in front of me, blocking anyone from getting in my way. I try to move around him, but he doesn't move.

"Why are you here?"

Frowning, I look up. He's so much taller than me. His blond hair tousled and messy, in complete contradiction to his immaculate and expensive tailored suit.

"I have a meeting." I don't want to tell him anything else. He'll stop me if I tell him, he'll tell me not to worry. That I'll be free soon. He won't understand how much I need to do this for myself. I don't want to argue; I want to get in there and get this done.

"With who?"

"That's none of your business, Cole." Stepping to the side, I start to walk around him, but he's quicker than me, getting in my way again.

"What's the meeting about?" his head ducks slightly, to be level with mine.

"It's a proposal. That's all you need to know."

"I'm intrigued now, Ari," Sweet Jesus, the way he says my name, it sends shivers down my spine. "Business or pleasure."

"Neither, please move. I only have a few minutes until my meeting starts." I can't read him. He's holding me up, and if I'm late, there's no telling what will happen.

"But if it's neither business or pleasure?" He's frowning now, but he moves out of my way as I make my way towards my father's offices on the third floor. "What is it?" He continues his relentless questions as he follows me, watching me intently. With each step closer to the office, my heart rate rises.

"What's in the bag?" I ignore him and keep walking up the stairs. "Ari," he almost shouts from beside me, stopping me for a second.

"I'll fill you in, just not now," I say, storming ahead, my bag clutched to my side.

When we reach the third floor my father's secretary is front and centre, sitting at the huge desk. Steeling my spine, I step up. This is it. She doesn't even grace me with a look, even though she watched me walk in, a look of disgust on her face.

"Name?" she asks aggressively. My fucking name? Am I really that none existent in his life?

"Arianna Byron," I tell her as politely as I can. If that's not embarrassing enough, she looks me up and down like I've just walked in poop, and rubbed it in her carpet on purpose.

"Take a seat." It's hard to keep my embarrassment to myself when my cheeks heat, giving me away. Sitting down in the chairs in front of her desk, she asks Cole if he would like a drink while he waits. He declines then turns to me, expecting her to ask me the same, but she walks off sitting back at her desk.

"What the fuck was that?" Cole says like he expects me to answer. I don't, swallowing down my nerves as they lodge themselves in my throat. I have a bad feeling that this meeting will go to hell. I know the feeling well, it starts in my stomach, then spreads like a disease into all my limbs as they go numb, preparing me for what's to come.

Cole doesn't say another word as we sit together, side by side. In a weird way, I'm glad he's here. I feel safe. Not so alone.

After waiting for thirteen minutes, his secretary announces my father's name in full with extended title, adding he's ready to see me. Cole's head snaps towards me, his eyes wide. I can't look at him.

"What?" he whispers, more to himself than to me. When I start to walk towards the huge oak door, he walks with me.

"You need to stay out here." Turning towards him, we stare at each other for a second, his chest rising and falling like he can't understand what I'm doing. I guess he can't. I need this. I need to do this on my own. As shit scared as I am, if I want to have any sort of life outside my father's walls, I need to ask.

"Ari?"

Placing my hand on his chest, his heart like a drum under my palm. I feel him everywhere. He looks down at where I'm touching him. Letting out a breath, I step away quickly.

"Cole, I need this, please?" Why does this feel so different? I can see the worry along with all the questions running through his beautiful hazel eyes. I don't give him a chance to say anything. I move to the door, leaving Cole behind.

Chapter Thirty-One

Hell

Arianna

Walking into my father's office, I hold my head up high. I need to be confidant. I can't let the emotions I have simmering under my skin show. He'll see them as weakness, pick them apart, and tear me down in the process.

Taking a deep breath, I step further into the room. The smell of old books and leather filling my nostrils. Scanning the large room, I see him at his desk. He doesn't even look up to greet me.

"Father," I say, not too loud, but loud enough to get his attention. Not daring to move, until he says so. Looking from his notes laid out across his desk, his eyes run over me.

"Is this some sort of fucking joke?" Leaning forward, he picks up the phone, ready to call his bitch of a secretary.

"No, I'm your nine-fifteen appointment," I say, my voice a little louder than I expected. He places the phone back down. Standing, he leans over his desk, fists bunched on the surface. If looks could kill, I'd be dead; like at the bottom of a river, tied to a concrete block.

"Get the fuck out, I'm working," he seethes through gritted teeth.

"Please? Hear me out. I have something I want to ask you." My voice is shaky, but I make a move to step towards him, then stop.

"You have got to be kidding me? You want me to listen to *you*?" It's like he hits me; his words hurt like a slap to the face.

"Yes, please." I plead. Taking out my laptop, I open it up and place it on his desk. I turn it towards him before he makes me leave, trying my best to ignore the death stare burning into my face. "Read this. It's a proposal," I stammer. *Shit, it's going badly.*

Sitting at the seat in front of his desk, I rush the words out. I know I don't have much time. "I'd like to learn to drive. In there," I point to the presentation, on his desk, "are the figures on saving versus costs on having a full-time driver." This catches his attention. "Just look over the numbers. You could save thousands."

Flicking through the presentation slides, he takes a few minutes to read though some of the financials I've pointed out. I'm so proud of myself right now. Even if he says no, he still looked at the work I've done. It's a step in the right direction no matter how small it is.

My stomach is churning with nerves as silence settles around us. Watching him read through what I've done, the tension in this room, simmers and it's all aimed at me

Closing the laptop, he leans back pulling it towards him. My hearts is in my throat, I swallow it down. He lifts the laptop, and I assume he's going to hand it back.

My heart rate picks up a notch from its already high rhythm.

It only takes a second before it plummets into its icy depths when he drops the laptop onto the floor. It cracks and I gasp, my hand flying to my mouth. When he stands, his foot smashes onto the silver metal, breaking it further. My heart breaks along with it.

Chills run over my body, my gut tensing. I don't know what's going to happen. Yes, I do, it's going to happen again. He's going to lock me up for trying.

"Why?" I question before I can stop myself.

He rounds the desk, my face frozen, attempting to portray some kind of confidence, disguising the true weakness that lies beneath. He smiles. I almost whimper. If I scream, Cole will come running. He'll burst through the door and take me away. I know he will, but I can't get the words past my lips. They're trapped in a spiked bubble in my throat, tearing me apart from the inside.

"I have an alternative proposal. It's the perfect fit for you," he says, eyeing me in such a way that I cringe, my skin breaking out like a thousand spiders running over my skin. "All my problems taken care of." Walking back, he sits back in his chair, looking full of himself.

"Your problems?" I whisper to myself. Is no secret he's always seen me as a problem.

"It's a means to an end," he states so casually, I want to cry.

"What does that mean?" I find my voice. It's not stable, but I want to know the truth.

"We never wanted you." He says it with such casual ease, my heart slices in two.

"We got you for a reason. It was an added bonus that made me money. A perfect look for when I stepped things up and run for mayor." My breath rushes out. I knew there was reason for everything I've done lately.

"Mayor?" I question. I was right. "You see, while you do earn me money, it's not enough. I need more. So, I struck a deal." My stomach sinks to the floor.

"What kind of deal?" My breathing shatters into fragments. I don't under-stand what is happening.

Move, Ari, move, run, get out, and never come back. It's a faded whisper at the back of my mind.

Only I can't. Fear grips me, holding me so firmly in place like I've been tied down.

Reaching for his phone again, he presses a button. "Cherry, could you ask Mr Carmichael to come to my office, please?" My fear chokes me, making me cough and gasp as it courses through my veins. My father's smile grows wider at my reaction. She must say something back and he laughs before saying, "She's about to find out," before he hangs up.

"Mr Carmichael?" I ask, gulping down the lump still lodged in my throat. I know I should stay quiet. I shouldn't provoke him.

Scream do something before he tells you, his plans. You don't want to hear this, you won't survive.

Standing, he kicks my now broken laptop before he walks over to his cabinet and takes out two crystal glasses, filling them with an amber liquid I can only guess is his favourite bourbon. I'd like to think he's going to offer me a drink. I could use one, but I'm not stupid. I'm the shit on his shoe, apparently. Taking a long sip from his glass, he tops it back up before standing behind me. A shiver running down my spine. His hand touches my shoulder and squeezes me just on the edge of pain. I try not to wince. "You're not worthy enough to be treated like an equal to earn yourself lessons, or an education of any sort. You have a place in this world, and it's firmly beneath men like me and Robert. Nothing to say?" I shake my head. I know better.

"Just as it should be, I would have thought you would have learnt last time, Arianna."

"I..." I don't know what to say. Moving my hands under my legs to stop the visible shake in them.

"You, what?" he spits, "It makes no difference. Your fate was always going to be sealed like this. But this worked out better than I could have ever imagined."

"My fate? I don't understand?" My voice is small and shaky.

"Your fate was decided when we found we were getting a fucking girl." He sneers. "Useless breed if you ask me. But we found a way to make it work for us." He just referred to me as an 'it'. Dying inside, I try to steady my breathing before I pass out, my mind going fuzzy.

"We just needed to decide who and how it would benefit us the most."

"Benefit you?" I'm scared. The creaking of my father's door is the only noise I hear. I know Robert's walked in.

"Robert." My father greets him with a greedy smile

"Thomas, is it time?"

I want to run; I don't want to hear what he has planned for me. I'm not sure I could take being confined again. If it keeps him from deporting Gianna, then I'll do it. I'd do anything for her, for them.

"I was telling Arianna how her fate has been sealed for a long time, Robert."

"I'm glad we met when we did, Thomas. It seems our fates have been combined, Arianna." My stomach rolls. "I've had my eye on you for a long time." He licks his lips, and I heave. "I think you're just what I need." Did I hear that right? Bile rises in my throat, but I manage to swallow it down, leaving a god-awful taste behind.

My father nods, smiling, as he hands Robert the second drink.

Move! I scream to myself.

I stand abruptly, moving behind the chair. I need a barrier between us.

"You have ten days, Arianna. Then you'll belong to me." I crumble, all the air leaving my body. I lean forward and my knees give way.

"Be... belong to *you*? What do you mean?" A wave of sickness washes over me, making me dizzy. *They can't mean that...*

No.

They wouldn't.

"Let me spell it out for you, *princess*. In ten days' time, you and I will be officially married. Consider this our official engagement." I don't move, I don't react, I can't.

Robert steps forward, skimming his fingers down my cheek, making my skin crawl.

"Ten days and you're mine. Everything about you will be *mine.*"

Chapter Thirty-Two
Waiting

Cole

There are so many questions running through my mind right now, I don't know where to start. I need to hash this out with someone. I'd call Owen, but I can't speak freely here, not in judge-fucking-Byron's waiting room.

Why the hell would his own daughter need to book a meeting with him? Taking my phone from my pocket, I shoot a message to Dec.

Me: Everything alright out front?

Dec: Yep. All clear.

Me: Can I ask you something?

Dec: Sure, what is it?

Me: Why is she here today?

It's a shit thing to do, to ask him about it. I feel like I'm going behind her back, but I need to be prepared for whatever's happening in there, and for whatever happens when she comes out.

It won't be pretty.

Dec: I don't know. She didn't say.

Me: Tell me the truth.

Dec: Fuck.

Dec: Okay, she didn't tell me anything, but I was told by Gi that she wanted to ask her father for something. I don't know what. She didn't say.

Me: Have you passed this information on?

Dec: No, give me some credit.

So many more questions, I'll have to wait to see what I can find out. See if she'll tell me first.

Me: Why would she need to book a meeting with her dad?

Dec: Because he's a dick. He'd never see her otherwise.

I want to storm in there. My gut's telling me to. I know she needs me, but I don't want to put my nose where it doesn't belong. She asked me to wait here, so, I will. I need to remain calm. I can't help her if I get taken away by security.

Me: I have a lot questions right now, and I need some serious answers.

Dec: I'll answer anything you have.

Me: Leave, go to the office, tell Owen we need to hurry things up. That I have a gut feeling, and you need to spill your guts.

Dec: Okay.

Me: I mean it Dec. Anything you know, I want it.

Dec: Will you make sure she gets home safe?

Me: She's safer with me than without.

When the phone rings at the sour faced cows' desk a few minutes later, I listen in.

"Mr Bryon, sir." I only get half of the conversation, but it puts the fear of god into me, and I'm not a religious man.

"Of course. I'll call him down right away. If you don't mind me asking, is it finally time to put her in her place?" She laughs, fucking laughs at whatever has been said. It has to be about Ari. What are they planning for her?

Just for my own piece of mind, I take out my phone and add Cherry to my shit list, I'll confirm she's involved before I delete everything about her, she'll regret that day she got herself involved with fucking with my woman.

My woman. I like that.

My black suit seems fitting for the way today's panning out, dishing out hell is my favourite thing to do. Although, watching as it unfolds in front of eyes as chaos consumes them comes pretty close.

I'll take her back to the office when she's done here. There's no way I'm letting her out of my sight until I know what they have planned for her.

Sitting back, I watch as the three people approach: two security guards, and the fucker that likes to hurt my Ari. Not moving from my spot, I watch as Robert Carmichael enters the office while his goons stay stationed at the door.

Me: I need the footage of Byron's office now. Live. Feed it to my phone.

O: Shit, okay.

Me: Record it all. I want everything they say and do. Ari's in there alone with Byron and Carmichael.

O: Double fuck.

O: Done. Here's the link.

If Thomas Byron and Robert Carmichael think they are above the law, they have another thing coming. They've never seen me in action. Connecting my phone to my earpiece, I press the link and it takes a moment to open. I think I'm too late to hear anything, but I get Carmichael's last words to her as she sobs silently.

"Ten days and you're mine. Everything about you will be *mine*."

She turns and runs, a hand covering her mouth. Lifting my eyes to the door, I wait for Ari to come out, chasing her down when she runs past me.

Chapter Thirty-Three

Salvation

Arianna

What do I do?

My father thinks he's sealed my fate. Is he right? Ten days. Walking without true sight, my vision is too blurred to see where I'm going. One step in front of the other, needing to get as far away from them as possible. Running

I just had this feeling, a deep urge to flee, to save myself.

I'm not sure I can.

Ten days. Is no time at all.

My own father, laughing at me. Finding joy in something that will undoubtedly end me, or destroy me. My father has to know of Robert's past inflictions or the rumours at least.

My own flesh and blood is handing me over to ruin me. For what, money? A proposed marriage.

I can feel the wetness on my cheeks. I have no idea where I'm going. I'm stumbling, my feet unsteady. I don't see anything other than Robert's face. His words penetrate my skin... a cold sweat covers my body, leaving me clammy.

There's nothing 'proposed' about any of this. That would mean I have an option to step away, he's as heartless and cruel as they come.

If I stop, I may never get back up again. I need time to think, to... to.

"Fuck," I don't swear. Rule one from my parents: never swear. Swiping the tears from my cheeks, I keep going. I'm in a bubble I can't pop, voices around me, muffled, distant. I don't know where I'm going and I don't particularly care right now. I know one thing for sure: he's right next to me. Cole, I feel him keeping pace. Maybe if I focus on him, I can distract myself from the villainous deed my father has just bestowed upon me.

I'm nothing more than a transaction.

Covering my mouth with my hand, I try to contain the fear that's clawing at me. Closing my eyes for the briefest of seconds, more tears trickle down my face

I try to breathe in, get another lungful of air. Even if he's not touching me, his scent wraps around me, making my heart beat so loudly it's all I can hear alongside my descending thoughts.

What can we achieve in ten days?

Cole said he wants to help me, but I'm not sure now. What will happen to Gi if I don't do it? Will he hurt Chrisy? Will he fire Ed? Dec? All these people. Can I watch as their lives fall apart because I deny my father what he wants?

Hands grip me on the tops of my arms, stopping me from wherever I was heading. Forcefully spinning me around, the action so quick I have to brace myself on his chest.

"Ari, what the fuck are you doing?" I can't say anything, resting my forehead on his chest, breathing him in as I try to figure out what I can say to him. "You almost stepped into the road," he roars. I cry so hard into his shirt. I can't stop.

"Baby, you're scaring me." His hands move slowly up and down my arms. It's such an intimate movement; a touch I want to commit to memory for the moments of darkness I know will come when I have to marry Robert Carmichael.

What else can I do? Ten days is no time to form a plan and execute it. I can't risk the few people I care about. I've had the most beautiful peek of the world I could have had. A life with Cole, friends, freedom.

There's a saying: it's better to have loved and lost than never loved at all. I'll feel loss in my heart forever. For the love I could have had. I'm not sure it's better. Maybe more painful, knowing what could have been.

"You're shaking. What the fuck happened in that office, Ari? Tell me. Did they hurt you?" He's the only thing keeping me together, holding me up.

Looking up through blurred eyes, I shake my head in answer. How do I tell this man who's kept me safe, who listened, and cared, that my own father has just given me, no fucking *sold* me, to a man who will quite possibly end my life? How can I tell him that? I can't, can I?

Cole's head lowers to the top of mine as his lips brush my hair tenderly. "Ari?" he pleads, his arms holding me against him in an embrace so tight I sob harder.

"Cole," I whisper, "take me to the gallery." It's the only place I know no one will bother me.

"I will," he says, reassuring me, his arm sneaking around my back to guide me. "Baby, I know what he said before you left the room. What does he mean?" His hazel eyes are vying for information.

I can't remove my hands from his shirt. "You know?" I'm clinging on. I don't care. When his hand wraps around mine, I expect him to pull mine away. When he holds them in place, my breath catches.

"I need you to tell me everything. I'll find out anyway." Pausing, he waits for me to answer. Can I do this? Ask for help, I mean? He moves, taking me under one arm while taking his phone from his pocket and makes a call.

"We're heading out." His stern gazes meet mine. "The corner of Knights Street, yeah." There's a pause. "The gallery by the beach." I can only assume it's one of the guys on the other end. "Full detail. Twenty-four-seven. I want it all. She doesn't leave my sight." My heart swells. "I don't know yet." He only knows a fraction of the story and he's already willing to keep me by his side. My heart may be torn to pieces, but there's a part of it that this man is beginning to own and rebuild.

Cole pulls a set of keys from his pocket, guiding me towards a carpark. My footsteps echo off the concrete floor as we move. Looking around, I don't see his truck, only his motorbike.

He holds his hands out until I place my palm in his as he nods towards the bike.

"You ready for the ride of your life, Cupcake?" I nod, happy to get as far away as possible.

"Yeah, I am."

Cupping my face, he leans in, kissing the corner of my mouth before he places a helmet on my head and fastens it securely.

Within a few seconds, the rumble of the engine is purring between my legs as I straddle the bike behind Cole, my arms around his waist, holding tight.

Chapter Thirty-Four

Idiot

Cole

I never thought I'd have anyone on the back of my bike. I like to ride by myself. Always have. When Ari swung her leg over my bike, gliding her arms around my waist, it felt right.

She's resting her head against my back as we pull up at the gallery, her breathing steady like she's fallen asleep. Only her hands have been on me all the way, her fingers caressing my stomach. Ethan said he'd call and get them to let us in.

I stay seated when we pull up, watching as she removes the helmet, shaking her hair loose

Jesus-fucking-christ. This woman.

Swinging her leg back over the bike, like she's done it a thousand times, she smooths her pink trousers down.

"What?" I ask, curious as to what she's thinking as she looks at me.

"Nothing that can't wait until this conversation is over," she says seriously, stepping back

"Don't hold back baby, what are you thinking?" I never want to stop listening to her.

"Fine." Her neck flushes. "Now that I've ridden on the back of your bike, does this make me your old lady?" My eyes flare as my mouth hangs open.

"Come on," she says, as I get off the bike, I think she mistook my silence for shock. It's not. I'm not sure she's ready for the answer I want to give. Fuck, I'm not sure I am. Gulping down the honest answer, I knock on the door.

"Let's move, baby. You ready?"

"Nope." She's trying to joke, but the glimmer of playfulness disappears as her eyes shift back to the reason were really here. She looks devastated, lost almost. I make a promise to myself that I'll fix whatever this is.

"I guess I have to be, don't I?"

"I'm not leaving you," I say, stepping into her space, I hold her to me. She tucks her head under my chin as I kiss the top.

"You'll have to at some point," she says as the back door to the gallery opens, revealing Owen and Ethan standing there.

"We weren't expecting you," I say with a frown, as we pass through the door, making our way to the silent gallery floor. "We're all in, Cole. Tell us what you need," Owen says.

"If it's okay with you all, I'd like a few minutes on my own before I fill you in," Ari says, her head hung low. Ethan turns around stopping in front of a huge painting of a dancer. His eyes flicker to it. "Take however long you need, Miss Byron."

"I think that's the most you've ever spoken to me, Ethan." She smiles but it doesn't reach her eyes. "Also, could you please call me Ari?"

"Of course. Ari, it is." Ari's eyes trail over the paintings that cover the walls until she settles on one where the sun is shining on the greyest of sky's, highlighting the clouds. With a bench in front of it. She sits, staring at it. I crouch down in front of her, my hands on her knees, her sad eyes on mine.

"Do you want me to stay?" I want to take her away from all of this, run for the hills, and hide her away.

"I need a moment to get my head together. As long as your close, I'll be fine," She says, brushing my fingers over her calf.

"Sure thing, baby," I add, before kissing her softly on the cheek, I stand and leave her there.

In the back room Owen and Ethan are leaning against the wall waiting for me.

"What happened?" they ask together.

"Honestly, I have no idea." I shrug. "I got the call from Dec to say she was heading out and to meet her at the courthouse."

"The meeting wasn't planned?" Ethan asks.

"No, she had a free day, the only update I had was the extra hour in the gym this morning. Until Dec called, I checked and they'd slotted in this meeting. No other details, nothing. When I checked the cameras, she was already heading out the door."

"Was the footage recorded from his office?" I ask them. It'll help whatever happens next.

"Yeah, but we've not looked at it yet," Owen says. "I'm giving her the chance to tell me before I find out anyway," I whisper, running my hand down my face.

"That's decent of you, Cole." Ethan nods in agreement.

"All I was able to hear were a few words before she ran out the room." I've had them on repeat since she left his office.

"From who?" O asks.

"Carmichael." My jaw clenches. "He said '*Ten days and your mine. Everything about you will be mine.*'" They both go still.

"Shit, what's that supposed to mean?" I don't want to think about it.

"It can't mean anything good from what I've found of Carmichael. He's a real piece of work. I think he's linked with Hex, the PR firm. There's snippets of information, but nothing solid yet," Ethan adds.

"There's something we're missing here. None of this makes any sense. Why would Carmichael want to control Arianna? And why would Byron let him have so much control over his daughter?" I say, confused I pinch my nose, to try and stem my impending headache.

"Let's not get ahead of ourselves before we know the facts. It could mean anything. Ari could tell us something that makes it all make sense," Owen offers.

"O's right," I add. "No speculation. Whatever it means—"

"It means, in ten days times I'm his." Ari's soft voice shocks me. We all look at her standing in the doorway. "My father's found a better use for his problem." She points at herself.

I might actually kill this man if I have the chance, treating her like she's a problem. She's my fucking solution. "Effectively selling me to Robert Carmichael. Ten days, and I'll be his wife. He'll own every part of me." She's lifeless, all her spark gone.

Before she can say another word, I'm taking her in my arms. "Never, Cupcake. If you're going to be anyone's, you'll be mine." I don't care who's listening. Cupping her face, I kiss her fiercely. I want her to feel how certain I am.

Raising to the tips of her toes, she kisses me back. She's crying. I can feel the tears on my skin as they fall over my hand. Pulling back, I rest my forehead against hers, breathless. "He can't marry you, baby," I whisper.

"Cole, they have threatened everyone I love. Unless you can save them in the next ten days, I don't have another choice." Her voice wobbles. She thinks that's her only choice.

"Yes, you do." I know what I'm about to say is fucking bat shit crazy, but who cares.

"No, I don't," she says stepping away. Owen and Ethan remain silent, watching intently.

"I don't have many people in my life who care for me, Cole. I won't jeopardise their, or your, safety and happiness." There she goes again, looking after everyone else.

"It's my turn to look after you. There's one huge thing you're forgetting baby," She needs to learn we're here. She doesn't need to watch out for everyone on her own. "You're not alone anymore. You have us." she smiles through her tears, sagging against me.

"Cole, I—" I cut her off with another kiss, taking her by surprise. When we come up for air, I step back, my mind made up.

"He *can't* marry you..." Taking her hands from my chest, I hold them in mine. "If you marry *me* first."

There's a choking noise behind me, and Ethan makes a sound similar to a laugh.

"Oh my god, you're an idiot," she shouts, pushing me back and storming away. "You can't be serious. Do you think that would stop someone like *him*, Cole? That man hurts me any chance he gets. For years, he's put the fear of God into me, while my father watches it all happen." She folds forwards, hands braced on her knees. "He makes me sick. He won't stop until he gets what he wants."

"Even more reason to marry me," I say, striding over to her, pulling her up and back into my arms.

"Cole, what we have..."

"Don't you fucking-dare finish that." My teeth clench in frustration. "What we have is just starting, but I know you feel it just like I do, Ari. Don't give up, let us try. Marry me, be with me."

"You're being... I don't know, something. We can't do that. How will it stop him?" Ari says, her voice picking up a notch, like she's trying to process what I've just said.

"If you marry me..." Fuck, the more I say, the more I want it for a whole different reason. "He won't have a legal leg to stand on."

"He's right, Ari," Ethan admits, appearing out of the other room.

"Stop god-damn-smiling." I had no idea I was. "Be serious, please."

"I'm so fucking serious. I'll marry you now." Her eyes go wide. She's not said no.

She's not fucking said no.

"There's a twenty-eight-day notice that needs to be filed before you can do that." Owen chips in. "I checked when Charlie asked me." I glare at him and his unhelpful comment.

"See, your plan won't work." That won't stop me. She has no idea how good I am at what I do. I can make his notice disappear, and speed ours through.

"I'll file for the licence and backdate it."

Owen rolls his eyes. Ethan just grins, knowing full well I'll do it.

"I haven't said yes, yet," she shouts. Her eyes go wide, realising what she said. Holding her head in my hands, I kiss her forehead.

"You said yet. You want to marry me?" I almost split in two with happiness.

"Not like this, Cole. One day maybe. We've only just started seeing each other. I don't want to ruin what we have by putting this pressure on us." This makes me want it so much more.

"Let's make a deal then. Marry me tomorrow. And in ten days' time when all this is over, and you're free from your parents, and Carmichael. You can choose what we do. Stay married or get a divorce." Either way, I'm not giving her up. She's the only woman that lights me up. I want to see her thrive. And I'll be there.

"You'll let me do that." She can do anything she wants.

"Yep."

"You'll let me walk away if I need it, you'll let me leave."

"No. We can get divorced, but I'm not leaving you, I'm going with you. If you need to run, if you need to leave, I'm with you." A small smile creeps onto her lips.

Cupping Ari's face again with my hands, my thumb stroking the line of her jaw. I need an answer, so I stand still, waiting for my beautiful queen to realise just how serious I am about this, about us. I think I'll file for the notice anyway. Even if we don't get married straight away, it'll happen eventually.

She doesn't say anything. Just looks at me like I've lost my mind. For her, I think I have.

"What do you need, Ari?" I question when I can't stand the silence anymore.

"I need a night with you, away from all this."

"Then you'll marry me?"

"Then I'll think about it." That will do. In my mind she's already in a perfect dress, walking down the aisle towards me, flowers in hand, rings in the pockets of my best men, ready for me to place on her perfect finger.

"Okay. We have some planning to do. And two arseholes to take down." I smirk, and she actually laughs before I wipe the smile off her face by kissing the fuck out of her sweet lips.

Chapter Thirty-Five
Rash Decisions

Arianna

We made a plan, a good one actually. Between the four of us, it should work. It includes distractions, escape plans, and at least three different contingency plans. All so I can spend some time with Cole before I say yes to this stupid plan.

Of course I was going to say yes.

How could I not? He's the only man I have ever had in my life that's willing to care and not give a shit who knows about it.

He's willing to risk everything. *For me.*

All I've ever wanted was to be out of this house. Not necessarily on my own, but to have the freedom to have my thoughts, my own voice. It's exciting. I'm willing to try it with him.

Now I'm planning on sneaking back out of my house, through the balcony door of my bedroom. Opening the door, I'm immediately greeted by Gi, busying herself with a fresh delivery of flowers from Magnolias.

"Arianna." She hands me a package. "This came for you while you were out."

"Oh, it's my new book for my collection." She looks so worried, like she's waiting to see me with her own eyes, after my meeting with my father. They have no idea what I'm doing and I'm not telling them. They were worried something had happened at the meeting. I had so many missed calls from Gi when I finally left the gallery. I rang her back, keeping it simple and telling her it didn't go as planned. She and Ed had thought the worst when I didn't answer. It was careless of me to make her worry. I couldn't tell her the truth. I know I'll have to at some point, but not now.

"I'm glad you're okay, honey."

"Me too. Sorry Gi, it's been a bit of a day. I'm going to stay in my room tonight. I don't need dinner."

"I understand. You need some time. I'll see you in the morning. You can show me your new book." She taps the expertly wrapped package.

Stepping back into my room, I lock the door behind me, only to find Cole already there, waiting by the window. I force my hand over my mouth to stifle my yelp of surprise.

Walking towards me, a bag in his hand. His lips meet mine in a not so quick, knock your socks off kiss. "I've already packed for you," he murmurs. "I hope you don't mind."

"No, but let me just check you have everything." Placing the bag on my bed, I look inside, seeing joggers, a jumper, along with a hoodie and jeans for tomorrow. I like his choice. I'll be back before Gi comes into my room tomorrow morning.

"Why the pink lipstick?" I say, holding the offending item up between us.

"I have some wicked plans for you, that pink lipstick and my dick later." He grins, his eyes already darkening. "The filthy things I've imagined your lips doing, wearing that shade of pink." I have no idea how we managed to keep away from each other for so long. It feels near impossible right now.

"You forgot underwear."

"Nope, I don't think I did." That dimple makes an appearance when the right side of his mouth hitches up. "You won't be needing any sort of underwear for the next twenty-four hours."

"In that case, I won't be needing these." Removing my trousers, I shimmy out of my knickers and toss them at him before I walk to my closet. Coming out with a pair of leggings. I slip them on while he watches my every move, my underwear gripped in his hand.

"I'm getting quite the collection of your underwear, baby," he adds, putting them in his trouser pocket and patting it. "Ready?" he asks, taking the bag from the bed.

"Let's go," I add, chewing the inside of my cheek.

"Don't be nervous, baby. We have Ethan, Leon, and Owen watching out for us."

"I'm not nervous, Cole. I'm excited for my first night away from the house." Well, that's not accurate, I've spent time away from, my room, just never in a place I wanted to be, or willingly went to.

"Shit, I love it when you give me one of your firsts."

"Home-sweet-home," Cole announces. He's smiling. He has been since I let slip the 'yet' to marrying him. It must be infectious, but I can't hide mine either. It feels oddly normal stepping back into Cole's house. His *home.* Warm and cosy, such a deep contrast to the house I live in. Photo's scattered everywhere, ones of his unit in the army, ones of another man, I assume to be his dad. They have the same eyes and dirty blonde hair.

Smiling as I pass the images hung on the wall in the kitchen. A warm sense of relief descends as I know I'm safe here. We have a team of guys outside, as well as Leon, Owen and Ethan monitoring the cameras around us and at my father's estate.

"I've already ordered the food. It's on the way," Cole says, putting my bag at the bottom of the stairs and walking into the kitchen.

"What did you order? I'm starving."

"*Everything,*" he states. "I ordered everything. I don't know what you like. I've only ever seen you drink shakes and eat half a steak before it was taken away for you." I realise I know nothing about him. This is why I wanted this. I like him a lot, but marriage is another level, even if it is just to keep me safe for the time being.

Is this the right thing to do? Marry Cole?

I hate the thought of using Cole like this. It's even more foolish to think he could be doing it because he wants this, us, I mean. Another thing to ask him later I suppose.

"What have you ordered that will satisfy my *food* needs?" I joke, trying to ease his anger at my state of constant hunger.

"You'll see." He moves around the kitchen, getting me a glass of white wine from a bottle chilling in the fridge. Handing me the glass, he gets himself a bottle of water. I take a tentative sip, not really drinking it, but letting the flavour coat my lips. Licking my top lip, I catch him staring at me.

"Why do you do that? Drink but not really drink?" he says, dipping his head towards me.

"You noticed, huh?" I do it again out of habit, rolling my eyes at myself.

"I notice everything, Ari. The way you order food and never eat it. How you hold yourself back in every situation. You don't pass any sort of comment, positive or negative, you sit around others hoping they don't see you."

"You really have been watching."

Putting his water down, he nods, his body tense. "I fucking hate it, baby. Because I see you, Ari, every glorious inch of you." My breath hitches, and I take another fake sip of my wine. I've never felt more seen.

"How can you see me? I don't even know myself, Cole."

"In the moments you think no one's watching. You watch the freedom everyone else has like you crave it. Your face softens when you see something you love; it's all in your eyes. They shine just a little brighter. You're quick to hide it, but I see it." My hand grips the counter behind me.

I close my eyes, unable to see the look of endearment in his eyes. "You're fierce when you want something, and you don't even realise. I've seen that spark in your eye when you're out with Chrisy, when I've dragged you away. The fight you've hidden inside you. Fuck, I love it when you fight back." I can't help the smile that ghosts across my lips.

Turning from him, I feel him at my back before I can catch my breath. He doesn't say anymore. His presence fills me with comfort and hope. Feather-light hands grace my hips, urging me back against him.

"I want to be her, Cole. I'm just not sure how yet." It's honest. I've shut that part of me away for so long it scares me.

"You're already her, baby, you just need to let her out." What have I done in a past life to deserve this man?

"I don't really drink." I admit, placing my glass down. I open my eyes, turning in his arms.

"What does that mean?" he says, taking a step back, but his hands still linked behind my back.

"When I was fifteen, there was a small drama. Chrisy and I got caught drinking a bottle of Champagne in my room. She'd snuck it in." I smile at the memory before it fades. "My father found out, he..." *Be honest.* "... called me some truly horrible names, then backhanded me across the face in front of Chrisy."

Shuddering at the memory of the tears in Chrisy's eyes as she had to watch it happen.

"I haven't drunk since. Apart from that night at Praise. My parents found a travel board me and Chrisy made years ago. I'd hidden it, but one of the staff found it. It was childish, but was a hope of a future I wanted. He tore it up in front of my eyes. The following day, they flew to Venice. It was on the top of our board," I say sadly. "I told Chrisy I needed a night out, and well, I had a few drinks. You dragged me away, back to the house. My father found out when he came back. I spent the following days curled up in my room after he forced me to drink a bottle of vodka," I say. Cole looks like he wants to kill someone.

"Fucking hell, I'm so sorry that happened to you, Ari." His eyes soften through his anger. "I tried my best to cover you," he says solemnly.

"What do you mean, cover me?" His shoulder bunch up to his ears. "Cole?" Groaning, he turns around to face me. *He looks guilty.* Worrying his lip, he takes a sip of water.

"If you want a cup of tea or a soft drink I can change the wine," he mumbles, trying to change the subject. He reaches for the glass in my hand.

"Don't you dare. It tastes too nice," I say, slapping his hand away. "Cole," I demand.

Placing his glass on the side, he closes his eyes, before running his hands through his hair.

"I may have been able to take care of all of those outings." His demeanour changes. Shoving his hands in his trousers, he juts his chin out like he's proud, but also a little embarrassed.

"I was told to look after your reputation, so I did."

"Oh my god. Who asked you to do this?" I squeal.

"Ed, in not so many words."

Eyeing him, I can't get my head around it. "What did you do?"

"I permanently removed images and footage, sometimes from social media and websites. And sometimes from the little bastards' phones. Or cameras in person."

"Cole," I'm gaping at him, his skills are so much more *skilled* than I could ever imagine. "It's humiliating," I mumble, "they would even ask you to keep me away from meeting guys." My hand comes to cover my face, before I slide it down. My cheeks warm with embarrassment.

"No-one asked me to do that."

"I'm confused, Cole. Right now, I want to head back and have it out with Ed for asking you to do those things when he has no right." He crosses the kitchen in two strides, hovering over me.

"No one asked me to do that, Ari. That was all me." My breath catches. He's so close, all I can do is breathe him in. "Even then we had this chemistry, I knew I would piss you off whenever I turned up to get your fine ass back home." There's a flash of something in his eyes, like he regrets taking me there. "And fuck, I got off on seeing you take the bait." His lip raises and I burst out laughing, I can't hold back. The truth is, I do too.

His knuckles skate down my cheek, his thumb parts my lips, as his other hand slides over my lower back, pressing me against his hard chest and divine abs. My hands skim his back, feeling the bunched muscles beneath.

His lips take mine in a soft kiss that undoes me.

By the time the food arrives, we've both changed; me into a t-shirt and a cosy pair of fleecy joggers. When Cole came down in a pair of grey joggers, I think my knees buckled. I don't think there's anything he could wear that he doesn't look mouth-wateringly hot in. Suit. *Check.* Joggers. *Check, check, check.* Bin-bag, *more than likely. Check.* And yes, you can see it all, every fine swinging inch of him. Big, thick... I'm internally groaning at the sight of him. It makes me question if he's wearing boxers or if he's hanging free.

Hanging free, he has to be the way that things move down there.

I'm not ashamed to say I keep looking. Clenching my thighs together, imagining sliding them down, freeing his length, watching it *pop* free, and taking him in my mouth.

I'm so horny.

Jumping up from the sofa, he runs to the door. Oh yeah, the food. *God-damn grey joggers.*

Listening in, it sounds like Owens delivered the food.

"Who the fuck needs this much food?" I hear him say. "I've had to go to four different takeaways to get this shit, plus The Manor to grab the stuff from Marco. Who also said he's doing breakfast for you tomorrow."

"The man's a saint. His eggs benedict is to die for," Cole says, ignoring his friend's protests.

"Learn to cook," Owen scolds playfully. I laugh before I hear the door close, and Cole walks in with four large bags and two pizza boxes.

"I'll get the plates," I say, walking to the kitchen. Trying and failing to keep my eyes away from his crotch as we pass each other.

"No plates, just grab some forks," he says, smirking at me with a raised brow. *Damn*, caught red-handed.

The array of food we have is pure gluttony. I just stare at it for a while, my mouth watering as Cole watches me.

Lifting the first box, he places it in front of me, handing me a fork. I take a peek inside the box. "It's not going to bite, dig in," he says, tipping his head in the direction of all the food laid out on the coffee table.

I shouldn't be surprised the food is delicious. Our conversation flows from subject to subject. I tell him all about growing up and that Gi and Ed practically raised me. That without them, I don't know what I would have done.

"Same as my dad," he says. "He'd love you. I can see the two of you sitting on the patio over the summer just chatting about anything." His smile seems genuine.

"You can?" A blush creeps up my neck at the thought of meeting his dad.

"Yeah, I told you, baby, I want this," he says it so easily. Holding my breath as hope swells in every cell of my body, I lean into where we're sitting on the floor, and give him a quick kiss.

"Why are you doing this?" I want to know why he wants to marry me. I'm sure there are *many* other ways he can keep me safe; this seems to be a little... I don't know, outside of the box.

"What?" he frowns at me, placing a hand on my thigh.

"Wanting to marry me? I don't understand. You have all the right resources to help me without having to marry me in the process." I shrug, brushing my fingers over his. Looking at our connected hands, the spark I feel causing my heart to flutter in response, every time we touch, still takes my breath away.

"I don't know why. You gave me an idea when you joked about being my old lady, then you told me why you ran from the court building. I knew if I got there first, he couldn't marry you. That he'd *never* have a hold on you."

"Never?" I question, picking up on a single word. My chest squeezes as I wait for him to answer.

"Never." He smirks. "I just know it feels like the right thing to do." I wince. Am I just a job? Is that what he means? "I don't mean it as part of my job," I *really* think he can read my mind. "Yes, I want to protect you any way I can. But this," he pauses, kissing our interlinking fingers, his warm mouth scorching my skin, "us, feels right. I want this with you. I want to wake up every morning with you and know you're safe. And if getting married helps to secure your safety while we sort this stuff out, then it's not even a question I have to ask myself. I'll marry you now and keep you safe forever." *God-Damn-it.* I'm a puddle. Swallowing hard as I digest everything he's just said. I drop his hand, lean forward and kiss him.

"I want this too; you make me forget about what's to come."

"Is that a yes, Ari? You'll marry me?" Apprehension and excitement line his features.

"Mrs Grant has quite a ring to it, doesn't it?" I say between kissing him and straddling his legs. Cole groans, gripping my hips, holding me to him. *Definitely no boxers.*

"*My wife* sounds so much better," he says, that dimple coming back to tease me. I kiss his dimple before I stand up. Grabbing the hem of my top, I lift it over my head, dropping it beside me, showing him that I'm not wearing a bra. My nipples pebble when Cole eye fucks me from his place on the floor. When he licks his lips, I slip my hands inside my joggers, pushing them down and taking them off.

"Stunning baby, inside and out," he says, my breath hitching. As he stands and takes off his hoodie, my eyes travel the length of his torso. Each defined ab, like carved stone, wanting to be felt, each ridge hot to touch as I move my fingers over them. He's so beautiful, toned, tanned skin, rippled with muscle on muscle. I'm lost for words.

Hooking my thumbs inside his joggers, I slide them down over his hips, only I go with them, kneeling in front of him. His cock sits heavy, hard, and proud in front of me.

"Ari," he questions and I lick my lips in anticipation. I love how he says my name. Tracing my hands up his thick thighs, I take his dick in my hand, feeling the weight of him. He feels good. Stroking him up and down, I add a little twist at the end, moaning again when he lets out a groan.

"That's it, baby, just like that." His hands rest on my shoulders, only moving to cup my jaw when I look at him. His eyes are hooded, his breathing laboured. Hesitating for a moment, nerves flutter in my chest like a butterfly trying to escape, I want this, I want this for him. Flattening my tongue, I lick up his shaft before swiping my tongue over the tip where pre-cum beads at the top. Like a fever running through me, I shudder at his salty taste. He tastes so good. Wetness seeps from my core. I never want to stop. *I love it*. It's like taking a piece of him.

"Tell me..." he grunts out when I take him all the way to back of my throat, hollowing my cheeks, "I'm your first." He hisses as I move my tongue around his shaft, enjoying every second. I hum when his hands grip the nape of my neck, tugging on my hair. He pulls me back to get my answer.

"Yes," I pant, "only you." I want him back in my mouth more than anything. Fisting him again, I lick over the head of his cock, listening as he groans.

"Then where the fuck have you learnt how to do this?" Wrapping my lips around him, he's so big I have to use my hand; pumping him as I take him as far as I can. Gagging when he hits the back of my throat, I ease him out a fraction. His hand gripping my hair tighter. Breathing through my nose, I try to take him a little further, a tear making its way down my cheek.

"Fuck..." He swells in my mouth but doesn't come, eliciting a moan from me that makes him thrust his hips, making gag me when he hits the back of my throat. I moan again, I want him to lose it. My hand at the base of his cock twists as I move my mouth up and down his length, his hand guiding me. Sneaking my hand between his legs I cup his balls.

"Fuck, baby, I'm…" His hand in my hair tightens. It stings, but only makes me want more. As he thrusts again, the sheer pleasure he's taking from me makes me shudder, my thighs clenching harder, trying to get the release I need.

His moans excite me more than I ever thought they could. Doing this for a man. Not just any man, my soon to be husband. It's over all too soon. He pulls out of my mouth. I actually whine at the loss of him.

"You liked that, didn't you, baby? Did you make yourself nice and wet?" Gripping himself, I watch his hand move, rubbing himself in front of me.

"Yes," I whisper. Kneeling with me, his lips meet mine, his tongue seeking access, before he murmurs, "Spread your legs, baby." I open them as wide as I can, closing my eyes as his rough fingers brush over my slick folds. I quiver from his firm touch. I want to close my legs, but I want this more. I rub myself on his hand.

"Fuck, you loved sucking my cock, didn't you?"

"Loved it." I breathe. Pushing me back so I'm lying on the rug, Cole leans over me in all his naked glory, sinking two fingers deep inside me. Gasping at the intrusion, my back arches, needing more.

"Oh… Fuck." It feels too good. He's slow as he moves them, twisting until he reaches that bundle of nerves. My hips jolting when he curves his fingers, stroking the spot that set fireworks off inside me.

"Cole." His fingers are replaced with his length, sinking into me, filling so deep I clutch his shoulders for support. Kissing his way back up from collarbone to the column of my throat, he leaves a trail of sparks in his wake. He starts to move, deliberately slow as his soft lips graze my mouth.

"Open your eyes, baby. Good girl," he whispers, his forehead resting against mine. "Show me how fucking beautiful you are when you come." Every inch of him sparks more intense waves to course through me. Each movement has my thighs shaking and tightening around him. He's swelling inside me, kissing me like there's no tomorrow. Passionate, easy, *mine*. My soon to be husband.

"Fuck, Ari, baby." His hot breath skates over my skin and the moment he comes, I fall with him, savouring each thrust.

"Do you feel it, baby?" He pants his lips tracing a path along my jaw a few moments later.

"I feel you everywhere." I do, inside and out, my heart, my head, my body.

"There's nothing like coming deep inside you. God-damn perfect." We stay here, on the floor of his living room, content.

That's how I feel. *Happy.* He makes me happy.

Chapter Thirty-Six

Dotted

Arianna

"What are you doing?" Looking down at myself, I think it's pretty obvious what I'm doing.

"It's pretty obvious," I say, looking around. "I'm in your gym. My tops sticking to me, I have a five kg weight in my hand," I say, sarcastically as I sit up from the mat on the floor, placing the weight next to me.

"I know you're working out. I just don't understand why?" He looks so confused.

"It's part of my routine. I do this every morning." Sighing, he comes and sits in front of me in his perfectly fitted dark grey suit. Legs bent, arms draped around them.

"It used to be part of your routine," he says, rolling his lips between his teeth. "Make a new one to stay in bed."

"Stay in bed?" It's a new concept to me. I don't remember a day I've stayed in bed. I wake up, never wanting to get out of bed, but I always do. Wake up, get up, workout.

"I'll even bring you herbal tea that you can *drink* in bed." I'm liking the sound of this more and more.

"Can I watch a film in bed?" I'm wiggling where I'm sitting with excitement.

"Baby, you can do whatever you want." Not really, not yet, I can't. I don't say that though. I don't want to ruin this.

"I want to get back into bed and have a do-over. Join me?"

"Tomorrow. Today, Cupcake, I get to marry you." He drops his gaze, making me wonder if he regrets that he asked me already.

"Today?" I panic. It's all happening so fast.

"Yes," he says weirdly. "*Technically…*" He looks nervous. "I did something. I should have asked you, or maybe involved you, as it involves you." Pushing himself from the floor, he holds out his hand, helping me up.

"Technically, what?" I ask suspiciously as I grab my water, taking a long sip.

"Technically, you're already my wife." My water sprays everywhere. Shock, hurt and excitement buzz through me. Choking back a cough, I wipe my face, watching him for any signs he's taking the piss.

"Say something, please." It's odd isn't it. I love fighting with Cole, more than anything. It sparks life in me. But this… actually hurts, and I don't want to say a word, nothing.

"Uh…"

"I need more than a sound, Cupcake." He breaths out, reaching for me

"I honestly thought I would be part of my own wedding, Cole." I'm gutted, rubbing my chest where it aches.

"Shit," he curses. I turn, ignoring his hand.

"Yeah, shit. You fucked up." Walking away, I slam the door behind me. How could he take that away from me? "How could we get married without *me*?"

Oh my god, is this how my life is supposed to go? Everyone making decisions for me? I don't know how he did it, and I don't want to know. Not yet anyway.

"Ari, please," he begs, coming through the door behind me.

"No," I shout, pushing his hands away as he reaches me again. "How does that make you any better than them? You took that away from me. Like everything else in my life, you took that decision away from me."

"I never thought, baby." No one ever thinks about what I want.

"Obviously," I yell in his face, tears stinging my eyes. Fuck, this anger simmering through me. I don't know what to do with it. I'm crying, releasing the overwhelm I feel.

"Did you even consider how it would make me feel, doing that without me?" I don't give him time to answer. "Fuck, Cole, I was excited to sign that certificate with you. *With You.*" I jab my finger into his chest. I knew I wouldn't be having a full wedding. I was happy to take what I could. *With him.*

I storm away up the stairs, locking the bathroom door behind me before I strip off my sweat-soaked clothes. "Ari, open the door," he says as I turn on the shower to drown him out.

I don't answer him as I step in. The noise fades away as I wash my hair. Either he's gone, or waiting. Either way, I'm not in any rush to face him right now.

How could he think I'd want it to happen like that? He took my *choice* away from me. I'm fuming. Placing my head against the tiles, I let my tears flow, watching as they wash away. Unseen.

The thought of being his wife. The way he said those two words. *My wife.* It sent a thrill right along my spine. I like it. Shit, I really liked it.

Staying in the shower longer than necessary, I wash my hair, exfoliate, and shave everything using his razor. I want my anger to deflate before I step out of this room.

Whatever reasons he has for doing it like that. I need to make him see that going behind my back without getting into an argument.

Mrs Grant. A little laugh floats to the surface, escaping before I can realise. It does sound nice. I want to be the strong, independent woman who keeps her name, but I hate my last name. It's a reminder of the family that hates me. It's a decision I'll proudly announce to the world that I'm a Grant and no longer a Byron.

When did you decide you were staying married to him? Standing still for a moment, I drop the razor onto the shelf beside me. Is that what I want?

Yes.

For real? Like a proper marriage?

Yes.

Maybe it's some sort of Stockholm syndrome. If you think you have it, do you have it or are you just trying to place the absurdity of the situation onto something? I have no idea.

I think I'll go with it. Not the Stockholm thing. I mean, I love him.

I love him.

I know that deep down in my bones. This would be the natural next step anyway. I should have had this conversation with myself before I said yes.

The answer's still yes.

What else do you want from your life Ari? Well, that's a looming question I have absolutely no intention of answering now. That's a sit down with a notepad kind of thing.

Opening the shower door, I step out, taking a towel from the heated rail. I wrap it around me, before wrapping a smaller one around my hair. Wiping the mirror to see myself, I take a breath in, I can do this, I mouth to myself. My hands shake as I reach for the lock and click it open, opening the door. I'm scared, not from fear, but from what my future could hold when I walk out this door.

It's all open to me. I just need to make the leap.

When I step out, Cole leaps from the floor like he's been waiting for me. Giving him a small smile, I walk to him.

"I'm sorry. Really fucking sorry. I'm an arsehole. I just…"

"You just what, Cole?" I seethe, lifting my hand to gesture my annoyance.

"I just got excited when you said yes." His whole body radiates just how excited he is and how sorry he is. "When you fell asleep in my arms, I knew I wanted to make it official. I wanted you to be my wife, Cupcake." Damn, he looks cute when he's worried.

"I have so many people that run my life, Cole. I wanted the start of ours to be different."

"Wanted." Instantly his eyes widen like I've hurt him.

"No, yes, actually. I wanted it to start out on a better footing than the rest of my life has. I wanted some control. And you took it *away* from me. What it doesn't change is the fact I still want to be your wife."

"But... wait, you still want this?" He looks so hopeful that I can't help but grin at him, tugging him by his tie to come a little closer.

"Yes. I want this. I want you to be my husband. But from here on out, *husband,* you will run every damn decision past me, whether you think you should or not." He leans into my space.

"Anything you want, baby. Does this also mean you want to stay married to me, even after the nine days is up?"

"Even after the nine days are up." I sigh, giving him my best eye roll.

I'm still not talking to him. Okay, only when I have to. As much as I want this marriage, as much as *he* knows I want this, I can't let him think I'll let this go so easily. He married us without me being a part of it, it's a huge failure on his part, he knows it. I just need time to stop being angry with his poor decision making. Even if he was over excited about marrying me.

I had to sneak out the same way I snuck in last night, creeping back into my room from the balcony before Gi had any clue I was missing. I was a nervous wreck, wondering what would be waiting for me.

Coming back out through the front door this time, on my way back out, fully changed into a pair of wide-leg trousers and a fitted jumper, green shake in hand courtesy of Gi, I find the car waiting for me. Only it's not Dec in the driver's seat, it's Leon as we make our way for deception two. One was my overnight stay. Maybe it's three, although I didn't know about the photo shoot at the time.

"What is that you have in your hand. It looks revolting," Leon asks as soon as the partition comes all the way down.

"My breakfast." I grimace, holding it up to get a better view of the bright green drink.

"No, this is your breakfast." Slowing down slightly, he hands me a bag.

"What's in here?" I ask as I open it.

"Avocado, bacon, and egg bagel. Coffee, and a herbal tea in the holder."

"Oh, my god. This is all for me?" I squeal. I'm so hungry.

"Absolutely. I had instructions this morning before I picked you up." Cole, no doubt, thinking of me. Maybe I can forgive him a little just for arranging breakfast.

"I can't remember the last time I had bacon or a bagel, come to think of it." My first bite tastes sensational. Crispy, smooth, delicious carbs. Moaning, I take a second mouthful. I think it may be the best thing I've put in my mouth in a long time. I grin when I remember what else I had in my mouth last night. Equally just as salivating, I let out another moan for a completely different reason.

"Are you two okay in the back there?" Chuckling at his comment, I almost choke. Leon pulls into the underground garage at Cerberus' building. "Do you need a minute to compose yourself?" Licking my fingers, I mock glare at him before he gets out.

Shifting to the other side of the car, I open the door to see Cole pull up on his bike. That sight will never get old. Boots, leathers, bike. The way he takes his helmet off, then runs his fingers through his hair. *Fuck.* I can feel the damp patch in my knickers already. It's only when he unzips his jacket and shows off his shirt and tie that I melt.

"Who's better? The bagel or Cole? Because right now I can't tell from the noises you're making." Leon's voice penetrates my visual, and I burst out laughing. Cole scrunches his eyebrows, not hearing Leon's comment.

"If you we were to put them together so I could eat them at the same time, then... *Boom.*" I laugh, using my hands to mimic the explosion. "Perfection."

Leon's belly laugh echoes through the small parking area. I think I like making Leon laugh.

"What's that about?" Cole asks when he reaches us.

"Your *wife* shocking the shit out of me, that's what." He called me Cole's wife. It's the first time someone else has referred to me as it, and I have to suck in a breath to calm my nervous excitement.

"Just telling the big guy how I'd like to eat you and the bagel at the same time," I say, walking away from him towards the elevator.

"*Cupcake,*" he groans. "You can't say shit like that to him. We'll never hear the end of it." I don't look, but I know he's behind me.

"I'm still not officially talking to you," I say, pressing the button as Cole swipes his card over the box thingy. I assume it's a safety thing.

"Trouble already?" Leon asks as we all step in and the doors slide closed, shutting us in.

"No," Cole says as I harrumph at him.

"What did he do?" Leon asks, leaning against the wall. He looks so imposing in the small space. Cole's hand sweeps down my back before tugging on my jumper, making me look up to him.

"Oh, this genius," I say, "decided to marry us without me."

"Yes, fine, we've already aired our shit. I should have included you. Sorry again, for the millionth time." He bends down, kissing my cheek and I poke his side again. "Ari still wants to be married, thank fuck. We're good." His hand trails up my back this time, just as we reach the office floor.

"We are good, but I'm still annoyed at you for it." I huff as he tugs on my hair this time.

"In that case, let me be the first to congratulate you guys on becoming husband and wife." We both look at each other and smile. Who am I kidding? I've forgiven him already.

Walking into the space where Cole works is like stepping into some kind of military operation. There are screens and gadgets everywhere. The back wall is covered with monitors displaying different things. I just stand, staring for a moment before Cole hugs me from behind.

"This is the system we use, the one that Owen and I built. We use it to monitor, find, and trace people and information." His finger toys with the button on my trousers.

"Wow, this is amazing. Is this how you married us?"

"Yes. I drew up the paperwork, then sent it over to a friend of mine to have approved."

"Don't they need witnesses or something?"

"Yes, I also added Leon and Chrisy's signatures to the certificate, along with yours and mine. I made the circumstances very pressing, with an incentive, so they couldn't resist." I don't want to know any more. I also kind of wish I hadn't asked.

"Okay. My best friend will be *thrilled* she missed my wedding." I sigh, "Have you looked me up on this thing?" I glance back at him when he tenses and doesn't say anything. "You're giving me the same look you did this morning when you told me I was already your wife. I'm not going to like the answer, am I?" I say, taking a step forward, out of his embrace.

"No, you're not. Full disclosure. I know everything about your life." Sinking down into the huge chair on wheels, I lay my face on the table. I'm not ready to deal with this. Closing my eyes, I count to five, letting the information sink in. Cole rubs my back, trying to soothe me.

"Sorry, baby," he adds.

"No, you're not," I counter.

"You're right, I'm not, but only for all the right reasons," he says when I shoot him a look.

"The right reasons? You think looking into my life, knowing everything about me without me knowing is okay? Just how much do you know?" I lift my head from the desk. It's kind of nice that he cares so much. I get why he's done it, but ask me. Don't do it behind my back.

"It might be easier to tell you want I don't know." My stomach sinks. "Holy shit."

It takes me a full thirty minutes to gather myself after that, not really believing he could know everything about me, until he showed me my file. Yes, I have my very own file. And it's a pretty big one. I walked out the room, leaving him in there.

I'm not sure I can cope with all this. I will, but I'm finding it hard.

Walking past Leon in their lunch room, after I've snagged my third cup of coffee, he takes me to one side. "Everything okay?"

"Define, okay? Because right now, that bagel is looking better and better."

"He's told you he knows everything?" he asks, making himself a coffee. Tears fill my eyes.

"Oh my god, you know too? Oh, my god, do you all know everything about me?" I feel so stupid. Embarrassed even, that these men know my secrets. It's like they're reading my diary; I don't like the feeling that comes with it.

"Sorry, it's part of what makes us good at what we do. Cole started looking because he was concerned about your safety... he can become a little too focused sometimes. Especially when it's someone he cares about." Guilt trip.

"Right, I guess I can't be angry at that, can I." I'm starting to worry even more for their safety. If they find anything on Robert or my father, the more it could swing back in their face. Especially with Cole hacking into the house and The Manor.

"Not really. Has he told you what we have on Carmichael yet?" Leon says, breaking my thoughts.

"No, I needed a few minutes after he showed me my file." This is a lot. One day, marriage, secrets and files baring all.

"Ah, understandable. Shall we? We only have you for another hour before your next real meeting." It's easy to forget I still need to be who I'm expected to be when you have these people around you. I guess it couldn't last forever. Leon points to a large table next door where a woman is setting out cakes and more coffee as we walk over. "This is Jill, our office manager."

I extend my hand. "It's nice to meet you, Jill." She shakes it.

"Likewise," she says before she leaves Cole, and Owen walk in. Cole takes a seat next to me, while Owen sits with Leon across the table.

The huge screen flares to life, and I watch as information on my father, Robert and me appears just as Ethan strolls in, taking a seat by Leon.

"Arianna," Owen offers, breaking my stare. "What we have found on Carmichael will send him away for a long time." Sitting up straighter, I listen harder. "He's been bribing judges, mayors, high ups in the police for a while, which is why he's managed to get away with so much. We can put him away for the murder of his first wife and the attempted murder of his second. There are other charges that will be brought against him by other women. He'll go away for a long time." I'm frozen at this info overload.

"You've done all that in a few days?" I ask, gawking at the four of them.

"Cole's done all that in a few days, Arianna," Owen admits. I take Cole's hand in mine under the table, our fingers link together, and I relax a little when he gives me a reassuring nod.

"That's a lot to take in. So, the rumours are true?" *Oh my god, the rumours are true.*

"Yes. He's good at covering his tracks, but I'm better at uncovering them." Cole gives me a sad smile.

"When will he be arrested?"

"We have to wait." Not what I wanted to hear, my shoulders sag. "All the information has gone to a contact of ours. They're compiling the case their end before they can arrest him, but it should be soon. These guys don't hang around." Right. I nod at Ethan.

"What about my father? What will happen to him and my mother?"

"We still need a little more info on him. He's up to something. We just can't prove what, yet." I don't know what I was expecting to hear, but that wasn't it.

"One's better than none, right?" I chip in, touching my temple, a tension headache coming on from all of this.

"We will get him, Ari." Cole's thumb grazes the skin on the inside of my wrist reassuringly as he speaks. "We have a lot of things in place already, some of which we'll need you to sign so we can get your assets back to you."

"My assets? I have nothing." It's not strictly true, but what I have, I give away, pay back money I know my father has taken from people.

"You have, or will have, everything, Ari. Your father may take your money, but he's not smart about it. He just takes it from your account. Directly to his. That's stealing. We'll have him arrested for that." This is really happening. My stomach churns with excitement and worry. I'm picking at the skin on my fingers, when Cole lifts our interlaced fingers, stopping me with a kiss to the back of my hand.

"This must be costing you a fortune," I say, looking around the table. They all frown at the same time. "Look, um, I'll pay you any extra for this. I don't want you charging this to Gi and Ed. I'm already repaying them back for the security you've been providing. They can't afford anymore. After I've paid Millie back some of the cost for the photoshoot," I wince, mentally calculating my allowance, "it doesn't leave me with a lot." Nothing, actually. "But I'll work something out. I won't leave you out of pocket."

"You won't be charged." They all say in varying forms.

"Yes, I will be. Send the bill to my new phone I'll have the money as soon as I can." I don't leave room for any more arguments. "What else do you need from me?"

"Baby, you'll never get a bill" Cole leans into me. "You're my wife now. That means something around here." The bubble in my chest grows, reminding me I have him now. Looking up I get similar looks from the others.

"Okay," I say nervously. I'll find a way to pay them back. "Do you need anything from me?"

"We just need you to be their version of you for a little while longer," Leon tells me.

"That's not hard to do. I've had a lifetime's worth of practice." I shrug, earning a growl from Cole.

"It'll be over soon, baby." I don't give an answer. I'm not sure I'll believe it until I see it. I've lived this life too long to live on hope.

Chapter Thirty-Seven

Like This

Cole

Seeing her like this, dressed up in a bright Teal dress that I know she feels uncomfortable in spikes my anger. Clenching my fist at my side, I move with her. Tonight, I'm by her side, and I don't plan on leaving it. Not even if she needs to take a piss. I'll wait outside the door. I know they plan to be here, her father and Carmichael. They won't get near her if I have my way.

Ari's still having to act like she's one of them because I can't find what I need. This is all my fault. I'm desperate for just a nugget of information on her father. Something I can roll with. Something I can pin him for life for. Stealing her money won't be enough. With his connections, I doubt he'd get a slap on the wrist.

The contrast between who she is now and who she was last night is startling. Today she owns the room, dressed for someone else, cool, calm, tense, on edge, scared. Last night dressed in joggers, an oversized t-shirt, hair in a plait over her shoulder, free, relaxed, and laughing. She cried with happy tears when I mentioned my first pet, Titty, I was three and couldn't say Kitty, and again with me when I told her it was a goldfish.

My wife was intoxicating.

This version of her, the forced version she's been for most of her life, is still intoxicating, but only because I've seen the real Ari. She's strong enough to endure this while she preserves her beauty underneath. She works the room like a fucking pro.

Looking over the crowd, I spot a familiar figure walking towards us.

"What the hell?" Stalling my steps, I have to take another look. I never expected this. How could I? My blood runs cold as my mother walks towards us, her dress, extravagant; a little too over the top for this place. Even I can see that. She's here to impress. Pressing my ear piece, signalling Owen and Ethan to keep eyes on us, I reach for Ari, who's been listening to some reality tv star chat shit about fuck all. She looks back, but I don't have a time to warn Ari of Tanya's approach, or warn her who she is to me, before my mother leaps.

"Arianna, darling," she coos, watching me as she tries to air kiss my wife. Ari has other ideas. Smiling sweetly, she avoids my mother.

"My apologies, but do I know you?" Ari says, stepping to my side, my mother looks perplexed.

"Not directly, of course, but—"

"Miss Byron," Ari's eyes flare at me for using her old name. What I want to call her, I can't: *Mrs Grant, my wife,* not yet anyway, not out loud. There will be a perfect moment for that, and I'll take it. "This is my mother." I don't make any more introductions. I told Ari all about her.

"Right, your mother. It's a pleasure to meet you." She smiles sweetly, but it doesn't reach her eyes. My stunning wife takes a step closer to me. *She's looking out for me, the way she's angled herself between me and Tanya, not blocking me, but fuck.*

"I hear you know, Mr Carmichael. I'd love to meet him." She doesn't pause for breath. "Do you think you could introduce me?"

"Mrs? I'm sorry, I don't know your last name," Ari says.

"Stevens, Tanya." She holds out her hand, expecting Ari to take it, but she doesn't. I bite my tongue to stop myself from smiling. Instead, Ari lowers her voice so only the three of us can hear.

"I hear that he's recently engaged, *Mrs* Stevens. But did you hear the rumour of what he did to his poor last wife or wives, I should say?" My mother looks annoyed at the insinuation, but listens anyway.

"They're just rumours, darling. You can't believe everything you hear." She tries to wave it off.

"Yet, he is a close personal friend of my father's. Would you be willing to risk it?" *Fuck me, she's good.*

"Still, you never know, do you? He may be open to meeting someone new." Tunnel vision, that is what my mother has. There's not a flicker on Ari's face; she remains impassive.

"Let me ask you this," Ari says, glancing around the room. "When was the last time you saw his wife? Or ex-wife, or the one before her? Can you divorce a dead woman?" her eyes flick to mine, gauging my reaction. I'm shocked as fuck at the way she's handling her. Putting her in her place but giving her a clear warning to stay as far away as possible. "Ask your son," she says, knowing full well we're putting a case together on him.

"She's right, Tanya, you should stay away," I add, my heart pounding in my chest at the woman standing beside me taking my side. *Fuck.* I want to take her into a private room right now and show her just how much I love this side of her. Even with so much at risk right now, she's willing to stand up and say something.

I love her.

It's not a shock, just a warming feeling throughout my heart, chest, fuck my entire body. I'm never letting her go.

Tanya doesn't say another word, just tuts and walks away. Hopefully out of this building and back to her husband. Poor bastard.

"Interesting mother you have there *Mr Grant.*" Oh shit.

"Don't be pissed, I had to," I whisper as she spins around, continuing her walk of the room. After a few minutes, I watch her shoulder sag, turning towards me, she places her hand gently on my arm, enough to get my attention. The corner of her mouth lifts in a gentle smile, showing me she's still there. Even if just for a split second.

"I want to be back in your living room," she murmurs.

"Later, baby. I'll have you out of that dress before we make it back through my door," I say, scanning the room in front of us. She's stayed in my bed every night since she gave me the news her father had essentially sold her.

Between me, Leon, Ethan, and Owen, we sneak her out every night and back in every morning have eyes on her twenty-four-seven, unless she's in her room. There are no cameras in there. Just me as soon as the door closes and locks behind her.

It seems I wanted Ari the day I met her, only she represented all the things I hated. I thought she was like Tanya, my mom. I made excuses for my action towards her, ripping her away from others. Fuck, it felt good pissing her off, seeing the anger in her eyes. Only I hated it when it faded and she made no argument to fight back.

It killed me.

So, I did it more. I craved her reaction. I wanted her anger, all while denying the real reason I wanted it. I could see deep down she wasn't herself. I fucking knew she was hiding something. It guts me I didn't dig into her past, or her life further. That while I waited, she was going through so much. On her fucking own, while I watched and judged. I'll make it up to her. She hid what was happening to help those she loved.

She's the queen of veils.

The queen of indifference.

The queen of keeping her darkest secret, only letting people see who they want her to be, not the person she is and has never been able to be.

Controlled, used, abused, and sold by people who are supposed to love her. Her parents are the ones responsible for the darkest moments of her life. I stood by and watched the illusion she set in place.

I've not told her yet, but she has no reason to worry about the people who love her anymore.

I'm here now, and now I know everything. I'll make sure she's safe to be herself. She'll have the freedom to do whatever she wants without judgment.

I can't wait to see her grow.

But this is so much more than protecting her; I want to be around her. I want to make her smile. I want her in my bed every night. I want to spread her legs and watch her come like the fucking queen she is. I want to be the only one to ever do those things.

It doesn't freak me out like I thought it would.

Love.

She stops walking abruptly. Halting my thoughts, a chill runs up my spine when I see why she's stopped. Her father and Carmichael stand side by side, drinks in hand. It's the first time she's seen them since she ran from his office three days ago.

Seven days to go.

"Don't go over there," I plead from behind her. I know she has to. Owen echo's in my ear, telling me to keep it together. I will. I nod, knowing he can see me from the balcony above us.

"I have to, Cole."

"I know, doesn't mean I have to like it."

Ari's arm moves behind her back. I glance down, she needs me. Her hand opens wide, as she flexes her fingers. I graze her palm with my finger, feeling her warm skin on mine. I watch the way her hand curls around my finger, holding it like she also needs the contact and reassurance. "I'm here," I whisper, and her shoulders relax a fraction before I let go of our connection.

A moment just for us in this crowded room.

"Father, Mr Carmichael." Ari greets them with a cool tone when she approaches the two men I hate most in this world. Robert looks over his shoulder at her, while her father makes no move to greet her back. Ari stands tall as she waits for one of them to speak.

"I think we can be a little more intimate in our greeting towards each other, Arianna." Carmichael conveys, talking to her cleavage, and I want to take him down right now... gouge his eyes out, and make him choke on them for even looking at my wife. I don't want to wait.

Seven days. It's like an echo. I hear it from Ethan in my ear as it rattles around my head. It's too long. We'll have it all in place, the fuckers going down. They both are.

"I don't think so, Mr Carmichael. That would be impolite of me." Ari's tone is icy but sweet as she delivers it. I have to bite my tongue for the second time tonight as my cheeks twitch while I hold back the smirk threatening to rise.

"Seven days, Arianna. What do you think will happen in seven days, when your take on this life changes forever?" He sneers, and it raises the hackles on my neck. I notice Owen in my peripheral. He must have come downstairs. Ethan flanking him on the other side.

Remaining still at my wife's side, I mentally go through anything else I can pin on them. They have no idea the world of pain he's in for. Yesterday, we managed to record, and find old footage, from his office cameras. Everything he's said in his office where he thinks he's safe from prosecution and prying eyes. That right now documents are being drawn to—

"Oh, Mr Carmichael. My take in this life will never change." Fuck, she's fire, my cock stirs at her feisty side, I love seeing her like this. Even with the mask firmly in place, she's letting them see her. I love it.

I love her.

"Father, *Mr Carmichael.* If you'll excuse me, I need to make the rounds." Her father moves, stepping in front of her, half blocking her path while he takes her arm in a firm grip, like he wants to remind her who's she's meant to be. I tense, my hand on his arm, gripping his wrist so hard he winces. His eyes flick to me before letting go.

"Try not to make a scene, Father. I'd hate for everyone to know that you just sold your only beloved daughter to a monster. How much did he pay you?" He lets out an angry grunt in a warning. "How would that look to all your constituents?" His eyes go wide. Irritation written all over his pale face. Fuck, I'm so proud right now.

I'm fighting not to laugh, shoving my hands in my pockets, before I take her in my arms, and kiss the ever-loving-fuck out of her.

"If you want this to go ahead," she gestures towards Carmichael, "without so much as a word to the press for the next seven days, I recommend you leave me alone. I'll do as you *asked* if you let me have the week," and the rest of her life, "then I'm all his." Never going to fucking happen. "And your little campaign will be safe."

Campaign?

"Fucking bitch." Carmichael says under his breath. "Just you wait," he seethes. Knowing he can't say shit here, he leaves her alone with her father.

"Seven days, and I'll be rid of you," he says. "You'll regret ever making a demand on me. I'll make sure of it."

"I won't regret anything. Be sure to cancel everything on my schedule for the next seven days. I won't be showing up to anything." She walks away, leaving her father behind in a fit of rage he can barely conceal.

Owen and Ethan mutter that they have eyes on both Thomas and Carmichael as Ari steams ahead. "Ready to leave?" I ask, walking into the hallway behind her. She looks tense as we retrieve her coat from the clerk.

"I'm so sorry." I'm taken aback. She looks ready to burst into tears. "I've ruined everything." Her hands fly to her face, covering her turmoil. "What have I done?"

"Come with me" Taking her hand in mine, not caring who sees, I pull her towards a room. Closing the door behind me, I watch as a single tear slips from her lashes.

"Ari, what you just did—"

"I know, I'm sorry, I'm so sorry. I don't know what came over me. I saw the way he looked at me and I wanted to be sick." She shivers at the thought. "I just thought, fuck you, you know, if I only have seven days, then they're going to be the best fucking seven days I've ever had." Her arms reach out wide.

"Baby, that was—"

"Stupid, reckless, oh my god what have I—" I cut her off this time.

"Baby, shit, it's—"

"What have I done, Gi, what if he deports her, I feel sick. Dec, he could fire Dec, he could lose everything, he's saving for his house. And Ed, oh no, Ed has no life outside of Gi, if she goes, then, then, I don't know—"

"Stop," I bark. Backing her against the wall, I grip her cheeks in my hand. "Don't," I say before taking her mouth in a rough kiss. "Seeing you like that, being you. Fuck, baby. It was everything. The people you love are already taken care of." Her hands slam against my chest, in an attempt to move me, but I don't budge.

"What?" Her eyes search mine for answers.

"From the minute you told me, I had them covered. They can't do shit to hurt them, baby," I murmur, tilting her head to the side to get better access to the delicate skin on her neck.

I hear a quiet 'Oh' as I lick her clavicle over the material of her dress. Reaching for the hem of her dress, I've never been so desperate to have someone like I do now with her. The soft fabric bunches around her waist, finding her thong drenched when I hold her heat in my hand. Pressing firmly on her clit, she whimpers.

"That was the fucking hottest thing I have ever seen, baby." Moving her thong to the side, I slid my fingers through her folds, pushing two fingers inside her, she groans, bucking her hips into my hand.

I want her to be proud of how she acted today. I'll show her just how fucking good it will feel.

"You loved every second of it didn't you?"

"Yes, sir." I almost come in my briefs. Thrusting my fingers harder, I hook them, swiping across her sensitive spot, making her buck her hips, again. "Cole," she gasps, sucking in a breath.

"You're fucking drenched, baby." I groan, looking down between us. She follows my gaze. "Look at how well my wife takes my fingers." Easing them out and back in again, I take it slow, breathing her in as she whimpers. The room's bathed in a dim light, and fuck, the look on her face says it all. She loves this just as much as I do.

"Look what happens when you stand up for yourself. It feels so fucking good, doesn't it?" Sinking my fingers further, she whimpers. Her legs clench together, gripping my hand like a vice as I brush over her clit with my thumb. She starts to shake. I love watching her rise, just as much as I love watching her fall.

"Yes," she screams as I pump my fingers in and out of her, faster this time. She's close; fluttering around my fingers. I curl them and suck on the sweet spot along her collarbone.

I feel her tense around me, her leg rising around my waist. She starts to come undone. The pleasure I feel just to be able to watch her; it's a fucking honour.

Her head falls back against the wall, her dark silky hair spilling over her shoulder as her tight bun unravels. Her lips part when I press against her clit. "Cole," she screams.

"Say it again." I breathe into her neck, my cock so hard it's painful against the zipper of my trousers.

"Cole," she whimpers. Looking into her eyes, I see the moment she crashes. Her breathing falters. Her beautiful, dark eyes roll back as a flood of arousal coats my palm.

"Fuck, baby." I undo my belt and zipper with a speed that could defy laws. Ari's still lost in the fall of her orgasm, as I push my trousers down, freeing my cock. Reaching for me, I bat her hand away. "If you touch me, baby. I'm going to come all over your pretty dress, and we still have to walk out here." Backing her up against the wall once more, she grinds her pussy into me. Fisting her thong in my hand, in a fierce tug, the fabric tears and I place them in my pocket. Pressing my cock up at her warm soaked entrance, I don't wait. I can't.

This mixed feeling of pride and protectiveness, mingled with love, lust and need overwhelms any rational thought I could have. Inch by inch, I slide home until there's nowhere else I'd rather be.

Pumping wildly into her, each stroke like a flash of lightning along my spine. Holding my shoulders as she takes what she needs, just as much as I do. Her walls grip me as we ride together. I'm losing control. Lifting my face from her chest, she bites my lip.

"Cole, I..."

"I know, baby, I feel it too." She's not telling she's about to come, even though she is. It's more. So much fucking more, I feel it with everything I am.

"I feel everything." Tears well on the rims of her lashes, her soulful eyes on mine, as I slam into her over and over again, until it's too much. The base of my spine tingles, my balls draw up, cock swells, sending her further over the edge. Ari moans as her walls grip me like a vice.

"I think I love you." And fuck I explode, hearing those three little words. I hold her tighter, cradling her in my arms, in this darkened room, like she's the only thing I care about.

"I fucking know I love you, Ari," I grit out, as another wave hits me, sending another stream of cum deep inside her. We fall together. Pulses racing, breathing slowly descending as we come down.

"You love me?" Ari says after she catches her breath. Still inside her, I press my softening cock into her. Making her laugh and groan at the sensitivity.

"I love you," I tell her.

"I love you." I reach the soft skin on her neck, sucking it to leave my mark on her.

"Cole," she gasps as I take the skin between my lips, my teeth.

"I don't care, baby, you're fucking *mine*." I'm grinning like a fucking idiot when she tilts her head to the side, giving me just the right amount of space to graze her skin and mark her flesh. I want the world to know she belongs to me.

Chapter Thirty-Eight
Who

Arianna

I spent another night in Cole's beautiful home.

That's the difference, isn't it. I've never called where I live home. It's never represented a home, but Cole's home is a *home*. Filled with his memories, rooms decorated to his taste, personal touches, evidence from a life he has lived in every space. I want to explore and spend my time in each and every part of it. With him.

Could I do that? My hand drifts over the frames of his life as I move through his bedroom. I think I could.

I think that's the plan. We've never said as such, but it's implied with each touch, each kiss, and every look we give. Not forgetting how he's taken my shit show of a life I've been hiding from the world, and showed me just how much I've been truly missing out on. The connection, the way I should be treated by people. Instead of the way I have to protect the few I hold dear. He's setting things right for me, letting me see what life will be like and love it. Every fucking second.

The peace I feel when I'm here, when he's with me, makes me smile so much my cheeks actually ache.

Taking a seat on the sofa, in his cosy living room I relax back. Yesterday, I asked Gi to pack a bag for me, with no explanation. I couldn't tell her over the phone, it's too risky. I know Cole told me they would be safe, but they still work in father's cold, sterile house, under his watchful eye. Until this is done, the less they know the better.

Ethan kindly packed it up my things from Gi and Ed's house after we got back. Not wanting anyone to find out where I am, he told them I was safe. When I opened the bag, she'd packed money, a passport I had no idea I had, and enough basics to see me through for some time.

I cried, broke down in the middle of Cole's living room.

My heart's broken at the idea of leaving them behind. I know I'm not, but I will never go back to spend another night there again.

When I woke this morning, I had to pinch myself, and I watched in awe as Cole soothed the sting with his tongue. I can't believe I spoke to my father like that and got away with it. *In* public. I freaked, almost had a full-blown panic attack when it sank in that I said those actual words to my father's face; that I stood up for myself with Robert. I daydreamed about moments like that for so many years. Actually, seeing it play out was incredible, knowing I actually did it, gives me the drive to do what's coming next.

Move on.

With my husband.

I slept in his shirt. That's what I'm in now. A shirt that smells like him, soft and freeing to dress how I want to for the day. After I calmed down last night, we talked some more, about nothing and everything at the same time. I fell asleep in his arms. Woke with Cole kissing me tenderly as he took us to bed.

I feel whole and lost all at once.

He's working from home this morning while I watch a movie on his huge ass telly. The fact that he's sitting in joggers and no shirt is divine. My eyes flick to him constantly. Sitting in front of me on the floor, with his laptop perched on his lap, working on finding something about my father to send him away with Carmichael. It all feels good. Really good.

He's not left my side.

Sitting here with nothing to do feels oddly strange but good and terrifying. Even when I had my own space in my room, I was still expected to make sure I looked my best, take care of myself with a daily routine. Workout, hair, nails, clothes. All of it. My free time planned. Or shut away, so I'd never bother anyone.

I kind of like that I don't have to do it, although I still feel like I should. Getting into my own routine is going to take some getting used to. *Why do you need a routine?* The question pops into my head unannounced, making me blink at the world that's open to me.

Give yourself time, Ari.

Six days.

The first thing Cole asked me this morning, after he made me come undone with tongue, was what I wanted to do. I said nothing and everything. He handed me the remote and told me to enjoy my morning. I know he's giving me space to think and I appreciate it. There's so much to process, but there's one thing that remains: I want out.

Out of my parents' house. Out of that life. Not just for six days, but forever.

I need my stuff, my books the small box hidden in my room filled with memories, and I need to be the one to get it. I don't want the guys at Cerberus doing it. Even though I know they would.

That's the only reason I'll step foot back into that house.

Maybe you could tell them that you'll never marry Mr Carmichael.

Even with the small-ish panic attack I had yesterday about standing up for myself with my father and Robert. I loved the feeling I got afterwards. My chest swelled with pride for myself. Cole made me realise I should be proud of myself, he really showed me how much he loved seeing me like that, how much he loved me.

He was determined to make me see it for myself, and I am proud of myself. I think, with an underlying fear, that I don't know what to do about. I did that. For the first time in my life, I took charge, said what I would normally hold back.

He loves me.

Stretching my legs out on the sofa, my hand lazily runs through Cole's hair at the back of his head. Perhaps that's it. Doing it myself, one final time standing up to him, them. Imagine how that would feel. I get a rush through my body at the thought.

"You thinking about last night again, Cupcake?" Twisting to look at me, his eyes roam over me.

"How can you tell?"

"Your smile. It's the same one you had while I fucked you against the wall last night, and when we walked out the door together. Come to think of it, it was on your face when I fucked you on this floor after you agreed to be my wife." Placing his laptop down on the coffee table, he stands and straddles me, the remote control clattering to the floor. Tipping my chin up with his fingers he kisses the corners of my smile. "I'd do anything to keep this smile on your face Ari."

"Anything?" I question, my arms circling his neck.

"Yeah, baby, anything. After watching you break last night, I never want to see that again." Glancing at my book by my side, one Cole admitted he stole from my room the other day, I get an idea.

I want to be more like them—the women in my books, who seem to take what they want. No fear. I want to act on something they did in the book but with my own take on it. It turned me on so much I had to put it down. Following my gaze, he squints his eyes. "That's a look I've *not* seen before."

"I have an idea, I'd like to try?" I say, snapping the waistband of his joggers against his warm skin.

"Is my naughty girl coming out to play?" he asks, looking down at his tented joggers.

"I think she might be." The deep rumble in his throat has my eyes fluttering shut.

"Good girl." Fuck the praise does it for me. My breath shudders.

"I'm going to need a few things before we start." Kissing his sweet lips again, I shove him off me. Laughing I get to my feet and head to the kitchen. "Wait for me in the bedroom?" I say over my shoulder. Making quick work of what I need, I make my way up the stairs slowly, anticipation thrumming through my veins. This is the boldest thing I have ever wanted to do.

The door's already open when I reach his room, the bed messy and unmade from this morning's activities.

Peaking in, I hide what I got from the kitchen behind my back, I don't want him to see. A feral grin hits my lips when I see him stretched out naked on the bed, one hand behind his head, the other touching himself in slow leisurely strokes. Eyes closed, his lips slightly parted, I take in the view. I know I could jump him right now, and we'd enjoy it, but seeing him like this, laid out waiting for me, looking like a horny god, carved from granite, turns me on so fucking much, I'm soaked just watching him play.

"Are you going to join me, or just watch?"

"Watch." His eyebrow raises, but his eyes remain shut. "Don't open your eyes" I say, as I tug his shirt over my head, dropping it to the floor. Placing the items on the bedside table, I grab his black tie from the chair, running the silk through my fingers, "I'm going to cover your eyes, lift your head," I tell him, trailing the tie over his chest making him still, his hand caressing his cock and his eyes screwed shut.

"Ari?" His breathing picks up as I climb on the bed. "What are you doing?" Straddling his stomach, my bare core connects with his abs, and I feel him tensing underneath me. "You're naked?" he asks. His breathing is slightly laboured as his hands come to my sides.

"I am," I tease as I cover his eyes with his tie, securing it at the back of his head. My breasts dust his face and I gasp when he takes a hardened nipple into his mouth, I moan, grinding myself into him. After a few seconds, I pull away, and he groans in disappointment.

"Hands to yourself, sir." His cock twitches at the command. I'll be a goner if I carry on. Staying where I am, I grab the tub from the side and open the lid.

"Ari?" he warns, but I want to play today.

"I want to do this for you, sir," I add. Strong hands kneed my arse, jolting me forward as I move picking up the spoon. "Hands off," I demand, plucking them away from me and dropping them to his side. "Or do I have to tie you to the bed?" I tease.

"Fuck." He swallows thickly. "If I can't touch you, where am I supposed to put my hands?" Taking a hand in mine, I place it on his stomach.

"Touch yourself. I like watching," I tell him.

"Ari, this is torture already." I know where I'm going to start. The spot that made him groan. Marked like an x on the spot, I grab the spoon as he reaches for his cock, taking it firmly in his hand. "Whatever you have planned for me, just know that I'll be doing it to you." Placing the spoon in my mouth to warm it up. I don't say anything, watching his body react to his own touch. I want to find all the places that make him moan.

Hovering over him, taking the spoon from between my lips, the warmth of the spoon melting the ice cream as I scoop some up onto the spoon. Letting it drip on his lips, he gasps, his tongue darting out to taste. "My favourite flavour." Dripping another on his lips, I kiss him before he can lick it away. It's long and sensual, teasing him with my tongue. Tasting him mixed with the chocolate ice cream just became my new favourite flavour.

Dragging the melting ice cream over his chest, I work my way down, licking the sweetness from his hot, silky skin as I go. His hips jerk as his hand tightens around himself. I drip the smallest drop onto his dick.

"Baby, if you keep doing that... fuck." I sit between his legs as he moans a little louder. I've not touched him yet. I want to, and it's setting my skin on fire just seeing him like this for me.

His knees come up either side of me, penning me in, as I reach for just a little more ice-cream. My hand sweeps down his stomach, dragging the cold chocolate down to the sensitive spot just to the side of his hipbone, watching it melt against him, dripping lower. I catch it with the flat of my tongue before I suck, leaving a mark of my own to match the one he gave me. His hand creeps to my hair as I lick and tease his skin. His hips move with a feverish need, his hand gripping firming around himself. I could come just watching him.

Lifting myself, he stills. Unable to see where I am, I drip more ice cream onto the tip of his cock. Sucking in a breath, he hisses through his teeth at the coldness, before I lean over, licking him up.

"Jesus-fucking—" he cuts off his own words, his hand coming to the back of my head, as I continue, savouring every drop. His hand and my tongue. "I'm going to come, baby. Fuck, take me in that pretty mouth." I do, I don't stop until he hits the back of my throat, squeezing his balls with my free hand, I feel them tense, jolting up, making me gag as his grip tightens in my hair. The sting making me moan.

"Yes, baby. Look what my fucking wife does to me." Holding himself at the back of my throat he comes so hard, it takes me a moment to swallow it all down. He pulls out, removing his tie and blinking at me. "That just makes me love you so much more." Laughing as I land on my back on the soft bedding, he grabs the tub, only he scoops it with his fingers. "Time to repay the favour, baby." Placing some in his mouth, he devours me. The cold on my skin, a complete contrast to the feel of his warm mouth.

"I love it." My breath dissipates as he drips ice cream over my core. My back arching so high at the overwhelming sensations, he places an arm over me to keep me in place. "Cole." My head spins and when his tongue rims my entrance, I lose it. Cresting my high as his ice- cream filled tongue sinks into me, his fingers circling my clit with precise movements he knows will send me flying.

Kissing his way up my stomach, he spreads my legs wide, his hot cock entering me so slowly, I gasp. Taking my nipple in his mouth, he sucks, and it's like my orgasm never stopped. My skin flares, my walls flutter when he sinks in all the way, stretching me wide.

His eyes meet mine, the flecks of gold shining in the light. Tugging his hair at the nape of his neck I move, but he doesn't, looking at me like I'm his world.

"Move, please, baby, I need you to move." But he's still just staring at me.

"This is us now, Ari. I'm never going to give you back."

"Good, I want this Cole, you. Us." Thrusting his hips forwards, I gasp again when he bottoms out. Pulling out, he sets a new rhythm, teasing, lazy strokes making me crazy. "Cole, oh-my—" His tongue pierces my lips as he fucks me harder, knowing my body better than I do, sending me over the edge. To send us over the edge. When he comes inside me, I come again. I never what to leave.

"Forever, baby," I whisper into his neck as we come down.

"Forever."

Chapter Thirty-Nine
Footage

Cole

The whole team's been working their ass off to put together a case to get Byron and Carmichael put away. Even Jack came through, telling me he wants to run for mayor. I don't think I've slept more than a few hours a night since Dec let slip about her parents and it's been a downwards spiral ever since.

Myself and Owen have set up notifications for every camera and device we've installed, ready to listen to anything, hoping to catch them out. I thought it was going to be hard. Carmichael seemed untouchable.

For years, there have been rumours about the way he treats his wives. His first was found dead in their pool, bruised and battered with drugs in her system. It was ruled as a break-in gone wrong as some things were missing, but nothing of value. Thomas Byron declared her death tragic and unnecessary, all part of a burglary gone wrong. The intruders were never found.

Was this the start of their friendship? Or was Byron hoping to have a hold over Carmichael's influence? Since then, Byron has risen through the ranks of social standing and become one of the better-known judges to take on high profile cases. Freeing the guilty, jailing the less fortunate. Reaping the rewards? That's what I'm doing tonight while Ari sleeps soundly in my bed. I'm going through her father's bank records. *I'll run away with her before I ever let her go back there.*

I've already set up the transfers from his to Ari's new accounts before they arrest him, but I'm finding a trail of bribes he's taken as I go.

I've discovered statements and transfers from off-shore accounts linked to those he's helped go unpunished. I have fifteen so far. I just need his connection to Carmichael. That's something I can't find. Owen found his second wife. She's alive and well, living under another name in the US. She gave us what she had on him. Photo evidence of what he did. Beat her to an inch of her life, then left her for dead. She was found by a stranger who hid her, nursed her back to health, then helped her move away. She's willing to help. My laptop dings with a notification from Bryon's office. It's three am. What the fuck is he doing there so late?

I guess evil doesn't sleep either. Pulling up the camera, I watch Carmichael take a drink from the cabinet and sit behind Byron's desk, propping his feet up like he owns the room. Bryon walks in a few minutes later, his expression full of anger at the man sitting at his desk.

"Byron, glad you could make it. We have something to discuss," he says, sipping his drink.

"I've told you already. She's yours," her dad says.

"I know that, my old friend. Nothing has changed with your sweet daughter becoming my third wife." His dark laugh churns my stomach. "What we need to discuss is how you're going to get her back, so that will happen." I'm clenching my teeth, so hard my jaw aches.

"Arianna's always does as she's told. Even with this little revolt of hers, she'll be there on the final day, walking right into your depraved arms." Carmichael licks his lips. Never fucking happening arsehole. You'll be long gone by then.

"Let's hope you're right. I'd hate for our friendship to end after all this time."

"What will you do with my dear daughter?" He looks intrigued, not concerned.

"I'll do what I've done to all the others. Only this time, it'll be agonisingly slow and beautifully torturous. She'll feel it all, and won't be able to do a thing about it." Images play out in my mind of what he would do to Ari if she was still in that house without my protection.

My stomach heaves as my hands shake, as my mind conjures up the depraved things he'll never get to do to my wife.

Heading to our room. Craving the feel of her close to me, I climb back into bed. Watching her sleep soundly, facing her, Ari moves into me. Even in her sleep, she wants to be near and I sigh in relief.

The sooner those men get sent away, the better.

Chapter Forty

Shit Together

Arianna

Over the last few days, I've realised I need a focus. I don't like not doing anything; it makes me uncomfortable, and it's just not me. It's been two days since I found my voice and I can't handle sitting around anymore.

Sitting in the Cerberus office, I've been waiting for Cole to come back. He's gone to meet a contact. Said it was the final piece for putting Dad away. Something about a hex? I don't know. I was only half listening.

I've been sitting here since. Just thinking. I'm going to tell Cole about going to get my things. I have an idea about how he'll react: not great. But I also think he'll let me do it because I need it. I just want my stuff and to say my piece.

"You're quiet," Ethan says, passing me a coffee.

Sighing, I take the coffee from his hands. "I am." I sound a bit flat.

"Let me get Leon. He's good at these things."

"No, it's okay. I don't need to talk; I just need to know what to do." He looks uncomfortable, but I carry on, not wanting to wait any longer to get this off my chest.

"I've never had time to do anything of my own. Is this what it's like? Having time?"

"Yeah, freedom's a good thing." It is, but this seems like torture.

"What can I do with it? *Anything?* I'm so stupid, I don't know what to do with myself. I've wanted this for years. But..." I don't know how to express it.

"It doesn't feel right?" Ethan suggests.

"That, yes, it feels odd. Unsettling. That's another word for it." sitting opposite me, he contemplates something, rubbing the stubble on his chin.

"When we came out of the Army, we all felt the same, or varying versions of it. It took a while to get used to." He leans forwards. "You don't need to do anything."

"You see, that right there scares me." I feel it in my bones.

"Hm, Leon," he bellows, and I laugh as the big guy pops his head out of the office, and comes to sit by me.

"She said she needs to know what to do," Ethan says, placing his phone on the table.

"I've never had the choice to do... anything really," I say solemnly.

"Tell him what you told me." Rolling my eyes, I get it he's not much of a talker, but seriously.

"All I said was that it scares me, not having anything to do, and not *having* to do anything." I flip my hands up in annoyance at myself.

"It's a lot, especially when you've lived a life like you have," Leon says, agreeing with me. They should know; they've seen all the evidence.

"Start small, work your way up. We have five days to semi-hide you before this shit hit the fan. Make a list." Sounds simple enough.

"Make a list?" I repeat.

"Yeah, when Millie was going through some stuff, she made a list of all the things she wanted to do but was never able to." Ethan nods knowingly.

"She does love a list." Ethan pipes up, sipping his tea.

"She does," he chuckles, "but it helped clear her head, and put it all into perspective."

"That does sound like a good idea." There's a lot going on in my head right now.

"I'll ask Jill to bring you a notepad and pen," Ethan says, taking out his phone and typing out a message.

"Try it, it may just work," Leon chimes in, before walking back to his office.

"Jill will bring it up in a minute," Ethan says, lifting his phone to his ear. "Gran," he says, before giving me a chin lift, leaving me alone again.

A few minutes later, I have a good idea what I can write down, when a woman I recognise walks up the stairs looking around like she's never seen the place before.

"Layla?" It's the girl from the flower shop.

"Miss Byron?" she questions when her eyes land on me.

"Please call me Ari."

"You remember me?"

"Of course." Standing, I walk over to her.

"Oh, I have this," she holds up the notebook and pen, "Jill asked me to bring it up."

"Thanks," she hands them to me, "just what I needed."

"It's so nice to see you." She hugs me, then steps back, worry on her face. "I'm so sorry, I over-stepped. My friend Aggie tells me I have issues with personal space." I laugh and hug her back.

"I liked it." I shrug, making her smile. "I think I needed that," I admit, and her eyes soften.

"You look different. I can't place it?"

"It's the outfit, jeans and jumper. I'm never seen like this," I say, glancing down at myself, feeling a little self-conscious.

"No, that's not it. There something about you?"

"Oh, um. Do you fancy getting a coffee sometime?" I ask. "I'll tell you everything, just not yet." Her beautiful dark honey eyes go wide.

"Do you mean it? I'd love that, like really love that." She's bouncing on her heals.

"What are you doing here, anyway?" Layla asks, blinking. I don't know what to say. Or how much to say. I don't want to say something I shouldn't.

"Don't say anything," Leon shouts as he comes back into the room. The look on his face when he sees her is priceless: shock, regret, admiration. "Layla, shit, sorry..." he stutters. "I didn't mean to shout at you."

The poor girl freezes, her whole body flushing before she turns pale. *What's that about?*

"I dropped off some flowers," she says quietly before turning and bolting.

"No, please don't go," Leon says as I call after her, "can I have your number?" but she's already down the stairs.

"Damn it." he curses, "I'll give you her number. But don't tell her anything."

"What was that?" I ask.

"No idea. Every time I say something she acts the same way. I've tried. But it's the same thing over and over again."

"How long have you been trying?"

"A while. I don't know what it is. She talks the ear off everyone else. But me, nothing." I feel a little sorry for him.

"Oh, you like her?" His eyes flash to mine.

"Write your list, Mrs Grant," he orders before he walks back into his office. A minute later, I get a message with Layla's number attached from Leon. Making a mental note to message her when all this is done.

I've filled almost three pages with things I want to do. From buying myself a sandwich and actually eating it in public, to walking up the high street. *I know, pathetic, right?* But when you've never done anything like it, there comes a time when you think, the normal stuff sounds exciting. Then there's the opposite end of the scale, like getting my degree in architecture, to travelling the world and all the places I want to see.

I'll have to earn some serious money. I know technically Cole said the money would be mine, but I can't bank on it. If they freeze my father's accounts when he's arrested, it could be years before I get anything back.

I like the thought of helping others. Millie said that just with my reach, I could do a lot. I can be an ambassador for her brand. *If she'll have me.* Maybe I can turn my account around to be mine? Tell them why I'm changing things. That would really screw my father up. Turning the page, I start to plot out what I can do. By the time Cole walks back into the office looking pretty pleased with himself, I'm done.

I feel different. I think I just gave myself a purpose. Placing a kiss on my cheek, he hands me my lunch and tells me what my father has been up to. While we eat, I tell him about the plans I've made. When I'm finished, he looks over everything, smiling and frowning.

"We can get some of these done easily, baby." I squeal. Then he slides his tablet from his bag and places it on the desk. "I have some news too, I'm not sure you'll like it, but it is what it is."

"Why won't I like it? What is it?" My good mood sinks as I watch Cole open up some information on the screen.

"I found out who owns, and runs Hex PR," he says, as I sit back in my seat waiting for the blow that's about to come.

"Who is it?" I ask tentatively.

"Carmichael," he says on an aggravated breath.

"He owns and runs it? You mean to tell me that he's been running my life for... I don't even know how long."

"It took me a while. It was all concealed under various subsidiaries of other businesses he owns. I finally found a name on a document, a pseudonym I found the same name on an online reservation that Carmichael's secretary booked. Watching the footage of the restaurant, it was Carmichael and some guy he uses to face the company."

"So, it's not directly Robert that's been doing it?" I ask and he grimaces, and I know the answer.

"Sorry, Cupcake. I hacked the company system and it's only him who has access to your schedule. He's been keeping tabs on you through the tracker in your phone too, as have your parents."

"I don't under stand why? All of this so he can marry me? It seems like a lot of effort."

"From what we've found over the past week, that guy thrives on control. He gets off on it."

"So, he used all of this," I point to everything he's shown me, "to control me, to do what he wants, when he wants. To keep tabs on me until he was ready to force me to marry him." I feel sick knowing that everything I have ever done as been conspired by him. All for his sick and twisted game of control.

Chapter Forty-One

Ride Baby

Arianna

Today is warm, given we are nearing the end of October. Cole suggested a ride on his bike, I suggested he teach me how to ride it. He didn't agree, but he didn't disagree either. It's one of the things on my ever-growing list. I also wanted to see the bike shop, Iron Viper, but standing here, I think I may have hyped it up too much in my head. It looks an awful lot like a car garage, but for bikes.

"So, this is the other side of you?" Glancing around the bike shop, there are tools, machinery, and lots of things I don't know the name of. It's all black motorbikes, grease, men in overalls, and only a few men with tattoos.

"I'm a little disappointed." My hand flies to my mouth. Oops, I didn't mean to say that out loud. "What?" I ask, chuckling to myself, when Cole swats my ass.

"Books, that's what this is. You read too many MC club biker books," Cole says, walking over to the small office at the back of the workshop. Looking at him today he fits this scene well. Wearing dark denim, a black t-shirt, and a red and black plaid shirt, and a black leather jacket to finish the look.

When he walked out of the bedroom wearing that this morning, I nearly took him back in there just to undress him. I had a fangirl moment of speechlessness, where I proceeded to make a mess of my knickers.

It also reminds me how much I miss my kindle.

Leaving him to get what he needs from the office, I stay rooted to the spot, taking it all in. I'm finding out I'm nosy. And now I'm able to look around without anyone commenting on my life, I will.

"Ari," Cole shouts, calling me over from the door of the office.

"I'm looking around," I shout back.

"For fuck's sake," he chides, leaving me to it.

"Miss Byron," a guy calls from the other side of the room. He's in overalls tied at the waist, a black t-shirt, and tattoos all over his arms and neck. No beard though.

"I'm Ryder, Trax's business partner," he shouts as he wipes his hands on a towel before he holds his hand out to me.

"Please call me Ari. Who's Trax?" I ask, shaking his hand. I'm also Mrs Grant. I don't add though. I really want to call Chrisy and tell her. She'd shit her pants at all this.

"Noted. Cole *is* Trax, it was his squaddie name in the army. Told me your name will change soon anyway. You're going to be his old lady?" My eyes widen. *He used a bike term.* Cole's obviously not updated him on our current relationship status.

"So, you do use terms like old lady and Pres?" I ask, grinning from ear to ear. I want to know everything.

"We do. So, is it true?" he says, tilting his head to the side in question.

"Answer me a few more questions and I'll tell you."

"Deal. He's not said much about you, but you have been seen on the back of his bike more than once." Ah, well we arrived on his bike, so that's a giveaway really.

"And that implies?" I question, tilting my head just like he did.

"That he's as serious about you as he is his bike." Grunting out a laugh, he starts to dismantle the front of a bike. Interesting.

"Strange comparison," I admit.

"Not really. We take care of our bikes like we do our women." Crouching down on the floor by the bike, he looks up at me, like he knows I want to ask more.

Don't ask, don't ask, don't ask. His eyes shine with amusement, waiting for me to bite.

"How's that then." Hearing a door close somewhere behind me. I stand waiting.

"You see, Ari, we care for them, treat them with respect, and make then purr like a god damn kitten." He winks and laughs while I blush all over.

"I like you," I say, knowing Cole's close. I can feel him.

"Fuck off." Cole's whipping me around and moving me away from Ryder before he or I can say anything else. "That's the line he uses on all his women. This one's taken arsehole," he announces.

"It was good to meet you, Mrs Grant," he shouts after us. Cole actually rolls his eyes.

"I'm never bringing you here again," he grumbles as we get outside.

"Don't be a spoilsport," I add, slapping his chest playfully.

"Ari," he warns, teasingly.

"Cole." Smirking, he pulls me over to the bike. Leaning against it, he pulls me between his legs.

"I like hearing them call you Mrs Grant." He captures my hand, brings my arm behind my back in a firm grip, and inches me closer to his chest. He hitches my leg to rest on his thigh, holding me impossibly close.

"I like it too." pushing a stray hair back behind my ear, our lips brush in a sweet, but seductive kiss. The heat of him on my skin, his hand in my hair as he parts my lips, teasing me with his tongue as he kisses me softly.

"I love you, baby," he murmurs.

"I love you too." I smile into our kiss.

"Good, I want you to move in with me." That's unexpected.

"Wow, we really are doing things backwards aren't we?" I say.

"Our way. Is that a yes?" he asks, kissing my jaw.

"It was on my list to get my own place. I've never lived on my own," I say sheepishly, unsure of how he'll take it.

"I never thought of that." His thumb is now stroking over the inside of my wrist. "I take it back. You need to have your own place."

"You can't take it back. It's out there," I say seriously.

"I can and I have. We'll look at a place close to mine. I'll call Em and see what she has." Letting go of my hand, be cups my face before kissing my forehead.

"Thanks. Who's Em?"

"She's Jack's sister." He looks at me like I should know all of this.

"Mr Lucas?" I ask.

"Yeah, Jack. Long time friend and client of ours." I wonder if I could meet with him? I'll add it to my list for when all this is done and dusted.

"You have so many people in your life, it's hard to keep up." I'm not used to any of this.

"You'll get there." His arm hangs over my shoulder. I love the feel of him this close.

"I've arranged a training session with Charlie for you."

"Who's Charlie?" I really can't keep up.

"The owner of the flower shop, she's also an ex- MMA fighter. Now she just likes to kick our asses. I have a training session with the teens at the gym later this afternoon. Thought you could tag along and do that." I'm staring at him.

I go to rattle off a few more questions lingering in my head, but there's too many. "You know what. I'd love to. I need to ask you something anyway."

"What is it, baby?" he asks, pecking me on the lips.

"I know that everything is prepped for... the things that will happen." I don't want to say the words out loud, just in case "Four days and it will all hopefully be over." I know he's not going to like this, but I have to gulp down my nerves. "But I want to do something before that, something you may not like given the circumstances." If it's possible for your whole face to frown, then that's what

Cole's tanned, handsome face scrunches into. His lips twist, then part, ready to say something. Moving quickly, I put my hand over his mouth, stopping him. Snapping his eyebrows up, he stays quiet.

"I want to see them, my parents, I mean. That came out wrong. I don't *want* to see them ever again. But I want to face them, Cole. I'd like to collect the things that are important to me from my room." *Am I conveniently not telling him that I want to speak with them, give them shit, and tell them they can find someone else to marry Carmichael?. Yes, yes, I am. He'd never let me do it if he knew.* "I think I need to do this for myself. I need it," I add, hoping to win him around.

"Fuck, it's not a good idea, baby," he says, his hand taking a firm hold of my waist.

"It may not be a good idea, but I want to grab my things, then tell them I'm leaving."

"Ari, I can't." I can see the fear in his eyes as his grip tightens. He knows he can't stop me.

"No, you can. You just don't want to."

"It scares the shit out of me, Ari," he says when I try to step away. "You in there with them."

"It terrifies me too, but I need to do this." Standing firm on this, I won't back down.

"I don't know, baby, it's dangerous. They want you back there. And if they get you in that house, they may never let you come back out. I don't know what I would do." So this is what it feels like to be wanted. My hand comes to my heart, checking it's still beating.

"I know," I say. "I know what you would do. The same thing you've done since you started this job, the same damn thing you've done every time I slip the net. You find me."

Standing straight, he takes the tops of my arms in his big hands and pulls me back to him.

"I would. I'd get you back. In fact, I'd never let them get you." Crushing me to his chest, he kisses the top of my head, holding just a little bit tighter. Cole breathes out a huff, his arms comforting me.

"Okay," he agrees reluctantly, "we'll figure it out, but you're having that lesson with Charlie first. She'll teach you to kick ass." I nod. You can hear him working on a plan in that big nerdy mind of his. "I'll be watching you the entire time. I'll be waiting for you to step out that door. I'll be listening in to every word they say." I feel bad, if this is the reaction for me just collecting my things, I'd hate to imagine what it would be like if I told him the truth. I think he'd be the one locking me up under twenty-four-hour surveillance.

"Overprotective much? But okay." I'm trying to lighten the mood.

"I'm not being overprotective. I made you a promise to never let them hurt you again. You're my wife. I protect what's mine." My heart does that flip-out thing. I love it when he says stuff like that.

"I appreciate it, baby," I say, kissing his palm as I raise it to my lips. He just groans at me

"You can ride up front. I'll sit behind. I'll show you what to do. Climb on." I almost scream with excitement when I swing my leg over, making myself comfortable in the seat. He watches me for a moment. I can't make out what's running through his head, but I see the care in his eyes. Sitting behind me, his warm frame at my back, he leans in, engulfing me. He feels amazing.

Pressing the button to turn on the engine, and watching as Cole as he shows me what to do, makes me tingle all over. Combined with his protective side, I'm an absolute goner, before we even take off. I keep grinding my ass into his crotch, each time a groan rumbles in my ear, as his grip on me tightens.

It's exhilarating

"Ride the damn bike, baby, before I fuck you over it." The warmth of the day is nothing compared to the heat racing down my spine.

"You think saying things like that will help? You're delusional," I say, grinding my ass against him.

"No, but it might make our ride home a little more exciting."

Chapter Forty-Two

Smack Down

Arianna

Shit, I wince again, watching Charlie fight. She's brutal. Brutal but amazing. Sitting on the bench against the wall waiting for my apparent training to start, I'm terrified.

Will she do that to me? If I can learn just a fraction of that, I'd be happy. I think I like her. She's clearly strong, quick, and knows what she's doing. The way she moves her body, anticipating what's coming, defending herself, attacking. Spectacular, terrifying, it's the same thing in my eyes.

She really does know how to kick ass.

Cole's ass, to be precise. When he got into the ring twenty minutes ago, Charlie got a wicked glint in her eye, laughed, and proceeded to floor him over and over again.

He's given as good as he's got, but Charlie definitely has the edge. I've winced, covered my eyes, and gasped at it all.

Right now, I can't stop laughing, my hand covering my mouth to hide the explosive snort that comes flying from me. *Me*, laughing in public. I feel lighter, all because Charlie floors him again, only this time she holds him down. Cole locks his eyes on me, smirking at my reaction to the way Charlie is scolding him.

"This is what you get, Cole Grant, when you don't tell me important information about your life." She pants as she holds his legs up, effectively immobilising him on his front while her knees pin his shoulder down to the floor.

"Sorry, it won't happen again," Cole whines. I actually think he's enjoying this when he hisses out a sort of grunt chuckle.

"What will you do next time?" she demands, her hair falling over her shoulder as she sways it out of her face.

"Tell you first."

"Good boy." Letting him go, she gets up leaving him lying on the floor to catch his breath. Turning to me, Charlie waves me up to join them.

A nervous sort of grunt comes from my throat.

I don't move. I'm not going to get in there. I'm not ready for this.

I mean, I'm dressed in my gym stuff. I've warmed up, I just need to move.

"Ari, get your arse in here," she sings. "I won't do that to you," she says, pointing at Cole who's rolled onto his back. "He deserved that for not telling me about you." Cole rolls his eyes. Getting up, he climbs between the ropes of the ring and jumps down, coming to sit next to me on the bench.

"Everything okay?" he asks, a little breathless. His hand rubbing up and down my thigh to comfort me.

"I'm not doing that," I utter, tilting my head towards the ring he just came from.

"I never asked you to, Cupcake."

"I think I have a girl crush," I admit, still looking towards Charlie, where she's leaning against the ropes, laughing at something.

"You're taken, and so is she." My head snaps to his, the serious look on his face making my insides tingle and my heart tilts a little.

"Are you jealous, husband?" I beam, standing. He smirks at the sound of me calling him *husband*.

"The fact you have a crush on a woman who just kicked my ass, yes." Grumbling, his words.

"Brilliant." I make it to the ropes and climb in, ducking between them rather than going over the top. In the background one of my favourite songs comes on, *'Billie Eilish, bury a friend'* spurring me on to a least give this a try, no matter how nervous I am on the inside. My heart thudding to the beat of the music.

"That's the first step done, Ari. I bet that once we're finished here you'll be booking another lesson." She's so sold on the idea I'll love it. I'm envious of how confident she is. I want some of what she has.

"You sound so sure of yourself," I tell her, jokingly.

"I am. Just you wait and see." She winks at me, untangling some of the nerves in my stomach.

"Why?" I ask as she looks at me. I'm not trying to be a bitch. I'm trying to understand how this will help me, not just make Cole sweat a little.

"What I'm going to teach you will make you feel incredibly confident, and in moments where we as women can feel," she pauses, tapping her chin, "less than. This will help you gain some control." Shit, well, when she put's it like that.

"Show me," I state, lifting my chin to her.

"This is all about survival." Her words make me shudder, hitting me in the chest like a spear. That's what I've been doing, nothing but surviving. "Your instincts."

"Survival instincts," I repeat.

"Exactly. This training is to help you defend yourself, disengage, and back away from the situation." I could have done with this months ago.

"Okay." And I'm back to shitting myself, shaking my hands out by my sides, trying my best to get rid of the nervous energy trapped in them.

"In the scenarios we'll go through, I'll be your attacker and your teacher. Showing you different ways to get out of holds, tricky situations, and get away as fast as you can." Gulping, my throat feels like sandpaper. "Number one rule in self-defence, get away. Never attack unless you have to. Ready?" she asks, eagerness written all over her face.

"No," I answer honestly. She comes to stand in front of me.

"We'll start with the basics."

An hour later, I'm buzzing, knackered, but absolutely high at what Charlie has accomplished with me. "One last go at the getting out of the chokehold?" Charlie asks, taking a breath.

"Yeah." It's the one I've struggled with. The others, like groin kicks, elbow blows and hammer fists, I got quickly. This one's a little trickier. Charlie comes behind me. I take calm breaths, steadying my breathing, my pulse wild with anticipation. There's a soft, warm breath at my back, then her arms tighten around my neck, her hands clamp together, holding me where I am. My hands fly up, gripping her arms, dropping my weight. Her hands break free of their firm hold on each other. Moving quickly, I step to her side, lowering my centre of gravity. I pull away, not before I let go, causing her to fall backwards in the process.

"Yes, Ari." She pumps her fist in the air and I sink to my knees, feeling the rush of getting it right. "Told you, didn't I," she says, staring at the ceiling.

"No idea what you're talking about." I grin.

"Liar," she teases. "Feels great, doesn't it?"

"Yeah, it does." Charlie turns her head to look at me.

"Just remember the basics for now. We can work on the rest." There's something serious in her eyes, like she knows the truth about me. I frown. Does she know? Before I can ask, she's up and out of the ring. "Book in for your next one," she shouts from across the busy room.

I don't say anything. Picking up my bottle of water I take a huge gulp, before I hit the showers, wondering what she really knows about me.

Chapter Forty-Three
Shoving

Cole

After our ride out on my girl—bike—this morning, Ari had her lesson with Charlie. She did well, but it took her a while to get the hang of a few of the moves. She seemed stuck in her head this afternoon. She said she was okay, but I'm not sure. I decided to distract her with orgasms. I wanted her to relax, to be free of her thoughts for a while. It worked. Ari seemed to relax after that, almost back to normal, but not quite.

When she leant over my desk when we arrived in the office, I knew what she wanted. Immediately closing and locking the door. She dropped her jeans and a shiver ran up my spine as I unbuckled my belt. This woman is going to be the death of me, and I'm right here for it.

Fuck, it was good. But I think all this is wearing her out, emotionally and physically. After making her list yesterday, I've memorised the whole thing. I already have at least three we can do this week. Ticking off riding my bike put's a huge smile on her face.

She's missed out on the simplest of things. Number ten on her list was to make a cake. I mean who, at our age, has never made a cake? Or at least tried. The things she wants to accomplish, the things she wants to see and let her life be like are uncomplicated, things that most people do in their average day. I'm right here for that too.

I went into full creep mode and watched her sleep for a full hour, before I got back to work. The way her hair is tied up, in a loose and messy bun, her soft snore, something I'll rib her about tomorrow.

I love having her here with me.

This case has become an obsession, I won't rest until I have everything I can on both Carmichael and her father. I never want them to see the light of day again.

"I have it," Charlie announces. "Cole, I have it. It's something anyway." She all but runs into my office, throwing an envelope at me. Catching it, I'm eager to know what she has and why, before she can wake Ari up, who's currently sleeping on the sofa.

Charlie backs up a pace when I launch myself at her, placing my hand over her mouth, shoving her back through the door before she can wake up Ari.

"Please be quiet." I whisper, as she grunts at me, then bites my hand. "That hurt." I groan, taking a seat out for her.

"Then don't put your hand over my mouth when I have some information for you on Arianna," she says wiping her face with the back of her hand before taking a seat.

"Charlie, what have you been doing? It's..." Looking at my watch, my eyes widen. "Shit, it's one am."

"I know, but my contact came through. I think this will help." My skin goes cold. I've known Charlie for almost eighteen months, and nothing will stop her when she gets an idea in her head. I should have known she'd take it upon herself to see if she could find anything on Arianna's father.

"Where does Owen think you are right now?" I look around expecting him to charge in.

"Don't worry about him. I'm sure he'll be fine with this; he'll be here when he realises I'm not next to him." She pauses, then says, "I actually think he followed me here." She says with a shrug.

"I'm not worried about you," I add, running my hands through my hair, "I'm worried about me," I say, my eyebrows shooting up to my hairline, knowing Owen will try to kill me if I inadvertently got the love of his life involved in this. *He'll think I asked her.*

"That might be too late." She squirms, tilting her head backwards, like she can sense him.

"Angel," Owen mutters angrily, bursting through the door. "What the hell are you doing here at this time? You do realise I'll fucking follow you everywhere." This is nothing new, Charlie has a habit of doing things the way she likes, and Owen will follow without question. Last year he hunted her down inside a burning building. Ended up saving her life.

"Calm down, I'll explain," she says when he stomps to her side, sitting next to her. "I found some information for lover boy here." She's not fazed by him or his reaction.

Owen's eyes land on me. A death stare. I tense waiting for it. He leans forward as his free hand clenched on the table in front of him like he's ready to punch me.

In fact, I can't blame him. How would I feel if it was the other way around. I'd be frantic if it was Ari.

"Sorry," I say, my full feelings of regret behind it. He gives me a nod similar to the ones Ethan hands out on occasion. Understanding.

"I should have known I couldn't keep you away from a case or sneaking around. I don't know why I even tried," he says, shaking his head like he knew it would happen eventually.

"Still, I'm sorry, I should have realised—" I start before Charlie cuts me off.

"You have nothing to be sorry for. I was doing it anyway as soon I found out you were together. I knew we needed some decent info on them. And I freaking have it. *I hope,*" she blurts, eyeing the envelope in my hand.

Tearing it open, I plug in the pen drive to the central system. I know this has come from Xander. He's like a brother to Charlie. I'm not a hundred per cent sure what he does, but he's high up in the covert ops world. He likes to play these little games with us and Charlie. Giving us titbits of information. A few seconds later, I'm looking at hospital documents for Ada Byron, Arianna's mum, for a small surgery.

"What am I looking at?" I ask, curious

"Well, my contact said, 'not is all as it seems'." She air-quotes. "Work it out from here."

"You know we know it's Xander, don't you." I sigh, scanning over the screen.

"Of course I know. It's just more exciting when I say contact or informant." She scowls at me while Owen tries to hide his smile.

"How long ago was this surgery?" I ask.

"From the date, it's almost twenty-six years ago," Owen says, reading the document. There's a niggle in my chest, telling me this is big.

"Arianna's birth certificate says she was born six weeks after that date. How is that possible if she was pregnant." I raise my eyebrows in Charlie's direction, knowing she's done a lot of digging if she seen her birth certificate.

"Before we jump to any conclusions, get Ethan on the phone," Owen says, dialling Ethan before I can even grab my phone. He's our medic. He'll be able to tell us if it was possible or not.

"If it's not possible to have that sort of surgery when you're pregnant," Ethan will tells us when we explain the situation. "Does that mean she's adopted?" Charlie says, pressing her fist to her mouth. She may be right—as much as we've been digging into her father and Carmichael, we haven't even thought about looking into her mom. Shaking my head in denial, she can't know about this, can she? My posture crumbles at what I'll have to tell her.

"Maybe. I don't want to overlook anything here. Let's get the facts first." I swallow as my voice cracks.

"Shit, okay. Oh, my god." Charlie looks worried.

Arianna

I'm not asleep. *I wish I was.* Then I wouldn't have to listen while they all talk about me. I woke the moment Charlie came in and now I'm frozen in place while I hear what they've discovered about me. I'm scared to listen but I can't not. Am I adopted? My chest hurts. It's just another blow that I shouldn't really be surprised about. But I am. I think I know it's true. I don't really look like them—my hair's dark like my mother's was originally, but that means shit.

My father even said the other day that they 'got me' not had me, or when I was born. Got me, like I was delivered to their house like an Amazon parcel.

I'm biting the inside of my cheek, to stay quiet, as they put Ethan on loud-speaker.

"It makes no sense. If she was thirty weeks pregnant they wouldn't have risked using a general anaesthetic for any sort of surgery. This was a knee op to repair tendon damage. They would have waited." There are a few murmurs around the room as they try and fail to keep their voices down.

I can't make it make sense. If they couldn't have children, and then adopted me, why would they treat me like shit? Surely, your need for a child in your life has to be out of love, not greed. But that's all it's ever been.

They went to the hassle to adopt me, for what? My chest tightens further, squeezing the more I think about it.

My head's already spinning when I hear Cole speak up.

"I can't find any adoption papers," he whispers. My hand flies to my mouth to cover the sob that tries to escape me. Staying silent. I daren't move. I want to hear it all before they can sugar-coat it. Would they even tell me? They've glossed over any sort of details on my father and Carmichael. Letting me know the basics. Of course he'd tell me. *Wouldn't he?*

"What does that mean?" Charlie asks tentatively. Good question. *What the fuck does that mean?* My skin feels clammy, my heart's racing, I'm struggling to hear through the thunder roaring in my ears, as my blood pulses.

I feel like I'm free-falling, and I can't find anything to grip on to.

My eyes snap open. If I'm not adopted and I'm not their birth daughter? What does that make me? As I struggle to comprehend what's just been said.

Abducted? Snatched? Holy fuck.

Tears silently roll down my cheeks, soaking the cushion below me.

I need some air. I don't want to face anyone right now. My chest hurts, like it's been stabbed with a barbed blade, then twisted to make sure it's in there.

Who do I belong to?

Cole sounds devastated on my behalf, I love him. I really fucking love him, but no one needs baggage like this—emotional and physical trauma. Homeless, parentless, penniless, and lost, a career I have no control over. Shamed... given away. I feel heavy, the weight of everything suddenly feels too much. This is too much for me to handle. I've already put them through enough.

Their words are kind, but I don't know these people. I'd like to. But they know everything about me, good and bad. Mainly bad. It feels weird. I'm not sure how to handle that, knowing they know my darkest truth. I've always been a private person. I've never let anyone see what's happening. I put on this front for a reason.

I don't need the pity that comes with the truth.

I can hear it with every word spoken in the room next to this office, taunting me.

"There's nothing. No trail. Ari's birth certificate looks real enough..."

"Real enough?" Cole asks.

"You know as well as I do, documents can be easily modified."

I'm trying to breathe through it, trying to focus on a positive, but I can't find one.

From the moment I was born, it's all been a lie, every second of my life. Never wanted, never loved, never theirs.

"I'll add this to what we already have, and the new footage we have of them from last night," Cole says dryly. My heart sinks. I asked him to share everything that he had. What does he have on my father? He promised. He said he would keep me involved. We've had all day together, and he's not said a word.

I can't let them share this with the world. I can't let them do that. That's too much. To personal, it would be an attack on *my* life as well as my parents. It's already hard enough. Moving from my place on the sofa, I stand on shaky legs, making my way to the half-closed door. Watching them for a split second.

"I can't let you do that," I say quietly, stepping into the room. "Cole, I'd like to go back now, please." I give them all a weak smile. I can't muster much.

"Ari." He looks shocked, seeing me standing there. "Please listen," he begs, shooting from his chair.

"Not this time, I heard it all, everything you openly discussed with your friends about me. You all had no right to do that, this is my life. It's already fallen apart. Letting the world know I was stolen as a baby, abducted maybe." I sob. "Only to be brought into a shitty life of control and…" The air gets stuck in my throat and my hand clenches on my stomach, pain searing through me at the reality of my life. Cole's next to me in a flash, his arms wrapping around me, but I don't want his touch. I want to be on my own. I need some space. I need to be able to breathe.

Because I can't breathe.

"No, don't touch me." I whimper, shoving his hands away, the hurt in his beautiful eyes almost kills me, but I feel like I'm being boxed in. Pushing him away, I watch them all watch me, Cole steps back, doing as I asked, but it makes me feel worse as I move around them, heading to the stairs.

"Arianna, wait. Please." His normally smooth voice, broken, trails after me like it has so many times before. Only this time, it's not to get a kick out of the chase. "Baby, let me take you home." Stopping on the stairs mid-run, I almost topple. Turning around to see him, my fingers tightening on the banister, Cole's only a few feet behind.

"I don't have a home, Cole," I state. "I have nothing. Everything I thought to be true, even the shit show of them actually being my parents. They were *my* parents, and now they're not." I heave a breath as the tightness in my chest constricts further, tendrils of fear, shame and deceit curl into every living cell of my body.

Standing on the step below me, stopping my escape, his hands reach for mine. The gold flecks in his eyes dulled by the situation.

"You do have a home, Ari, right here," he says softly, bringing my hand to cover his chest, his heart beating steady under my palm. "Me, I'm your home," he says, his voice so sure, as his hand covers mine. "Where you are, I am." His voices wavers, trying to get through to me.

I break, tears tumbling down my face, so fast and free I can't stop them. His muscled frame wraps around me, cocooning me in his love. Holding me as my legs give way to the shock cursing through me.

Chapter Forty-Four

Solitude

Arianna

I have forever in front of me and yet I feel like I can't move. The news yesterday about my parents has me in a complete spin. Cole said he'll tell me everything today, everything he knows, everything they have planned, but I'm not ready to hear it.

I need to have my say before I can think clearly.

I don't think I could go back into my parents' house, to collect my things, and tell them what I really think, knowing what was going to fully happen to them; knowing what they have planned for me, and still act like nothing is happening. If I don't know, I can't let anything slip. And I'm terrified I will.

Pacing the kitchen, my fourth coffee in my hand. I hit the button to make Cole another before I take it to him in his office. His office reminds me of a den. It's not the kind of office I would have: dark, screens everywhere, and one chair. That's the only reason I'm not in there with him. It's more like a cave.

Sliding the cup in front of him, he looks up at me. "Thanks, Cupcake. I'm sorry about this," he says, sweeping a hand over my side as I perch on the desk beside him. "I need to get everything ready, make sure there's no loopholes to what we've found."

I've not talked much about what happened yesterday. When we got back, I took myself to his spare room and stayed there. I needed space. It was lonely. I never slept; all I did was listen to Cole wander past my door every few minutes. It killed me being apart from him, but I can't let go of the fact that they were all discussing me and my issues like it was a just any other job, and not my actual life. I'm trying my hardest to see past it, that they're helping me get out of this.

I just can't.

I hate that they all know so much. My chest caves as I close my eyes, savouring his touch.

"I get it, I want to be air tight too," I say softly. "I— "

"Good. When I'm done, we'll have lunch, then we'll talk. I promise," he says, squeezing my hip.

"About that—" His phone rings and Cole looks away to glance at the screen. I know he's doing all this for me, and I can't and won't hold it against him, but he's the only one I have to talk to right now. My sore heart pinches a little more when he reaches for it, giving me a brief apologetic smile as he answers before I get a chance to speak.

His hand leaves my side, and he turns back to the screen. My mind wonders if it will always be like this. Once all this is over and done with. Will I be set aside for his work? I give him a sad smile, even though he's not looking.

Closing the door behind me, I walk back to the kitchen. God, I hate this feeling of nothing. I need to talk things over with someone. Cole asked me not to tell Chrisy anything, but he just shut me down to take a call. Maybe I could gloss over a few things just to say my bit.

I pull out my phone, my new one. And dial Chrisy. Slipping my key-card from my bag into my back pocket.

"Hello?" she answers after a few rings.

"Hi, trouble, it's me," I say quietly, so Cole can't hear me.

"Ari?" She sounds busy. The noise in the background is loud.

"The one and only," I say, making my way outside to the back door.

"It came up as a private number, what's going on?" I want to blurt it all out, but I won't. I think I made up my mind when he turned to answer the call. I need to get this over with. I just want someone to know where I will be while I have my say. And maybe give me the extra encouragement to do it on my own.

"So much. I can't wait to tell you when I see you. But right now, I don't have time."

"Not this again. What are you up to?" she asks with caution. I take a quick glance back at his office.

"I just need to talk to you. I think I'm about to do something that's both courageous and a little stupid." Opening the back door quietly, I step out, walking down the steps to the back garden. Smiling lightly as I spot two of the guys who are watching the house for us while I'm here. I point to the beach path, indicating where I'm heading, they nod and carry on walking.

"If it lets you be you, even for a short while, Ari, I'm all for it." I think if she really knew, she'd be telling me to walk back into the house and close the door behind me. Not head down the garden path towards the linked pathway. Slipping below the arch, I walk across to the pebbled beachfront and continue my walk. Cole said he'd break for lunch, that gives me two hours-ish. My heart's going ten to a dozen, causing me to swallow loudly.

"Thanks, I needed that." Pressing forward, I pause when I see another one of his guys, taking the path I've just walked down. Sitting down on a large piece of driftwood, I look out over the sea. Ignoring him as he passes me by then loops back up to the garden. "I'm hoping it won't be fleeting, more of a permanent fixture." My hand shakes as I check the time on my watch.

"This sounds like something I can get behind. Tell me more."

"I can't. I'm headed back to my parents' house." She doesn't know I've not been there in days. She has no idea I'm married. Or that my life has fallen apart. In a good way, I think. Apart from the whole stolen child thing, arranged marriage, having nowhere to live, or any money, but it'll be fine. It has to be.

"As long as everything is okay?" she sounds cautious, "Go be courageous, sweet-cheeks. Will you call me when you can? I need the details of whatever you're going to do." I think she's happy for me on some level.

"I will, love you," I add for good measure.

"Love you too." Hanging up I stretch my legs out as the same guy makes another round. When he passes back up towards the garden, I run.

Chapter Forty-Five
Ready

Cole

Sliding my finger across the screen, I answer the phone to Xander. He helped Owen and Charlie when they needed it most a few months ago. He's an undercover op's guy. I'm glad he's on our side. Holding the phone up to my ear, I listen as Ari slips out the door and closes it behind her. I'll have everything in a few hours. I'll be able to tell her everything.

"What do I owe the pleasure" I ask, moving my chair back a fraction.

"You know I like to get myself involved. Boo asked if I had anything a few days ago and I decided to look into it myself a little." Boo's Charlie's childhood nickname. They've known each other a long time.

"We know, but you never call. What's up."

"They're moving in." So matter of fact.

"What? Shit, when?" Standing, I look at the screens in front of me. I only have a short amount of time to get this done, tying up loose ends.

"Just getting our gear ready." He's so relaxed about it all. "Intel says they are both in the house. We can do this without two separate raids." Oh shit, thank fuck she's not there. Relief washes over me, knowing she's around the house somewhere.

"Thanks, I appreciate it. You have everything we have?" I'll send him every-thing in an hour or so anyway.

"Yeah, I logged into your system, I got it all. Keep tying up those loose ends. I'll catch what you have later." Motherfucker.

He laughs and hangs up, leaving me to deal with the security issue we now have on the system we use. It takes me a full forty mins to see where he entered and to erect a new more intricate firewall in its place. Taking my headphones off when I hear the door to the office open, I expect to see Ari, not one of the guys who are meant to be outside.

"Cole, we have an issue." Standing, I walk towards him as his eyes dart to the monitors behind me. I've not looked at them while I've been sorting the breach. "She ran."

"Ran? Ari? What do you mean?" My heart plummets. I knew there was something wrong when she walked out. She tried to tell me something. Shit. I answered my phone instead of listening.

"Fuck, where?" Turning back to the screen behind me, I search the surveil-lance for her. I can't see anything, nothing outside, nothing inside. Pushing him to one side, I race up the stairs, my fist crashing into the doors, checking the rooms I don't have cameras in. All fucking empty. No sight of her. *Where is she?*

My heart's in my throat, my mind racing at all the possibilities. Why would she run? Why would she leave without me?

My vision blurs, resting my head on the wall, I need to focus, you can do this, it's what you do. *Find her.*

What did she want to tell me earlier? A million things run through my mind, Chrisy's too far away, and has no idea what has been going on. She'd never put her in danger like that. Ari has no-one else.

Her stuff.

She said she needed to do it for herself. She's been so unsettled, she hates doing nothing.

She wouldn't have gone there, would she? Not alone? Not without telling me? The only tracker I have is on the new phone I gave her.

"Where did she go? Where was she seen last?" I yell, coming back down the stairs.

"Last seen sat on the beach out the back." I could punch him, but I shoot him a look of warning instead. "She walked to the beach on the phone to someone. We did the rounds. I walked it twice on the third she'd gone," he tells me. He's pissed with himself, fisting his hands at his sides.

"Who did she call?"

He shrugs and it pisses me off. I know he can't know, but I can find out. Picking my phone from the desk, I open up the tracker app and grab my keys from the side. It feels like a lifetime before it gives me her location.

She's inside her parents' house.

"Fuck," I curse, fisting my hair.

Pulling up the feed for her father's house, I scan every room, finding her leaving her father's office, heading upstairs. She looks okay. Thank fuck. My heart's pounding as I try to swallow the fear down.

She needs to get out before Xander's team heads in. I hit call, but she doesn't answer. My guy stood next to me, waiting. He wants to know what to do.

"Sit in there," I grunt, pointing at my office, "and call me. I need updates on where she is and what each and every person in that house is doing." With quick nod, he's in the chair, as I run for the front door.

My heart trips when I remember an armed unit's just about to head in. They're both there, Byron and Carmichael. They're both at the house the love of my life has just walked into.

I send an SOS to the guys, knowing they have my back.

Running down the front steps, I grab my helmet, straddling my bike. I rev the engine before I move out, leaving a trail of dust and dirt clouding the air behind me.

Chapter Forty-Six
Redemption

Arianna

Closing the door of the Uber behind me, I look up to the gate of the house I've lived behind all my life. Letting out a shaky breath, I punch in the code on the entry keypad and watch the gate slowly open. Stepping through small gap between them for what I hope will be the last time, I walk down the drive towards the house, the gravel crunching beneath my trainers.

Looking at the exterior with fresh eyes, it's stone façade and large windows only make the house darker, and if I'm being honest, creepy. The false turrets, added a few years ago give you the impression it should be something more than it is.

It's like the richer my father became the more he wanted it to show in and around the house.

Not how I would build my dream home.

I don't feel a thing for this house. No loss of a home I once had, only a few memories from the few who made my life worth living.

Taking the steps two at a time up to the front door, I grab my key-card from my pocket and let myself in. I've long thought about what I want to say to my father. Even more so in the last few days. I want to cut all ties. I'll deal with the fallout when it comes. Money and somewhere to live can all be sorted out when

I leave. It's so simple, knowing that Chrisy, Gi, Ed and Dec are safe no matter what happens. It feels like a weight has been lifted. I feel like I can breathe for the first time in my life.

I think he's home. His coat's on the coat rack when I walk in. If not, I'll wait. This has to be my moment. My heart racing as I step forward. I have to try.

I made a mental note of everything I want to take with me. It won't take me long to pack.

"Arianna?" Gi whispers when I step inside, her hand coming to her mouth. "What the hell are you doing here?" She hugs me close. "I didn't think you would come back. Why are you here, Ari?" She looks me over me like I've been forced to be here. "I was just about to leave. Ed's got the day off. I'll stay." Hugging her back, I take a breath of her familiar, comforting scent.

"I've come to say my piece. He wants me to marry Mr Carmichael in two days' time." Gianna's hand comes to her chest as tears well in her eyes. "It's not going to happen," I say, trying to reassure her as best I can.

"Oh, dear god. Ari, please leave before they know you're here. Turn around," she says, pushing me back towards the door, panicking. But I feel so calm, I know I'm right where I need to be.

"Not this time," I say, taking her hands in mine.

"Does anyone know you here?" she mouths, facing away from the cameras in the hallway.

"No, I need a little time. Can you let them know for me, then can you leave?" I don't want her to see anything if it gets ugly.

"I'm not leaving this house without you, Ari, I can't." her Italian stubbornness shines through.

"Okay, I need you to wait a bit before you call Cole. He'll come charging in before I manage to say anything. But I need him to know I'm here." I bite my lip, knowing my husband would walk into the lion's den just to get me out. I love him so much.

"Ari, has something else happened?" she questions.

"I'll tell you everything tomorrow. Go and stay in Ed's office. I'll come and find you when I'm done." I say, looking over her shoulder towards the surveillance room.

"Is my father in his office?" She just nods. "Thank you. Gather your things. We'll be leaving soon." Kissing her on the cheek as I pass, I walk down the dimly lit hallway towards my father's office, leaving her behind.

I don't bother knocking when I place my hand on the cold gold handle. I straighten my shoulders. One more show, then I'm done.

My father's sat in his large leather recliner chair, next to his bookshelves. I smile.

"I wondered how long it would take you to come grovelling back." He sneers.

"Oh, Dad," I say sarcastically because I know he hates it. "I'm not here to grovel." Hearing a noise behind me, I turn, heart in mouth, to see my mother walk in, eyes on me. I clasp my hands in front of me, like I'm holding my own hand through this.

"You'll grovel, girl," he says, not looking at me. My mother comes to stand by his side, hand on his shoulder.

"No," I say simply, "I've come to tell you, I'm never marrying Robert Carmichael. I'm leaving this house today." I point to the floor. "And never coming back." My mother's eyes go wide and her nostrils flare, but my father doesn't move. The corner of his mouth tilts up like he knows better.

"You ungrateful little bitch," she spits out at me, her face reddening with anger. "You have no right, no ground to stand on here. We own everything about you." My father smirks at her words. I know he agrees with them, but it's their mistake. Standing my ground, I remain unflinching.

"You can have the money, the image. I don't need any of it."

"Don't you dare speak to us like that, you worthless piece of shit," she screeches. I don't feel the sting of her words like I used to.

"I have every right to speak to you as I see fit, considering you're not actually my parents." My father's black eyes snap to mine. I seem to have hit the nail on the head with that one. "I know everything," I state. My mother raises her hand and slaps me. My head snaps to the side as tears well in my eyes from the force of the blow. My hand comes to my cheek, daring to touch it.

"I'll be glad to see you gone. Robert's going to show you just how you should have been treated all this time. He's going to ruin you, damage you beyond repair, and enjoy every second." She actually looks happy about it.

"Too bad it'll never happen," I counter. The quicker I get my things, the better. I don't want to spend another second here.

"I can't wait to learn how long you lasted in his hands." Holy shit. The calm and numbness I felt before slips away.

"Wow, Mom, that's low." I feel it like a blow to the stomach. "You're forgetting one huge thing. None of it is going to happen. I never have and never will want to marry that fucking monster just to line the pockets of people like you." She scowls at my use of the word *fuck*, then walks back to my father's side.

"People like us? You should be grateful for what you have." Her hand gripping the chair my fathers still sitting in silently.

"I'm going to grab my things, then leave. You won't see me again. It's that easy." My father just laughs as his eyes flick behind me, but when I glance over, I don't see anything.

"Do what you want. This isn't over, Arianna. You forget who I am, what I do. I control everything you do." He really believes he has all the power. "You will never be free, not from us, but especially not from Robert." There's something in the undertone of his voice that I don't understand. *Get out.* The sooner I leave the better.

I thought I wanted to say hurtful things. I wanted to spit fire and hurt them just like they have hurt me, but nothing I will say will damage them like me leaving and showing the world who they really are.

'Let them see,' Cole said. This is it, I'll show them.

"We'll see," I say.

Chapter Forty-Seven

Shake

Arianna

Opening the door to my room, nothing's changed. It's exactly as I left it eight days ago. I'm not really sure what I expected. It just goes to show how sure they were that I would come back and live under their roof.

My hands shake a little after the confrontation downstairs. It felt good, so freeing to tell them I'm putting an end to all this. I didn't raise my voice like I thought I would either. I thought I would scream and shout, get angry, and cry. But even when she slapped me, I kept my calm. I think I've surprised myself as well as my parents. *Can I call them that now I know the truth?* Shrugging off the thought, I smile at the wave of pride I feel in myself.

"I'll never go through with that sham of a marriage; how could they think I would?" I whisper to myself, stepping into the centre of my room. It's reassuring that they have no idea I've married Cole.

I'm married to Cole.

The best bit being that it's no longer part of a backup plan like Cole first suggested, to make sure Robert could never marry me. *I love the man I'm married to.* Grinning, I let a small laugh slip out at the thought. It's something I never could have imagined for myself. What we have is real. I want to keep it.

Rushing to my closet, a grin still sitting proudly on my face. I pick up a small case from one of the top shelves, crouching down to open my underwear drawer. Dislodging the bottom revealing my real treasured items. Pictures, so many of them, ones that kept me sane in my low moments. Images of me and Ed, Gi, and Chrisy. Chrisy would print them off for me, never framed, but that's something I can look forwards to when I have my own place. *I get to have my own place.* I want to squeal with excitement.

Laying them in the bottom of the case safely, I pick up some t-shirts, jeans, more underwear, not that Cole would approve, but they go in anyway. I've hardly worn any the past week and when I do, they seem to end up in his pocket. I add a pair of boots Chrisy bought me a few Christmases ago.

Walking back to my bed, I open the large drawer underneath it and take out the small book collection I have, reaching to the back to get my private smutty, morally grey collections I love so much. My newest special edition purchase sitting proudly on top. I place them all in my case, zipping it up. I stand, taking a look around at the room that's been my sanctuary and my own personal hell.

Walking to the door, case in hand, I turn the handle but nothing happens. Did I lock it? I don't remember doing it. Pulling against it harder, it still doesn't move. Shit.

I'm locked in.

Resting my head on the cold door, trying to stem the overwhelming panic, the tingling in my chest increases. I breathe, slowly, in and out. I can get out. I can. *I will.* I'm not trapped.

I won't be locked in again.

Closing my eyes, my determination flirts with the idea of climbing down the balcony. My room's on the top floor, I can do it. I've only done it a few times before with Cole but he always helped. I'm sure I could. But with my case? I can throw it over. There's nothing breakable inside. It's that or stay here. Where they'll keep me locked away until I marry Carmichael. Hurt me, and no doubt end my life at some point.

Balcony it is.

I hear a shuffle behind me, and freeze, hoping to fuck it's Cole lurking behind me, but knowing it's not. I can't feel his sense of calm. I don't want to turn around. I can smell his vile aroma from here. Trying desperately to remember what Charlie told me in that one lesson I had with her, something about... shit, why can't I remember? My mind's gone blank.

"Looking for this?" The tone of his voice stills any movements I was considering making, my blood roaring instantly in my ears. I know who it is. He's in my room. A pained sob breaks from my throat. I drop my case by my side and try the door one last time in some desperate hope that I imagined the whole thing. There's no escaping it.

Robert Carmichael has locked us in my room. *Trapped.*

My breathing escalates. I should have known.

It was too easy. I knew it. But I ignored all the signs, my father let me walk away.

Stupid, stupid, so fucking stupid.

That's what he was smirking about, my father. That's why he never moved, he knew he was going to come to my room, as soon as I said I was getting my things, he knew, I watched his eyes flicker to the door, only assuming Carmichael was listening, and smiled about it.

Nausea rising at the unwanted images of what he has planned for me.

Turning slowly, I see him. Standing there, tan jacket, one hand in his trouser pocket. White shirt untucked and scruffy, tie loosened around his neck, his crooked smile pulled over stained teeth.

"Yes," I say, answering his question, looking at the key dangling in his hand as he walks from my en-suite bathroom shrouded in darkness. I do my best to hide the shiver that runs over my skin.

I'm scared, trembling.

Placing the key in his pocket, he stalks towards me. He's too close. I can smell the unsettling concoction of drink and smoke, mixed with something so stale, my stomach twists painfully.

His eyes lock on me, lifting his other hand, I track the motion before he brings the back of his hand down in harsh and unyielding smack access my cheek, his ring catching on my lower lip. Whimpering, my head snapping to the side, as I fall back to the door behind me with a thud. My fingers catch the trickle of blood as I try to control my breath.

It's nothing like the temper fuelled blow my mother gave me. No, this is him. Disciplined, exercising his rule over me. Controlled and dangerous.

There's not an ounce of remorse, no flinch, no nothing at what he just did, just a sickening smile.

"This is just the start, *princess*." My stomach rolls at the word. "Deny me again, refuse me, and you'll see how much I like inflicting the consequences. You. Are. Mine." He gets in my face, the stench of his breath causing me to heave. Swallowing it down, I stand straight. I'm not backing down now. I don't care how much he hurts me. I'm fighting for me today.

"Am I fuck," I say, my voice shaky, "I will *never* be yours." I spit, shouting the words. My lip stings with the movement, already swollen and bruising. I shove my hands into his chest, trying to get around him. Only he doesn't move. He's the only thing that stands between me and the balcony.

"That's where you have all this wrong." He laughs maliciously. "You've been mine for a long time." Grabbing my shoulders, he shoves me back against the door, his dirty fingers bruising my skin, his hand smashing against my face, forcing my head to hit the door. I try again, but he's too strong. His full body presses into mine. My hands claw at him, yet he still doesn't move. "I like it when they fight back." Another cry leaves my lips. His hand moves, encasing my throat, squeezing so tight. Choking out a strangled breath, my hands reach for his arm that's cutting off my air, digging my nails in as hard as I can, trying my best to loosen his grip. It's no use. I'm using everything I have. My legs kick out, but there's not enough space to hurt him.

I'm starting to feel dizzy.

"I'm going to enjoy calling you my wife." He's enjoying this.

"Never," I choke out, my throat on fire.

"I hope you last longer than the last one. She *was* disappointing." His tone is ice cold at the mention of his ex-wife.

My mind blank of anything but the lack of air I feel as his hand tightens, my lungs burning and my eyes watering, streaming down my sore cheeks.

"Your father signed you over to me when you were just a sweet six-teen-year-old girl." Black dot edge into my vision, "I should have had you then," he says, licking his lips.

Remember Ari, what did Charlie tell you? I hear Cole's voice in my mind like he's trying to help me, even when he's not here. My mind rattles, coming up blank as I try to breathe. Robert's other hand brushes back my hair from my face. "How I wanted to take that innocence as mine." Whimpering, struggling to move, my grip on his arm sagging as I lose my strength. Relieved he never had the chance to even get close.

Use everything to your advantage.

"I will never marry you, you... you..." I manage, sounding weak, my throat tight with his grip. He takes something from his pocket: a small bottle of clear liquid in his hand. His knee comes to my stomach, digging in, pinning me painfully to the door behind me.

Gripping my jaw in his hand, he forces my mouth open. I'm powerless to stop it, letting go of my neck, I'm gasping for air. He takes his chance, tripping the liquid down my throat.

I try not to swallow, but when he squeezes my neck again, I can't help my body's reaction. I swallow. Choking it down, it's tasteless. I spit out what I can. He's so close, some drips into his mouth. He sputters, taken aback.

"Bitch," he shouts, involuntarily licking his lips. Taking my chance, when he blanches back, dropping the hand on my neck, I snag the key chain from his pocket without him noticing.

I'll worry about what he gave me once I'm out that door.

Crashes and bangs rain from downstairs, somewhere from the front of the house, distracting him. He turns his head to look at my only escape. I hold it behind my back, while my other hand grasps my neck as I suck in lung-fulls of air.

Lifting my leg in a quick motion, my knee connects with his dick and he slumps over me, stumbling back, his arms reaching out, almost taking me with him. Kicking him again, he falls back.

Spinning round, my head dizzy from the movement, I slip the key into the lock as quickly as I can. Turning the key, I feel it click. I'm yanked back before I can reach the handle, my world tilting, my mind becoming foggy. I'm thrown to the floor. I have no idea how to fight, but I do. Moving my body any way I can, but my arms and legs don't seem to be working like they should. They are heavy, sluggish. I kick out again as Robert kicks me. Grunting from the pain in my hip, I swipe his other leg with mine, watching him fall heavily to the floor.

"Motherfucker," he slurs.

Why is this so hard? What's happening to me?

I'm not going down easily, my mind fighting with my body.

My foot connects with some part of him I can't see as we scramble. Me desperate to escape, him desperate to do unspeakable things to me. My vision blurs. *What the fuck did he give me?*

I think I hear voices. They're muffled, tainted by the ringing I hear in my ears as he lands a blow to my head.

"I'm going to enjoy this."

"No!" I use everything I have to kick him away. I shove as hard as I can, turning to my side, my elbow connecting to the soft tissue of his neck. He moves back, coughing and spluttering. Twisting, I shift as quickly as my sluggish body will allow, feeling like I'm being pulled to the floor, my own weight too much to keep me upright. Stumbling forward, fighting at black spots that dance at the edge of my vision, I feel my body going limp, trying to give up. I won't let it. I can't.

How could I have been so stupid to think I could do this on my own. Crying, willing myself to move forward, getting to my feet.

Get out of this fucking room, I scream to myself, crashing to the door, struggling to grip the handle, my focus waning. I open it. Relief surges me forward, falling into the hallway as my legs start to lose feeling.

Moaning as I hit the floor, my shoulder screaming in pain. I can't stop, I need to keep moving. He'll come after me, he'll take me away.

"Fuck," he roars, and I know he's seconds behind.

Getting to my hands and knees, I try my best to move, but whatever he gave me is most definitely having an effect. I can still hear everything going on, but my body falls short of what I need it to do. I hit the ground again, and again. Determined to get out of this fucking house. My hands scrape at the cold, hard floor.

"Come on, Ari," I whisper, "Try again." Loud cursing comes from behind me as I crawl forward. Closing my eyes, I hear them, shouts, protests, things smashing.

"This isn't over, you fucking little whore."

Then I see him, and all my fight leaves me.

Chapter Forty-Eight

Good Timing

Cole

Coming past the wide-open gates, Ed's men are being taken in for questioning. Xander's people everywhere. Skidding my bike to a stop in front of the house, leaping from the seat, I let it fall to the gravel. Not caring about it one bit. I have to make sure she's okay. Why she left on her own I have no fucking idea. I would have come with her.

You should have listened to the stubborn woman when she tried to talk to you earlier.

I search for Xander while the guy in my office confirms she's still in her room, and can't get a visual on Carmichael. I spot the bastard's security being loaded into the back of one of the vans.

"Back track the footage, find him," I demand to the voice in my ear.

Fuck. It's not lost on me that the only place we don't have cameras is my wife's room. My heart pinches, what if he's in there. Fuck, I need to know.

Spotting Xander sitting in his custom truck, I run over. "She's in there, Ari, she's in there," I shout, pointing to the house. He rolls his eyes, shaking his head like I had one fucking job to keep her away and failed.

I did fail. I got too engrossed in what I was trying to find, rather than taking the time to listen to her.

"Tag one, daughter in the vicinity, location..." Xander pins me with a look, waiting for an answer. I mouth where she is. "Bedroom."

"Gear up, head in, get your girl." As he turns to the other side of the van, not wasting a second, I grab the vest he offers, strap a gun to my side, as Xander hands me an earpiece, and run in the direction of the house after the team that's just burst through the doors.

They storm the house, moving through with fluid and precise moments. Leaving them to find their targets, I head for the stairs. Three guys follow me as we take the steps two at a time, guns drawn, checking our surroundings as we go.

A crash comes from the hall as we reach the top of the stairs.

Using my hand to motion them to stop, we still our movements, not knowing who's up here.

Listening intently, I hear a whimper, then a series of small thuds from down the hall. My chest tightens as gulp down the nervous tension that's rising. "Fuck it," I announce, getting closer. My pace picks up when I see Ari on the floor, crawling. Her face is red, blood dripping from her lips. My hands grip my gun tighter, scanning her body. Her hair is a mess, but there's something else. Something's really wrong. She can't lift herself. My stomach almost bottoms out as I run to her, something's not right. The moment she sees me her whole body giving up as I watch on.

"This isn't over, you fucking little whore." I hear a voice behind her. A second later, Carmichael staggers from my fucking wife's room and my blood boils with all the vile things he could have put her through in there.

My body tenses with anger, as adrenaline surges through me.

Protect what's mine.

"Watch what you call my fucking wife," I seethe, enjoying the look of shock on his face as his eyes widen, darting to Ari as he sways backwards.

Running forward, I step between them, raising my fist in one fierce, controlled movement. I give him everything; his nose pops, sending blood gushing everywhere, I don't watch as he falls. Spinning around. I'm on my knees, gathering her in my arms.

"Cole," she mumbles. My brows furrow trying to think. I go to kiss her but she moves away. "Can't," she slurs.

"What is it, baby, tell me," I plead. Gently rolling her onto her back, she looks up at me, pressing her finger to her lips. "Something, liquid, drug…"

"He injected you with something?" My body shakes.

"No," she pants, sounding breathless, her eyes closing. "Drink."

"Shit," pressing my earpiece, "Xander, I'm bringing her out, she needs a medic. Is Ethan here yet?" There's a crackle before I hear his response.

"The whole team's here, Cole." He sounds pissed.

"Cole, it's me, Ethan. Tell me what you can."

"She's been drugged, something he made her drink."

I lift Ari into my arms. Her arms fall to her sides, almost lifeless, as I cradle her to me. *What has that arsehole given her?* Her head rolls to my chest. She groans, and I can't run fast enough to get her to Ethan. My eyes barely leaving her as we move back through the house. As I list every visible injury, giving Ethan anything I can on how she's limp in my arms, before we get outside. I leave them all behind to get her out, away from this fucking house for the last time. Running out the front door, I spot the guys and run faster. My throat thick with fear, I have no idea what happened to her, I just want to make it all right. I need her to open her eyes, I need to hear her words. I'm shaking when I reach the front steps, Leon, Ethan and Owen come rushing forward.

"What happened?" Ethan asks, taking her wrist in his hand, checking her pulse.

"I don't know the full story, not yet." My voice breaks. "Somethings not right, Eth," I shout, looking down at her motionless body, all my focus on her slowed breathing. "What's wrong with her?" Looking between them, I need answers. I can't stand this.

"I need to know what it was before I can treat her." He's lifting her closed eyelids, checking their response. She flinches. Is that good? *It has to be good.*

"Ari, can you hear me?" he says and she moans in response. My hands grip her harder, need the contact, I'm never letting her out of my sight again.

Leon takes off into the house, coming back a moment later with a small plastic bottle in his hand, followed by Xander's men, shoving Byron, and his wife down the steps, towards the waiting police cars that must have arrived while I was inside.

Laying Ari as gently as I can down on the stretcher a paramedic brings over, I hold her hand. "I'm here, baby, I'm not leaving you. You're safe," I whisper in her ear as her head falls to the side.

"How can we test it?" I ask, my eyes snapping to Ethan.

"There's a kit in my bag, I need to confirm it, but it looks like some kind of sedative." Placing a hand on my shoulder, he squeezes. "If it is, she'll be fine. She'll have the biggest hangover she ever had, but she'll be okay, Cole." My eyes wander over her, noticing the bruising on her face darkening, as clear as day a mark shaped like a hand print around her neck. Leaning closer to her, I bring my forehead to hers, touching it as softly as I can. I don't want to hurt her any more than she already has been.

"I'm sorry, baby," I whisper.

"What the fuck was he planning to do to my wife?" I heave, burying my face into her neck, inhaling her scent, and holding her as close as I can. I don't care who's watching.

"Leon?" Ethan nudges.

"Shit, sorry, doing it now." Grabbing his bag from the van they must have arrived in, he picks up the test.

Carmichael comes out last, cursing, stumbling, as he's pushed forward, his face blood-stained and his hands cuffed behind his back as they move him to a separate police car.

I'd like to feel relieved, watching him like that. It would have been so much more satisfying to watch with Ari, while she witnessed the people responsible for the misery, get taken away. Turning away I concentrate on what's more important right now, my beautiful wife.

Chapter Forty-Nine

That's It

Arianna

It's the strangest sensation, like being in a dream only knowing what I'm hearing is real. My mind's fuzzy but I feel warm and safe as I open my eyes.

I think I know what's happened, there's no need to ask if it's over. I know it is.

Cole came after me, he found me. It's the last thing I remember. He gave Robert what he deserved. That's all I need to know for now.

The next few months will be difficult. I need to rebuild my life, so I can actually live it.

Opening my mouth to speak, I can't. It hurts so much my eyes water. *What the hell*? My eyes widen in panic. My trembling hand coming tentatively to my neck, flinching when I feel how sore it is, along with my entire body.

"Try not to speak, Cupcake," Cole softly warns from beside me, where I'm cocooned into his side. "You'll be fine in a day or two, but it's going to be sore for a while." His fingers brush the hair away from my face. Looking around, I expected to be in hospital. "My house. I didn't want you in hospital." I go to speak but remember just in time. Cole gives me a concerned smile, his fingers linking with mine on his stomach as he kisses my forehead softly. How the fuck can I communicate if I can't talk?

"I got you this," Cole says, moving across the bed, looking fine as always, shirtless and in a pair of joggers. He picks up a tablet. "You can write on this until your voice comes back." Smiling, I nod again. Taking the pen thingy and tablet, I scribble a note.

I knew you were a mind reader. My tongue comes out to lick my swollen lip. It could have been so much worse. I think I got away lightly.

"No, baby, I can just read you like a book." I roll my eyes at that. "Leon found the case you packed at the house. He dropped it off earlier." My eyes widen, sitting up, I wince, remembering the kick to my ribs and the fall on my shoulder. He sits next to me as I hug him.

"So many books, I'm going to have to get Owen to build you a bookcase." He's watching me closely.

Why Owen? I scribble down. *Why not you?*

"Oh, baby, you have so much to learn about me. Owen banned me from his workshop a long time ago when I almost destroyed it and his tools in the fifteen minutes I was there.

You're serious? I write, arching my brow at him.

"As serious as a snake."

You can't cook? I write, and he shakes his head. *You're no good at DIY?* I write next, and again Cole shakes his head his dirty blond hair falling perfectly over his forehead as he gives me a teasing, sad smile, *Why did I marry you again?* I draw a winky face and circle it with a heart.

"Harsh." He laughs, putting his hand over his heart. I laugh with him, even though it hurts. "If it wasn't for your condition, I'd show you exactly why you married me. Unfortunately, that will have to wait a few days." I pout, and his eyes flare. I write out my response.

There's no need to wait, there's nothing wrong with my vagina. Cole bursts out laughing and grabbing the tablet off me, he writes his own message.

You and your vagina can wait two days. I huff when I read it. Slowly sinking back into the bed, Cole moves with me into his plush covers.

"I've never been so scared in my life baby, when I saw where you'd gone." I look up frowning. "I'm sorry, I didn't listen when you needed to talk to me." I'm shaking my head at him. Grabbing the tablet and pen, I write.

Don't. None of it matters now. It's all over.

"It is. I'm just happy to have you here." He sighs.

There's nowhere else I'd rather be, I scribble.

"I love you, baby," he says kissing my lips softly, I don't need to say it back, the smile across my face says it all. Instead, I draw a heart.

Epilogue

"Are you ready, baby?" I ask as we finish setting up for Ari's first live video from the living room. She squeezes my arse as I walk past.

"As I'll ever be." She's not stopped smiling all morning, I know she's nervous. That's why, over breakfast this morning, I gave her a small token of encouragement. She was missing two vital things in becoming my wife.

I placed her engagement and wedding ring on top of her chocolate-covered pancakes and waited for her to see them. I've never heard someone squeal so loud, then cry. We have matching bands. Each engraved with a Cupcake and heart on the inside. For our eyes only.

She thanked me by covering my cock in chocolate and licking it clean at the dining table.

She surprises me every day.

"Going live in three, two, one," I say, sitting back on the chair and watching. She presses the button on the screen, and there she is. My wife. Fucking hell, I'm the luckiest bastard on the planet to have her. Pride doesn't even cover how I feel when I see her, to have her with me every day.

Checking the sound and connection from my laptop, I watch as she goes live across her social media channels for the first time since the mess with her father hit the news. Over the last three weeks, she been healing and making plans for her new life. Which still includes me, *thank fuck*. Although I'm giving her three months of living on her own before I drag her ass home where she belongs.

She's rented the flat above Charlie's flower shop. Charlie insisted when she mentioned she was looking for a place.

Today she wanted to tell her side of the story, not the full truth, some of those will die with us. But she's had so many of her followers reaching out, wanting to know what's happened, how she was, and how they can help. She had thousands of messages of support and she wanted to deal with it all in one go.

"Hi." She waves into the camera. The ring light gives her a bright glow. "If you don't know me, my name was Arianna Byron. You may have seen a few things over the last few weeks about me and," she takes a deep breath, "my *parents*, and Mr Carmichael. A lot has changed for me in such a short time, the first being my name. I'm no longer a Byron." My eyes shoot up at this I had no idea she was doing this. "I'm Mrs Arianna Grant." Leaping up, I lean into view. Cupping her face, I kiss her smack on the lips. Fuck, I want to take it further when she moans against my lips, but we're live. I'll have to wait until she's finished. My smile stretches wider than ever before. She just announced to the world she changed her name, and I had no fucking idea. Puffing my chest up, I'm fucking happy.

> **Dad**: I'm watching, son.

My smile spreads further. My dad's besotted with her like I knew he would be. The first time they met while she was recovering in bed. He just sat with her, hugging her like they'd known each other a life time. When she eventually stopped crying on his shoulder, he told her that if I loved her, he would too. They've not stopped talking since, daily phone calls, messages and endless meals with each other. The three of us together, if we're not with the guys and she's not with Layla.

That's a friendship she loves now that Chrisy's working more than ever in Liverpool. Layla's helped her move; she even brings her flowers every few days.

Gianna and Ed visit so much, she feels like she has a real family around. After some talks with Owen, Leon and Ethan, we gave Ed a job working for us, and Gianna decided she never wants to work again, and is enjoying her time fussing over Ari any chance she gets.

Me: She looks good doesn't she.

Dad: Stunning son, inside and out.

Me: Yep.

Dad: Mrs Ari Grant has a good ring to it.

I laugh and Ari frowns at me, pointing to my phone she see's it my dad, and rolls her eyes.

"I have so much to tell you," she says to the millions of viewers currently watching, "but I wanted to reassure you all I'm okay. Better than I ever have been actually. I have a new family, one that care's for me. The Byron's were not who they seemed. They hid secrets and lies from me, and the world."

Dad: I'm so proud.

Me: Me too, Dad.

Dad: I'm talking about you son.

Well shit. Clearing my throat, I move away from Ari to check the feeds okay.

Dad: Always have been, but especially how you've handled all this.

[right-aligned message bubble] **Me:** Thanks,

I don't know what to say, not over a message anyway. He's coming over later, I'll hug the old man then.

"I've been controlled my entire life. All for nothing that's important to me, but to be used as pawn in a bid to gain status and money by my parents, and Mr Carmichael." She hangs her head, and I move next to her again, out of view, holding her hand in mine. "Someone once told me to let them see." She pauses, looking at me. "So, as of today, I'm changing what you see, starting with this account. I'll show you who I really am, and what I care for while I get to live."

Taking a sticky note from the pad on the coffee table, I scribble what I want to say, holding it above the camera so she can read it.

I'm so fucking proud of you.

Ari gets that look in her eyes to say stop it or she's going to cry. I attach it to the ring light, so she knows I mean it.

My phone vibrates in my hand, looking down reading the new message from my dad. I'm shocked, but not surprised.

Dad: I heard from your mom last night. She said to pass on her thanks to you and Ari. She's giving it anther go with Clive.

Dad: I've also blocked her number. I need a break.

[right-aligned message bubble] **Me:** It's about time.

The day I let Ari get out of bed after she was attacked, I told Owen and the guys I wanted more time off. We've agreed to me only working a few weeks a month. I still have to do my things every week, but I want to enjoy what me and Ari have right now, and on the top of her list is a holiday. I've booked us a two-week holiday to the Amalfi Coast in Italy. Only we'll meet Chrisy there. Ari has no idea and I want to keep it that way.

Arianna

Looking into the screen all I can see is myself, and the hundreds of comments coming through. "I'll get to each one of your comments and messages as soon as I can." I may have to hire someone to help.

"Down to business," I announce, distracting Cole from his phone. "I'd like to share something close to my heart. A company I recently had the honour of working with." Since Cole set up all of the money my father stole to be transferred back to me, I have enough to do what I want and then some. "Millican," I say. Cole grins, knowing I've spoken with Millie about becoming an ambassador for her brand. I like keeping secrets from him, only good ones of course. One will make him smile when I eventually tell him.

"I'll be donating back what she paid my father to have a few hours of my time. Plus, an extra million. You'll be seeing so much of Millie's products and everything she does to help victims of abuse. I hope you'll join me in supporting such a worthy cause." Cole's phone starts ringing and I can hear Millie on the other end as soon as he answers. I want to cry, the bubble in my chest swelling beyond belief at how good it feels to do this. All of this.

There's still so much I need to get through, but this makes me happy.

Clicking off the live feed a while later. I slump back in my chair, exhausted.

"Millie's beyond excited and floored at what you announced. She said you need to be there for Friday night dinner next week.

"Okay, I'd love that." I yawn. Pulling me from the seat, to stand, he wraps his arms around me.

"Let get you fed, then we can go to bed." He teases, kissing my neck.

"It's only three in the afternoon, Cole." He shrugs like he doesn't care.

"I know." The dimple shows on his cheek as his smile grows. "But seeing that ring on your finger has me hard as iron, baby. I've had to watch you wear it all day and I've not been able to do anything about it." His hands run down my sides, lifting me as he walks us out of the living room towards the stairs. "Then you go and announce you've changed your name to the world when I couldn't touch you."

"What are you doing to do about it, Mr Grant?" I tease, kissing his neck, the scratch of his stubble feels rough against my skin.

"I'm going to watch you wrap your delicate ringed hand around my cock, while I fuck your pretty pink mouth."

The end

Also By Bekki

Other books in The Protected Series

I Dreamt Of You

No Matter What

Let Them See

Echoes Of Me

I'd Bet My Life

Novella

More Than Tempted

About the Author

Bekki Vowles writes romantic suspense filled with tension, emotion, and characters you can't help but root for. Her stories blend twists, danger, and heat with strong, complex leads who fight for the love and healing they deserve. She is the author of The Protected Series, an elite ex-military romance world packed with high stakes and heart.

Bekki lives in a small UK village with her husband, two energetic boys, and her beloved fur baby. When she's not writing, you can usually find her curled up with a spicy romance and a glass of wine.